N E LINCS LIBRARIES

D0279725

8 4

NORTH EAST LINCS
LIBRARIES
WITHDRAWN
FROM STOCK

AUTHORISED:

LONDON BELLES

Annie Groves lives in the North-West of England and has done so all her life. She is the author of *Ellie Pride, Connie's Courage* and *Hettie of Hope Street*, a series of novels for which she drew upon her own family's history, picked up from listening to her grandmother's stories when she was a child. Her most recent novels are *Goodnight Sweetheart, Some Sunny Day, The Grafton Girls, As Time Goes By, Across the Mersey, Daughters of Liverpool, The Heart of the Family, Where the Heart Is* and *When the Lights Go on Again*, which are based on recollections from members of her family who come from the city of Liverpool. In *London Belles*, the first in a new series, she introduces a new set of characters that live in Holborn, London. Her website, www.anniegroves.co.uk. has further details.

Annie Groves also writes under the name Penny Jordan, and is an internationally bestselling author of over 170 novels with sales of over 84,000,000 copies.

Also by Annie Groves

The Pride family series

Ellie Pride
Connie's Courage
Hettie of Hope Street

The WWII series

Goodnight Sweetheart
Some Sunny Day
The Grafton Girls
As Time Goes By

The Campion series

Across the Mersey
Daughters of Liverpool
The Heart of the Family
Where the Heart Is
When the Lights Go on Again

ANNIE GROVES

London Belles

HARPER

This novel is entirely a work of fiction.
The names, characters and incidents portrayed in it are
the work of the author's imagination. Any resemblance to
actual persons, living or dead, events or localities is
entirely coincidental.

Harper
An imprint of HarperCollins*Publishers*
77–85 Fulham Palace Road,
Hammersmith, London W6 8JB

www.harpercollins.co.uk

This paperback edition 2011
1

First published in Great Britain by
HarperCollins*Publishers* 2010

Copyright © Annie Groves 2011

Annie Groves asserts the moral right to be identified as the author of this work

A catalogue record for this book is available from the British Library

ISBN: 978-0-00-736149-6

Set in Sabon by Palimpsest Book Production Limited,
Falkirk, Stirlingshire

Printed and bound in Great Britain by
Clays Ltd, St Ives plc

All rights reserved. No part of this publication may be
reproduced, stored in a retrieval system, or transmitted,
in any form or by any means, electronic, mechanical,
photocopying, recording or otherwise, without the prior
permission of the publishers.

This book is sold subject to the condition that it shall not,
by way of trade or otherwise, be lent, re-sold, hired out or
otherwise circulated without the publisher's prior consent
in any form of binding or cover other than that in which it
is published and without a similar condition including this
condition being imposed on the subsequent purchaser.

Mixed Sources
Product group from well-managed
forests and other controlled sources
www.fsc.org Cert no. SW-COC-001806
© 1996 Forest Stewardship Council
FSC

FSC is a non-profit international organization established
to promote the responsible management of the world's forests.
Products carrying the FSC label are independently certified
to assure consumers that they come from forests that are managed
to meet the social, economic and ecological needs
of present and future generations.

Find out more about HarperCollins and the environment at
www.harpercollins.co.uk/green

I'd like to dedicate this book to all those who throughout WW2 made do, mended and somehow kept together the fabric of everyday life.

NORTH EAST LINCOLNSHIRE COUNCIL	
00976688	
Bertrams	14/02/2011
SAG	£20.00

Acknowledgements

Susan Opie, and Victoria Hughes-Williams, my editors at HarperCollins. Yvonne Holland, copy editor extraordinaire, who, as always, has done a magnificent job.

All those at HarperCollins whose hard work enabled this book to reach publication.

Tony, who contributes so much to my books via the research he does for me.

PART ONE

August 1939

ONE

'So what are you going to do now that old Bert has finally gone, Olive? I mean, you won't have his pension any more, will you? Your Tilly might be working up at the hospital as an assistant to the Lady Almoner, but I dare say she isn't bringing in very much,' Nancy Black sniffed.

As Olive knew, Nancy had a keen interest in the business of her neighbours and an even keener nose for 'problems' of any kind. She was the kind of person who liked spreading doom and gloom; the kind of person who would complain about the noise children made playing innocently together in the street and then go on to extol the virtues of her own daughter and only child. Some people were inclined to call her a bit of a troublemaker but Olive always tried to give her the benefit of the doubt.

The afternoon sunshine sparkled on the immaculately clean windows of Article Row, the narrow byway that wound between the close interweaving of London streets, within the boundaries of Chancery Lane to the west, Farringdon Road to the east, Fleet Street to the south and from High Holborn to Holborn Viaduct to the north.

Nancy stood, leaning on the broom with which she had been sweeping the short path to her front door whilst she waited for Olive's answer to her original question about the loss of her father-in-law's pension.

The row of fifty narrow three-storey houses, with the addition of their attics and cellars, clinging together as though for mutual protection, had been built, so it was said, by a wealthy East India merchant in the seventeen hundreds, whose fortune had been saved for him by the keen eye of a poor articled clerk working for a pittance for his lawyer. In recognition of his good fortune the East India merchant had had Article Row built, with the houses in it to be rented out for peppercorn rents to help the struggling. After he had lost his money in the South Sea Bubble débâcle, his estate, including the Article Row houses, had been sold, as a result of which Article Row was one of the few places in Holborn where an ordinary working-class family man bringing in a steady wage might buy his own home. Separated by class and stature from the inhabitants of the Inns of Court, and artistic, some said slightly louche Bloomsbury beyond, and by respectability from their poorer neighbours towards the East End and the river, Article Row was a world almost unto itself, its inhabitants living by their own set of rules and observances, one of which was that a front path must always be spotless.

Across the road from the front of the houses

were the blank windowless high walls of a succession of buildings that housed various small businesses, some of which employed inhabitants of the Row. These ivy-covered brick walls gave the Row a vague semirural aspect, much cherished by some of the long-standing residents, who felt that Article Row being one single row of houses gave it a special air of gentility.

'Well, I've been thinking about that, and what I've a mind to do is take in lodgers.' Olive looked her neighbour firmly in the eye as she delivered this information. Married at eighteen, widowed a year later when her husband, weakened by the dreadful rigours of the First World War had died from TB, Olive had learned as a young wife how to deal tactfully but firmly with bossy members of her own sex.

Olive had spent all her adult life living under the roof of her husband's parents, who had taken them in when Jim, their only child, had been poorly, and Olive and Jim's daughter, Tilly, only a baby. Although Olive would never have said so to anyone, especially a gossipy and sometimes forthright neighbour like Nancy, it hadn't been easy for her, left motherless at sixteen, and an only child herself, to deal with a strong-willed mother-in-law who adored her only son. Olive's mother-in-law had not been above hinting that Olive had seized her chance to improve her lot in life by marrying her son, and that that marriage had drained him of what strength he had left, thus hastening his death.

Jim, though – dear kind, gentle person that he

had been – had always sworn that their love for one another had given him strength and the desire to hold on to life, especially once he knew that there was to be a baby. How he had loved Tilly. And his mother had softened towards Olive once she had become a grandmother.

Olive had repaid her in-laws' kindness by nursing first her mother-in-law through ill health to her death, and then more recently her father-in-law, Bert.

A better daughter-in-law than Olive it would be impossible to find, her late mother-in-law had been given to saying in her later years.

'Lodgers?' Nancy queried sharply now, breaking into Olive's thoughts, her narrow face beneath her greying hair taking on an expression of pursed-lipped disapproval. 'Well, I don't know about that. That's not the kind of thing we do round here. I don't want to disappoint you, Olive, especially with you needing to replace Bert's pension – after all, no one can live on fresh air – but I'd think twice if I were you. After all, you don't want people thinking you're lowering the tone. Of course, if you was to think of selling the house, then I reckon that my daughter and her husband might be willing to take it off your hands.'

Aware that Nancy was trying to manipulate her, Olive smiled pleasantly and pointed out, 'There's plenty of houses in the Row already owned by a landlord and rented out.'

'Yes, but they're respectable types. After all, most of them work in the civil service for the Government, and they're decent families who rent the whole house, not just a room. You get all sorts when you just let out a room: young men – and young women – behaving like they shouldn't. There could be all sorts of goings-on going on.' Nancy sniffed again, her pursed mouth becoming even more prune-like with disapproval. 'Anyway, I don't know how you could take in lodgers, seeing as you've only got two bedrooms, same as the rest of us, and there's you and Tilly living there already.'

'There's the attics: that makes two more,' Olive pointed out calmly. 'I've made up my mind to give it a try, Nancy. Like you said, our Tilly doesn't bring in that much.'

'You could go back cleaning, like you did before Bert got took bad. There's still plenty staying on in the Inns of Court, despite all this talk of war.'

'Well, that's another thing, Nancy,' Olive responded, playing her trump card. 'Tilly's been telling me that the Lady Almoner, up the hospital, has been saying that if there is a war then anyone with spare rooms is going to have to take in other folk on the Government's orders, and to my way of thinking it's better that I let my rooms now whilst I've still got a chance to choose who I have living in them.'

For a few seconds Nancy was silent. But never one to give up on an argument she wanted to win, she announced triumphantly, 'Well, I'm not saying that I don't admire you for thinking of it, but you'll have to be careful, you not having a man around. You don't want the wrong sort. Like I said before, this is a respectable street and you'll have some saying they don't want anyone lowering the tone.'

Yes, and you'd be one of the first to complain, Olive thought wryly.

Nancy shook her head. 'And as for there being a war, well, I'm telling you now there won't be one. It's all just talk, you mark my words.'

'I hope you're right, Nancy,' Olive answered quietly.

Olive knew perfectly well that her plans to let out her spare bedrooms to bring in the money they would need to live on now that her father-in-law had died, and his pension with him, would be all over the street within a couple of hours. It was all right for Nancy, Olive thought wryly. She had a husband who brought in a good wage from his work at a factory where they made artificial limbs, close to Barts Hospital, a business that had boomed, thanks to the Great War. Of course, Nancy would have been delighted if she could have persuaded her to sell her house to Nancy's daughter, who was married with a child of her own, Olive knew. But Olive loved the neat little house in Article Row she had inherited from her father-in-law, and had no intention of selling it.

'So how are you going to get these lodgers then?' Nancy wanted to know, obviously still eager to disapprove of Olive's plan.

'I've thought of putting a notice in the papers, and probably in the bakery, if Mrs Macharios will let me.'

'The bakery? But that's run by them Greek foreigners. We don't want any of them coming living here in Article Row, thank you very much.'

Olive suppressed a small sigh. She liked the

Greek family – members of Holborn's Greek Cypriot community – who owned and ran the small bakery two streets away.

'The Macharioses aren't just foreigners, Nancy, they are refugees. And very nice and pleasant they are too. Besides, you won't get any of their girls wanting lodgings, because they are very strict with them and keep them at home until they get married, you know that.'

Nancy gave another sniff. 'Refugees, is it? We've got a sight too many of them already without getting involved in a war with Hitler that will bring in some more.'

Olive kept her peace. She suspected that in the eyes of most of the other inhabitants of Article Row, she herself was something of a 'refugee and a foreigner' since she had not been born and brought up in the area. She personally liked the mix of people living in the small houses that filled the narrow backstreets of the area: Greeks, Italians, Jewish people, flood tides of the lost and desperate, washed up by the Thames and left to make lives for themselves as best they could, clustered together in their small communities, clinging to the ways of the countries and homes they had left.

Nancy's sharp tongue, though, was a small price to pay for the pleasure of living in Article Row, Olive admitted half an hour later as she poured boiling water onto the tea leaves she had spooned into her warmed teapot. Olive's kitchen was her pride and joy. The upstairs of the house was filled with the heavy late-Victorian furniture that her in-laws had inherited from their parents, but after her mother-in-law's death, Bert had allowed Olive to modernise the kitchen and the front room, even paying for the new gas oven, and the coal-fuelled stove, which not only heated the kitchen but provided hot water as well.

In addition to her gas oven, Olive had a whole wall filled with cupboards just like some she'd seen in the newspaper that had seen on display at the Modern Homes Show. Bert had always had an eye for a bargain and a clever tongue for getting himself a good deal, and he had bartered with a friend of a friend who worked at a wood yard, and who knew someone who could knock up the cupboards for them at a quarter of the price of some fancy factory.

Olive had painted them herself, a really pretty duck-egg blue, which went with the kitchen's cream walls, and the curtains of pale blue, apple green and white gingham. Ever so proud of her kitchen, she was. Her heart swelled with pride every time she walked into it. From the stone sink under the window she could look out into the garden – a long narrow strip, at the bottom of which was the blank brick wall that separated her garden from that of the house beyond. The floor of Olive's kitchen was covered in a good practical mosaic-patterned linoleum that didn't show the dirt. Not that there was any dirt on Olive's kitchen floor – certainly not. She swept and washed it every single day. Very house proud, Olive was, putting her back into whatever task she took on. That was something that, like her domestic skills, she had learned from the grandmother, who had taken her in after her mother had died and her father had then disappeared from her life. Not been very lucky in their dads she and her Tilly hadn't. But she'd been determined right from the start to make sure that her daughter had the very best mum she could possibly have and that she would grow up knowing how loved she was.

That was why, over the years, Olive had gently but determinedly turned down several men who had tried to court her, some perhaps for her own sake, but some, she suspected, because of what they had hoped she would bring them, be it a good housewife and a stepmother for their children or, in one or two cases, the hope of the inheritance she might one day get from her in-laws. Well, that day had now come and if there was one thing that Olive was determined on it was that she wasn't going to have any man coming along and disrupting her routine or her life.

It was ten to five. Tilly would be home soon. Tonight, after they'd had their tea and listened to the news, they could sit down together and talk about her plan to let their spare bedrooms.

'Come on, Tilly, it's finishing time. Thank heavens. I've never known the Lady Almoner be as sharp as she was today. We've got more than enough work on our hands here without her giving us even more,' Clara Smith grumbled as both girls pulled the covers onto their typewriters, the office clock having reached five o'clock.

Clara and Tilly were the most junior members of the Lady Almoner's office staff, Clara being the previous 'dog's body', as she referred to Tilly's role, before Tilly herself had been taken on. Clara was just coming up for nineteen, whilst Tilly was just a few weeks short of her seventeenth birthday.

'We can't blame her for us having to type up all these new lists,' Tilly pointed out patiently. 'The Hospital will need them if there's a war and patients have to be moved.'

'A war. I'm sick and tired of all this talk about a war,' Clara complained, 'and all these things the Government keep making us do, like buying blackout material, having to have gas masks, putting up Anderson shelters, and the like. My dad's only gone and joined the local ARP, and with all the drills we're having to do here anyone would think we were at war already.'

'I know,' Tilly agreed, 'but the Hospital hasn't stopped making plans in case there is a war, no one has, and the Government has said that if Hitler invades Poland, they won't stand for it.'

The girls looked at each other in bleak and sober silence, their shared apprehension showing in their tense expressions.

'They're still calling up the lads for that six months' National Service training,' Clara admitted reluctantly. 'My Harry's had his notification.'

In April the Government had passed a law to make it obligatory for all young men of twenty and twenty-one to undergo six months' military training.

Clara tossed her head so determinedly that her carefully curled brown hair bounced.

'Well, I know one thing,' she announced. 'If

there is to be a war, my Harry better look smart and get an engagement ring on my finger before it starts. Him and me are going to the Hammersmith Palais tonight, seeing as it's a Friday. Are you doing anything?'

Tilly shook her head. Her mother considered her too young to go out dancing at places like the Hammersmith Palais, which was where all the boys went to size up the girls.

Five minutes later, on her way down the staircase of St Barts' main hall, Tilly paused as she always did, unable to stop herself from gazing in awe at the paintings. It had been Clara who had told her importantly during her first week at Barts that the Biblical murals had been painted by William Hogarth and were over a hundred and fifty years old. But that was nowhere near as old as the hospital itself. Barts had been the very first hospital to be established in London, though the original buildings had been replaced in the eighteenth century. Tilly marvelled to think how old the hospital was: hundreds of years. She had found the sheer size of the place a bit overwhelming at first, and feared getting lost whenever she was sent to one of the wards to get the details of a patient from the sister there, but she could find her way around with relative ease now.

Tilly felt that she was very lucky to be working at St Barts, which had a special place in the hearts of Londoners, and whose nurses liked to claim was London's very best hospital. And to be working for the Lady Almoner too. There was never a day when Tilly didn't think gratefully of her old headmistress, who had recommended her for the job, her being a second cousin or something of the Lady Almoner. Miss Moss, her headmistress, had come to number 13 Article Row herself to tell them about the job. Tilly's eyes filled with tears now when she remembered the happiness and pride she had seen on her mother's face when Miss Moss had told them that she considered Tilly to be the right kind of person for the job, because she had been a good hard-worker at school, clean and neat, with a sensible head on her shoulders, and Miss Moss knew that her mother had sent her off to learn shorthand and typing after she had left school instead of her having to get a job in a factory. Tilly hadn't really known what a hospital Lady Almoner was but Miss Moss had explained that it was someone who was in charge of the social care of a hospital's patients – everything from finding out who a patient's relatives were, if they came into hospital because of an accident, to making arrangements for a patient to be looked after properly at home once they were discharged. From making up and sending out bills, to dealing with all those charities and insurance companies who provided funds for patients and their health care – running the Almoner's office, Miss Moss had explained, involved an awful lot of administration work, the kind of work for which Tilly, with her shorthand and typing skills, would be ideally suited.

Tilly knew she would never forget how hard her mother had worked to get the money together for her secretarial school lessons, taking in laundry and sometimes even cleaning rooms at the nearby Inns of Court.

Tilly was proud of her mother and she knew that her mother was proud of her. Having pride in yourself and your work was something her mother had taught her from an early age. Tilly and her mother were much closer than many of the girls she had been at school with were to their mothers, but then those girls had had siblings, and . . . and fathers. Tilly caught her breath. She had never known her own father, just as she had never known what it was to be part of a large family.

The hall was busy with comings and goings, nurses in their crisp uniforms walking at that swift pace that nurses had, that was almost as fast as running but without actually doing so, porters pushing patients in wheelchairs, doctors, white coats flapping, heads down, one hand clasping papers, stethoscopes round their necks, Consultants, in their smart suits and their bow ties, and, of course, the patients themselves.

All sorts came to St Barts to be treated, from the poorest to the wealthiest, and Tilly's heart swelled with joy at being part of such a wonderful organisation, with its proud history of caring for those in need.

As she passed under the main entrance to the hospital she hesitated and then turned back to look at the painted head of Henry the Eighth, before joining the teeming mass of Londoners homeward bound after their day's work.

* * *

Tilly wasn't the only one passing through Barts' main hallway to pause and consider the history of the ancient building and all that it stood for.

Sally Johnson paused too, still acutely conscious of her new Barts uniform, with its distinctive high nurse's hat. She still half expected to look down and see that she was wearing her old and dearly familiar Liverpool hospital uniform. She could feel forbidden tears pressing against her eyeballs, her eyes themselves gritty and tired, and not just from the long shift she had just worked. She missed Liverpool, her home city, so very much. She missed the smell of its salt air, the sound of its voices, the humour of its citizens, the familiarity of its places and faces . . . She felt . . . she felt like an outcast, alien, a person cut adrift from all that mattered most to her, but she had had no choice other than to leave. She couldn't have stayed. Not after what had happened. Not after such a betrayal. The very thought of it caused her pain as sharp as a surgeon's scalpel felt, but without the comfort of anaesthetic. That it should have been her best friend who was responsible for her agony only made the pain harder to bear.

Right now, though, instead of thinking about the past, she decided she should be thinking about the present and the future. She had been granted temporary accommodation in a nurses' home close to the hospital, but as she was on only a short-term contract – she hadn't decided yet whether or not she would stay in London – she needed to find lodgings reasonably close to the hospital. She was, though, Sally freely admitted,

16

perhaps too particular about where she was prepared to live. In Liverpool she had lived at home as soon as her initial training had come to an end, and it would take somewhere very special indeed to come up to the high standards of cleanliness and comfort her mother had always maintained. A small spasm of pain tensed Sally's body. Those at home in Liverpool who had known her as a happy, fun-loving, sociable girl who loved going dancing at Liverpool's famous Grafton Ballroom, who was a keen tennis player and who had a wide circle of equally lively young friends of both sexes, would probably hardly recognise that Sally now in the withdrawn unhappy young woman she had become. Sometimes Sally barely recognised herself any more, she admitted, dragging her thoughts away from her own unhappiness to the miserable situation the country now faced.

In the event of the country going to war against Germany plans had already been made for most of the hospital staff and the patients to be moved out of London, partially for safety, and partially to make sure that there would be operating theatres and beds available for the injured should the city be bombed. Only a skeleton staff would remain here in London with Barts doctors and surgeons travelling between the evacuated patients in the country and the hospital here in the city. As a temporary member of Barts' staff, Sally had volunteered to stay in London for the duration of her one-year contract. Right now she felt that she preferred the anonymity of working hard in a busy city where people came and went without their lives really touching, to making close friends.

It wasn't easy, though, to think about making a new life and home for herself here in London when her heart yearned for Liverpool and her home. No, not *her* home any more. Her home, like her father, now belonged to someone else who had far stronger claim on them than she did, despite all the false protestations and pleas that had been made for her to stay.

Stay? When she had been so betrayed? Now she *was* going to cry . . .

She stared up at the Hogarth scenes as though in doing so she might be able to force back her emotions, oblivious to the fact that she herself was being watched until a quiet male voice beside her remarked, thoughtfully, 'As a surgeon I can never pass this painting without reflecting on Hogarth's skill in understanding the needs and desires of the human race.'

Sally whirled round, dumbstruck with chagrin at the familiar sound of the voice of one of the hospital's most senior consultants, the world-famous plastic surgeon Sir Harold Delf Gillies. Sally recognised his voice so easily because only a matter of days ago she had been on theatre duty when the great man had operated for the benefit of his students on a young child with a hare lip. Now overcome with self-consciousness and the fact that so great a personage should deign to speak to her outside the operating theatre, she could only nod her head.

'There is a great deal to be learned from history,'

Sir Harold continued. 'It is said that when Hogarth learned that St Bartholomew's Founders were going to engage an artist from overseas because they could not afford the fees of a British artist, he immediately offered to provide the hospital with two paintings free of cost, thus echoing the same charitable impulse that had led to the hospital coming into being in the first place, and possibly with the same practical eye for the future, knowing that just as the Founders' charitable donations to the hospital would carry their names and their charity into the future, so his paintings would be here for us to see and marvel over. It is a foolish or perhaps overproud man – or woman – who does not sometimes reflect on how history will judge them.'

Knowing the pioneering work Sir Harold had undertaken, Sally could only swallow hard and nod again.

'You have a natural bent for theatre work, Nurse, and I think the temperament for it.'

Sally was still trying to come to terms with the gift of his compliment several minutes after he had gone. Merely to have had the famous surgeon speak to her was more than any well-trained nurse ever expected, never mind being recognised by him and then praised for her ability.

It wasn't so much Sir Harold's praise that lingered on in her thoughts as she made her way to the nurses' home where she was living, though, as much as his comment about how a person might be judged.

Did her father ever worry about how he might be judged? Did her ex-best friend?

'Take in lodgers?' Unwittingly repeating the words of their neighbour, Tilly stared at her mother in astonishment, over the deliciously scented and gently steaming serving of fish pie that Olive had just dished up for her.

Her mother was a wonderful cook, and even though they were C of E, not Catholic, they always had fish on Fridays. Fish pie with lovely creamy mash, parsley sauce and peas was one of Tilly's favourite meals. Now, looking at her mother, her shiny almost black curls – which Tilly had inherited from her, along with her sea-green eyes and pale Celtic skin – caught back in a neat bun, a faint flush warming her skin, Tilly felt the urge to protest that she didn't want them to have any lodgers, and that she had been looking forward to it just being the two of them after the long years of her mother nursing her in-laws.

But before she could do so her mother told her gently, as though she knew what she was feeling, 'We have to, Tilly, love. Bills don't pay themselves, you know, and without your granddad's pension coming in, I'd have to go back to cleaning or taking in washing, and I reckon that I'd be better taking in lodgers than doing that.'

'But it will mean you looking after them, Mum, just like you did with Gran and Granddad.'

Olive shook her head, dislodging a small curl from her bun, which she tucked back behind her ear. At thirty-five, her figure as neat as it had been the day she'd met Tilly's father, she was glad that Tilly had inherited her own looks from the Irish side of her family, and her own trim figure with them. Though with that kind of beauty, Olive would never want Tilly to use her looks in the cheap kind of way that some young women did. A pretty face could bring trouble on a girl who didn't stick to society's rules. Even here, on respectable Article Row, there had been daughters who had been married with unseemly haste, and babies born 'at seven months' whilst weighing as much as any full-term infant. Not that Olive was in any hurry to see Tilly married. Her own experience as a young wife, a young mother and then a young widow meant she felt it was more important right now that Tilly was equipped with the means of earning her own living because you never knew what the future might hold. Of course, Olive would never share those views with anyone else. Good mothers were expected to want good marriages for their daughters, not financial independence.

'No, what I'm thinking, Tilly, is advertising only for respectable female lodgers, young women who will keep their rooms tidy and look after them.'

'But we've only got two spare bedrooms.'

'And an extra bathroom – don't forget about that. I know I said at the time that I couldn't see why your grandfather wouldn't have his bed moved downstairs to the front parlour, which would have been much easier for me, but now I think having that will help us to get the right kind of young women wanting those attic rooms.'

Olive went over to her daughter, smoothing her

curls back off her face and dropping a kiss on her forehead as she told her, 'You'll see, it will all work out for the best.'

'But what if there's a war, Mum, and the lodgers and us get evacuated?'

Olive's expression firmed. 'No one's going to evacuate me from this house, Tilly, I can tell you that, and we don't know yet that there will be a war.'

'But what if there is?' Tilly persisted. 'I'm not a child any more, Mum. I read the papers and listen to the news. There's all that blackout material you bought for us to cover the windows with, and our gas masks. No one's said anything about us handing them back, have they? And boys are still having to do their military training. Clara in the office said only tonight that her Harry is going to be starting his soon. I don't want you worrying about things and not telling me, Mum. I want to share them with you.'

Olive smiled both sadly and proudly, as she stroked the silky darkness of her daughter's hair.

'You're right,' she agreed. 'You aren't a little girl, you're a young woman, Tilly, and if there's to be a war, then we'll deal with whatever it brings us together.'

They smiled at one another, and then Olive added briskly, 'Meanwhile, as soon as we've finished eating and washed up, you and me are going to sit down and write out an advertisement to let the attic rooms. I was thinking that if you could get permission to type it on your typewriter at work then it would look properly businesslike and attract the right kind of lodger. Now eat your fish pie before it goes cold.'

Later that evening, in her bedroom, cold-creaming her face before she went to bed, Olive paused. There would be those Olive knew who would disapprove of her plans and even be opposed to them. A small tremble, part apprehension and part determination, ran through her body. Her father-in-law had been fond of boasting that he had got this house at a good price because of its number – thirteen. Thirteen was lucky for some, he had often said, giving a wink as he added, 'Especially for those who have the good sense to make their own luck.'

Now with the respectable silence of the Row settling round its inhabitants, Olive hoped desperately that it would be lucky for her as well in her new venture. Because if it wasn't then she would face having to sell the house, and she and Tilly would have to take a step down in the world.

TWO

'David, do come along, otherwise we're going to be late meeting Emily and Jonathon at the Ritz.' The sharp female voice was accompanied by an equally sharp and pointed glare in Dulcie's direction, as the smartly dressed brunette placed a very possessive and expensively leather-gloved hand on the arm of the dashingly handsome man Dulcie had been flirting with from behind her makeup counter in Selfridges cosmetics and perfume department.

'You'll be for it now,' Lizzie Walters came out from behind her own counter to inform Dulcie. 'You know who she is, don't you?'

'No. And I don't care either,' Dulcie informed the other girl, tossing the blonde hair that swept down onto her shoulders as she did so, her attention more on her own reflection in the nearby mirror than on what Lizzie was saying to her. And hers was a reflection well worth any man's second look, Dulcie knew. She was, after all, a looker. Everyone said so. It was her looks that had got her this very desirable job at the department store in the first place. Women customers looked at Dulcie's flawless complexion, and the way in which the makeup she was wearing emphasised her dark brown eyes and her pouting lips, and wanted to look like her, whilst men listened mesmerised when Dulcie sprayed her wrist with scent and then invited them to 'test' the fragrance. It was perhaps no wonder that in the six months she had been working in Selfridges, Dulcie's sales had earned her praise from their supervisor, but Dulcie herself had become unpopular with some of the other girls. Not Lizzie, though. Lizzie, small, plain and good-natured, worked on a counter selling bath salts, favoured by the store's more elderly Home Counties customers.

'Well, you should care,' Lizzie warned, 'because her dad's one of the directors here. Arlene wot works on the Elizabeth Arden counter and whose dad is one of the managers is pally with her.'

Dulcie tossed her head again. 'You mean that Arlene sucks up to her. Well, I'm not going to. And anyway, it's not my fault that her beau was gentlemanly enough to pay me a compliment.'

Lizzie gave her an old-fashioned look. 'Wasn't it? I mean, the way you put that lippy on yourself and then pouted at him like you did . . .'

'I was just showing him how it looked on,' Dulcie defended herself virtuously. 'So who is he anyway, then?'

Lizzie knew everything about the store and those who worked there. She'd been there herself for over ten years, after all.

'David James-Thompson, his name is, and he's

proper posh. Lydia Whittingham met him at a house party in Surrey, according to Arlene, and the talk is that she's going to land him and that they'll get engaged this Christmas.'

'Well, good luck to her, but I can't say as I'd want to get engaged to a chap who's always going to have an eye for other girls and flirt with them.'

'You encouraged him.'

'He didn't need encouraging; that kind never does,' Dulcie retorted smugly. 'You can take my word for it.'

It was true. One look into David James-Thompson's laughing hazel eyes and she'd known exactly what sort he was. Her sort, with his good looks, his thick wavy brown hair, his dashing man-of-the-world air, and most of all the devilment she had seen glinting in his eyes when he had looked at her so appreciatively. Whatever else David James-Thompson was, it certainly wasn't good marriage material.

'I must say, I envy Lydia being taken to the Ritz,' Lizzie continued.

'Well, I don't. If he was to ask me out, I'd want to go somewhere like the Hammersmith Palais where we could have a bit of fun, not the Ritz, with all those posh types and snobs.'

Lizzie laughed at her. 'The Palais? You'd never get a man like him going somewhere like that.'

'Want to bet?' Dulcie challenged her. Everyone knew that the Hammersmith Palais was simply the best dancehall in London. That was why Dulcie was prepared to make the trek from the East End to Hammersmith every Saturday night, instead of going somewhere local.

'Don't be daft,' Lizzie said, but Dulcie persisted.

'Come on, bet you five bob I can get him to meet me at the Palais, and before Christmas.'

'You're never serious.'

'I certainly am.' It was just the sort of challenge that Dulcie loved; daring, reckless, breaking the rules, pushing against boundaries, and using her looks to get her own way.

Born into a noisy cockney family, with an elder brother and a younger sister, Dulcie had learned young that she had to fight and use what nature had given her to get what she wanted, and to hang on to it once she had.

Two hours later Dulcie had left Selfridges and Oxford Street behind her, along with her white overall with its pink collar and trimmings. An admiring look from a motorist in a rakish-looking soft-topped car had her pausing to admire her reflection in a nearby shop window, and reflect that the bows she had added to the dress she was wearing, and which she had had copied by a local dressmaker from her own sketches of a dress in Selfridges Young Ladies Models Department looked much fancier than the original. The dress had small puffed sleeves and a close-fitting bodice, the bows adorning the ends of the long seams that ran from the bust down to below the waist. The fabric – silk, no less – had a dark plum background and was covered in a pansy print in a variety of hues from pale lilac through off-white to darkest purple – colours that suited her dark eyes and nicely tanned arms and legs, as well, of course, as drawing attention to her blonde hair.

White opened-toed high-heeled sandals and a white handbag completed her outfit, and Dulcie wasn't in the least bit surprised that men turned to look at her and other women cast her assessing and very often antagonistic looks. She was nineteen now and she'd known from being fourteen that she was a head-turner. She'd had more boys asking her for dates than any of the other girls in the bustling street where her family lived, but Dulcie wasn't daft. They could take her out but they weren't going to take her for a ride. There was no way that she was going to end up married to some no-hoper and a new baby on the way every year, like the girls she'd been at school with and her own mother. She would marry one day, of course – every woman had to have a husband to keep her – but first she wanted to have fun. And fun for Dulcie was flirting and dressing up and going out to the pictures, or a dance hall. Once she agreed to be someone's steady girl, all that would have to come to an end, and she wasn't ready for that – not yet.

Gleefully she imagined her triumph when she won her bet with Lizzie. A double triumph since in achieving it she would be getting the better of Miss Hoity-Toity, with her stuck-up airs and graces. Dulcie had no doubts about the success of her plan. David James-Thompson would come back to the shop. She knew men and she knew what that gleam in his eyes had meant. He was up for some fun and so was she, although their ideas of what fun was might not be exactly the same. There was no way she would let him get into her knickers. She wasn't daft. He was the sort that would run a mile if he thought he'd got her sort into trouble. But that wasn't going to happen.

She joined the queue waiting for the bus that would take her home to Stepney in the East End. Her father worked in the building trade as a plumber, and the family had a better standard of living than many of their neighbours, with a whole house to themselves, though Dulcie and her sister had to share a room and a bed.

When she did get married she wasn't going to be like her mother and have three children – six, if you counted the three that had died before being born. Dulcie didn't really want any children at all.

The bus was crowded and Dulcie had to stand, strap hanging and receiving an admiring look from the young conductor, who had to squeeze past her as he collected everyone's fares, whilst the bus lurched away from the kerb and pulled out into the traffic.

Dulcie was glad when the bus finally reached her stop and she was able to get off. There'd been an old man coughing away the whole time Dulcie had been standing close to him. A really poor sort he'd looked too, smelling of drink and his clothes shabby. Dulcie wrinkled her nose as she left the bus stop.

There was a pub on the corner of the street up ahead of her. Automatically Dulcie crossed the road to avoid having to walk past the group of men and women standing outside it. There were two families in their street who were notorious for the rows and fights they had when they'd been drinking. The Hitchins at number 4 and the Abbotts at number 9. It was nothing unusual to see both husbands and wives sporting bruises and black eyes. Ma Hitchins, all twenty stone of her, loved nothing better than a good set-to, rolling up her sleeves at the drop of a wrong word, ready to go into battle, and her children, as thin and cowed as she was fat and aggressive, knew better than to approach their mother when she'd had a few drinks. 'Poor little ragamuffins' was what Dulcie's own mother called them.

The house Dulcie's parents rented was halfway down the street at number 11. Cheaply built and mean-looking, the houses cast shadows over the street that stole its sunlight.

The street was busy with its normal early evening summer life; children playing with hoops and balls, grandmothers sitting on front steps and gossiping, men returning home from work. Dulcie knew everyone who lived there and they knew her.

'Fancy going down the pictures tonight, Dulce?' one of a group of young men called out to her as he sat astride his bike, smoking a cigarette.

'Not with you and them roving hands of yours, I don't, Jimmy Watson,' Duclie called back without stopping.

She and Jimmy Watson had gone to school together, and he was a friend of her older brother, Rick.

'Heard the news, have you?' Jimmy carried on

undeterred. 'About me and your Rick getting our papers.'

'So what's news about that?' Dulcie challenged him 'Every lad's getting called up.' She had reached her own front door now, which, like most of the doors in the street, was standing open.

'It's me, Ma,' she called out from the hall.

'About time. I need a hand here in the kitchen, Dulcie, getting tea ready.'

'It's Edith's turn. And besides, I've got to go upstairs and get changed.'

Edith and Dulcie didn't get on. Edith had aspirations to become a professional singer. She did have a goodish voice, Dulcie acknowledged grudgingly, but that was no reason for their mother to spoil and pet her in the way that she did, letting her off chores so that she could 'practise' singing her scales. Dulcie suspected that Edith was very much their mother's favourite.

'She's got an audition tonight, down at the Holborn Empire, and with Charlie Kunz, as an understudy for one of his singers,' her mother told Dulcie importantly. Charlie Kunz was a very well-known musician and band leader, who had made many records.

Dulcie, though, refused to be impressed, puckering up her lips to study her reflection in the small mirror incorporated into the dark-oak-stained hat and coat stand. That new lipstick sample she was wearing suited her a real treat. She'd have to find a way of making sure it got 'lost' and then found its way into her handbag, she decided, giving her full cherry-red lips another approving look.

31

Everyone at home had laughed at her when she had first announced that she wanted to work in the makeup department of Selfridges.

'You'll never get taken on by a posh place like that,' her mother had warned her. 'If you want fancy shop work then why not ask Mr Bryant at the chemist's if he'll take you on?'

'Work in that musty old place, handing out aspirin and haemorrhoid cream? No, thanks. I will get a job at Selfridges, just you watch.'

And of course she had, even if it had taken her six months of persistence to do so, first turning up and hanging about chatting with the cleaners and the like, finding out what was what and, more importantly, who was who.

Once she'd got all the information she needed, the rest had been easy. Ignoring the disapproving looks of the female lift attendants in their dashing Cossack-style uniforms, every day for a week she'd 'accidentally' ridden up in the lift with the manager of the ground-floor cosmetics department, on his way to have his morning coffee in the managerial restaurant, until, via a carefully planned process of acknowledging his presence with a shy smile, through to a welcoming smile that lit up her whole face, he finally asked her which department she worked in. That had been her cue to explain, fake modestly, using the 'posh voice' she had learned to mimic, that she didn't actually have a job at Selfridges, and that she rode in the lift every day hoping to pluck up the courage to put herself forward for one.

The manager had been totally taken in. Her

pretty face and perfect skin would be a definite asset to his department. Dulcie had been whisked through the formalities of becoming an employee, but although she might have charmed and taken in the manager, the girls she worked with were not as easily won over. Middle-class girls in the main, and protective of their own status, they were quick to sense that Dulcie was not really one of them. It wasn't just because they thought of her as lower class that they kept her at a distance, though. In Dulcie's eyes the truth was that it was because she was by far and away the best-looking girl on the whole of the cosmetics floor. Not that their hostility bothered her. She had wangled things so that her counter, the 'Movie Star' range of makeup, was almost the first that people – men – saw when they walked onto the floor, which meant that she got plenty of customers. Traditionally, Selfridges had its perfume counters close to the main doors on Mr Selfridge's instructions, so that customers coming in would receive a delicious waft of perfume. The idea was that this would tempt them to the counter to buy, as well as adding to the allure and exclusivity of the store itself.

It wasn't just her pretty face that kept Dulcie's sales up, though. She knew how to sell, and how to make 'her' customers want to come back to her. The reality may be that 'Movie Star' makeup was made in a factory not very far away at all from Smithfield Market, but its management, like Dulcie herself, were determined to ensure that their cosmetics reflected the glamour of Hollywood films and encouraged customers to think that by buying

33

it they too could look like their favourite movie star – or, failing that, the pretty girl who had sold them their precious new lipstick. The manager was very pleased with his decision to take her on, and Dulcie was equally pleased with her own success. Even the senior buyer for the cosmetics floor, Miss Nellie Ellit, had made it her business to seek Dulcie out and give her the once-over. It was thanks to Miss Ellit that Selfridges was well stocked with lipsticks ahead of war potentially breaking out, with more orders soon to be delivered.

So much for her brother, Rick's, teasing that the only job she was likely to get in Selfridges was scrubbing its floors.

Dulcie headed for the kitchen. Unlike some in the area, who only had a couple of rooms to house a whole family and so had to buy hot food from one of the many small shops in the area, Mary Simmonds had her own kitchen. Today the kitchen smelled of cooking fish, making Dulcie wrinkle up her nose. Now that she was working at Selfridges she had a good dinner there in the canteen, and so she wasn't particularly hungry.

'Rick called by Billingsgate on his way home and brought back with him a nice piece of hake,' her mother told her.

'I passed Jimmy on my way home. He said that him and Rick had got their papers,' Dulcie informed her mother.

'That's right,' Mary agreed. 'I don't know why they're making them all do this training when there isn't supposed to be going to be a war.' She was frowning now.

34

Dulcie knew, from the photographs of her as a young girl, that her mother had once been pretty, but now she was thin, and her hair turning grey, and her frown was caused by her anxiety for Rick and what might happen to him if there was a war.

The Government had bombarded them all with that many leaflets and warnings about blacking out windows, getting fitted for gas masks, children being evacuated to the country, not to mention filling the streets with sandbags and the parks with trenches, and setting up Air Raid Precaution posts all over the place, but at the same time the Prime Minister had said that they weren't going to go to war with Germany.

Germany was going to war with other countries, though, and now the same Prime Minister who had said there would not be a war was saying that if Germany went ahead and invaded Poland then Britain simply wouldn't stand for it. Dulcie didn't think she trusted Germany – or the Prime Minister.

'Come on, Dulcie,' her mother instructed sharply now. 'Get that oilcloth on the table and get the table laid, will you? I'm in a bit of a rush tonight, what with Edith upstairs getting ready for her audition. It's lucky that Rick's around to go with her because your dad would never have let her go on her own.'

'Not in my good frock, Mum. I'll have to get changed first,' Dulcie protested.

Although her mother sighed, she didn't argue, but then, as Dulcie knew, her mother was a stickler for keeping her home and her family clean. She'd been in service before she'd met Dulcie's father and married him, a country girl brought up to London by the family she worked for, and she had what she called 'my standards'. Those standards meant that unlike many of their neighbours there were no bedbugs in their beds, even if that did mean standing the feet of the beds in jars of water, and Dulcie's father regularly putting a coat of lime wash on the bedroom walls.

As she reached the top of the stairs, Dulcie saw Rick coming out of the bathroom, his chest bare and damp, his trouser braces hanging from his waist, and his face obviously freshly shaved, a towel slung over one shoulder.

'It's Edith who's being auditioned,' she mocked him, 'not you, or are you hoping that one of the chorus girls might take a fancy to you?'

'Can't see why they shouldn't take a shine to a good-looking chap like me,' Rick grinned back, not in the least bit put out by his sister's taunt. But then nothing and no one ever got under Rick's skin, Dulcie was forced to admit.

Over six foot tall, broad-chested and strong-armed from the local lads' boxing club he'd attended when he'd been at school, Rick, like Dulcie, had inherited their mother's family's good looks, although his hair was much darker than his sister's. Easy-going, with a sense of humour, Rick liked taking the mickey out of his sisters, especially Dulcie, who had such a high opinion of herself.

'Well, seeing as you've got your papers to go and do your training, and that means you getting a short back and sides, I don't reckon much to your chances.'

Rick laughed and winked at her. 'Much you know. Girls love a chap in uniform. Why don't you come with me and Edith down to the Empire?'

'What, and have to listen to her caterwauling and then banging on about her ruddy singing for the rest of the evening? No, thanks.' Her mother and her brother could fuss round Edith as much as they liked, Dulcie wasn't going to join in.

Turning on her heel, Dulcie pushed open the door to the bedroom she shared with her sister, and then froze, as she saw what Edith was wearing as she sat at their shared dressing table, brushing her hair.

'What do you think you're doing thieving my new blouse?' she demanded furiously, dropping her handbag onto the bed and going over to her sister.

'I'm not thieving it, I'm only borrowing it.'

'On, no, you aren't. You can take it off right this minute.'

As she spoke Dulcie reached out and grabbed hold of her sister, who immediately tried to push her off, yelling as she did so, 'Mum, Mum, Dulcie's being rotten to me.'

'That's my blouse and you aren't wearing it.' Dulcie had to raise her voice to make herself heard above her sister's screams of protest as Dulcie tried to unfasten her blouse. 'You're always thieving my things, helping yourself to them, and then ruining them.'

'No I'm not.'

'Yes you are. Now get my blouse off.'

'Dulcie, I've got to borrow it. I'm going for my audition this evening and I haven't got anything decent to wear. I'm not like you, working at

Selfridges. Oww!' Edith screamed as Dulcie grabbed her hair and gave it a furious tug.

'What's going on?'

Both of them turned to look at their mother, who was standing in the open doorway.

'It's her, she's pinched my best blouse.'

'It's Dulcie, Mum, she's being mean to me.'

'Oh, for goodness' sake, Dulcie, why shouldn't she borrow your blouse? She won't harm it. She is your sister, after all.'

'Sister? She's a thieving nuisance, and she's not wearing my blouse,' Dulcie insisted, her temper well and truly up now. 'I'm sick and tired of her treating my things like they're hers, borrowing my stuff without so much as a by-your-leave.'

'That's enough, Dulcie,' her mother told her sharply. 'Look how you've upset Edith.' She gestured to the younger girl's tear-stained face. 'I thought better of you than this, I really did.'

'That's it,' Dulcie exploded. 'I've had enough of this and her treating my clothes like she owns them. Do you know what I'm going to do? I'm going to find myself somewhere to live. Somewhere I've got a room of my own, with no thieving sister sharing it.'

'Dulcie!' Both her sister and her mother looked shocked.

Rick came in to join the fray, shaking his head and warning her, 'It's all very well saying that, Miss Hoity-Toity, but who's going to rent you a room? Mind you, I'm not saying that this place won't be a lot more peaceful without you around.'

As always when she was challenged, Dulcie

immediately dug her toes in and refused to back down. As the elder girl in her family it was her opinion that her younger sister should look up to her, and their mother should put her first and not fuss over Edith like she did. Dulcie's pride was smarting, and even though right now she had no idea how she would get herself a room of her own, she was determined that she would do so.

The sound of their father's voice downstairs, demanding to know where his tea was, had them dispersing, her mother hurrying back down, whilst Rick retreated whistling to his own room and Edith went back to brushing her hair, an expression on her face that to Dulcie was unbearably smug and triumphant.

Sibling quarrels were part and parcel of their shared home life, and normally blew over, but during the evening, the more Dulcie thought about renting a room of her own, the more appeal the idea had. She resented the cramped space she shared with her sister almost as much as she resented the way Edith thought she could help herself to her clothes, and, what was more, her pride was still stinging from the fact that their mother had taken Edith's side in the quarrel. Didn't she give her mother a whole two shillings a week for her keep more than Edith did? The trouble with her mother was that she didn't appreciate her like she should, and the trouble with her sister was that she didn't respect her like she should.

Dulcie might not have thought anything of the two of them sharing a bed before she had started to work for Selfridges, but now, from listening to the other girls, she recognised that most of them lived in rather better circumstances than her own, middle-class girls in the main, whose parents had neat houses on the outskirts of the city, instead of growing up at its heart as she had, in what was unpleasantly close to being a slum area. Dulcie could well imagine how Lydia, whose father was a director, would look down on her if she knew how Dulcie's family lived. She couldn't imagine David James-Thompson walking her home here after that date she intended to have with him. No, that certainly could not be allowed to happen. She'd have Edith hanging out of the window, gawping at him and then her mother insisting that he come in and listen to Edith's caterwauling, she was that proud of her. No, finding a room of her own somewhere a bit more respectable would suit the image she decided she needed to project if she was to win her bet with Lizzie.

First thing tomorrow she'd buy herself a paper and start looking for somewhere. With a room of her own, she could do what she wanted. There'd be no parents wanting to know where she was going and who she was seeing; no brother poking his nose in and warning her about not egging lads on, and knowing her place; no irritating sister. In her mind's eye Dulcie pictured herself dressed up to the nines, and going off to the Hammersmith Palais dancing with handsome David, the director's stuck-up daughter's beau, her clothes immaculately washed and ironed and not salvaged from her sister's disrespectful treatment of them.

*　　*　　*

Gratefully Tilly picked up from her desk the 'Rooms to Let' notices she had been given permission to type out – and not just to type, but also to place on the notice board in the corridor outside the Lady Almoner's offices.

The office Tilly shared with Clara was in reality more of a long narrow corridor than a proper room. Its one small window overlooked an inner yard where waste bins were stored. Panelled in dark wood from floor to ceiling, the room was dark and smelled musty from the contents of the files stored in the ancient filing cabinets that lined both the long walls. To reach Tilly and Clara's desk, at which they sat on opposite sides to one another with their heavy typewriters, it was necessary to squeeze between the filing cabinets and the desk itself. Tilly's typewriter was old and very well used, its 'd' key inclined to stick unless you knew just how much extra pressure to apply to it to make sure that it didn't. Each girl had a set of drawers in which she kept her stationery: Official-looking notepaper with the Lady Almoner's name and title printed on it, as well as Barts' address for official letters, thin copy paper and plain white paper for typing up patient notes, memos and envelopes. Here too were kept their very precious pieces of carbon paper, which had to be used until one could barely read the copy they made. Fresh supplies had to be pleaded for from Mr Davies, who was in charge of the stationery cupboard, and who, so Clara claimed, counted out every single sheet of paper he gave them.

The doors at either end of the office were never

closed. There was normally a trail of people coming in and out: junior clerks carrying or wanting files for their superiors, senior clerks bringing in hand-written letters and notes that had to be typed immediately, or sometimes requesting that Tilly or Clara took down their dictation in shorthand. Tilly and Clara were certainly kept very busy. Once a week Miss Evans, the Lady Almoner's personal secretary, would march into their office, her greying hair swept back into its tight bun, the jacket of her tweed suit on over her blouse, no matter how warm it was, her eyes, behind her rimless glasses, seeming to notice immediately a typing mistake or a file that was in the wrong place, as she went through the week's diary with the two girls.

Now, grabbing some drawing pins, Tilly headed for the corridor outside the main office where the clerical staff worked, narrowly avoiding bumping into a senior nurse, and dropping her typed notice as she did so.

Both Tilly and the nurse, a tall slender girl with glorious dark copper-coloured hair drawn back under her cap, lovely cream-toned skin and eyes so intensely blue they were almost violet, came to a halt.

'I'm so sorry,' Tilly said.

'It was my fault.' The other girl smiled, both of them bending down to retrieve Tilly's notice.

The nurse reached it first, a small frown creasing her forehead as she read it.

'Is this your notice?' she asked Tilly. 'I mean, are you the one who is advertising the rooms to let?'

'Yes. Well, my mother is. My grandfather died recently and since we've now got two spare bedrooms and a bathroom standing empty my mother thought we should let them out.'

'Where? I mean, is your house within easy reach of the hospital? Only I'm looking for somewhere myself.'

Tilly recognised immediately that the other girl was exactly the type of lodger her mother was looking for. Tilly guessed that the nurse was older than she, perhaps in her early twenties, and that she had that air and manner about her that said she was responsible and reliable.

'Yes. We live on Article Row in Holborn, at number thirteen. It isn't far away at all.'

Sally had been doing her own assessment. The young girl in front of her was well turned out and spotlessly clean, her manner bright and energetic, the kind of girl who quite obviously came from a good home. A home that would be clean and properly looked after, Sally judged.

'Well, bumping into you looks like being a piece of good luck for me,' she announced. 'I'm Sally Johnson, by the way.' She held out her hand for Tilly to shake.

'I'm Tilly – Tilly Robbins.'

'Look, Tilly, I'm really keen to see your rooms. How about if I came and had a look at three o'clock on Sunday afternoon? I'm off duty then.'

'Yes. I'm sure that will be all right. I'll tell my mother.'

Sally gave a brisk nod of her head, and then turned on her heel to hurry away, thinking what a stroke of luck it had been to bump into Tilly like that – fate, almost. Sally considered herself to be a good judge of character and she had liked Tilly straight away. Not that she was going to get her hopes up too high until she had seen the room in question. She'd certainly feel more comfortable if she wasn't easy accessible to anyone who might take it into their head to come down from Liverpool and enquire for her at Barts' nurses' home, and she was conscious of the fact that her room there was only temporary. She'd meant what she'd said before she left when she'd told her father that she didn't want anything to do with him in future – him or his new wife.

THREE

'The vicar's wife has just told me that she thinks she knows someone who'd be exactly right for a lodger,' Olive told Tilly as they walked home together arm in arm after the Sunday morning service. 'I mentioned to her that I wanted to let a couple of rooms at our Women's Voluntary Service meeting on Wednesday night, and now it seems she's heard of a girl who's looking for a room.'

Despite the warm sunshine Tilly shivered as she glanced down a side street to see a convoy of army lorries loaded with men in uniform rumbling along the Strand. The signs of preparation for a war that Mr Chamberlain had assured them would not happen were all around them, from the sandbags piled up around buildings, to the men in ARP uniforms, and the ongoing work on preparing public bomb shelters. In Hyde Park work was underway to dig trenches for shelters and war defences, and Tilly and her mother were doing their own bit 'just in case' it came to war. Tilly had joined her local St John Ambulance brigade, and her mother had joined the local Women's Voluntary Service group – the WVS for short – run by Mrs Windle, the vicar's wife.

There'd been a smattering of young men in uniform in church this morning, with their families, and Tilly had stopped to speak with one of them – a boy who had been ahead of her at school and who was home on leave from his obligatory six months' military training.

The last time she'd seen Bob had been early in the summer, before he'd started his training, and the difference in him had really struck her. Gone was the soft-featured, faintly shy boy she remembered and in his place was a thinner, fitter, tougher-looking young man who spoke proudly of his determination to do his bit for the country, and his belief that Hitler would not stop merely at invading Czechoslovakia, no matter what the Prime Minister might want to think.

After church the talk had all been of the prospect of war.

Now, though, feeling her mother's slight squeeze on her arm beneath the smart little white boxy jacket trimmed with navy blue she was wearing over her Sunday best frock, Tilly turned to her to listen.

'The girl Mrs Windle has in mind is your own age, Tilly, and an orphan. Apparently she's spent virtually all her life in an orphanage run by the Church, but now she's too old to stay there any more. They've kept her on to help with the younger children but the Church has decided to evacuate the orphans to the country, they can't take her

46

with them. They've found her a job working on the ticket desk at Chancery Lane underground station and now she needs somewhere to live where she'll feel comfortable and safe. She'll be coming round to look at the room at four o'clock this afternoon, after the nurse you were telling me about. They both sound ideal lodgers for us. I'm looking forward to meeting them.'

'Sally, the nurse, is a bit older than me, Mum, but I think you'll like her.'

Like Tilly, in her navy-blue, white-spotted dress, Olive was wearing her Sunday best outfit, an oatmeal linen two-piece of neatly waisted jacket and simple straight skirt, made for her by a local dressmaker from the Greek Cypriot community. Both women were wearing hats, a girlish white straw boater with navy-blue ribbons in Tilly's case, a neat plain oatmeal straw hat for Olive, which she was wearing tilted slightly to one side, in the prevailing fashion.

'I feel sorry for the orphan girl, though. How awful never to have known her parents,' Tilly sympathised, earning herself another maternal squeeze on her arm.

'Yes, the poor little thing was left on the doorstep of the orphanage as a baby. According to Mrs Windle, she's very shy and quiet,' Olive approved. 'She'll be good company for you, darling. You'll be able to go to church social events and dances together, I expect. Young people need to have fun, especially now, when there's so much to worry about.'

Because it was such a warm day neither of

them felt like a heavy traditional Sunday lunch, and so instead they were going to have a nice salad made from a tin of John West salmon Olive had splashed out on, and some lettuce, cucumber and tomatoes bought from Alan, the barrow boy from Covent Garden, whose pitch was just off the Strand. Eaten with some thin slices of buttered brown bread from the local bakery, it would be a feast fit for a queen, so Olive had pronounced before they had left for church. As an extra treat they were going to have a punnet of strawberries, again bought from Alan, with either some Carnation milk or possibly some ice cream from one of Italian ice-cream sellers who sold their wares from the tricycle-propelled mobile ice-cream 'vans' they drove round the streets.

The houses of Article Row didn't have large back gardens, but at least there *were* gardens and not merely back yards, like those of the poorer quality houses in the area.

Olive and Tilly's garden had a small narrow strip of lawn surrounded by equally narrow flowerbeds, with an old apple tree down at the bottom of the garden almost right up against the wall.

The Government had been urging people to think about growing their own salad and vegetables, but Olive wasn't keen. She was city born and bred and didn't know anything about gardening. The garden had been her father-in-law's preserve before he had become too ill to work in it, and although she and Tilly kept the lawn mowed, pushing the small Wilkinson Sword lawn mower over the grass in the summer, and weeded the flowerbeds Olive didn't fancy her chances of actually being able to grow anything edible.

'We could take a walk over to Hyde Park this evening, if you fancy it,' Olive suggested to Tilly as she unlocked their front door. 'We might as well enjoy this good weather whilst we've got it.'

'Yes, I'd like that,' Tilly agreed immediately. 'Bob was saying after church this morning that some of the men will be parading and drilling there – you know, being put through their paces a bit.'

'We'll go then. We have to support our young men in uniform.'

It was dead on three o'clock when Sally knocked on the well-maintained dark green front door of number 13. She had liked the look of Article Row the minute she had walked down it, after exploring a little of the area. Article Row might be different from the neat semi in Liverpool's Wavertree area where she had grown up and lived with the parents, but she could see that here the householders were every bit as proud of their homes as her parents and their neighbours in Lilac Avenue had been of theirs.

Her keen nurse's eye saw and immediately approved of Olive's sparkling windows, immaculate front path and tidy little front garden. Sally liked too the way that the door was answered within seconds of her knocking on it.

She would have known that the woman stepping

49

to one side to invite her into the clean fresh-smelling hallway was Tilly's mother because of their shared looks, even if Olive hadn't introduced herself with a warm but businesslike smile and a firm handshake.

The hall floor was covered in well-polished linoleum in a parquet flooring design, with a red and blue patterned carpet runner over it, the same carpet continuing up the stairs and held in place by shining brass stair rods.

'I'll show you the room first and then you can see the rest of the house afterwards,' Olive suggested. 'It's this way.'

As she followed Olive up the two flights of stairs to the upper storey, Sally took note of the clean plain off-white-painted walls and the well-polished banister rail. On the first landing the doors to the bedrooms were closed, as were the doors on the upper floor, but she liked the fact that Olive opened both bedroom doors, telling her, 'Both these rooms are more or less the same size. The front room was my late father-in-law's until he died. It was his idea to install a bathroom up here. I must say, at the time I thought it was a lot of work for nothing, but now I'm glad that he did. Whoever takes the rooms will share the bathroom between them.'

'Your notice said that you wanted respectable female lodgers,' Sally checked as she stepped inside the front-facing bedroom. It was simply furnished with the unexpected luxury of a double bed, a shiny polished mahogany wardrobe and a matching dressing table, and a square of patterned beige carpet over brown patterned lino, the walls papered with a plain cream paper with a brown trellis design. A dark gold satin-covered bedspread and eiderdown covered the bed, and when Sally lifted them back she could see that the bed linen underneath was immaculately white and starched.

In addition to the bed, wardrobe and dressing table there was a comfortable-looking chair and a small bookcase.

'That's right,' Olive confirmed. 'We've got another girl coming to look at the rooms at four this afternoon, an orphan, recommended by the vicar's wife. She's just started working at Chancery Lane underground station.'

Sally nodded.

'And this is the back bedroom,' Olive told her, stepping across the narrow landing, its floorboards stained dark oak.

This bedroom overlooked the garden and was rather more feminine in décor, with its pale lemon wallpaper decorated with white green-stemmed daisies. Its furniture was very similar to the furniture in the front room, though its coverlet and eiderdown were more of a lemon yellow than gold.

This time Sally paid her would-be landlady the compliment of not checking the bed linen.

The bathroom was as immaculately clean and fresh-looking as the bedrooms, half tiled in white, blue curtains hanging at the windows and a blue-patterned lino on the floor.

She liked it. She liked it very much, Sally acknowledged.

'If you were to take the room you'd be expected to keep it neat and tidy, although of course I'd given it a good clean once a week,' Olive told her.

'And the rent?

'Ten shillings a week. That includes an evening meal as well as breakfast, although I dare say, you being a nurse, you'll be working shifts.'

'Yes,' Sally agreed as she followed Olive downstairs and into the kitchen, which she wasn't surprised to see was as clean and tidy as the rest of the house.

'There are no gentleman visitors to be taken up to your room, but I do not rule out the possibility of you inviting a male friend into the front room to wait for you,' Olive continued.

Sally didn't have any problem with that.

'And the kitchen?' she asked. 'As I work shifts I'd want to be able to make myself a hot drink and have something to eat when I get back from my shift.'

Olive pursed her lips. She didn't like the thought of anyone else making free with her kitchen but she could see that Sally, as Tilly had said, was the sort who could be trusted and who had the right kind of standards.

'Yes, I'd be happy to allow that,' she agreed.

'Good, then in that case I'll take the room.' Sally informed her, specifying, 'The front room, please. I like to see what's going on.' What she really meant was that she didn't want to be surprised by any unexpected visitors from Liverpool coming in search of her.

'It will be one week's rent in advance,' Olive

told her. Although she was striving to sound businesslike, inwardly she was delighted to have found such an ideal lodger, and so quickly. If the little orphan turned out to be as good then Nancy was going to have to admit that she had been wrong complaining about the prospect of lodgers bringing down the neighbourhood.

'I'm living in the nurses' home at Barts at the moment. I'd like to move in as soon as possible, if that's all right with you? Say, Tuesday? I'll pay you then.'

'That will suit me nicely,' Olive confirmed.

'I'll aim to be with you at ten in the evening, if that suits you?' Sally offered, as she extended her hand to shake on their agreement.

'You mean she's taken the room already? That means that if the orphan girl says she wants the other room when she comes then you'll have let them both straight away,' Tilly praised her mother, after Sally had gone.

'Yes, and I must say that it's a relief. I was anxious whether we'd actually get anyone interested, never mind exactly the right type of person. I like your nurse, Tilly.'

'She's not my nurse, but I liked her too.'

Dulcie pushed off her forehead a stray curl that had escaped from her smooth Veronica Lake hairstyle to curl damply against her skin. In her right hand she was holding her best handbag: white leather, bought off a market trader, probably, she imagined, having been 'acquired' by dubious means. Or at least that had been her interpretation of the way in which the stall holder had looked warily up and down the street before producing the bag from a sack tucked away out of sight, when she'd asked to see 'something good quality'. Dulcie didn't mind where it had come from. What mattered to her was that it looked exactly like the classy and expensive bags on sale in Selfridges, at prices way beyond her slender means. Dulcie didn't consider what she had done to be dishonest. It was part and parcel of the way of life for many of those who had the same hand-to-mouth existence of her own family. The fact that her dad and her brother both worked as plumbers in the building trade meant that they both suffered periods when they weren't working, and Dulcie had grown up knowing that one penny often had to do the work of two. Dulcie had ambitions for herself, though: nice clothes, which, along with her good looks, attracted the attention of men and the envy of other girls, and having a good time.

She wasn't having a good time right now, though. She was already beginning to regret having said that she would find somewhere else to live. Initially, when she'd looked in the newspaper there had been so many rooms advertised that she thought it would be easy. But now, having spent over two hours of her precious Sunday – the only day she had off work – crisscrossing the streets between her parents' home in Stepney and Selfridges where she worked, she decided she really wanted something a bit closer to Selfridges than

Stepney. But one look down some of the streets in the advertisements had been enough for her to dismiss them as not the kind of places she wanted to live at all, and that was without even asking to see the rooms. She wasn't going to give up, though; slink home with her tail between her legs, so to speak, and have Edith get one up on her because she'd failed.

Two young men on the opposite side of the road – Italian, by the looks of them – were watching her as they smoked their cigarettes. The trouble with Edith was that she was an out-and-out show off, who always wanted to be the centre of attention, Dulcie decided crossly, as she stopped walking, as though she was unaware of the men's presence as she pretended to check the seam of her stockings. The result was a gratifying increase in their focus on her. They were good-looking lads, no doubt about that, with their olive complexions, crisp dark wavy hair, and their dark brown gazes, which were paying her such flattering attention.

Reluctantly she straightened up and continued down the street. All she'd heard ever since Edith's audition was how impressed they'd been at the Empire by her singing, and how Mr Kunz had said that he'd be a fool not to give her a chance. Dulcie would certainly be glad to get away from that – and from her sister.

Her feet, in her white sandals, were beginning to swell up, her toes feeling pinched, the August sunshine hot on her back. As a concession to the fact that it was Sunday – and she'd felt obliged to accompany her family to church after her father had started laying down the law about the importance of still being a family even if she was planning to move out, and that her elder brother could end up having to go to war, thanks to the Government telling Hitler that he wasn't to invade Poland, and that if he did the British Army would go to its aid – she was wearing a very smart white hat with a deep raised flat brim, trimmed with a bow made from the same fabric as her favourite silk frock. She'd been lucky with that piece of silk, and no mistake, snapping it up when she'd seen it on sale as the last couple of yards on the roll in Selfridges' haberdashery department. It hadn't been her fault that the Saturday girl had thought that it was one shilling and sixpence a yard instead of the four shillings and sixpence it should have been because the price written on the inside of the roll had been rubbed away a bit. Dulcie hadn't rubbed it away.

She was hot and beginning to feel tired and hungry. She looked at the paper again. Only three ringed notices left, the next one advertising a room to let somewhere called Article Row, Holborn.

Well, she was in Holborn. She saw a couple of children playing hopscotch out in the street and called out to them, 'Article Row, where is it?'

'Right behind you, miss,' one of them answered her, pointing to the narrow entrance almost hidden by the shadows thrown by the surrounding buildings.

Cautiously Dulcie approached it, stepping into the shadows and then out of them again as Article Row opened out ahead of her, her spirits lifting as she realised how much better the houses were here than in the other streets she had visited. Number 13, the paper said. Determinedly she started to walk down the narrow street of uniformly neat tall houses, with their shining windows and painted front doors. Here and there she noticed a lace curtain move slightly.

'The orphan girl is very late – it's gone five o'clock now – do you think that she's changed her mind or found somewhere else?' Tilly asked her mother as they sat together in the kitchen, listening for the sound of anyone knocking on the front door. The kitchen door was open to the warm summer air, and Tilly's faint sigh as she looked towards it had Olive saying lovingly, 'You go out and enjoy the sunshine, Tilly love, I'll hang on here a bit longer just in case she does turn up. Oh!' They both looked towards the door into the hall as they heard the knock on the front door.

'That must be her. Now you stay here because I want you to meet her. From what Mrs Windle said, she's a bit on the shy side and I think she'll probably welcome seeing someone of her own age.'

'Yes, Mum,' Tilly agreed. Pulling open the front door, Olive stared in bemusement at the appearance of the young woman who was standing on her doorstep. A quiet shy orphan was how the vicar's wife had described Olive's prospective lodger, but this young woman looked anything but quiet or shy, and she was dolled up to the nines, wearing clothes that were just a bit too stylish and attention-attracting for Olive's taste.

'I've come about the room you've got to let,' Dulcie announced without preamble, stepping forward so that Olive was forced to move back and admit her into the hall.

'Well, yes . . .' Olive began, taken aback by both her prospective lodger's appearance and her manner.

'It's this way, I suppose?' Dulcie continued, heading for the stairs without waiting for Olive to invite her to do so.

From the kitchen Tilly goggled at the passing vision, taking in the close fit of Dulcie's silk dress and the stylish brim of her hat with a tinge of envy laced with excitement. Tilly was a dutiful daughter and she understood that her mother's protective attitude towards her was for her own benefit, but sometimes she did yearn for a bit more excitement in her life. The girl whose heels she could now hear on the stairs was, Tilly knew immediately, someone who knew how to have fun, the kind of girl that secretly she half envied and would like to have as a friend even though she suspected that her mother would not be too keen on their friendship.

'These rooms are on the top floor, are they?' Dulcie demanded on the first landing. 'That will play hell with my feet, especially with me standing on them all day.'

Standing on them all day and wearing such high heels, Olive thought wryly, but all she said was, 'Actually, there is only one room now; the other has been taken.'

It had, had it? Well, Dulcie thought that was

58

probably a good sign, although she certainly wasn't going to be fobbed off with the second-best room. She'd insist on seeing them both, she decided as they reached the top landing.

'This is the room that's left,' Olive told her.

As she stepped into number 13's back bedroom, for once Dulcie had nothing sharp to say. The room was easily half as big again as the one she shared with her sister. It had a double bed that she would have all to herself, a large wardrobe for her clothes, a dressing table, the glass top of which was shiny and clean and empty of the clutter that Edith spread all over their own small chest with a mirror stuck on the wall above it. There was even a chair, and a sort of shelf thing.

Dulcie walked over to the window, barely glancing into the garden below, her mind racing, calculating. If this was the room the other lodger hadn't chosen then what must that room be like?

'I'd like to see the other room before I make up my mind,' she told Olive firmly.

'That room's already been taken,' Olive repeated.

'I'd still like to see it,' Dulcie insisted, pushing past her to go and open the other bedroom door, and then frown as she looked inside and saw that whilst it was the same size as the back bedroom, its décor was nothing like as good. Fancy anyone deliberately choosing all that dull beige and brown over the lemon and daisy-patterned wallpaper of 'her' room. Her room and she was determined to have it, but Dulcie wasn't going to let anyone know that and give them the upper hand.

'Somewhere a bit better than what's normally

59

on offer is what I'm looking for,' she announced. 'I work at Selfridges, see, and Mr Selfridge, he likes them as works for him to keep up their standards,' she told Olive, stepping back onto the landing.

The mention of the well-known and very smart Oxford Street store and the information that Dulcie worked there would normally have pleased Olive and been a point in Dulcie's favour, but on this occasion Olive felt dismayed, and not just because she didn't think that Dulcie was the kind of young woman she wanted under her roof.

'You *are* Agnes Wilson, aren't you?' she asked her. 'Only the vicar's wife told me that you were going to be working at Chancery Lane underground station, when she said that you were looking for a room.'

Someone else was after 'her room'? Dulcie wasn't going to allow that to happen.

'No, I'm not Agnes Wilson. My name's Dulcie Simmonds,' she told Olive. 'I saw the advertisement for this room in the paper.'

'Oh!' Olive felt both relieved and uncomfortable. 'In that case, I'm sorry, but I'm afraid I can't let the room to you. I've as good as promised it to Agnes. In fact, I was expecting her to come round this afternoon, that's why I thought you were her.'

The very thought that she might lose the room to someone else was enough to make Dulcie, used to having to compete with her younger sibling, all the more determined to have it.

'Well, you might have been expecting her but

she hasn't turned up, has she? And even if she did, there's no saying that she would want the room,' Dulcie pointed out, adding acutely, 'I can't see a landlady wanting to let out a room to someone who isn't reliable. It's all very well her not turning up to view the room when she was supposed to, but what if her rent started not turning up when it was due?'

Dulcie had a point, Olive was forced to admit. Even so, she wasn't keen on letting the room to someone she suspected could be a disruptive influence on the household.

'It should be first come, first served,' Dulcie insisted. 'I am here first, and I've got the money to pay my rent.'

As she reached down to open her bag, Olive recognised that Dulcie wasn't going to be dissuaded and that she was going to have to give in.

'Very well,' she agreed, against her better judgement. 'It will be a week's rent of ten shillings, including breakfast and an evening meal, in advance, payable the day you move in. I don't allow gentleman callers to visit my lodgers in their rooms, so if that's a problem . . . ?'

She was half hoping that Dulcie would say that it was, but Dulcie merely shrugged her shoulders and told her, 'That suits me. If a lad wants to see me then he can prove it by taking me out somewhere. I'm not courting anyone and I don't intend to start courting either. Not if there's to be a war. You never know what might happen.'

Somehow Olive didn't think that Dulcie was referring so much to the potential loss of a young man's life as the potential opportunity for her to amuse herself with the variety of young men a war could bring into her life.

As they went back downstairs it was hard for Olive not to feel rather unhappy about the prospect of having Dulcie as a lodger. So much for her belief earlier that everything had worked out really well.

'Before you go I should introduce you to my daughter, Tilly,' Olive told Dulcie. 'She works at Barts in the Lady Almoner's office, and my other lodger is a nurse from the hospital. A very respectable young woman indeed,' she emphasised, causing Dulcie to grimace inwardly, imagining what a dull pair her landlady's daughter and the nurse sounded, as she responded to Tilly's shy smile with a brief handshake.

Not that that bothered her. Dulcie wasn't one for girl friends unless for some reason it suited her to have one, like when she wanted to go dancing and neither Rick nor Edith would go with her, and she certainly wasn't looking for a bosom pal. That kind of thing was for soft schoolgirls.

'So that's that then,' Tilly announced after Dulcie had gone, with a final, 'Right then. I'll be round Tuesday evening then, about eight o'clock, if that suits?'

'Now we've got two lodgers.'

'Yes,' Olive agreed. 'Although I'm not sure that Dulcie will fit in as well as Sally.'

Working in the orphanage kitchen buttering bread for the orphans' tea, Agnes hoped desperately that Matron would not take it into her head to come in.

Because if she did, she was bound to ask her how she had got on this afternoon going to look at that room she had been supposed to go and see.

She had intended to go. She'd got the directions to it from Cook, whose husband worked on the London trams and knew everywhere, and she'd told herself that it was silly for her to feel so alone and afraid. After all, she was seventeen, and most of the orphans had to leave the orphanage at fourteen. She'd been lucky that Matron had taken pity on her and allowed her to stay on and work to earn her keep.

To Agnes the orphanage wasn't just her home, it was her whole life. The orphanage had taken her in when she had been left on its doorstep as an almost newly born baby, left in a shopping basket wrapped in a shabby pink blanket, which she still had, and wearing a flannelette nightdress and a nappy.

All of the other orphans knew something of their parentage and many of them had family, even if that family could not afford to house and feed them. Agnes was unique in the fact that she had no one. There'd been articles in the papers about her, Cook had once told her, attempts made to find the mother who had abandoned her. Sometimes even now Agnes looked at her reflection in the mirror and had wondered if she bore any resemblance to that mother, if her mother also had pale skin that flushed too easily, a pointed chin, pale blue eyes and light brown hair that sometimes refused to curl and at others curled where she didn't want it to. Had she been thin, like Agnes herself was? However much she thought and wondered, even ached privately about her mother, Agnes never thought about her father. Cook had, after all, come right out with what no one else would lower themselves to say, especially Matron, who was so good and who had been a missionary in Africa in her youth, and that was that a baby who had been abandoned on an orphanage doorstep probably did not have a father, at least not a respectable married-to-her-mother kind of father, a father who would want to acknowledge that Agnes was his daughter.

Agnes didn't really mind being an orphan. Not like some of the other children, who came into the orphanage when they were older and who could remember their parents. Those children had been Agnes's special little ones before she had been told that she had to leave. She had comforted them and assured them that they would come to like being at the orphanage and feel safe there, like she did. Agnes feared the outside world. She feared being judged by it because of her birth. She rarely left the orphanage other than to go to church and to walk with a crocodile of children escorting them on some improving visit to a museum or a walk in Hyde Park. At fourteen, when other orphans her age were boasting about the fun they would have when they were free of the orphanage's rules and restrictions, she had cried under her bedclothes for weeks, she had been so miserable at the thought of leaving.

That had been when Matron had said that she could stay on and work to earn her keep. She had been so grateful, feeling that her prayers had been answered and that she would be safe for ever. But now this war they might be having meant that the orphanage was being evacuated to another church orphanage in the country and that there wouldn't be room for Agnes, or for some of the other staff either.

Matron had explained it all to her and had told her that they had found her a job working at Chancery Lane underground station, selling tickets, and a room in a house owned by a friend of a vicar's wife.

'You'll like it at the station, Agnes,' she had said. 'And you know it well, from taking the little ones there on the underground. As for the landlady, she has a daughter your own age, and I am sure that the two of you will quickly become good friends.' Matron had told her this in that jolly kind of voice that people used when they didn't want you to be upset and cry.

Agnes had nodded her head, but inside she had felt sick with misery and fear. She still did, but now those feelings were even worse because this afternoon, instead of going to see Mrs Robbins at 13 Article Row, she had gone and sat on a bench in Hyde Park, where she had wished desperately that she didn't have to leave the orphanage and that the orphanage didn't have to be evacuated to the country. Agnes had never hated anyone in her life, but right now she felt that she could hate Adolf Hitler. She would have to go and see Mrs Robbins eventually, she knew that. And tomorrow morning she would have to present herself at

Chancery Lane underground station, ready to start her new job. She wouldn't be able to escape doing that, because Matron was going to take her there herself.

FOUR

'So you're going ahead then with this taking in lodgers business?'

Nancy had caught Olive just when Olive was in the middle of hanging out her washing, coming to the hedge that separated their back gardens and obviously determined to have her say.

'Yes. I've got lodgers for both rooms now,' Olive agreed as she pegged out the towels she had just washed. There was a decent breeze blowing, so they should dry quickly.

'And one of them's from the orphanage, so I've heard.' Nancy's voice was ominously disapproving. 'You wouldn't catch me taking in an orphan. You never know what bad blood they might have in their veins.'

'According to the vicar's wife, Agnes is a very quiet, respectable girl.'

'Well, that certainly wasn't her I saw coming walking down the Row yesterday afternoon then, all dressed up to the nines and on a Sunday too. Anyone could see what sort she is. Too full of herself for her own good. I hope you won't be giving her a room.'

'I think you must mean Dulcie,' Olive felt obliged to say. 'Yes, she is going to be moving in. She works in Selfridges.'

'She might work in Selfridges but it's plain where she's come from, and where she's going to end up if she isn't careful. I don't want to worry you, Olive, but there's going to be a lot of people in the Row who won't be at all happy about what you're doing. You know me – I like to mind my own business – but I wouldn't be being a good neighbour if I didn't warn you for your own good. It's like I was saying to Sergeant Dawson after church yesterday: we've got standards here in the Row.'

Olive nodded but didn't say anything. Inwardly, though, she suspected that she hadn't heard the last of her neighbour's disapproval.

Agnes had had the most terrible day, the worst day of her life, starting from when Matron had left her in the charge of Mr Smith, the portly, moustached, stern-looking man who was in charge of the ticket office at Chancery Lane station and thus in charge of her.

Her new dull grey worsted uniform piped in blue, which London Transport supplied for its female employees working on buses, trams and the underground, was too big for her. They hadn't been able to find anything to fit her when she'd been taken to the large supply depot where the uniforms were handed out because she was so small and thin. Agnes knew she'd only been taken on in the first place because Matron had spoken up for her, and that had only made her feel even more as though she wasn't really good enough. The grey serge didn't do anything for her pale complexion and mouse-brown hair, her uniform somehow making her face look pinched and thin, and she'd seen from the look that Mr Smith had given her that her appearance hadn't impressed him.

She'd felt sick with anxiety before she'd even tried to follow Mr Smith's brisk instructions, but that had been nothing to the horrible churning feeling that had gripped her stomach when a customer had complained loudly about her slowness and then she'd gone and given him the wrong change.

After that the day had gone from bad to worse, leaving her filled with panic and despair. She'd seen from the look that Mr Smith had given her at five past five, when he'd told her to clock off because the evening shift was about to start, that he was angry with her because of all the mistakes she'd made. She'd let Matron down, she knew, and soon she was going to have to admit to her that she'd deliberately not kept her appointment with Mrs Robbins in Article Row.

Now, still wearing her second-hand uniform, her head down, and tears not very far away, Agnes headed for the steps that would take her out of the station and into the daylight, gasping as she was almost knocked flying.

Immediately a pair of male hands gripped her,

a male voice saying, 'I'm sorry. Are you all right?'

Those words – the first of any kindness she had heard all day – were too much for her and to her shame she couldn't stop herself from bursting into tears.

Immediately the young man – she could see through her tears that he was a young man – pulled her into the privacy of a shadowy area against the wall and announced, 'You must be the new girl that started at the ticket office this morning. I'm Ted Jackson, one of the drivers. What's wrong?'

'Everything,' Agnes told him tearfully. 'I made a customer cross because I was too slow and I got his change wrong. Mr Smith is really angry with me, and I know he'll give me the sack and then Matron at the orphanage will be upset because I've let them down.'

'Orphanage?'

'Yes. I'm an orphan but I can't stay at the orphanage any more because they're going to be evacuated, and anyway you can't stay once you're fourteen. I was lucky that they let me stay for so long.'

The poor kid looked as pathetic as a half drowned kitten he'd once rescued from the river, Ted thought sympathetically.

'Look, I'm not due to start work yet, so why don't you and me go upsides and have a cup of tea? It will help calm you down,' he suggested, putting his hand under her elbow and leading her back towards the steps.

Agnes experienced another surge of panic, but

a different one this time. Matron was very strict with her girls, and Agnes had never ever been alone with a young man.

'Come on, it's all right, you'll be safe with me,' Ted assured her as though he had guessed what was worrying her. 'Got two sisters of me own at home, I have.'

They'd reached the top of the steps and somehow Agnes discovered that she was being bustled into a small café where the woman behind the counter greeted Ted with a broad smile.

'Your usual, is it, Ted?'

'Nah, just two cups of tea this time, Mrs M.' He glanced at Agnes and then added, 'And a couple of toasted teacakes.'

A toasted teacake – Agnes's mouth watered. She hadn't been able to eat the egg sandwiches she'd brought with her for her dinner because she'd been so worked up and upset.

The café was only small but it was homely and looked clean and welcoming. It smelled of strong tea and hot toast. The counter had a glass display case in which there were some scones and sausage rolls and sandwiches. Opposite the counter was a window with a sign in it saying 'Café'. A row of wooden tables and chairs ran the length of the wall from the doorway, past the window and into the corner of the room. There were red and white checked cloths on the table and the same fabric had been used to make curtains for the window. Brown linoleum covered the floor, and the two women behind the counter serving the customers were large and jolly-looking.

'You don't want to take too much notice of old Smithy,' Ted advised Agnes once they were settled at a table, their mugs of tea and toasted teacakes in front of them. 'His bark is worse than his bite.'

'But I got everything so wrong.'

'That's only natural on your first day.'

'I couldn't remember which line was which, or any of the stations,' Agnes admitted in a low voice. 'I'll be sacked, I know I will, and then Matron will be cross with me as well, especially when she finds out that I didn't go to Article Row like she told me.'

'Article Row? What were you going there for?'

'To get myself a room. The vicar's wife had told Matron that there was a room there for me and I was supposed to go round yesterday to see it but I didn't . . . I couldn't.' Her eyes filled with fresh tears. 'I don't want to go anywhere. I want to stay at the orphanage.'

'What, and end up stuck in the country? That's daft. I'll tell you what, why don't you go round to this Article Row after you and me have finished our tea? You can tell the landlady that you made a mistake and that you thought it was tonight you were supposed to go. That way you won't get into trouble with your matron and you'll have some-where to live.'

Ted made it all seem so simple and so sensible. He made her feel better, somehow.

'I'll still lose my job. Mr Smith told me that I'd got to learn the stations on every single line, or else.'

'Well, that's easy enough to do,' Ted told her.

Agnes's eyes widened with hope and then darkened with doubt.

'I mean it,' Ted assured her, adding, 'I could teach them to you if you wanted. See, my dad worked on the underground as a driver all his life, and now I'm doing the same. Grown up with knowing what the lines and the stations are, I suppose. Dad used to sing the names to me when I was a kid and lying in bed.'

'Sing them to you? You mean like . . . like hymns?' Agnes asked in amazement.

'Well, not hymns, perhaps, but like what you might hear down at the Odeon, you know . . .' He cleared his throat and began to sing in a pleasant baritone, as though to a marching tune that he had made up.

'Here's to the Piccadilly –
Cockfosters, Oakwood and Southgate,
Arnos Grove, Bounds Green and Wood Green,
Turnpike Lane, Manor House and Finsbury
   Park,
Ar – sen – al
Holloway Road, Caledonian Road
King's Cross and Russell Square,
Holborn, Covent Garden and Leicester Square.'

Agnes was entranced. Ted made learning the names of the lines and their stations seem such fun.

Her obvious awe and delight had Ted's chest swelling with pride. He was an ordinary-looking lad, of only middling height and a bit on the thin side, with mouse-brown hair and vividly blue eyes.

His smile was his best feature in his opinion, and his ears his worse because they stuck out so much. He had long ago accustomed himself to the fact that his looks weren't the sort that girls made a beeline for, so he'd learned to compensate for that with his friendliness – not that he was the kind to go chasing after girls. He'd got his mum to help out after all. But something about Agnes's plight, coupled with her awed delight, touched his heart. Ted reckoned that the poor little thing needed someone to look out for her and give her a hand, and he'd as soon do it himself as see her taken in by some lad who might not do right by her. There were plenty of that kind about, and she obviously hadn't a clue about how to look after herself properly.

'Look, I'll tell you what,' he offered. 'How about you and me meet up every teatime when you come off work, and I teach you the names of the lines and their stations?'

'You'd do that for me?' Agnes didn't even try to conceal her disbelief.

'I've just said so, haven't I?'

For a moment euphoria filled Agnes but then her ingrained lack of self-confidence swamped it.

'It's very kind of you but I just don't think I'll be good enough to learn them properly.'

'Course you will,' Ted assured her. 'If my old man could teach me and I could learn, then I reckon I can teach you and you can learn.'

'Does your father still drive the trains?'

Ted shook his head. 'He's dead. Got killed upsides in an accident six years back. It was a foggy night and he got hit by a bus. Didn't stand a chance. Killed him straight off.'

He said it so matter-of-factly that Agnes could only stifle her shock to say politely, 'How awful.'

'Knocked us all for six when it happened, but we've got used to it now. Course, it's meant that I've had to help Mum out with my own wages and take a bit of a firm line with the girls when they start giving her their cheek, and acting up.'

'How old are your sisters?' Agnes asked him shyly. She didn't really know anyone who had a real family. She'd never met someone who was as frank and open as Ted was. His frankness enabled her to ask the kind of questions she would never normally have dreamed of asking.

'Marie, she's the eldest, she's ten, and then there's Sonia, who's eight.' He paused and then added, 'In case you're wondering how come I'm so much older, it's because there was a couple of others – both boys – that died young. Talks about 'em still, Ma does, and then gets herself in a state about them, poor little tykes. Now, I've got to get on duty and you've got to get yourself over to – what was it? – Article Row, and get yourself sorted out. Then tomorrow teatime you and me will meet up here and get started off learning you your lines and stations.'

He was already standing up so Agnes did the same, telling him emotionally as they left the teashop, 'You've been so kind coming to help me just when I thought . . . You're like a Good Samaritan.'

'Aw, get away with you, it was nothing,' Ted

told her, looking embarrassed. 'I'd do the same for any kid that was in the state you'd got yourself into. Now you remember, tomorrow teatime here. Right?'

'Right,' Agnes told him.

The warm happy glow she felt from Ted's kindness accompanied her as far as the entrance to Article Row, but once she could see how nice the houses in the Row looked, she felt her confidence start to slip away, and at the same time a feeling growing in her that if she couldn't stay at the orphanage then this would be a lovely place to live. Out of the corner of her eye she could see two women walking on the pavement on the other side of the street, going in the opposite direction to her, both of them glancing at her, their curiosity making her feel self-conscious and awkward. Number 13, she'd been told; that was the next house. Now her tummy had begun to cramp nervously.

Inside her kitchen, Olive had just sunk down into a chair to drink the very welcome cup of tea Tilly had brewed for her. Although she was glad to have both her rooms let, she would really rather not have had a girl like Dulcie as one of her lodgers. Her maternal instincts told her that Dulcie was not likely to be a good influence on Tilly, who was just at that age when she wanted to be grown up and go out to dances, and, of course, meet boys.

The unexpected knock on the door surprised them both.

'I hope that isn't Nancy from next door coming

round to complain about something,' Olive sighed, getting up to go and see who it was.

The thin mousy-haired and obviously anxious girl, standing outside in her grey serge underground uniform immediately broke into nervous speech.

'Please, miss, I'm Agnes and I'm ever so sorry. I was supposed to come yesterday only I didn't. It's about the room. Matron at the orphanage said that you had a room for me.'

Olive's heart sank. The girl looked so on edge, and so much more the kind of lodger she had expected and wanted than Dulcie, who had now taken her room.

'I'm sorry,' she said with genuine regret, 'but the room's already gone, I'm afraid. When you didn't come yesterday, I thought you didn't want it.'

Olive's words made Agnes feel as though a bucket of icy cold water had been thrown over her, drowning the hopes she had begun to build up and leaving her feeling as close to tears as she had done when Ted had found her on the stairs.

Poor girl, Olive thought, seeing the shocked despair on Agnes's face. Tears weren't very far away, Olive could tell.

'Look, why don't you come in and have a cup of tea?' she offered kindly. 'It's a warm evening and you'll have been working all day.'

'Oh, no, you're very kind but I don't want to be a nuisance,' Agnes began, but before she could turn to walk away, Olive was reaching for her arm and drawing her inside, guiding her down the hallway and into the kitchen, where a girl of her own age, but much prettier than she, with her dark curls and cherry-red lips, was standing in front of the sink, drinking a cup of tea.

'Tilly, this is Agnes who was supposed to come yesterday about the room. Agnes, this is my daughter Tilly,' Olive explained, adding, 'I've told Agnes that I've already let the room, but she's going to have a cup of tea with us before she goes home.'

Tilly nodded and set about removing a clean cup and saucer from the cupboard and filling the kettle with some water to make a fresh pot of tea, setting it on the stove and then lighting the gas.

The girl who her mother had brought into the kitchen looked dreadfully upset, and so small and thin that Tilly immediately felt sorry for her.

'I don't know what Matron is going to say to me,' Agnes told them both once she had been coaxed into a chair and a fresh cup of tea put in front of her. 'She'll be ever so cross. I should have come yesterday, but all I really wanted was to be evacuated with them. You see, the orphanage is all I've got – the little ones and Matron and everyone – but like Matron says, they can't take me with them because really I shouldn't be there at all, me being seventeen.'

A tear rolled down her face and splashed onto her hand, followed by another.

'Oh, I'm sorry, acting like this. It was just that

I'd got my hopes up. And now I'd better go.' Agnes looked agitated and even more upset as she finished her tea and then stood up. 'You've been ever so kind.'

She was trying to be brave but Olive could see how upset she was. There was nothing she could do, though. Dulcie was the kind who would make a first-class fuss if Olive tried to persuade her to give the room up, Olive knew.

She walked with Agnes to the front door. Then, just as she was about to open it, Tilly called urgently from the kitchen, 'Mum, can I have a word? Now!'

Olive frowned. It was unlike Tilly to be forgetful of her manners, and not wait to say whatever it was she wanted to say until their visitor had gone.

Agnes was waiting for her to open the door. Feeling desperately sorry for her, Olive did so, watching as she walked down the garden path, her head down, no doubt to hide her tears.

'Mum!' Tilly's voice was even more urgent now.

'Yes, Tilly?'

'I've been thinking. There's two beds in my room, and if Agnes doesn't mind sharing with me then we could double up.'

Olive could almost feel her heart swelling with love and pride. Her wonderful kind daughter had not been rude; her impatience had been caused by her desire to help another girl whom she had recognised was desperately in need.

'Well—' she began.

'Please, Mum,' Tilly pleaded. 'She hasn't got

anywhere else, and if she doesn't like sharing with me then at least she'll have somewhere until she finds another room.'

'It won't be easy, Tilly,' Olive warned. 'You've always been used to having your own room.'

'I know, but I really want to, Mum. Can we?'

'Very well. If you're sure,' Olive agreed.

'I am sure.' Tilly flung her arms round her mother and kissed her before running to the front door and pulling it open.

Agnes had almost reached the end of Article Row when she heard the sound of someone running behind her. She stopped and turned round, surprised to see Tilly, her black curls dancing in the early evening sunshine.

'Agnes,' Tilly called out breathlessly, 'wait. I've got something to tell you.'

Silently Agnes waited.

'I've spoken to my mother and, if you're in agreement – that is, if you want to – you can share my room. There's a spare bed, and it's a good size. I know it won't be the same as having your own room, but I thought that, well, for now, until you find somewhere better, it might do?'

Somewhere better than number 13 Article Row and Tilly and her mother? Could such a place exist? Agnes didn't think so.

'You really mean it?' she asked, hardly daring to believe it. 'You'd really share your room with me?'

'Yes,' Tilly assured her, taking her arm and leading her back.

*   *   *

Half an hour later, after another cup of tea in number 13's kitchen, it was all arranged. Agnes would return to the orphanage to inform Matron that she was moving into Mrs Robbins' house.

Her heart flooding with joy and gratitude, Agnes thanked her saviours, and this time when she headed back down Article Row she held her head high, her tears replaced by a smile.

FIVE

'So you're doing it then? You're really going to go ahead and move out?'

Despite the fact that she could hear disbelief and censure in her brother's voice, Dulcie tossed her head and demanded, 'Yes I am, and so what?'

They were in the cramped shabby living room of their home, empty for once apart from the two of them.

'So what?' Rick repeated grimly. 'Have you thought what this is going to do to Mum? We're a family, Dulcie, and in case you've forgotten there just happens to be a war about to start. That's a time when families should stick together.'

'That's easy for you to say when you're leaving home to go and do six months' military training. Have you thought about what that's going to do to Mum?' she challenged him, determined to fight her own corner.

'I don't have any choice. It's the Government that's said I've got to go,' Rick pointed out.

'And I don't have any choice either, not with Edith treating my things like they belong to her

82

and Mum backing her up.' There was real bitterness in Dulcie's voice now. 'Mum always takes Edith's side; she always has and she always will. All she wants me for is my wages.'

'Aw, come on, Dulcie, that's not true,' Rick felt obliged to protest, but Dulcie could see that he was looking uncomfortable. Because he knew the truth!

'Yes it is,' Dulcie insisted. 'Mum's always favoured Edith, and you know it. It's all very well for you to talk about families sticking together, but when has this family ever done anything for me? Mum hasn't said a word to me about wanting me to stay. If you ask me she's pleased to see me go. That way she can listen to Edith caterwauling all day long.'

There was just enough of a grain of truth – even though Dulcie had deliberately distorted and exaggerated it – in what she was saying for Rick to fall silent. During their childhood his sister had always been the one who seemed to get it in the neck and who had borne the brunt of their mother's sometimes short temper, whilst Edith was indeed their mother's favourite. Despite all that, though, he felt obliged, as the eldest of the family, to persist doggedly, 'We're family, Dulcie, and families like ours stick together.'

'Fine, but they can stick together without me.'

'You'll regret leaving,' Rick warned her, 'and I'm only telling you that for your own good. Moving in with strangers – no good will come of it.'

'Yes it will. I'll not have a thieving sister helping

herself to my clothes, nor a mother always having it in for me. Besides, it's a really nice place I'm moving to, and you can see that for yourself 'cos I need you to give me a hand getting my stuff over there tonight.'

Rick sighed. He knew when he'd lost a fight, especially with Dulcie, who had her own ideas and opinions about everything, and who was as sharp as a tack when it came to making them plain.

'All right, I will help you,' he agreed, 'provided you promise me that you'll come home every Sunday to go to church with Mum.'

Dulcie was tempted to refuse, but she needed Rick's help if she was to get her things to her new digs in one trip, and besides, something told her that her new landlady was the sort who thought things like families and going to church on Sunday were important. If she didn't accept Rick's terms she could end up finding herself dragged off to church by Olive. It would be worthwhile coming back once a week, if only to show off her new – unborrowable – clothes to Edith.

'All right,' she conceded.

'Promise?' Rick demanded.

'Promise,' Dulcie agreed.

Sally looked round her small Spartan room in the nurses' home. The few possessions she had brought with her from Liverpool – apart from the photograph of her parents on their wedding day, in its silver frame – were packed in her case, ready for her to take to Article Row. As soon as she'd come off duty she'd changed out of her uniform, with its distinctive extra tall starched Barts' cap, much taller than the caps worn by any nurses from any of the other London hospitals. Sisters' caps were even taller, and even more stiffly starched, Sally guessed.

Workwise she'd fitted in quite well at Barts. She loved theatre work and had been welcomed by the other theatre staff, most of whom were down to be evacuated should Germany's hostile advances into the territories of its neighbours continue and thus lead to a declaration of war by the British Government. Normally, of course, Sally would not have been allowed to 'live out' but these were not normal times.

Not normal times . . . Her life had ceased to be what she thought of as normal many months ago now.

She sat down on the edge of her narrow thin-mattressed bed, nowhere near as comfortable as the bed waiting for her in Article Row, and nowhere near as comfortable as the bed she had left behind her in Liverpool in the pretty semi-detached house that had always been her home. The house that she had refused to enter once she had known the truth, leaving Liverpool in the pale light of an early summer morning to catch the first train to London, with nothing but a recommendation to the matron at Barts from her own Hospital, and the trunk into which she had packed her belongings. Heavy though that trunk had been, it had been no heavier than the weight of her memories – both good and bad – on her heart.

She hadn't told her father what she was

planning to do. She'd known that he would plead with her and try to dissuade her, so instead she'd asked the taxi driver to take her first to her parents' house, from her temporary room at the nurses' home, where she'd put her letter to her father very quietly through the letter box, before going on to Lime Street station.

Her father would have read her letter over breakfast. She could picture him now, carefully pouring himself a cup of tea, sitting down at the blue-and-white-checked-oilcloth-covered table, with the paper propped up against the teapot, as he read the words that she had written telling him that she wanted nothing more to do with him.

Pain knifed through her. She had loved her parents so much. They had been such a happy family. *Had been*. Until the person she had thought of as her closest friend – close enough to be a sister – had destroyed everything.

A mixture of misery and anger tensed her throat muscles. The death of her mother had been hard enough to bear, but the betrayal of her closest friend; that had left a wound that was still too poisoned for her even to think of allowing it to close. As with all wounds, the poison must be removed before healing could take place, otherwise it would be driven deeper, to fester and cause more harm. Sally could not, though, see any way to remove that poison or to salve its wound with acceptance and forgiveness. She couldn't. If she did she would be betraying her poor mother, who had suffered so dreadfully. She reached for her photograph and held it in both her hands as she looked into the faces of her youthful parents, her father so tall and dark and handsome, her fair-haired mother so petite and happy as she nestled within the protective curve of his arm.

Her mother had been such a happy, loving person, their home life in their comfortable semi so harmonious. Sally had grown up knowing that she wanted to be a nurse and her parents had encouraged her to follow her dream. Her father, a clerk working for the Town Hall, had helped her to enrol for their local St John Ambulance brigade as soon as she had been old enough. Those had been such happy days, free of the upsets that seemed to mar the childhoods of others. In the summer there had been picnics on the sands at Southport and Lytham St Annes; visits to Blackpool Tower and rides on the donkeys, trips across the Mersey, of course, in the ferry boats that plied between Liverpool and New Brighton, whilst in the winter there had been the excitement of Christmas and the pantomime.

And then when she had started her formal nurse's training at Liverpool's prestigious teaching hospital she had felt as though all her dreams had come true, especially when she had palled up with Morag, the pretty girl of Scots descent, whom Sally had liked from when they had first met up as new probationers.

Sally could still remember how awkward and excited at the same time she had felt when Morag had first introduced her to her elder brother, Callum, with his dark hair and piercing blue eyes. Callum, who looked as handsome as any film star and whose smile had made her insides quiver with delight.

Morag and Callum had become regular visitors at her parents' home, welcomed there by her mother once she learned that they had lost their own parents, when the small rowboat they had taken out on Loch Lomond during a holiday there had sunk, drowning them both. That had been two years before she had met them, and before Callum's job, as a newly qualified assistant teacher, had brought them both to Liverpool, where Morag had decided to train as a nurse.

They had all got on so well together, her father and Callum sharing an interest in natural history and often going off on long walks together, whilst Morag had shown Sally's mother how to make the Scotch pancakes they all learned to love too much, small rounds of batter cooked on a flat skillet and then served warm with butter.

But then her mother had become ill, and had felt too sick to want to eat anything.

It had been Morag who had held her tightly after the doctor had broken the news to them that her mother had stomach cancer, Morag who had so willingly and, Sally had believed, lovingly helped her to nurse her mother through the long-drawn-out and heart-searingly hard to bear pain she had suffered in the last weeks and days of her life. Morag who had comforted Sally before, during and after the funeral, and not just Morag but Callum as well, both of them standing staunchly at her and her father's sides to support them through the ordeal of her mother's loss and burial.

In the weeks that had followed they had all become closer than ever, Callum calling regularly to spend time with her father, Morag too calling at the house to make hot meals for her father when she was off duty and Sally wasn't.

Sally had been grateful to her then, loving her for her generosity in treating Sally's father almost as though he were her own and helping to ease their grief.

Only it hadn't been as another adopted 'daughter' that Morag had been comforting her father at all.

Sally closed her eyes and put the photograph face down inside her case before closing it, as though she couldn't bear to have her mother 'face' the betrayal that still seared her own heart. It was time for her to go; her new life beckoned. It might not be what she had hoped for in those heady days when she had first felt the thrill of excitement that came from having her hand held in Callum's, nor the warmth she had felt at believing that Morag was her best friend and as close to her as any sister, but it was her life and she had to live it, doing what she had been trained to do and remembering always what she owed to the mother she had loved so much and who had loved her. How her father could have done what he had she didn't know, but she must not think of him. She must think instead of what lay ahead. There were those who had warned her that what she was doing was reckless when she had announced that she was leaving Liverpool to go to work in London, and right at its heart, the very place that would be most exposed and at risk if they did end up at war with the Germans. Sally had said nothing. What could she say, after all? That she didn't care whether or not she lived or died, that part of her actually wished that she might die rather than go on living with the feelings that were now tearing her apart, the memories of her father's voice, at first defensive and then angry when she had told him how shocked she was by his betrayal of her mother and the love they had shared? She had pleaded with him to change his mind and not to go ahead with his plans to marry Morag. How could her mother and she herself mean so little to him now when they had been everything to one another before? How could Morag actually expect her to 'understand', as she had pleaded with her to do? How could Callum – how dare Callum – have stood there and told her that she was being selfish and cruel and that her mother would have been ashamed of her?

Whilst she didn't want Barts or its patients, or indeed anyone, to suffer the horrors of war, if there was to be war then she might as well be in the thick of it, she might as well risk her life in the place of another nurse who might have more reason to want to survive than she did. The truth was that she no longer cared what happened to her. Barts, like the rest of London, had laid its contingency plans for war. What could not be moved to a place of safety must stand and bear the onslaught of that war, and she fully intended to stand with it and to play her part. Better if anyone were to die that it was someone like her, with nothing and no one to live for.

'And then when I told Matron what had happened she actually hugged me and told me that she was proud of me.'

After rushing headlong into her story the moment she had seen Ted waiting for her outside the café, now that they were inside sitting at 'their' table, their tea and teacakes in front of them, Agnes finally paused for breath.

'You were right to tell me to go and see Mrs Robbins. She's ever so nice, Ted, and Tilly, her daughter, has offered to share her room with me. She's lovely, and so pretty. It was awful at first, me thinking that I'd lost the chance to have the room, but then when Tilly came running down the road after me, well . . .'

Ted listened sympathetically whilst Agnes told him yet again of her astonishment and gratitude. When she was all sparked up like she was right now, Agnes was a pretty little thing, her cheeks flushed and her eyes shining.

He'd told his mother about her over breakfast this morning when he'd finally got in from his late shift. She'd pursed her lips and said that she wasn't sure she held with orphans, on account of it being odd that someone shouldn't have any family at all, but Ted had insisted that Agnes was all right.

'Look I've done this for you,' he told her after taking a bite of his teacake and chewing on it, reaching into his pocket to remove some sheets of folded paper. Spreading them out on the table, he explained, 'See, this is a map of the underground, and these different colours, well, they're for the different lines.'

Impressed, Agnes studied the complex inter-linked coloured lines, all drawn so carefully.

'This here dark blue, that's the line I was telling you the stations for last night. And see, I've written down all the station names in the same colour as the lines.'

'You shouldn't have gone to so much trouble on my account,' Agnes said.

'It wasn't any trouble,' Ted fibbed. His mother had had a real go at him, telling him off for missing out on his sleep to sit up and 'draw lines for a daft girl who could be anybody'. But Ted had wanted to do it, and the look of delighted gratitude on Agnes's face was more than enough payment.

'See here,' he continued, producing another sheet of paper and putting it down on the table on top of the first one. 'I've listed all the stations again and I've written them down in the same colour as I've drawn the different lines, so as you can remember them better.'

'I'll never be able to remember them all,' Agnes told him, shaking her head. 'I got two tickets wrong again today and Mr Smith wasn't at all pleased.'

'His knees were probably bothering him. Suffers something rotten with his knees, old Smithy does. It comes of playing football when he was a young-ster, so he says. He was a likely-looking junior for Arsenal before he went and broke a bone in his foot.'

Mr Smith, as wide as he was tall, had been a football player? Agnes's eyes widened in amazement. Ted knew so much. He knew almost everything there was to know about the underground and those who worked there, she felt sure.

'And here,' Ted produced a third sheet of paper, 'see these squares I've drawn over the map of the underground? Well, they tell you the different charging areas and where they change. Red's the cheapest 'cos them's the stations nearest to us, and them blue's the next and then green . . .'

'Ted, I'm ever so grateful to you. I don't know what I can do to thank you.'

She was so earnest and so innocent, Ted thought protectively, well able to imagine what another lad, a lad who wasn't him, might have to say to an offer like that.

'Well, the best thing you can do is get them stations learned,' he told her, mock reprovingly, finishing his teacake and then draining his teacup with noisy enthusiasm before saying casually, 'So I'll see you here again tomorrow so that we can run through some of them stations, shall I?'

'Oh, yes, please – that is, if you've got time?'

'Course I've got time. I'll make time, but mind you look at them drawings and lists I've done for you and get learning them.'

'Oh, I will,' Agnes promised him fervently.

Later, hurrying along High Holborn towards the orphanage, Agnes acknowledged that somehow seeing Ted made the knowledge that this evening would be the last she would ever spend at the orphanage easier to bear. Matron had said that she would walk with her herself to Article Row to see her settled in. Agnes's heart swelled with pride as she remembered how Matron had praised her for her honesty and her courage when she had told her that after initially being too cowardly to go and see the room when she should have done she had then gone back and been rewarded with Tilly's generosity.

'I can see already that you and Tilly are going to become good friends, Agnes,' Matron had said.

Agnes certainly hoped so. She had never had a close friend of her own before, just as she had never had anyone like Ted in her life before, or a room she would have to share with only one other person, and in a proper house.

She hoped the two other lodgers would like her. Tilly hadn't said much about them other than that one of them was a nurse, who worked at Barts, as Tilly herself did, and the other – the one who had claimed the room that was to have been Agnes's – worked at Selfridges and was, in Tilly's own words, 'very glamorous and exciting'.

From her mother's bedroom window Tilly surveyed Article Row eagerly, looking to see if any of their lodgers were on their way, even though it was only ten past seven. She had come upstairs using the excuse of needing to use the bathroom, knowing that her mother would disapprove of her hanging out of the window, so to speak, just as though they lived in some common rundown area where the inhabitants did things like that. Of course, her mother was being very matter-of-fact and businesslike about the whole thing, and because of that Tilly was having to pretend that she wasn't excited, especially when it came to Dulcie, whose imminent presence in their home her mother was regularly verbally regretting.

Disappointingly, though, the only people Tilly could see were Nancy from next door, who was standing by her front gate with her arms folded and a scarf tied round her head, talking to the coalman. He had sent a message earlier in the week via the young nephew who worked for him that he had received an extra delivery of coal and that if his customers had any sense they would take advantage of this, though it was summer, and fill their cellars 'just in case'.

There had been no need for anyone to ask, 'Just in case what?' The prospect of war was on everyone's mind. Now, watching as his horse, obviously bored with his master's delay, moved on his own to the next house, Tilly gave in to one of the delicious shivers of excitement she had been feeling ever since Dulcie had marched into number 13 and staked her claim on the back bedroom, imagining how much fun Dulcie was going to bring into their previously quiet lives.

Further down the road, right at the end, Sergeant Dawson was opening his front gate and stepping out onto the pavement, the buttons on his police uniform shining brightly in the evening sunlight. The Dawsons went to the same church as Tilly and her mother, and tended to keep themselves to themselves. They didn't have any children, their only son having been sickly from birth and having died in his early teens. Tilly could only vaguely remember him, a thin pale boy several years older than her, in a wheelchair she'd seen being pushed out by Mrs Dawson.

The Simpson family at number 3 had four young children, two girls and two boys, and Tilly could see the boys taking turns riding their shared bicycle whilst the girls played hopscotch. Not that the children would be around for much longer. Barbara and the children were evacuating to Essex to stay with Barbara's cousin, whilst Ian Simpson, who worked on the printing presses of the *Daily Express* in Fleet Street, would continue to live in the Row during the week and spend the weekend with his family.

Even so, if Nancy saw that the children had drawn on the pavement in chalk they'd be for it, Tilly reckoned. Nancy didn't approve of children making the Row look cluttered and untidy, not when they had back gardens to play in.

Most of the inhabitants of Article Row were around Nancy's age, with children who had grown up here and moved on, and some of the houses, mainly those further down from them, were all owned by the same landlord who rented them out to people who came and went, people who, in the main, worked at one of the local hospitals, the nearby Inns of Court, or the government offices on and around the Strand.

Downstairs, Olive's thoughts were occupied with their lodgers every bit as much as Tilly's, although in a different way. She'd spent the day, making sure that the house was immaculate, wiping a damp cloth over the insides of drawers and wardrobes, then leaving them open to the warm summer air to dry, before replacing inside the small bags of lavender she'd carefully sewn and filled at the end of the previous summer. The previous week she'd taken the last of her late father-in-law's clothes down to Mr Isaac just off the Strand, carefully paying the money he'd given her for them into her Post Office book.

This morning she'd been up early to give her windows an extra polish with crumpled-up pages of the *Daily Express* dabbed with a bit of vinegar, and then this afternoon, she'd made up the beds with freshly aired sheets. She and Tilly had made do with a scratch tea of freshly boiled eggs, brown bread and butter, and some summer pudding she'd made earlier in the week. Now, as she surveyed her sparkling clean kitchen and smoothed a hand over the front of her apron she just hoped that she was doing the right thing, and that Nancy wasn't right to disapprove and warn her that no good would come of her actions.

In the event Sally was the first of the lodgers to arrive, bringing with her only one small suitcase, her calm organised manner soothing Olive's anxieties. For a girl still only in her early twenties, Sally had a very mature manner about her, Olive recognised, deciding that this must come of her being a nurse.

'Yes, I'd love a cup of tea, please,' she replied to Olive's offer, 'but I'd like to take my case up to my room and unpack first, if that's all right with you.'

'Of course,' Olive agreed.

Upstairs in what was to be her new home, Sally unpacked quickly and efficiently pausing only to linger over and touch her parents' photograph before making her way back downstairs to the kitchen where Olive was waiting for her with the kettle on the boil.

'I've had keys cut for you all,' Olive informed Sally. 'My neighbour seems to think I shouldn't have done but in your case especially, with you doing shift work, it seemed to make sense and I felt I couldn't offer you your own key and not do the same for the two other girls.

'Two other?' Sally queried, smiling approvingly at Tilly as Olive explained what had happened.

Once they had their cups of tea they gravitated out into the back garden, Sally explaining, 'It seems a shame not to make the most of this warm weather, especially as we don't know how much longer we'll be able to enjoy it. It was noticeable how many young men in uniform there are in London, as I made my way here, and of course no one can avoid noticing the sandbags and other precautions.'

'No,' Olive agreed unhappily. 'I've already got my blackout curtains done. Me and Tilly did them together a few weeks back.' She nodded towards the bottom of the garden. 'As you can see, we've got an Anderson shelter in place. Sergeant Dawson from number one, and my neighbour from next door's husband, came round and put it up for me. Sergeant Dawson said that I'll be able to grow some salad greens on the top of it, with all the earth we've covered it with, but I don't know the first thing about gardening, as you can see.'

'My parents loved gardening,' Sally smiled, 'and I don't mind having a go at turning part of the garden into a veggie patch, if you want me to?'

'Would you?' Olive was delighted. 'I must say that I've been feeling a bit guilty that I haven't got a clue when all the neighbours seem to be doing their bit and growing all sorts. There's a small shed on the other side of the Anderson, and a bit of a greenhouse, but you can't see them right now for the apple tree.'

Gardening had been something Sally and her parents had always done as a family, and although it would be painful to take it up again because of the memories it would bring back it would also be something she would enjoy, Sally knew.

'I'd be happy to do what I can, although I dare say with Covent Garden so close you aren't short of fresh veggies.'

'Not normally,' Tilly joined in, 'but I overheard Sergeant Dawson telling Mrs Black from number fourteen the other morning that if we do go to war then it mightn't be so easy to get fresh food. Smithfield Market has already been moved, and . . .' Tilly hesitated and then, because Sally was after all a nurse and working at Barts herself, she continued in a small rush, '. . . and they were saying in the Lady Almoner's office this morning that they wouldn't be surprised if the evacuation of the hospital didn't start soon.'

'That's true,' Sally agreed, finishing her tea, which had been strong and hot, just as she liked it.

*   *   *

'Are you sure you really need all this stuff? After all, you'll be coming home every week,' Rick complained as he was forced to sit on the bulging suitcase that Dulcie had borrowed from one of their neighbours in order to transport her personal belongings to her new home.

'Of course I need it, otherwise I wouldn't be taking it, would I?' Dulcie responded scornfully.

Her brother was wearing his new army uniform, collected only that morning prior to him going off for his six months' military training in a few days' time. The heavy khaki clothes and sturdy boots, which often looked uncomfortable and unwieldy on other men, seemed to fit Rick quite well, but Dulcie certainly wasn't going to boost her brother's ego by telling him how surprisingly good-looking and well set up he looked. Even with his new short back and sides haircut.

When they went downstairs, the family were all gathered in the kitchen, her mother's pursed mouth making it plain what she thought of Dulcie's decision and her behaviour, whilst, typically, her dad had hidden himself behind his evening paper as he sat at the kitchen table drinking his cup of tea, whilst Edith, smugly virtuous as always, was doing the washing up.

'That's it, then, I'm off,' Dulcie announced from the open kitchen door.

Her mother's look of disapproval deepened, but then, at the last minute, just as she was about to turn away, her mother came over, telling her with maternal concern, 'You just look out for yourself, Dulcie. You like to think you know all there is to

100

know. It's all right thinking that when you've got the support of a family behind you but it's a very different matter when you're all on your own. You just remember as well that we are your family, and if you aren't back here on Sunday morning to go to church with us then I'll have something to say about it, I can tell you, and so will your dad.'

It was the longest speech her mother had made to her in a good while, and to her own astonishment Dulcie discovered that there was an unfamiliar lump in the back of her throat as she tossed her head and pretended not to be affected by this unexpected display of affection.

It might not be a long distance as the crow flew from Stepney to Article Row, but just given that they were not crows or able to fly, and given, too, the bulging weight of Dulcie's borrowed suitcase, Rick quickly discovered, as he manhandled the suitcase onto the bus, that he had been right to suspect that it would not be an easy journey. Dulcie, of course, had jumped on the bus ahead of him and was right now slipping into what looked like the last vacant seat, leaving him to strap hang and keep an eye on her case. Mind, there was one advantage to helping his sister, since the four girls squashed into the long seat at the back of the bus meant for only three people were now all looking approvingly at him.

Rick winked at them and joked, 'How about making room for a little 'un, girls? One of you could always sit on my knee.'

The girls giggled whilst pretending to

101

disapprove, and Rick was just on the point of taking things a bit further when Dulcie turned round in her seat to call out, 'You can pay for me, Ricky, and make sure you keep an eye on that suitcase.'

Having realised that he was 'with' Dulcie, the four girls looked disapproving at him, obviously jumping to the conclusion that they were a couple, and were now studiously ignoring him.

'Trust you to flirt with the likes of them,' Dulcie told him scornfully, once they had got off the bus in High Holborn, Rick having to tussle with the case to get it past the queue of people pressing forward to get on the bus. 'Common as anything, they were, and if you carry on like that you'll end up having your name written against the name of a kid that might not be yours, on its birth certificate.'

Unabashed by this sisterly warning, Rick shook his head. 'No way would I fall for anything like that. When I do write my name on a kid's birth certificate, it will be my kid and its mother will be my wife. But I'm not up for that yet, not with this war, and plenty of girls fancying a good-looking lad in uniform. Fun's the name of the game for me.'

Dulcie couldn't object or argue since she felt very much the same, although in her case there was no way she was letting any chap think she was going to take the kind of risks that got a girl into trouble. Being tied down in marriage with an unwanted baby on her hip wasn't what Dulcie wanted for her future at all.

Everywhere you went London's buildings were now protected by sandbags, the windowpanes covered in crisscrosses of sticky brown tape, which the Government had said would hold the glass together in a bomb blast and prevent people from being cut by flying fragments.

Outside one of the public shelters a woman was haranguing an ARP warden, demanding to know whether or not Hitler was coming and when, whilst a gaggle of girls in WRNS uniform hurried past in the opposite direction, carrying their gas masks in smart boxes.

'Cor, look at those legs,' Rick commented appreciatively, taking a break from carrying the case, to flex his aching arm muscles as he turned to admire the girls' legs in their regulation black stockings. Out of all the services, only the WRNS were issued with such elegant stockings, but Dulcie eyed them disparagingly.

'You can get better than that in Selfridges' hosiery department,' she sneered.

'Maybe so, but I'll bet they cost a pretty penny.'

Dulcie nodded, feeling smug that she'd had the good sense to snap up half a dozen pairs from a consignment in which the boxes had been damaged, rendering them unfit for sale in Mr Selfridge's opinion and so sold to his staff at a discount price.

Dulcie had heard that it wasn't entirely unusual for some consignments of luxury goods to end up being 'damaged' thanks to an arrangement between the delivery drivers and the men who unloaded them, and that most of the damaged stock was then sold in one or other of the East End markets.

'This way,' she instructed Rick, indicating the turning that would eventually lead to Article Row.

She hadn't said much at home about Article Row and so she had the satisfaction of seeing her normally unimpressable elder brother come to a halt and stare around himself to take in the well-tended line of houses.

'Bit posh, isn't it?' was all he allowed himself to say, but Dulcie knew him and she knew that he was impressed.

Sergeant Dawson, leaning on his front gate and watching the world go by, spotted them and straightened up. He'd heard initially on the Row's grapevine via its best gossip, Nancy, that Olive from number 13 was taking in lodgers; he'd seen Sally arrive, and then the thin little waif accompanied by the larger older woman, guessing that the girl must be the orphan recommended for a room by the vicar's wife, but this young woman walking toward him confidently now, well, Nancy and the other old biddies would have something to say about her, the sergeant reflected, not altogether unappreciative of the slim length of Dulcie's legs in her nylon stockings, or the way in which the skirt of her fitted poppy-red dress, with its white collar, just reached to her knee, its white belt showing off her narrow waist. He didn't think, however, that Mrs Dawson would be equally appreciative, and he felt sorry for Olive, whom he knew and liked, having to deal with the kind of lodger this one looked as though she could turn out to be, and accompanied by a lad as well. The Row would not approve of that! Respectable single ladies was what Olive had advertised for, not too-pretty young girls of a type that would attract men like honey attracted bees.

He nodded a brief welcome in their direction though, causing Rick to respond with a smile, and gesture toward Dulcie's case.

'You'd think she'd got enough clothes in here to fit out the whole street.'

'Row, lad,' Archie Dawson corrected him. 'You won't be very popular round here if you call Article Row a street.'

'See, I told you it was posh,' Rick told Dulcie as she gave him a warning look and determinedly marched past the policeman.

It was Tilly who saw them first. The orphanage matron had left, her mother was showing Sally the garden, so she'd come upstairs to help Agnes unpack, feeling sorry for her when she saw how little she had, and all of it looking second-hand. Poor girl, Tilly thought as she watched Agnes hang her uniform and her other small collection of clothes in the half of the wardrobe Tilly had cleared for her. The dull brown dress Agnes was wearing didn't do anything for her, making her look thinner than ever because it was too big for her, and turning her skin slightly sallow.

'I'll be downstairs, when you're ready,' Tilly had told her, thinking that Agnes might want to use the bathroom or perhaps unpack a few personal treasures in privacy, but then with her foot on the top stair, she'd turned back to go into her mother's room and look down the Row again.

And that was when she saw Dulcie, in her smart red dress and her white high-heeled peep-toed shoes, followed by the best-looking young man Tilly had ever seen carrying a large suitcase.

As though he sensed that he was being studied, the young man looked up at the window, causing Tilly to step back, clasping her hands over her chest to calm her excited heartbeat as she did so.

Was he Dulcie's young man? He must be, Tilly decided, racing downstairs and out into the garden to warn her mother breathlessly, 'Dulcie's nearly here.'

Although she smiled and turned to make her way back to the house, Olive wasn't happy about her daughter's obvious excitement. This was just what she had feared. Tilly was at an impressionable age. Because there weren't any other young people in the Row of her age, and because her mother had been so busy nursing Tilly's late grandfather, Tilly hadn't had the opportunity to go out and have fun as much as other girls might. Olive was aware of that, just as she was aware of the increasing restlessness she had seen in her daughter over the summer months. There was fun and fun, though, and Olive did not want her quite naïve daughter getting involved in the kind of 'fun' she suspected someone like Dulcie enjoyed.

When Olive opened the door to Dulcie's firm knock, though, it wasn't the sight of Dulcie that set maternal alarm bells ringing inside her so much as the sight of the far too handsome young man standing behind her, one arm draped loosely around Dulcie's shoulders. Her mouth firmed, her expression cooled, but before she could say anything Dulcie forestalled her.

'It's all right. Rick here is only my brother. He's come to help me move in on account of my case being heavy. Rick, this is Mrs Robbins.'

Her brother and not a boyfriend. Olive allowed herself to relax a little. Rick's smile was open and warm, his handshake firm and his uniform indicating that it was unlikely that he was going to be around very much, to Olive's relief, as she recognised the effect having such a very good-looking and friendly young man in and out of the house could have on her daughter. Rick had the kind of smile, looks, and easy charm that would melt any girl's heart.

'I'll show them up, shall I?' Tilly suggested happily from the hallway, having just learned that the handsome young man was Dulcie's brother and not her boyfriend.

But to her disappointment her mother told her, 'I'm sure that Dulcie can remember which is her room and you'd only be in the way of her brother getting her suitcase up the stairs. Go and put on the kettle instead, please, Tilly, so that Dulcie and Rick can come down and have a cup of tea when they're ready.'

'Well, I have to admit that you've fallen on your feet here,' Rick pronounced after he had dragged the heavy case up to Dulcie's room and thoroughly inspected her new living quarters.

'Told you,' Dulcie reminded him. 'I've got a whole room to myself and my own wardrobe, and there's a bathroom on this floor that I only have to share with this nurse that's taken the other room.'

'All right, but don't you forget that promise you made me,' Rick warned her as he picked up the now empty case.

Olive was waiting for them at the bottom of the stairs, ushering them into the kitchen, ruefully aware of just how pleasant and charming Dulcie's brother was in contrast to Dulcie herself. Pleasant and charming and far, far too good-looking for the peace of mind of the mother of an impression-able girl, especially when that impressionable girl was currently gazing at him with the kind of dazed expression girls her age normally reserved for matinée idols, Olive thought with a small sigh. She directed Tilly to fetch some milk from the larder, and then to go and bring Agnes and Sally in from the garden so that they too could have a cup of tea.

When the three young women returned Dulcie's eyes widened at the sight of Agnes in her dull ill-fitting brown dress, and then narrowed with hostility when Olive told her pointedly, 'This is Agnes, who should have had your room. Luckily she doesn't mind sharing with Tilly. Come on and sit down, Agnes,' Olive coaxed the hesitant-looking girl, her voice and expression warming as she welcomed her.

Her new landlady's obvious approval of the shabbily dressed orphan and her equally obvious disapproval of her raised Dulcie's hackles and brought out the same fighting instinct that her mother's favouritism of Edith always aroused. The orphan was nothing compared with her so why should Olive make such a fuss of her? Deliberately and very disdainfully Dulcie brushed off the skirt of her own dress as Agnes's shabby frock touched it, the pearl-pink nail polish she was wearing catching the light as she did so.

Little madam, Olive thought grimly, treating poor Agnes like that, although fortunately the other girl hadn't noticed Dulcie's deliberate slight. Dulcie, though, noticed Olive's reaction and immediately her dislike of Agnes for her shabbiness hardened into dislike of the girl herself, because Olive obviously favoured her. Agnes was another Edith, 'a favourite' to be fussed over whilst she was pushed to one side and ignored.

'Just been called up?' Sally asked Rick, whilst Tilly looked on, envious of the older girl's calm ability actually to speak to Rick whilst she could only stare at him in speechless awe.

'Yes,' Rick acknowledged. 'I leave in a few days to start my training, and I reckon that we'll be at war before I finish it, from what they've been saying in the papers.'

'I don't think there's any doubt about it,' Sally agreed.

'The sooner we get Hitler sorted out and put in his place, the sooner life can get back to normal. I reckon we'll give him the roundabout and boot him back to Germany in no time at all,' Rick assured her confidently. 'He'll never get past the Maginot Line, even if he does dare to try and invade Belgium.'

'That's what the Government is saying,' Sally confirmed.

Olive hugged her arms around her body. 'I hate all this talk of war, after what our men went through the last time,' she said, 'but if it has to come then it has to come. Turn on the wireless, will you, Tilly? It's almost time for the news.'

Obediently Tilly went to switch on the wireless, feeling all fingers and thumbs and very self-conscious as she did so, because Rick was sitting closest to it.

The announcer's voice, when it did come through, was slightly fuzzy, and immediately Rick turned in his chair, leaning over to Tilly. 'It needs a bit of tuning – want me to do it for you?'

Before she could answer, he was reaching out towards the control knob, so that his fingers brushed against hers as she moved away.

Scarlet colour dyed her skin, her heart flipping over like an acrobat whilst her pulses raced with excitement and delight, mixed with even more self-consciousness.

'There, that's it,' Rick told her as his small adjustment brought the sound back in balance, his smile for Tilly warm and friendly. She was a very pretty girl, but very young, not much more than a school girl. Had she been a couple of years older he might have been tempted to tease her a little and really make her blush, before he asked her out and kissed her – had she not been Dulcie's landlady's daughter and had he not been about to leave London. Right now, as far as Rick was concerned, Tilly was just a nice kid.

All of them fell silent whilst they listened to the news, even Dulcie. Not that there was much to learn unless you were interested in the fact that Poland had mobilised all its reservists and France had called up all of hers which Dulcie wasn't, not really She was more interested in wondering when she was next going to see David James-Thompson. *When* she was going to see him, not if, because she knew that she would. She really could do with getting hold of a decent bit of material and having a new dress made, Dulcie decided, because when David James-Thompson took her to the Hammersmith Palais de Danse she wanted to look her best, so that he'd know that every other man there was looking at him and envying him because he was with her. Dulcie loved that kind of admiration; that feeling of knowing that she was the best.

The newsreader was talking about Britain's plans for evacuating children from the cities, and whilst Olive and Sally sighed and said how awful that was going to be for their mothers, Tilly sat with her chin in her hands pretending to listen intently, whilst in reality what she was looking at was Rick.

It had been such a busy evening she hadn't had any time at all to study Ted's lists, Agnes acknowledged, but she could start reciting them to herself in the morning whilst she walked to work. She'd expected her new surroundings to feel alien and a little bit frightening but Tilly and her mother had made her feel so welcome. It felt funny not to be in the large orphanage kitchen, washing up or helping cook. Tilly's mother had stopped her when she had gone to wash their teacups earlier, saying that there would be time enough for that another day and that anyway, she was a paying lodger and not here to work.

Olive nodded as she listened to Sally whilst inwardly thinking that she would have a word with Tilly and see what she thought about passing on a couple of the dresses she was growing out of on to Agnes. Matron had more or less admitted to Olive before she had left that it was difficult getting second-hand clothes for Agnes because she was so much older than the other girls, and the clothes that people passed on to the orphanage were for younger children. Olive had decided there and then that she would do her utmost to make sure that poor Agnes had a few better things. She would see if she could get a decent bit of material from one of the markets, Petticoat Lane perhaps, to have something new made up for both Tilly and Agnes. She could afford it now that she was getting three lots of rent money in, even if she had reduced what Agnes had to pay because she was having to share with Tilly.

The news had finished. Rick got to his feet, having assured himself that his sister had indeed found somewhere comfortable. It had been daft of him secretly to worry about her. Trust Dulcie to fall on her feet. Not that he liked what she had done. Families should stay together – that was how people like them lived – but Dulcie had always been awkward, wanting to make things difficult for herself and for others.

112

Dulcie saw Rick to the front door.

'And don't you forget about going home on Sunday to go to church?' he reiterated yet again.

'Will you stop going on about that?' she complained. 'I've said I'll come, haven't I?'

'Well, you just make sure you do,' Rick warned her, as he set off in the direction of Stepney with the now empty case.

It was gone eleven o'clock, she could see from the tiny illuminated hands of her alarm clock, but Sally still couldn't sleep. Being back in a proper bedroom in a proper house had brought back too many memories.

Memories of before the betrayal, when Morag had been invited home by her mother and had stayed overnight with them; memories of the laughter and happiness that had filled the kitchen as Morag easily and naturally fell into the household routine, helping with the chores; memories of the Christmas before her mother had fallen ill that they had all spent together, Morag, Callum, her parents and her. She could see herself now pulling a cracker with Callum and then wearing the silly hat he had put on her head before reading out the equally silly riddle that had been inside the cracker along with a plastic heart charm, which he had given to her with the words, 'Here's my heart, Sally. I want you to look after it for me.' Silly words, and yet to her at the time they had had such meaning. It was pointless thinking about that now, she told herself, rolling over and punching her pillow as she reminded herself that she was on duty in the morning at eight o'clock, and that the ENT surgeon had a full list of tonsillectomies to get through, the final batch before the majority of the operating staff were evacuated. These urgent operations were now to be carried out in the basement theatres the hospital had organised, the top-floor theatres closed down because of the threat of war.

Liverpool . . . She would always miss her home city, Sally knew, but she would not miss the pain she hoped she had left behind there. A pain she was determined should not follow her into her new life.

SIX

'Come on and sit down, Mum. I've got the kettle on.'

Olive gave Tilly a grateful look as she sank down into the most comfortable of the kitchen chairs – the one that originally belonged to her father-in-law, and which had arms and a couple of cushions, and which she had re-covered in the spring at the same time as she and Tilly had run up the pretty kitchen curtains.

It was Friday afternoon and Tilly had been sent home early because the hospital was completing its evacuation programme ahead of the war that everyone was now not just dreading but also expecting. As Tilly was remaining in London, she would continue to work as part of the skeleton staff in the Lady Almoner's office.

'My feet,' Olive complained as she eased off her shoes and surveyed what looked like the beginnings of a blister. 'Although I shouldn't complain, not when I think of those poor children and their mothers.'

In her role as a member of the WVS, Olive had

been on duty all day today and the previous day, helping to get small children onto the evacuation trains organised to take them away from danger and into the country.

Newspapers were full of photographs of lines of children being marched away from their homes and their parents, many of them escorted by their teachers, ready to be handed over to waiting groups of volunteers once they reached their destinations. Only mothers with very young children and babies were being evacuated with their children. As Agnes had said the previous evening, after going straight from work to the orphanage to help with the evacuation, it really broke your heart to see the children's tears as they were taken away from everything and everyone they loved, unable to understand that it was for their own sakes and their own safety.

Olive watched her daughter as she made the tea, worried about her safety.

As though Tilly had guessed her thoughts she said quietly and in a very grown-up voice, I'm glad we're staying here, Mum. It would be awful if we all deserted London, and those who can't get away were left on their own. And besides, if anything does happen, if Hitler does bomb us, then I want to be with you, because you're the best mum in the world. When I listen to poor Agnes talking about growing up in the orphanage and being left on its doorstep, I try to think how I would feel if that was me; if I hadn't been lucky enough to have you as my mother.' Her voice broke slightly, causing Olive to blink away her own emotion.

'Oh, sweetheart, we mustn't blame Agnes's mother too much. We don't know what she might have gone through, poor girl. No mother gives up her baby willingly, I can promise you that, and as for us staying here in London, well, I hope I am doing the right thing, Tilly, and that I'm not just being selfish wanting to be here in this house. A home means a lot to a woman but it never means more than her children and those she loves.'

'We'll be all right, Mum, I'm sure of it. Besides, how could Hitler bomb London when we've got all those barrage balloons and anti-aircraft batteries, never mind everything else, and the RAF?'

Sally, coming into the kitchen in time to catch Tilly's fiercely patriotic words, exchanged a brief look over her head with Olive, before agreeing firmly, 'That's right, Tilly. This city, and this country, are well defended and we'll stand firm when the time comes, no matter what Hitler might try to do.'

'Has everyone gone now?' Tilly asked her as she removed an extra cup from the cupboard to pour Sally a cup of tea. 'It seemed so strange when I left earlier, coming through the main hall and it almost being empty. It felt funny, sort of ghostly, making me think how old the hospital really is. I'd never felt it before today.'

'I know what you mean,' Sally agreed, 'and yes, everyone who's going has mostly gone now, and we've sorted out the operating theatres in the basement.' She didn't add that she'd heard that orders had been given for thousands of cardboard coffins

117

to be made for the dead the authorities were anticipating should the city come under attack from
Hitler.

'I almost don't want to do this,' Olive announced
as she switched on the wireless for the six o'clock
news bulletin.

'Come on, Dulcie, it isn't like you to hang on after
we've closed for the day,' Lizzie teased good-
naturedly. 'We're the last on the floor by the looks
of it as well.'

The cosmetics floor was indeed deserted, and
had been unusually quiet all day, allowing Mr
Selfridge to order each floor to do a practice run
of its fire-watching duties, a new regime instituted
earlier in the week and which Dulcie loathed.
Who wanted to go up onto the roof and act as
a look out for non-existent fires started by equally
non-existent bombs being dropped from non-
existent German planes? But Mr Selfridge had
said they had to, just like he had said they all
had to learn how to use a stirrup pump as well
as know the correct evacuation procedure from
the store, should that be necessary, and his word
was law.

She couldn't hang around here any longer,
Dulcie admitted, even if this morning she had
woken up feeling sure that today would be the
day she saw David James-Thompson again. She
had even planned how she was going to give him
a big hint about how he could find her at the
Hammersmith Palais tomorrow night, sitting at
her favourite table, the one in the middle of the

118

front row, facing the band. There was always a crowd of knowing girls who headed for that table, so there was no risk of her ending up sitting there on her own, and they were all there for the same reason: so that they could be seen to advantage by everyone else. Dulcie was so on edge she felt like smoking a cigarette, something she didn't do very often. Ciggies cost money, and meant that if she bought them she'd have less to spend on her clothes, so normally Dulcie only smoked if someone else offered her a cigarette.

'Oh, come on then,' she said to Lizzie, who had now finished putting away her own stock, 'I just hope we get a few more customers in tomorrow, otherwise I'm going to be dying of boredom. You'd have thought with all this fuss about there going to be a war on that every lad in the city would be coming in here with his girl to treat her to a bit of something, and that every woman without a chap would be coming in to get herself a lipstick so that she could get one before they all go off to war.'

Lizzie gave Dulcie a wry look. 'I dare say that most people will have more on their minds than buying lipstick, Dulcie.'

'Such as?' Dulcie demanded as they walked towards the staff exit to the stairs that led down to the basement-level staff cloakroom.

'Such as worrying about their children being evacuated if they are young enough, and worrying about their sons going to war if they are old enough. Same thing goes for courting couples. They'll be wanting to spend what time they've got together, not coming in here. Ralph and I are going looking at engagement rings tomorrow,' she added. 'Funny but when I was growing up I imagined that when my boy took me to buy an engagement ring it would be the most exciting and happy thing in the world but now it feels like the most frightening and upsetting, because I know that we're getting engaged now and married at Christmas, just in case.'

Dulcie heaved a bored sigh as they reached the cloakroom and she removed her overall and put it out for the laundry. Mr Selfridge insisted that his staff presented an immaculately clean appearance, which meant that a laundry service was provided for their overalls and uniforms. She was fed up with all this talk of war. Every night at number 13, when everyone else gathered round the wireless to listen to the news, she felt like stamping her foot and saying why didn't they have some music on instead so that they could have a bit of a dance. Not that that suggestion would go down well with Olive. Dulcie reckoned her landlady would have her out of the house if she gave her the smallest excuse to do that. Well, she wasn't going to give her that satisfaction. And she certainly wasn't going to give up her comfortable room, or her big bed, and definitely not the wardrobe she had all to herself. Tilly was daft for going soft and sharing her own room with the orphan. She wouldn't have done that, especially not with a plain dull girl like Agnes, forever creeping around in that shabby brown dress, making Olive feel sorry for her. Well, *she* didn't feel sorry for her; if anything, she felt sorry for herself for having to put up with her.

'So what is this blitzkrieg that everyone's going on about?' Dulcie demanded, the four of them – Agnes was still at the orphanage – sitting round the wireless that Olive had just switched off. Everyone apart from Dulcie herself had left their tea virtually untouched, and there was an almost palpable air of grim acceptance in the kitchen.

'It means lightning war, Dulcie,' Sally explained. 'That's the kind of war that Germany inflicted on Poland when the German army invaded Poland this morning.' When it invaded Poland and swept all before it, she thought emotionally, including the brave but hopelessly outdated Polish cavalry, which still waged war on horseback. They had been utterly unable to stand against the might of the Wehrmacht force of over a million men with armoured and motorised divisions. The Luftwaffe had blown up Poland's railways and blown its air force out of the sky. It was over: Poland's defences lay in ruins, and Poland as an autonomous state had ceased to exist.

Seated across the table from Sally, Olive removed a handkerchief from the sleeve of her blouse and blew her nose firmly, blinking hard as she did so.

'So why should we have to bother about Poland?' Dulcie asked, apparently unmoved by the emotion gripping Olive, Sally and Tilly.

'Why should we bother?' Sally's normally calm tone had sharpened to real anger. 'Why we should bother, Dulcie, is because thousands of brave men have died trying to protect their country from an unprovoked attack; even more thousands of innocent women and children have also been killed or injured or taken prisoner. Even if we weren't honour bound by treaty to support the Poles, even if there wasn't the fear that Hitler might decide to attack us, as human beings we should bother about the cruelty to so many innocent people. As hard as it might be for you to lift your mind from such important things as selling lipstick, I would advise that you try to do so, Dulcie, because where Poland lies defeated and bloody today, we could lie tomorrow.'

When Tilly made a small sound of anguish Sally looked at her and apologised. 'I'm sorry, Tilly, I didn't mean to frighten you.'

'It's best that we all know and face the truth,' Olive answered for Tilly.

'Our Government can't ignore what has happened.'

'Does that mean that we're going to be at war with Germany?'

'I'm afraid so, Tilly,' Olive answered quietly, brushing her hand over her daughter's head. A sad smile touched her mouth when Tilly put her head on her shoulder, plainly overcome by her own emotions.

There was no need for Sally to get on her high horse and start lecturing her, Dulcie thought crossly. And besides, lipsticks were just as important as Hitler and his blitzkrieg. At least they were to her.

'When do you think we'll hear – officially, I mean?' Olive asked Sally.

Somehow she had fallen into the habit of treating Sally as though they were closer in age than they actually were, finding it comforting to have Sally in the house to talk to. Secretly, in her heart, Olive was beginning to think of all of them here in her small all-female household as a sort of family. Already she felt protective of the girls – except of course Dulcie, who did not need anyone to protect her. Quite the opposite, in fact. In Olive's opinion it was others who needed protecting from Dulcie.

'I don't know, but it's bound to be soon,' Sally answered.

There had been so much talk about war in all the newspapers, so much preparation for it, what with the Government producing so many leaflets about the dangers they would all be facing, that Tilly thought she had grown used to the fear that stalked them, but now, in her mother's warm comfortable kitchen, with the sun still shining outside, she realised that she had not and that she had not known what fear was at all really until she thought about the fate of the poor Polish people and faced for the first time the true enormity of war.

Standing outside their church on Sunday morning, with everyone going on about the war, no one in her family would even have noticed if she hadn't turned up this morning, Dulcie thought grumpily as she watched the worshippers leaving, all the

123

young men in uniform grouping themselves together, passing round their cigarettes, not joking and indulging in horseplay as they had on previous Sundays, like children let out of school, but instead exchanging brusque words, spoken from the sides of their mouths, frowns replacing smiles. Even her own brother, Rick's, normal smile was replaced by a look of determination. She hadn't bothered going to the Palais last night after all. She hadn't felt like it somehow.

Moving a little away from everyone else – in part because her mother was still going on about Edith's singing and how she'd been clapped through three encores at a local working men's club the previous night, and in part because she liked standing out from the crowd – Dulcie caught the now familiar words being spoken grimly into the warm September air, words like 'devastation', 'POWs', and 'blitzkrieg', mingling with phrases like 'it will be us next', 'thousands left for dead', 'poor bloody bastards'. . .

Then one of the boy messengers that worked with the ARP men came cycling up full pelt, yelling out as loud as he could, 'It's happened. We're at war. Mr Chamberlain has just said.'

Of course, uproar followed, with the ARP lot grabbing hold of the boy and hauling him off to question him, whilst the lads in uniform followed after them. Wives and mothers, sisters and sweethearts, clung together, whilst the older men, including her father, looked smaller and shrunken somehow.

'Well, that's all I need, isn't it?' Dulcie could

hear Edith complaining. 'A war, just when my singing career is looking like taking off.'

'Oh, I shouldn't worry too much. Perhaps you'll be able to sing to Hitler. Course, you'll have to learn German first,' Dulcie taunted her.

'Dulcie, that's enough of that,' her mother stopped her, giving her an angry look. 'There's no need to go upsetting people more than they need to be upset.' She looked across to where Rick was standing with a now much larger group of men.

A shiver of foreboding went through Dulcie. Thousands the soldiers had killed in Poland, thousands of young men just like her brother. For the first time since all the talk of war had started Dulcie felt its ice-cold fingers clutch at her heart and grip it painfully hard. She might argue with her brother, she might mock him and taunt him, but of all her family it was Rick to whom she was the closest, Rick who she secretly thought was the best brother that any girl could have, with his handsome looks and his easy-going charm, his way of somehow always being there to calm things down when she felt hard done by. Rick might look so tall and manly and indestructible in his army uniform, but he wasn't indestructible, he was human flesh and blood, and vulnerable. A huge lump blocked her throat, feelings and thoughts she had never had to worry about before swarming through her head like wasps provoked by someone deliberately stirring up their nest.

'The next thing we know, the ruddy Germans will be bombing us out of our houses and gassing us all to death,' one elderly woman was screeching.

'I can remember what it was like the last time, our lads coming back from the trenches with their lungs rotting from the Germans gassing them.'

Dulcie looked down at her own side. She'd tossed her gas mask to the back of her wardrobe, but of course Edith had hers and was now clutching the strap of its box tightly.

Rick came over. 'Forget about dinner for me, Ma. Me and some of the other lads are going to see what we can find out. Sid Winters – you know, him whose cousin is a regular in the army – reckons that those who've already done their training will be shipped out to France pdq, and that our training will be rushed through now.'

Her brother seemed excited now that the initial shock of the announcement had faded, Dulcie recognised, her earlier concern changing to resentment that he could look so pleased when she was worrying herself sick about him. Her mother's pinched expression became even more strained but she didn't say anything, simply nodding and then turning to put her arm round Edith and draw her close to her in a manner similar to which Olive had drawn Tilly close the previous evening.

Mothers fussing over their favourites – well, let them, Dulcie thought acidly; she didn't care.

'I'll have my dinner at Article Row,' she told her mother tersely, turning on her heel without waiting for her to respond.

'So it's happened then?' Olive found that she was automatically speaking in a lower voice as she

126

asked the vicar's wife the question to which she already knew the answer.

'Yes. The Prime Minister has already made a formal announcement. I expect we'll be able to hear what he said on the news at twelve o'clock.' The two women exchanged tense white-faced looks.

The news that Britain was now formally at war with Germany hadn't come out of the blue but it was still shocking, making the heart race and the stomach tense.

'So many of our young men are already in uniform,' Mrs Windle continued with a nod in the direction of the young men standing together outside the church in their khaki, their Royal Navy dark blue and their RAF blue serge. 'And now thousands more will be joining them.'

Their small, well-attended church had been built at the same time as Article Row, by the same philanthropist, and stood on the site of a much older church, along with a neat little rectory, a church hall, and the orphanage, the congregation coming from Article Row and the surrounding area. Olive's husband and in-laws were buried in its graveyard, and on the anniversaries of their deaths and at Christmas, Olive always made a special point of placing fresh flowers on their graves. She could see the graveyard from where she was standing, sunlight dappling through the shade of the yew trees standing sentinel over the dead. Her heart lurched, a shiver striking through her as she looked from the graveyard to the eager young men in their uniforms.

'We lost so many in the last war, I can't believe there's to be another,' she said sadly. 'Look at them. They're all standing so tall and proud, so determined to do their bit, but they're so young.'

And so many of them would die, was what Olive was thinking but could not say, especially when one of those young men in air-force blue was Mrs Windle's own nephew.

At her mother's side, Tilly held on tightly to her gas mask in its smart box, which she and her mother had covered with some scraps of lace to make it look more attractive, a fashion that many young women in the country were adopting, according to *Woman's Weekly*.

'Everywhere is so quiet without the children,' Tilly commented as they walked home together.

'Their poor mothers were besides themselves with grief last week when they sent them away, but I dare say now that they will be feeling that they have done the right thing. Hitler is bound to target London.'

'If you're going to say that you wish that I'd been young enough to be evacuated, then please don't,' Tilly begged her mother. 'I want to be here with you, Mum.'

As they passed the ARP station on the corner, Sergeant Dawson was standing outside it smoking a cigarette.

'You'll have heard the news, I expect?' he asked.

'That we're at war? Yes.' Olive shivered a little despite the warmth of the sun flooding between the buildings at the entrance to Article Row.

'I never thought I'd say this, but right now I'm

128

sort of glad that our lad's already been taken,' the sergeant told Olive quietly. 'There's many a young lad I've seen this morning proud to wear his uniform and do his bit for this country. It's diffcrent for those of us who saw something of the last war. I was only in it for the last few weeks, but that was enough.'

'Yes,' Olive agreed, thinking of her own husband, his bravery and his death.

On Article Row, the leaves on the clipped privet hedges standing sentry between the low walls at the boundary of each front garden were beginning to look dusty and tired after a summer of exposure to London's sooty air. Soon it would be autumn and the leaves would die and fall, just like so many of the young men who today were full of vigour and life. Tears blurred Olive's vision.

A troop from the local Boys' Brigade marched past the end of the road, their young faces shining with excitement and anticipation. For them war was something to excite them, whilst for those who had lived through the last war, it was something to fear.

'Come on,' she told Tilly firmly, increasing her pace as they headed down Article Row after saying goodbye to Sergeant Dawson. 'I've got that joint in the oven that will need seeing to, and —' Olive stopped speaking to stare up in horrified disbelief at the clear blue sky in response to the wave of sound that was rising to a deafening warning wail.

For a second neither she nor Tilly could move, simply standing staring at one another until Tilly broke their stillness by grabbing hold of Olive's arm and yelling, 'Mum, it's the air-raid siren. Come on we need to get in the shelter.'

They were four doors away from number 13. Holding on to her mother's arm and almost pulling her along, Tilly started to run, her heart thudding with dread, the wail of the air-raid alarm sending its warning to every part of her terrified body.

Dulcie heard the air-raid siren when she was walking along High Holborn and got caught up in the frantic rush of people reacting to its sound, the panic of the growing crowd as some ran one way and others another, squeezing her up against the sandbags protecting the walls of one of the buildings. The rasp of the sandbags against her legs made her feel grateful for the fact that she wasn't wearing her precious stockings, but that relief gave way to fear as the crowd swelled and she was pushed again, this time half losing her balance in her high heels. She would have fallen if it hadn't been for the male hand reaching out to grasp her arm, its owner hauling her to her feet and insisting, 'The shelter's this way.' He was running so fast, his hand still holding her arm, that she was lifted off her feet.

'Stop, I'm losing my shoes!'

'Better that than losing your life,' was his response, as he slowed his pace just enough for her to get her feet back in her shoes, before tugging her along again to where a crowd of people were trying to push their way into the concrete air-raid shelter she had walked past so often, deriding its presence and its ugliness, but which now had never been a more welcome sight. Not that she was going to admit it. Even as she edged inside, Dulcie was sniffing disdainfully as the scent of stale concrete, male sweat and female anxiety filled the air, ignoring the ARP warden's instruction to, 'Move down inside, miss. We don't want people blocking up the entrance.'

'Hitler hasn't wasted much time, has he?' a woman standing close to her observed in a cockney accent, causing several others to give way to the relief of shaky laughter.

Now that they were inside the shelter and safe, Dulcie had an opportunity to look at her rescuer properly for the first time. Around her brother's age, and of middle height and square muscular build, and wearing an army uniform, he had mid-brown curly hair, hazel eyes and a plain but kind face. Not the kind of male looks to set a girl's heart beating with excitement, Dulcie decided ungratefully, not like David James-Thompson. Now there was someone she would much rather have been rescued by.

In their Anderson shelter at the bottom of the garden, Olive and Tilly sat opposite one another on the garden chairs they'd put in there, along with an old card table, a pack of cards in its drawer, which stuck now because of the damp. Olive had lit the paraffin lamp, which had been on the list of 'essentials' *Woman's Weekly* had advised all well-prepared housewives to have inside their Anderson. Spare bedding, warm clothes and food were things that should be kept close to hand in the home, ready to be carried into the shelter when needed, but the paraffin stove, matches, wrapped in a piece of waterproof material, and a waterproof box containing games, a couple of favourite books and some candles could be safely left in the shelter.

Olive had made sure that hers was kept swept and tidy, its door opened on sunny days to make sure it was aired, and the vexed question of 'needing to go' sorted out via a discreet curtain with a bucket and a wooden seat behind it.

'Will we hear the German planes?' Tilly asked Olive nervously.

'I should think so, but they won't get as far as London, Tilly, I'm sure, not with all the defences the Government has put in place.

'I'm glad I thought to dash into the kitchen and turn down the gas, otherwise that nice piece of beef I've got in the oven will be ruined.'

It was easier to talk about mundane, everyday things than to let one's mind be filled with the horror and fear of what was happening.

'Oh, don't talk about food, Mum,' Tilly groaned. 'I'm scared, but I'm still hungry. Do you think the others will be all right – Agnes and Sally and Dulcie?'

'They'll be fine, love,' Olive reassured her. 'Sally will be at the hospital and they've got a big shelter there, I'm sure.'

'She'd probably have to go down into the basement,' Tilly told her.

'Agnes is helping tidy up the orphanage before they hand it over to the council to use for extra billeting for refugees and that, so she'll be able to go into the cellar there,' Olive continued, 'and as for Dulcie, well, I'm sure she'll find somewhere.' Olive's voice hardened slightly, the thought in her mind that Dulcie would be safe because she was that sort, the sort that always fell on their feet.

'You don't like Dulcie very much, do you, Mum?' Tilly asked.

For a moment Olive was tempted to fib and say that she didn't know what Tilly meant, but her daughter was growing up. She herself had been married at eighteen and a mother not long after, and although the last thing she wanted was for Tilly to grow up too fast, Olive knew that it wouldn't be fair to lie to her and treat her as a child. So she admitted quietly, 'No I don't. She isn't the sort of person I was thinking of when I thought of us having lodgers.'

'You mean because she's pretty and likes makeup and goes out dancing a lot?'

Olive could hear not just the questioning in Tilly's voice, but also, more worrying, a hint of rebuke.

'No, not because of those things,' she defended herself. 'After all, you are pretty and although young skin like yours doesn't need anything more than a dash of lipstick and a brush of mascara on those lovely long eyelashes of yours, you too wear makeup and I dare say you would go out dancing a lot yourself if I let you. No, Tilly, it isn't because of any of those things that I feel the way I do about Dulcie.'

'What is it then?'

Moving closer to her daughter, Olive put her arm round her, smiling, filled with maternal love, when Tilly put her head on her shoulder just as she had done as a child.

'It's the way Dulcie speaks to Agnes, the way the things she says and does show that she doesn't have the kind of . . . of consideration and compassion for others that I hope I have always encouraged you to have. There's a . . . a selfishness about Dulcie that makes it hard for me to warm to her. Tilly, I know you find her exciting and glamorous – of course you do, and at your age I dare say I would have done as well – but think of this, sweetheart. Her own family live within walking distance of here and yet she's chosen to turn her back on them.'

'Because there isn't enough room, and her sister borrows her clothes.'

Olive's heart sank a little. Plainly Dulcie had had more of an effect on Tilly than she had realised if Tilly was already willing to take Dulcie's side and defend her.

'I do know what you mean though, Mum,' Tilly acknowledged. 'But don't you think that Dulcie might be the way she is because people haven't always been, well, kind and considerate to her?'

Hard on the heels of Olive's jolt of surprise that Tilly could be so acutely perceptive in pointing out something she hadn't yet recognised herself, Olive felt a surge of love and gratitude that she had been lucky enough to have such a special daughter.

'I don't know, Tilly, you might be right. We shall have to see,' she answered.

'Cigarette?' Dulcie's rescuer offered her, from the safety of the air-raid shelter, its dark interior illuminated by the lamps that had been lit by one of the three ARP wardens who had taken charge of the place. The lamps gave off a strong smell of paraffin, making Dulcie wrinkle her nose before she shook her head and started to turn away from her rescuer, but he refused to take her hint.

'I'm Jim Andrews, Private Jim Andrews, 3rd Battalion The Rifles.' He gave her a rueful smile. 'I was supposed to be on leave but I reckon with this lot happening, we'll be recalled before I've so much as got me feet back under me mother's kitchen table, and be on our way to France.'

'Regular soldier, are you then, son?' an older man sitting on one of the narrow benches down the side of the shelter asked.

'Joined up six months ago after I'd done me training,' Jim confirmed.

He was looking at Dulcie as he spoke, and she suspected that if she gave him half a chance he'd end up asking her out, which wasn't what she wanted at all. He looked the settling-down type, and Dulcie wasn't interested in anything about settling down. To her relief, just as he opened his mouth to say something, the sound of the all clear reached their ears, causing a wave of relief to surge through the shelter. Then those inside gathered up their belongings and started queuing up to leave.

''Orrible place. You won't get me going back

in one. I'd as soon die in me own bed,' one elderly woman was telling anyone who would listen as they started to file out past the ARP wardens, who were now trying to write down everyone's names and addresses.

'No point in giving him mine, seeing as I won't be here much longer,' Jim told Dulcie.

'Me neither,' she agreed, it being Dulcie's nature not to want to oblige officialdom in any of its many forms.

'You mean you're going into uniform?' Jim asked her as he stood back to allow her to step outside and then rejoined her, sticking firmly to her side.

'No. I mean you'd never get me back in a place like that again even if you paid me,' Dulcie informed him pithily. 'It smelled to high heaven, and all them old women going on about the last war and us being gassed got on my nerves. Anyway I shan't need to, seeing as we've got our own shelter in the garden. Thanks for looking out for me,' she felt obliged to say, 'but I'd better run, otherwise I'll get what for, for missing dinner.'

'I dare say you've already got a chap, a pretty girl like you,' Jim was saying, but Dulcie pretended not to have heard him, deliberately turning away and plunging into the growing crowd thronging the pavement, and then hesitating. The siren going off like that would have given her mother a real fright. Perhaps she should take the bus back home just to check that everyone was all right, and to reassure them that she was too. Not that they'd care. Her mother would probably be too busy having palpitations worrying about ruddy Edith and her singing to even notice she was there. And besides, if there was to be another air-raid warning then she'd rather spend it in number 13's Anderson shelter than in the public shelter her family would have to go in.

Turning on her heel, Dulcie headed for Article Row.

In the kitchen of number 13, Agnes was listening wide-eyed as Sally told them, 'I saw the police sergeant who lives at number one on my way here.'

'Sergeant Dawson,' Olive and Tilly said together, Olive turning her attention from the potatoes she was putting into the hot roasting tin as she did so to look at Sally.

'Yes, Sergeant Dawson,' Sally confirmed. 'He was standing by his gate when I walked past and he said that he'd heard that the sirens going off had just been a false alarm, that was all.'

'A false alarm!' Olive exclaimed. 'Well, of all the things, nearly giving us a heart attack just for that. It's just as well I dashed in here to turn the oven down. This piece of brisket wouldn't have been worth eating otherwise. Is it twelve o'clock yet, only the Prime Minister's announcement is bound to be on the news.'

'Nearly, just a couple of minutes to go,' Sally told her.

As Olive had guessed, Sally had sheltered at the hospital when the siren had gone off, thankful that because it was a Sunday no operations were scheduled, and no emergencies had come in. They'd had a busy enough night in the operating theatre with an appendix that had to be taken out, followed by a lad with a piece of glass from a broken bottle stuck in his leg, which had only just missed severing an artery, and another with a badly broken arm after a fight had broken out at a local pub.

'It's twelve now,' Sally warned, as Olive slid the roasting tin back into the oven and closed the oven door, wiping her hands on her apron before slipping into her chair just in time to hear the wireless crackle and buzz as Tilly frantically adjusted the reception.

Then, after comment from the announcer, they could all hear the Prime Minister saying, 'This country is now at war with Germany. We are ready.'

The sound of the kitchen door opening distracted them all, Dulcie coming in, saying crossly, 'I've nearly ruined my best shoes and now I've just heard one of your neighbours saying that that ruddy air-raid warning was just a false alarm . . .'

'Shush . . .'

'The Prime Minister's on.'

Dulcie glowered as both Olive and Sally spoke at once, demanding her silence. What was the point in listening to the Prime Minister telling them what they all already knew?

The announcer was back on the air, telling them that the King would be broadcasting to the country that evening.

'So it's really happening then?' Agnes asked uncertainly. 'We really are going to be bombed by the Germans?'

'We're certainly at war with them, Agnes,' Sally answered her briskly, 'but as for them bombing us, well, I dare say the RAF will have something to say about that.' Her eyes felt gritty from lack of sleep with being on nights. Thank goodness she started back on days tomorrow. There was nothing like night duty to drain a person of energy. Yes, it was definitely lack of sleep that was making her eyes sting and her throat ache, nothing else, and certainly not the thought of three people in Liverpool who now mattered as little to her as she obviously did to them.

It was a sombre group of women that sat down to the Sunday dinner Olive dished up later than its normal time of one o'clock, thanks to everything that had been going on.

Afterwards, whilst Tilly and Agnes washed up and Dulcie perched on the edge of the kitchen table watching them, Sally and Olive went into the garden so that Sally could discuss with Olive her plans for starting up a vegetable garden.

'Huh, growing veggies, is it?' Nancy from next door demanded, popping her head over the fence, obviously having heard them talking. 'My Arthur thinks it's a daft idea trying to grow stuff when we've got Covent Garden so close by. He reckons that the Government's got itself a load of seeds it wants to get rid of.' She sniffed disparagingly as she spoke, causing Olive to suppress a small sigh.

Sally, though, shook her head and told her calmly, 'I agree that you can't get better veggies than those from Covent Garden, but the veggies have got to be got into the country and up to

139

London, and that won't be possible once this war gets going properly, so it makes sense for us all to do our bit and grow what we can for ourselves.'

'Well, I suppose there is that,' Nancy agreed grudgingly, after a brief pause, 'although I hope you aren't thinking of fattening a pig like some seem to be doing down on the allotments by the railway.'

Sally laughed. 'I certainly can't see us going that far, although I suppose we could think about having a few chickens.'

'Chickens? Nasty dirty things. Bring rats, they do.'

'Not if you keep their food out of the rats' reach, and think of the lovely fresh eggs.'

Sally was dealing beautifully with Nancy, Olive recognised, treating her neighbour with the respect that was due to her seniority in years, but at the same time making it abundantly clear that she could and would stand her own ground. Nancy was inclined to be a bit of a bully and, like all bullies, if she sensed weakness or fear that only made her worse.

Changing tack, Nancy told Sally, 'I saw you stop and talk to Sergeant Dawson earlier. I feel sorry for him, I really do, with that wife of his.'

'There's nothing wrong with Mrs Dawson, Nancy,' Olive protested. 'I know she keeps herself to herself but that's because of them losing their son. At least that's what Sergeant Dawson hinted to me.'

'Well, she won't be the only one here with a son to mourn, now,' Nancy predicted direly. 'And have you seen how fast them houses further down that are let out to civil servants and the like have emptied? Cowards, they are, the lot them.'

'Mrs Windle told me that the Government have evacuated lots of civil servants. I expect that's why they've gone. They wouldn't have had any choice. Not if they wanted to keep their jobs.'

'Well, you would say that, you being the charitable sort. I'm not so easily taken in. Before you know where we are we'll have them empty houses filled with refugees wot don't know how to live amongst decent folk. It's bad enough us having them Greeks or whatever they are living so close.'

'They're Greek Cypriots, Nancy,' Olive explained patiently, 'and they don't do any harm. They keep themselves to themselves, you know that.'

Nancy, though, was plainly not in the mood to be appeased, her mood perhaps reflecting that of the whole country in its refusal to be appeased by Hitler's offers and explanations of why he had invaded Poland, Olive thought.

'How do we know them Greeks aren't on Hitler's side, that's what I want to know. They could be spying for him,' Nancy told Olive with the air of someone who was determined to have the last word.

'Nancy can be a bit difficult, I'm afraid,' Olive told Sally after her neighbour had returned to her own house, leaving them to continue their discussion about Sally's vegetable bed. 'She does tend to get a bit of a bee in her bonnet about things, so it's best not to tell her too much.'

141

'I know what you mean. We had a neighbour who was much the same. My mother always used to say that she loved finding fault with others. Sadly some people are like that.'

Such a sad look crossed Sally's face that Olive instinctively reached out and patted her arm.

'You must miss your own folk,' was all she could think of to say, not wanting to pry.

'Not really.' Sally's voice and expression changed and hardened. 'My mother is dead, and . . . and my father remarried and has his own life now. I had the most happy childhood, thanks to my mother, but that's in the past. Shall we have the veggie bed here, do you think? It's a good spot with plenty of sunlight?'

Recognising that her lodger did not want to talk about her family, Olive nodded.

'I noticed a decent-looking hardware shop a couple of streets away when I was walking back the other day,' Sally continued, changing the subject. 'I'll call in there and get some string and some other bits and pieces so that we can mark the bed out.'

'You might find there's everything you need in my late father-in-law's shed,' Olive told her. 'He was a keen gardener before he got too poorly to work. When we go back inside I'll find the key and then you can have a look. Mind you, if you are going to call in at Hargreaves you might see if you can buy some extra torch batteries, if you don't mind, and some more candles. I'll give you the money.'

'Good idea. We'll all be needing them once the

nights draw in and we've got to deal with the blackout.'

'Yes. I'm going to sticky-tape the windows tomorrow now that it's official and we're at war. I got the tape a while back when the Government started sending out those leaflets about gas masks and evacuating the kiddies and all that.'

Whilst Olive chatted to Sally in the garden, in the kitchen the washing up had been finished and the dishes put away – by Tilly and Agnes. Dulcie, who had watched them without offering to help, was sitting on the table, swinging her long slim legs and eyeing them with a bored look.

'I suppose your brother will go straight into service now, once he's finished his army training?' Tilly commented.

'I suppose he will,' Dulcie agreed. Agnes had removed the apron she'd been wearing whilst she helped with the washing up, and now what looked like several pieces of folded paper had fallen out of the pocket of her too large dress and onto the floor.

'What's this?' Dulcie demanded, swiftly picking up the papers.

'Oh. It's what Ted gave me.' Immediately Agnes reached out for the paper, her obvious anxiety making Dulcie taunt her, holding it up out of her reach.

'Ted? So who's he, then? A boyfriend? Been sending you love letters, has he?'

Dulcie was astonished that any male would show an interest in someone as drab and dull as Agnes, never mind write to her, as well as feeling just that little bit put out that Agnes, with her love letters, had stepped into territory that Dulcie considered to be more properly hers. It wasn't that she wanted a boyfriend, especially not one who was keen on someone like Agnes, but it still aroused her competitive spirit and galled her a little that plain Agnes should be the first one of them in the house to have a male in tow.

Her face scarlet with anxiety and mortification, Agnes denied that as quickly as though Ted himself were there to hear Dulcie's comments.

'It isn't like that. Ted isn't my boyfriend.'

'So who is he then, and why is he writing to you?'

'He's a driver on the underground, and he's helping me to learn the names of all the different stations on each of the lines, so that I don't get confused when people ask for tickets. Ever so kind and nice he is.'

'So you are sweet on him then?' Dulcie pounced.

'No.' Agnes could imagine how embarrassed Ted would be if he thought that someone as dull as her was getting ideas into her head that had no right being there.

Listening to their exchange, Tilly could see that Agnes was getting upset and couldn't help wishing that Dulcie would stop teasing her.

'Learn all the stations? Oh heavens, Agnes, I don't think I could do that!' Tilly exclaimed. Dulcie's behaviour was making her feel uncomfortable. She admired the older girl but at the same time she felt protective of Agnes and didn't like to see Dulcie making fun of her.

Giving Tilly a grateful look, Agnes explained, 'Ted's been teaching me this tune so that I can sing them 'cos that's how his dad taught him to remember the stations. We have a cup of tea together every day just before he clocks on. He does the late shift.'

'Well, you'd better not let Tilly's mother know that you're being so familiar with a man, otherwise you'll be out on your ear, 'cos she doesn't approve of her lodgers having gentlemen friends, does she, Tilly?' Dulcie demanded, determined to have her pound of flesh.

'Oh, no. It's nothing like that,' Agnes protested, looking even more distressed and anxious.

'Dulcie's just teasing you, Agnes,' Tilly tried to calm her, insisting to the other girl, 'Aren't you, Dulcie?'

Dulcie gave a dismissive shrug, tossing the folded pages over to Agnes and laughing as she failed to catch them and had to scrabble on the floor for them.

'If you say so.' It irked her that Tilly had taken Agnes's side. They were just a couple of know-nothing kids, the pair of them, who'd end up being 'best friends' and sticking to one another like glue. She'd left all that kind of thing behind her when she'd left school. In this life it was everyone for themselves, and them that put themselves first did best. Not that she'd actually had a best friend at school, she was forced to admit. But then that had been because the other girls had been jealous of her, and them that had palled up with her had only done so because they were soppy over her brother. Besides, once you started palling up with other girls they started wanting to know every bit of your business, and then they started threatening to tell on you if they didn't like what you were doing. No, the last thing she needed was a best friend.

SEVEN

'Six weeks we've been at war with Germany now, and I'm getting that tired of not being able to sleep properly at night for waiting for Hitler to bomb us that it would almost be a relief if he did.'

Automatically Sally nodded her head in agreement with the views expressed by the other nurse seated beside her in the canteen whilst they ate their lunch, but the reality was that for once her mind was not on the war. Her heart thudded against her ribs. She'd only come to London and Barts to get away from Liverpool, and until today, if anyone had suggested that she had become attached to Barts and would be unhappy at the thought of leaving, she would have told them soundly that they were wrong.

Now, though, to her own surprise she was forced to admit that she had developed a love for the old place. But it looked as though she was going to be asked to leave.

Just before she'd come for lunch, Theatre Sister had told her that Matron wanted to see her as soon as she'd eaten.

Of course, she hadn't said why, and Sally was far better trained than to ask. She'd searched her mind and her conscience and so far had not been able to come up with anything she'd done wrong that merited a summons from Matron, and she was glad that Sister had waited until they'd finished work for the morning before telling her. Not that they'd had any serious ops this morning, just a girl who'd come out of the pictures in the blackout and fallen over a sandbag, breaking her ankle, which had had to be properly set, and a young, newly enlisted soldier who'd been fooling around with a friend and ended up with a bullet in his arm.

All she could think was that there'd been a change of plan and that her services were no longer needed, with most of the hospital being evacuated. She knew that she would be able to get another job – somewhere – but she'd just begun to settle in at Barts and at number 13.

There was no point in delaying things. She couldn't finish her meal she was so apprehensive. Getting up, she made her way first to the nearest ladies' where she stared anxiously at her reflection in the mirror, checking to make sure that her nurse's tall hat was on exactly as it should be, with no wisps of hair escaping, before removing her cuffs from her rolled up sleeves and then unrolling them. She'd removed her apron before leaving the ward and now, trying to calm the nervous butterflies swarming in her tummy, she left the ladies' and headed for Matron's office.

Her hesitant knock was answered immediately by a firm, 'Come.'

Sally went in. Officially Matron was now based with the evacuated Barts in the country, but she still made regular visits to London, and Sally, who greatly admired her, found that despite her nervousness there was something reassuring about the sight of her familiar figure.

'Ah, Nurse Johnson. Good. I dare say you're finding our ways here at Barts are different from those in your previous hospital, and I hope that you feel that you are benefiting from your time here.'

'Yes, ma'am,' was the only thing that Sally dared allow herself to say. Had someone complained that because she wasn't Barts trained her standards were not as high as they should be? Naturally her loyalty to her own training hospital in Liverpool had her mentally up in arms at the thought of it, or of her being found wanting, but of course she could not say so. All nurses, and no doubt matrons too, felt the kind of loyalty for the hospital in which they had trained as members of a family did towards that family. They might criticise and even occasionally find fault, but outsiders certainly must not.

'Your employment here is, of course, only for one year.'

Sally's heart began to sink. This was it. Matron was going to tell her that her services were no longer required. Well, at least she hadn't done something so heinous that she was going to be called to order for it.

Matron was looking down at some notes on a piece of paper in front of her.

'Although most of the hospital has been evacuated, that does not mean that we don't have to maintain our traditional Barts high standards here. If London is bombed, then this hospital will be one of those at the forefront of dealing with the injured.'

'Yes, ma'am.'

Sally's muscles were beginning to ache from standing up so straight, but she dare not relax her pose, even had her training allowed her to do so.

'You have been on duty in the operating theatre whilst our consultant plastic surgeon, Sir Harold Gillies, has operated.'

'Yes, ma'am,' Sally agreed.

'Sir Harold has extremely high standards and is very particular about the nurses who work in his operating theatre. He has made a point of informing me that he thought that you, Nurse Johnson, are a first-rate theatre nurse.'

Matron had summoned her here to her office to *praise* her. Sally felt so dizzy with relief and disbelief that she was quite light-headed.

'Of course, it is my role as Matron to decide which of my nurses should be recommended for further training and responsibility, and mine alone. However, in this instance . . .' Matron paused and looked directly at Sally. 'The evacuation has created a lack of senior nursing staff. What I have in mind, Nurse, is to promote you to the position of theatre staff nurse, with a view – with further training – to you eventually taking on the role of sister.'

Sister! Back in the early days of their training

she and Morag had talked of the impossibility of either of them ever doing well enough to become ward sisters. Fierce pain caught at Sally's chest. Once Morag and her parents would have been the first people she would have wanted to share her news and her excitement with, knowing how well all three of them, but especially her friend, would understand what it meant to her.

'If you wish to accept the post of staff nurse I shall require you to change from temporary to permanent staff here, Nurse. Do you wish to do that?'

'Yes, ma'am, please. And . . . and thank you, ma'am.'

A small smile touched Matron's mouth. 'It is a great deal of responsibility that this hospital will be placing in you and, more importantly, so will its patients, but I have every confidence that you are capable of carrying that responsibility, Nurse, and carrying it as befits a Barts nurse. Thank you, Nurse. You may go. You will be informed of when you are to take up your new duties in due course.'

Not even once she was outside in the corridor did Sally dare to lean against the wall and give way to her own shaken exultation. She was going to be a staff nurse. And maybe ultimately a ward sister. She could hardly believe how wrong she had been about the cause of her summons to Matron's office. And it was all thanks to Sir Harold Gillies, whose handiwork she had now had the opportunity to admire on several occasions as she watched him work on surgery in children born with cleft palates.

Sally knew that there were nurses who openly admitted that theatre work was not for them, but she truly loved it. Staff Nurse Johnson – how proud her mother would have been to learn of her success. Sally's happiness was replaced by the familiar tight ball of mingled anger and pain that thinking of her mother, and the manner in which her former best friend had usurped her mother's role, caused. She could never forgive Morag for what she had done. Her father's loneliness she could understand but not her friend's taking advantage of it.

She looked at her watch. Officially she should have been off duty from midday as she was due to start working nights from tomorrow, but of course Matron's summons had meant that she had not been able to leave, and now that she was here she might as well look in on the ward where the patients operated on this morning would be recovering.

She was within sight of its doors when a young doctor, whom Sally recognised as being a would-be surgeon, came through them at speed, his white coat flying, his stethoscope dangling round his neck, one of the files he was holding escaping from his grasp and falling to the floor, dislodging its contents.

Sally bent to pick them up just as the doctor did the same.

'It's Nurse Johnson, isn't it?' he surprised her by saying. 'I recognised you from the operation on that cleft palate patient last week. I was in the gallery watching Sir Harold operate.'

'You're from New Zealand, like Sir Harold?' she guessed, recognising his accent.

He beamed her a warm smile. 'Yes. My father is in general practice there. He trained here at Barts himself. I'm George Laidlaw.'

'Sally Johnson.'

He was an attractive-looking, open-faced young man, with brown curly hair, blue eyes and a warm smile. Sally guessed that he was around her own age and he reminded her of a large gangling puppy, eager to make friends.

He was looking at her in a way that told Sally that he found her attractive. Normally this would have put her off him as the last thing she wanted was to get involved with a young man. She wasn't looking for romance, and not just because there was a war on. Her heart was still bruised from her quarrel with Callum over his sister's marriage to her father. However, there was something so hopeful and pleading about the look in George Laidlaw's eyes that Sally found her defences melting a little.

She returned his smile, surprised to discover how easy it was and how pleasant to bask in the warmth of such easy and unaffected male appreciation.

'Look, you can tell me if I'm out of order, and you're either not interested or already hooked up, but I'd really like to take you out one evening. Just for a getting-to-know-one-another drink.' When Sally hesitated, he added coaxingly, 'I've seen how kind you are to the patients. How about taking pity on a poor lonesome and far-from-home Kiwi?'

'It's my duty to be kind to our patients,' Sally pointed out mock severely, before adding truthfully, 'Besides, I'm just about to start on nights.'

Even so, she couldn't help remembering the fun she and Morag had had when they had first palled up as trainee nurses, especially at the Grafton Ballroom, where they had never been short of eager partners. Those days had been filled with so much youthful happiness. Barts and London were her life now and it was up to her what she made of that life. She rather liked George Laidlaw. He had a nice smile.

'Well, it doesn't have to be now,' he was persisting. 'Any night will do. I mean, I can fit in with you.'

He was flatteringly keen. Perhaps it would do her good to say 'yes'. Her mother would definitely have thought so, Sally recognised with a small pang. Even so, in time-honoured female tradition she felt duty bound to test him.

'If Sir Harold's taken you under his wing, I'm surprised you've got time to take nurses out.'

'Not nurses. Just one nurse – you,' he responded simply, the look he was giving her making the colour rise up to turn Sally's cheeks a soft pink. 'And you're right about Sir Harold, he does keep us busy. It's a privilege to watch him operate. His protégé, Archie McIndoe, is working over here as well.'

'Yes, I know.'

It was obvious to her that both Sir Harold Gillies and Archie McIndoe were much admired by the young doctor. George himself confirmed this to her when, unable to keep the admiration out of

154

his voice, he told her, 'During the World War, when Sir Harold first got the British Government's permission to set up a plastic surgery unit, he used to send out labels with the ambulances going over to France so that potential patients could be sent back to him as quickly as possible. He did the most wonderful things for some of those chaps. I dare say if this war gets going he and Archie will be doing a lot more.'

'Yes, I suppose they will,' Sally agreed, with a smile.

'So you'll come then? Out for a drink with me? When we're both free?'

He was persistent, Sally had to give him that. 'Maybe.'

The answer seemed to please him because he gave her another beaming smile as they both stood up and went their separate ways.

Sally was still smiling when she eventually made her way out of the hospital and into the October sunshine, and not just because of the praise Matron had given her.

The newspaper vendors along Holborn Viaduct selling the early evening editions of the papers, were crying out, 'British Expeditionary Force in France. Read all about it.'

Sally paused and glanced at the headlines. All young men of over twenty were now being called up, and everywhere one looked one could see men in uniform, the sound of their marching feet a warning, drumming in the war that so far had remained safely distanced from British shores. But for how much longer?

Sally hugged her uniform cloak tightly around herself. The leaves on London's trees were already turning and soon they would fall. Please God that a similar fate would not befall the country's fighting men.

Dulcie eyed the smart luxurious luggage on show on the luggage department's floor: trunks and cases of every kind, hurriedly being bought by those wealthy enough to afford them, as they made plans either to leave the country themselves or to send their children away to somewhere like Canada for their own safety.

Dulcie was particularly attracted to a cream leather vanity case, bound with tan straps. Its lid was open to show off its interior, with its mirror, silver-topped glass jars and silver-backed hairbrushes. It was placed on top of a series of different sized matching trunks. She was sure she'd seen a similar case being held by Gracie Fields in a photograph in *Picture Post*. The vanity case cost more than she earned in a whole year, but Dulcie loved it. She'd come up here every day during her dinner hour just so that she could look at it and imagine herself parading around with it. She looked round assessingly. The department was very busy. It wouldn't do any harm for her just to hold the case to see how it felt and how she looked with it. A girl could dream, after all. Quickly she reached out and closed the lid, securing it with its own special key, and then she reached for the case. The leather-covered handle fitted her palm perfectly.

There was a mirror not very far away. She'd

slipped off her overall before she'd come up here, because you weren't supposed to mingle with the customers. The tan woollen skirt she was wearing complemented perfectly the leather straps on the vanity case, just as its cream leather complemented perfectly her cream silk blouse. She'd had the skirt made up from a roll of fabric she'd spotted on a stall in Portobello Market, which the stall holder had told her with a nod and wink was French. More like fallen off a lorry, Dulcie suspected. The cream silk blouse had come from a second-hand shop in posh Kensington, which Dulcie had heard about by eavesdropping on a conversation between two of the other girls who worked in the perfume department.

Together with her brown leather shoes, she reckoned that she looked every bit as good as Gracie Fields. In fact, she thought she looked a good deal better, seeing as she was far prettier and much younger than the famous singer.

The mirror wasn't very far away, but as she turned towards it Dulcie suddenly heard a sharp female voice exclaiming, 'David, call the manager. That girl is trying to steal that case. I recognise her from the perfume department. She's got no right to be up here.'

In the mirror Dulcie could see David James-Thompson standing behind her, a purse-lipped Lydia Whittingham at his side.

Angrily Dulcie turned round, but before she could defend herself David James-Thompson was saying calmly, 'I'm sure, Miss . . . ?' He looked enquiringly at Dulcie, who obliged with a pointed dagger look at her rival, 'It's Dulcie, Miss Dulcie Simmonds.'

'I'm sure that Miss Simmonds has a perfectly good reason for being here, Lydia.'

'That's right, I have,' Dulcie agreed.

Lydia Whittingham flashed her a venomous look of female dislike, insisting, 'I doubt that. It was plain to me what she was up to. Another few minutes and she'd have been walking out of the department with that case. Not that she would have got very far. It's perfectly obvious to anyone with eyes in their head that she simply isn't the sort who could ever afford such an exclusive and expensive item. I'm going to call the manager, David. He can deal with her, and you can buy me that lizardskin handbag you promised me for my birthday.'

Never one to back down from a challenge Dulcie drew herself up to her full height and tossed her head, her confidence boosted by the appreciative look she could see David giving her behind Lydia Whittingham's back.

'You can call the manager if you like, and if you don't mind making a fool of yourself when I tell him that I got sent up here officially to look in this here case to see how much makeup could be packed into it.'

'You're lying,' Lydia proclaimed immediately.

'No I'm not.'

'So who sent you up here then – and be aware that I shall check.'

'Mr Selfridge,' Dulcie told her with aplomb and without the slightest concern for the fact that she

158

was lying. 'And you can go and ask him yourself if you want. He said that the case was a gift for a young lady of his acquaintance.'

To one side of her, Dulcic could hear David James-Thompson's muffled laugh.

Lydia opened her mouth to challenge her and then closed it again, and Dulcie knew perfectly well why. It was an open secret to the staff that, despite his advancing years, Mr Selfridge was prone to passions that led to him indulging the current recipient of his feelings with expensive gifts from the store.

Delighted by Lydia's heightened furious colour and obvious inability to refute her lie, Dulcie carried the case back to where she had got it, placing it carefully on top of the pile.

'Come along, David,' Lydia commanded her escort in a sharp voice, turning on her heel so that her back was towards both Dulcie and David.

Seizing her chance, Dulcie turned to him and told him nonchalantly, 'If you was ever to feel like dancing, I go dancing at the Hammersmith Palais most Saturday evenings.'

The look he gave her in response was one of amused admiration. Miss Iron Knickers might think she'd got him well and truly hooked, Dulcie thought with some satisfaction, but she, Dulcie, certainly didn't think so.

'David . . .'

'Coming,' David answered as he turned to follow Lydia.

The little shop girl didn't hold back when it came to putting herself forward, and there had been a look in her eye that he had liked. David had a weakness for girls like Dulcie, no doubt because his paternal grandmother had been a Gaiety Girl before she had 'snared', to use his own disapproving mother's word, his grandfather. His paternal grandfather's regrettable lapse of good taste was not something David's mother approved of. Her family was stoutly county and rigidly proper. His father might be a judge and his mother's family might have come over with William the Conqueror, but there was no money in the family, which was why his mother in particular was so keen to see him engaged to Lydia, whose father might be merely a director at Selfridges but whose mother came from a family of wealthy mill owners and was likely to inherit a very nice sum of money indeed when her own elderly father died.

The basket she had filled with the new season's root vegetables from Covent Garden was beginning to weigh heavily on her arm as Olive headed for Article Row, so when Sergeant Dawson came out of the police station just as she was passing it and offered, 'Let me carry that for you,' she was rather grateful to hand the basket over to him.

'I hadn't realised how heavy the veggies would be. I got a piece of scrag end of mutton yesterday and I thought I'd make a nice tasty mutton casserole with it for the girls, and thicken it up with some veggies.'

'Sounds good.'

Tall, well set up, and just turned forty, his dark brown, slightly curly hair now covered by his helmet, Sergeant Dawson looked very smart in his police uniform. Despite everything he and his wife had been through with the illness and then the loss of their son, Sergeant Dawson always had a kind look in his hazel eyes and a friendly word for everyone.

Olive felt very sorry for both him and his wife. Nancy might complain that it was unneighbourly of Mrs Dawson to keep herself to herself in the way that she did, but Olive felt that that was the sergeant's wife's way of dealing with the sorrow of her loss, and that they shouldn't talk about her behind her back.

'I must admit I'm partial to a good mutton casserole,' Sergeant Dawson confided to her. 'My ma used to make it. Thickened it with barley, she did.'

'I do the same,' Olive told him with a smile.

'I miss Ma's casseroles, but Mrs Dawson – well, she doesn't see the sense of making a big bowl of casserole when there's just the two of us to eat it. Working out all right, is it, having your lodgers?'

'Very well,' Olive answered. 'My Tilly and Agnes – that's the little orphan girl – get on really well together, and if Sally – that's the nurse – has her way we'll be eating our own veggies next year as she's taken over the garden.'

'The other one looks a bit of a flighty sort,' the sergeant opined.

'Dulcie.' Olive sighed ruefully, appreciating the sergeant's understanding tone. 'I dare say she doesn't mean any harm, but I do worry about the effect she might have on Tilly and Agnes. Tilly has already started hinting that she and Agnes are old enough now to go out dancing, but I'd rather see them going to dances at the church hall than the Hammersmith Palais, which is where Dulcie likes to go.'

'It must be hard work for you, having the four of them to cook and clean for.'

They both paused to cross over the road and then Olive answered, 'Not really. Tilly's very good, and Agnes of course is used to helping out with being at the orphanage. I have to tell her off sometimes for wanting to do too much. After all, she is paying me to have her lodging with us. To be honest I like having the house filled up a bit; makes it seem more like a home than there just being me and Tilly there. And they're no trouble really. Sally, with her being a nurse, keeps her room spotless, and even Dulcie is the tidy sort. Mind you, she is prone to taking more than her fair share of the hot water, especially on Saturday when she's getting dressed up to go out.' Olive sighed, remembering how envious Tilly had looked when she'd watched Dulcie setting off for her evening out. 'I dare say that if I hadn't got the girls lodging with me I'd have been asked to take in a couple of refugees. Not that I'd have minded that, although Nancy next door to me is dead set against them.'

'No, she's never liked foreigners, hasn't Nancy.'
They exchanged smiles.

'Tilly's got Agnes going to St John Ambulance with her, so that should keep them out of too much mischief, although I have to admit that I do worry about them being out during the blackout. I've got them both little torches and warned them to keep away from the pavement edge. Sally says they've had several injured people come into the hospital since the blackout started, because of not being able to see where there're cars coming, with them having to have their lights covered. It's going to get worse as well at the end of this month when the clocks go back and we stop having British Summer Time.'

'Had to attend a nasty accident myself last night, as it happens,' Sergeant Dawson told her. 'A young lady had driven straight into a cyclist and killed him. She was beside herself, of course, and had to be taken to hospital for the shock.'

'Oh, what a dreadful thing to happen, and there Mrs Morrison from Floris Street and I were both wishing that we could drive when the vicar's wife told us that we've been offered the use of a small van for the WVS, but as none of us can drive we'd have to pass up on it. There's quite a bit of competing between the WVS groups to be the best equipped and of course those groups that have drivers and transport are very much top of the heap.' Olive laughed. 'Now, though, after what you've just said I'm rather glad that I can't drive.'

'You mustn't say that. In fact, if this war gets as bad as some reckon it will, the Government will be wanting women to learn to drive.' Sergeant Dawson paused and then said hesitantly, 'If you and Mrs Morrison were wanting to learn to drive, and since you're saying that you've been offered the use of a van, I could teach you, if you like?'

'You can drive?'

A rueful smile curled his mouth, making him look younger and far more carefree. 'Learned almost as a kid at the back end of the last war, and once you've learned it's something you never forget.'

'Well, it's very generous of you to offer. Of course, Mrs Morrison's husband would have to agree.'

'Of course, but the offer's there if you want it.'

They had reached Article Row now but instead of handing her basket back to her when they arrived at number 1, the sergeant shook his head when Olive made to take it from him.

'I'll walk you to your gate with it.'

'I'll send you and Mrs Dawson a bowl of the casserole, as a thank you, seeing as you've carried the veggies home for me,' Olive told him with a smile of her own.

He was such a kind man, offering to teach her and Mrs Morrison to drive, Olive thought five minutes later as she went into her kitchen. Mrs Windle would be pleased if he did succeed in teaching them, Olive knew. She had been quite crestfallen at the thought of having to turn down the offer of the van.

From the kitchen window she could see Sally working in the garden and she went out to her.

'I'm just going to put the kettle on and make a cuppa before I start on the veggies for the mutton stew. Would you like a cup?'

'I'd love one,' Sally admitted. It hadn't felt particularly warm when she had initially come out into the garden but now, after lifting the turf from the plot she had marked out, she was feeling very warm – and very thirsty. 'I'm ready for a break so I'll come back with you.'

The minute Olive opened the kitchen door, Sally could smell the wonderful aroma, sniffing appreciatively as she removed her Wellington boots and left them outside.

'I put the stew in this morning to let it cook slowly,' Olive told her.

'My mother used to make a delicious stew and she always swore by cooking it slowly all day.' A sad nostalgic smile tugged at Sally's mouth and to her own surprise she heard herself telling Olive, 'I had some good news today. Matron is upgrading me to the position of staff nurse and she's recommended that I train to be a sister. I'm thrilled, of course, but I couldn't help wishing that my mother was still alive so that I could tell her.'

Lighting the gas beneath the kettle she had just filled, Olive turned to look at her. Sally, for all her maturity, wasn't really that much older than her own daughter and she knew how she would have felt in Sally's mother's shoes, so it seemed completely natural to her to go over to Sally and give her a firm hug, before telling her gently, 'That's what your mother would have wanted to do, I know. I'm so sorry you've had such sadness to contend with, Sally.'

Olive's unexpected tenderness brought tears to Sally's eyes. It had been so long since she had felt the warmth of a caring maternal hug.

'Your father is still alive, though, you said,'

Olive began carefully, but immediately Sally shook her head.

'I know what you're going to suggest but there's no going back. I couldn't. I couldn't stand in the kitchen that used to be my mother's and watch the person who was my best friend usurping my mother's role. They didn't even wait a decent length of time. I don't know how they could do what they've done, but I do know that I don't want anything to do with them any more.'

Poor Sally, Olive thought compassionately. The kettle had started to boil, the steam activating its shrill whistle. As she went to make the tea, tactfully Olive changed the subject.

'I don't know what you think but I'm to have driving lessons. Sergeant Dawson has offered to teach me. Our WVS group have been offered the use of a van. It belongs to the Lords, from the drapers in Norfolk Street, or rather it belongs to their son, Gerry, but he's been called up. They don't need it because Mr Lord has his own van that he uses for the business and Mavis, Mrs Lord, flatly refuses to learn to drive so Mr Lord has offered it to the WVS.'

'I think it's an excellent idea,' Sally approved immediately.

'Of course, it won't just be me he's teaching,' Olive hastened to add, pouring them each a cup of tea. 'There'll be two of us. Me and Mrs Morrison.'

'It's a great opportunity – for you and for the war effort,' Sally enthused.

*　　*　　*

166

'Mum, can I have a word with you, just between us?' Tilly asked her mother quietly as Olive checked on the dumplings she had added to the stew earlier.

'Of course you can, love. Why don't you go upstairs to my room and I'll follow you up there in a tick?' Olive told her daughter just as quietly.

With the wireless on and Dulcie complaining about the difficult customer she'd had in who'd insisted that Dulcie had sold her a shade of lipstick that didn't suit her and that she wanted to change, Olive knew that the others wouldn't have overheard, although what it was that her daughter wanted to discuss, she had no idea.

Wiping her hands on her apron, Olive went up and found her daughter, standing in front of the window in Olive's own bedroom.

Sitting down on the edge of her bed, automatically smoothing the soft, slightly faded blue satin coverlet, she patted it and invited 'Come and sit down here, Tilly. Is something wrong?'

When Tilly shook her head and answered firmly, 'No,' Olive admitted to feeling relieved.

'So what is it that you want to talk to me about?'

'It's just, well, you know that there's to be this dance at the church hall and you said that I could go, and Agnes is going to go too?'

'Yes? Have you and Agnes fallen out and you don't want her to go with you?'

Tilly laughed. 'No, Mum, it's nothing like that. I like Agnes, I really do. She's so sweet and kind. No, what it is, it that . . .' Tilly had bent her head and was plucking at the hem of her navy-blue cardigan – a little giveaway habit that was familiar to Olive from her daughter's childhood and which meant that Tilly felt uncomfortable about something.

'Well, it's just that poor Agnes only has hand-me-down clothes. I know I've given her a couple of things, but what I was thinking, Mum, was how she is going to feel when we go to the dance and everyone else there is wearing something nice and she isn't. And it isn't because I'll be with her and I'm bothered about what people think. Agnes is my friend now and it wouldn't bother me if she went to the dance in that awful brown dress she first came here in. It's for Agnes's sake, Mum. I don't want her to feel out of things and uncomfortable.'

What her daughter meant was that she didn't want Agnes to be hurt, Olive recognised. Maternal love and gratitude filled her. She had been so lucky with Tilly. She'd grown from a happy loving baby into an equally loving young woman.

Modestly Olive gave no thought to the fact that she might have been instrumental in helping to form her daughter's concern for others, instead taking Tilly's hand in her own and giving it a loving shake as she told her, 'You're right, Tilly, and I'm cross with myself for not thinking of it.'

'The thing is, Mum, I know that Agnes doesn't earn very much and that she sends money to the orphanage because she feels she wants to help them for bringing her up, and I was wondering if we couldn't perhaps get her a pretty frock as a bit of a present?'

'Oh, Tilly . . .' Olive hugged her daughter tightly. 'You are so like your dad. He was generous to a fault and always thinking of others as well. Look, I'll tell you what we'll do. I'll tell Agnes that I'm taking you out to get some material because you need a couple of new things since you've grown out of last winter's clothes, which is true, and that I've been putting a bit of money to one side from Agnes's rent because I thought that she'd probably need things as well but that she wouldn't have thought of it with always having had the orphanage to provide clothes for her.'

'Mum, can we really?' Tilly's eyes were sparkling as brightly as any stars, the delight and excitement in her expression melting Olive's heart. The income from their lodgers was bringing in a modestly comfortable sum and, always thrifty, Olive had been putting money to one side just in case one or more of her lodgers left. She had more than enough saved to be able to afford to buy a couple or so lengths of fabric for both girls, and to get the clothes made up.

'Yes,' she confirmed with a smile, 'we can.' What she'd got in mind was a couple of lengths of woollen fabric, so that a nice costume could be made up for Tilly – perhaps with two skirts to make sure she got her wear out of the jacket – something she could wear for Sunday best now and for work next winter, along with a length for an everyday skirt for each of the girls, and then something pretty for winter frocks for them both, which they could wear to the Church's socials and dances. If she went about it the right way she felt sure she could get Miss Thomas, the local dress-maker, who also attended their church, to give her a special price for such a good order.

'We'll go and have a look for the fabric tomorrow.'

'Could we go to Portobello Market?' Tilly begged her excitedly. 'We could make a real day of it. That's where Dulcie got the fabric for her skirt. She says you can get ever such a good bargain there if you know who to ask. We could ask her where she got hers.'

Olive forced herself to smile, pleased that, since Dulcie worked on Saturdays, Tilly would be unable to suggest that they asked her to go with them. 'Well, I was thinking of somewhere closer. Portobello Market is a bit of a trek, I'd thought of somewhere like Leather Lane.'

Tilly's disappointment was immediate and obvious as she pleaded, 'Oh, please, Mum. I really would like to go to Portobello. We could set off early.'

Tilly's plea tugged on Olive's heart, and with a small sigh she amended, 'Well, maybe, let me think about it and then we'll see. Meanwhile,' Olive stood up, 'I'll have a word with Agnes. I want to make it plain to her that it's her own money that will be paying for her new clothes.'

When Tilly looked questioningly at her, Olive explained, 'All Agnes has known all her life is charity, Tilly, and the need to be grateful to others for that charity. That was all very well when she was in the orphanage, but that sort of attitude in the wider world could lead to other people not

170

treating her as respectfully as they should. It's only right and fair that Agnes should be able to feel proud of buying her own clothes. Now, we'd better get back downstairs before those dumplings get too well done.'

EIGHT

Nearly six o'clock. At six Selfridges would be closing to customers, although it would be closer to half-past before she eventually got away, Dulcie knew. She was hungry and looking forward to her evening meal. One thing Dulcie could say for her landlady was that she was a good cook, who didn't cut corners on their meals or the portions she served.

'Lydia Whittingham was in here earlier with that chap of hers,' Lizzie told Dulcie, coming over to her whilst Dulcie was tidying up her counter. 'Arlene Watts from Elizabeth Arden makeup said that Lydia told her that they're getting engaged on her birthday.'

Dulcie gave a dismissive shrug. 'So what?'

'So what? Have you forgotten that you said that you were going to get her beau to go dancing with you?'

'Of course not,' Dulcie answered scornfully, 'not when I put a bet on it – and he *will* go dancing with me.'

'You mean that you'd go out with an engaged man?'

'I want to go dancing with him, not get married to him,' Dulcie replied. It was the truth. And a large part of the reason she wanted to go dancing with David James-Thompson was because she wanted to rub Lydia Whittingham's nose in it a bit.

She'd disliked the other girl, with her snooty airs, from the minute she'd set eyes on her and it would be amusing to know that she'd persuaded her fiancé to go out with her behind Miss Snooty's back.

'You mean you aren't sweet on him? Why do you want to go out with him then?'

''Cos he looks like going dancing with him would be fun.'

That was the truth too.

'If you aren't careful you'll get yourself a bad reputation and then no decent lad will want to marry you,' Lizzie told her warningly.

Dulcie laughed. 'There'll always be lads who want to marry me, but they'll have to prove to me that they're worth marrying before they get to put a ring on *my* finger. Besides, I don't want to get married for years yet.'

Lizzie was aghast. 'Every girl wants to get married,' she protested.

'I've seen what happens to a girl when she gets married,' Dulcie defended her intention. 'She ends up running round after her husband, being told what to do, and then being lumbered with squalling kids. That's not for me. When I do decide to get married it will be to someone who puts me first, not himself.'

Twenty minutes later, as she sauntered out of the store into the sharpness of the early evening, the camel coat she was wearing over her tweed skirt and silk blouse showing off her blonde hair, she was so busy mentally planning what she was going to wear for tomorrow night's dance, that she didn't see David James-Thompson until he stepped in front of her.

'You're taking a risk, aren't you?' she taunted him. 'Waiting for me when you'll soon be an engaged man.'

Unabashed, he laughed and bent his head to tell her quietly, 'I like taking risks and something tells me that you like taking them as well.'

He was carrying a large Selfridges bag, and unwilling to let him see how impressed she was by both his nonchalance and his response, Dulcie pointed to it and demanded, 'What's in there, her ladyship's lizardskin handbag?'

Again he laughed, shaking his head as he told her, 'No. This is for you by way of apology for the fact that I'm afraid I won't be able to accept your invitation – at least not this Saturday.'

'It wasn't an invitation. I was just saying that I go dancing of a Saturday,' Dulcie insisted. 'And what do you mean, it's for me. What is it?'

'Have a look,' David smiled, handing her the large bag.

For all her confidence with young men, Dulcie was not used to receiving gifts from anyone outside her family. And even when presents were given and exchanged they were small modest things, that most definitely did not come in large Selfridges bags. When a man who wasn't part of your family, or who you weren't courting, gave you a present, though, Dulcie knew exactly what that meant. For all her enjoyment of riling other young women by flirting with their partners, Dulcie had neither the desire to nor the intention of allowing any man to take things further than that.

Looking David James-Thompson squarely in the eye she told him bluntly, 'If you're thinking that by giving me some kind of present I'm going to let you take liberties with me, then you're going to be disappointed, because I won't.'

'That isn't why I'm giving you this.'

Dulcie looked searchingly at him, and then, sensing that he was telling her the truth and after a brisk accepting nod of her head, she opened the carrier bag and looked cautiously inside. When she saw what it contained, though, her head came up and she looked speechlessly at David before looking back into the carrier again at the cream and tan leather vanity case she had coveted so much, and which now so unexpectedly was hers.

'I told them not to gift wrap it because I wanted to see your face when you saw it.'

'I wasn't going to pinch it. I just wanted to see what it looked like. Gracie Fields has got one. I saw a photo of her in *Picture Post* carrying it,' Dulcie defended her actions earlier.

She meant it, David recognised, contrasting her blunt outspokenness with the coy but unmistakable promise Lydia had made him earlier about showing him later, when they were alone, how pleased she would be if he bought her the handbag she wanted. A coyness that had repulsed him every bit as much as Dulcie's bravado delighted him. Right now she was like a child at Christmas desperately trying not to look as excited as she felt, David thought, laughing as she immediately folded up the paper bag and then opened the vanity case to put the discarded bag and her own small handbag inside it, before triumphantly locking it and taking a couple of steps holding onto it.

Without having to discuss it they'd both automatically moved into the shadows away from the store as they spoke and out of view from anyone else leaving.

David had only bought the vanity case for Dulcie on impulse after Lydia had left him to go home with her father, but now he recognised that he was glad that he had.

'I suppose you're taking Miss Iron Knickers Lydia somewhere posh tonight, are you?' Dulcie asked him.

He shook his head. 'No. I'm going back to my rooms to study some briefs. It's a legal term meaning papers,' he explained when he saw her looking puzzled.

'Does that mean that you're a judge, like your dad?' Dulcie asked him, remembering that Lizzie had said that his father was a judge.

David grinned. 'No. I'm actually a barrister, a very newly qualified and junior barrister,' he added wryly. He'd taken off his hat when he'd first greeted her, but now he put it on again.

'A barrister? What's that?'

Both her naïvety and her lack of self-consciousness about questioning him appealed to David. They spoke of a freedom from the constraints of 'correct behaviour' and a zest for life. Things sorely lacking in both his mother and Lydia.

'Basically a barrister is someone who is instructed by a solicitor on behalf of that solicitor's client to present and plead or defend a case that is put before a judge and jury. In my case it means grubbing around in a second-rate set of chambers, hoping that the clerk will throw me a few scraps in the form of a brief.'

'You don't like being a barrister then.'

She was sharp, David thought ruefully, he had to give her that.

'It isn't a matter of what I do or don't like.'

'Well, it should be,' Dulcie told him stoutly. 'Are you really going to get engaged to Miss Iron Knickers?'

'It's what my parents and hers expect.'

Dulcie gave him a look. 'So you're almost an engaged man but you've given me this.'

'To make up for the unpleasantness this afternoon.' He paused and then told her, 'I'm sorry – about not being able to go dancing with you.'

'Don't be. I've got lads queuing up to dance with me,' Dulcie told him truthfully, thinking gleefully to herself that being given the vanity case was far better than winning her bet with Lizzie. She just couldn't wait to see the other girl's expression when she told her about the case.

'Where are you going now then?' she asked him.

'Like I told you, I've got to read some briefs.

The senior partner wants my notes on them in chambers first thing on Monday morning.'

'Chambers?'

'That's what they call the . . . the offices that barristers work from. Mine are at Gray's Inn. 'Look, I'm sorry but I've got to go.'

Before anyone saw them he meant, Dulcie recognised as she saw the quick look he gave over his shoulder. Well, she certainly wasn't going to ask him to stay.

'Suit yourself,' she responded. Then giving him a dismissive shrug, Dulcie turned on her heel and walked away from him without a backward look.

Who'd have thought that he'd buy her the vanity case, she thought gleefully. She certainly hadn't. Oh, she'd known from the look he'd given her this afternoon that he had a bit of an eye for her, but then she'd known that the first time she'd seen him. But buying her the vanity case . . . That would be one in the eye for Miss Stuck-Up Lydia Whittingham.

She wasn't going to take her vanity case out with her when she went dancing tomorrow night, though, Dulcie decided, immediately protective of her new acquisition. All sorts went to the Hammersmith Palais and she didn't want some other girl nicking it when she wasn't looking. She would take it with her to church on Sunday, though. She couldn't wait to see Edith's face when she saw it, Dulcie thought happily, unconcerned both about the fact that a vanity case was hardly the kind of thing one would take to church and the fact that she wasn't going to win her bet about dancing with David James-Thompson.

For much longer after he had left her than was wise or sensible David was still thinking about Dulcie and the way that talking to her had made him realise how little he wanted the future his parents had planned for him, and how constraining it felt, like wearing someone else's clothes. But he had no choice; he had to wear them, just as he had to marry Lydia, or risk being labelled a complete cad – something his determined and icily proud mother would never tolerate or accept. Marriage was marriage, and if his was going to be a duty rather than a pleasure, well then, he'd just have to find his pleasure elsewhere. His parents moved in the same social circles as the Whittinghams. They were neighbours, living on the outskirts of the same small market town. He had known Lydia for ever, and his mother had made it plain that she wanted Lydia as her daughter-in-law. Or rather, that she wanted the money Lydia's mother would inherit to come into their own family. His parents were comfortably off but not as well off as his mother would have liked. Her own grandmother had had country connections to the aristocracy, and she was an out-and-out snob, who never lost an opportunity to make it plain that she felt she had married down in marrying David's father.

Until now David hadn't really given much thought about whether or not he actually wanted to marry Lydia. Marriage was marriage, and marrying the right sort of girl was something a chap just did. When it came to having fun, that fun was something one found discreetly outside one's marriage and away from one's home. David was someone who liked living on the surface of life, skimming it like a pebble skimming across a flat calm pool. The emotional turmoil and danger of the depths that lay below that surface held no interest or appeal for him. He was obliging and easy-going, preferring to pay lip service to what he was supposed to do, rather than challenge the status quo. He preferred amusing flirtations to passionate affairs, risqué conversation to risqué relationships, going with the flow rather than swimming against it. Dulcie tempted him but she was a temptation he could easily resist because she was the sort who would cause him trouble. Meeting her this evening had merely been an impulse decision, his gift to her something that amused him, just as she did. As they went their separate ways David reflected cheerfully, that he would probably not even be able to recall her name in a month's time.

It was gone midnight according to the illuminated face of Tilly's alarm clock, and she and Agnes should have been asleep, but instead they were lying in their separate beds in the darkness facing one another as they whispered excitedly about their promised shopping trip. Olive, having given in to maternal love, had agreed that they could make the longer journey to the Portobello Road Market.

The Portobello Market. Tilly hugged her excitement and delight to herself, enjoying the grown-up feeling it gave her that her mother had accepted her argument that travelling to it could be cost effective in the end, given that they were bound to have a wider choice of fabrics, and possibly at better prices.

Typically, Nancy next door had nearly brought an end to Tilly's hopes, when the proposed shopping trip had been mentioned to her and she had sniffed in that disparaging way she had and said that you wouldn't get her travelling all that way just to get a length of fabric, adding for good measure that she'd heard that half the stalls in Portobello Road sold things that had been acquired illegally. Tilly had held her breath whilst Nancy had been sounding off over the garden fence to her mother but, to her delight, Olive had merely nodded her head and then told her and Agnes, once Nancy had disappeared, that they might as well take a look along the Portobello Market, even if in the end they ended up buying something from Leather Lane.

Tilly knew exactly what kind of new dress she wanted: one that was properly grown up. The kind of dress that someone like Dulcie's brother, Rick, would see a girl wearing and immediately want to ask her out. Quite what shape and colour that dress would be Tilly hadn't made up her mind yet, she just knew that it had to be a magical, special kind of dress that would transform her from a girl into a young woman.

Not that she'd said anything about that to her mother. Instinctively Tilly knew that Olive might not agree with Tilly's own plans for her new dress, and that a certain amount of coaxing and pleading might be required in order for her to get what she wanted. One thing Tilly did know, though, and that was that it would be far more exciting and much more fun looking for fabric for her dress at the Portobello Market than it would be in dull familiar Leather Lane. Thanks to Dulcie the Portobello Market had taken on an allure of glamour and excitement, the sort of place, in Tilly's vivid imagination at least, where all sorts of enticingly new things might happen. Like finding the perfect fabric for THE dress. The one that she would come downstairs in and that Rick, who would just happen to be visiting number 13 to see his sister, would see her in. He would look up at her with the kind of bedazzled expression she had seen on the faces of heroes at the cinema. She would smile graciously at him whilst she finished descending the stairs, and then . . . Tilly's heart gave a thump of mingled excitement and apprehension at the romantic possibilities of such a scenario (her mother would, of course, be at a WVS meeting and thus not there to witness the scene and possibly banish Tilly back to her room), which was so intense that she had to cover her heart with her hand to calm it down.

Agnes's ecstatic whispered, 'Oh, Tilly, I'm so happy I could burst,' echoed Tilly's own feelings so exactly that she reached across the narrow space between their beds to find Agnes's hand and squeeze it.

'Me too.'

Agnes expelled a deep sigh of delight. 'Your

mum is that kind, Tilly. I was that worried and upset when Matron first told me that I'd got to leave the orphanage, but now, well, there's no place I'd rather live than here at number thirteen.'

She could hardly believe it. She was going to have something new to wear. Something of her very own that no one else had ever worn. The very thought made Agnes tremble with humble delight. She'd never had anything that was her very own, excepting her underwear. She dare not even imagine how she might look. Not as nice as Tilly, who was so much prettier – that wouldn't be possible – but if she could just look, well, not like an orphan, but like an ordinary girl who came from a proper home. Not that she wasn't grateful to the orphanage, of course. She was. Matron had been ever so good to her, she knew that, but to have her own outfit . . . She scarcely dared to believe that it was really going to happen.

NINE

Early the next morning, before it got too busy and all the best bargains were gone, Olive and a very excited Tilly and Agnes set off for Portobello Road.

They'd decided to take the tube from Chancery Lane tube station to Nothing Hill Gate and then to walk the rest of the way. Agnes, of course, since she worked for London Transport, would be able to travel free.

'Will we get to see your friend Ted?' Tilly asked Agnes.

'No, 'cos he's on nights,' Olive heard Agnes answering, as she increased her walking pace to keep up with the girls, who were so excited that they were almost running. Their excitement was infectious, Olive admitted, and she was beginning to feel quite excited herself. Treats like this one had been rare occurrences in her life as a widow who was virtually financially dependent on her in-laws. She and Tilly had never gone without anything, but she'd certainly never felt able to splash out on things, not even for Tilly, which made today's outing all the more special and something to be enjoyed, she told herself, smiling at Tilly as her daughter linked arms with her on one side and Agnes on the other.

'He told me on Thursday when we had a cup of tea together that he's really proud of how well I've learned all the stations,' Agnes continued.

She spoke a great deal about the young man who had been helping her, and although Agnes's emotional and sexual welfare were not strictly speaking her responsibility, Olive couldn't help feeling a maternal twinge of concern as she listened. Agnes was virtually the same age as Tilly, and she was naïve. It wasn't her business to interfere, of course, but since Agnes had no one to stand as a caring parent for her, and since Olive felt morally obliged to keep a protective eye on her young lodger, listening to the two girls chatting she decided that she needed – discreetly, of course – to find out a bit more about this young man.

'Since he's been so kind and helpful to you, Agnes,' she announced. 'you'll have to ask him to come and have his tea with us one evening, as a thank you.'

Immediately Agnes looked a bit uncertain. 'I don't think I could do that. You see, Ted's mum likes him to go straight home from work when he's on days so that he can give her a hand with his younger sisters, with her being widowed.'

Olive could only accept what Agnes told her, though it raised her concern. It sounded plausible enough but who knew if this Ted was telling the truth, and he wasn't just leading Agnes up the garden path, her being such an innocent sort.

They'd almost reached the end of Chancery Lane. Olive pulled her warm winter coat firmly around herself as a sharp wind buffeted them when they turned onto Holborn, heading for Chancery Lane tube station.

It was definitely time that Tilly had something new, she acknowledged, as she looked at the hem of her daughter's coat, which barely touched her knees. Tilly must have grown at least a couple of inches since she had bought her the dark green coat with its velvet collar in an end-of-season sale at a shop on Oxford Street.

The grumpy-looking individual from whom they bought their underground tickets, wasn't as grumpy as he looked, Agnes told them in a whisper as they hurried along the tiled corridor, heading for their train.

'Ted says he just gets a bit cross because of his gout,' she explained, adding proudly, 'Ted knows everything about everyone at the station, and all about the trains as well.'

Although she smiled, Olive sighed to herself. She definitely needed to find out a bit more about this young man that Agnes so plainly admired.

In her room at number 13, Sally tried to sleep, reminding herself that she was starting night duty this evening, but she'd been dreaming about Liverpool and her mother, and she didn't want to go back into the dream from which she'd just woken herself. She turned over, thumping the pillow, knowing that she'd be cursing herself later on this evening if she didn't sleep now. Sleep remained elusive, though, so she tried to focus her mind on something else. During a snatched meal in the nurses' canteen earlier in the week, one of the ward nurses on men's surgical, a girl called Rachel Horseley, who was around Sally's age, had invited her to join a group of nurses who were planning to go to the pictures together. Sally had had to turn down the invitation because she would be on duty, but remembering the other girl's overtures of friendship made her smile.

She had made the right decision in coming to London to have a fresh start. The loss of her mother and what had followed would always cast its shadow over her, she knew, but her mother would have wanted her to be as happy as she could be and to enjoy life. Slowly, something of her old *joie de vivre* was coming back. She had laughed out loud at a joke one of the other girls had told them all yesterday, and she had hummed to one of her favourite songs when it had been played on the wireless, her feet starting to tap in time to the music. She'd even begun to wonder if George Laidlaw was a good dancer. Smiling to herself, Sally settled down to sleep.

It was just over two and a half hours after they had first arrived at Portobello Market, and the whole street was now a seething mass of enthusiastic bargain hunters, the cries of the stall holders, trying to attract custom, mingling with bellowed warnings from porters bringing up fresh barrows of goods, and even the ring of bicycle bells from those cyclists brave enough to try to ride through the busy throng of people filling the narrow streets.

Tilly and Agnes had been almost beside themselves with excitement from the moment they had arrived, Tilly especially as she had dragged them from stall to stall, calling to Olive to look at some fresh marvel that had caught her eye.

Olive couldn't really blame her. The market was far bigger and better than she had expected, and she was obliged to admit mentally, if somewhat reluctantly, that Dulcie had been right about the quality of fabric for sale. The problem was that the bargains were almost too tempting.

They'd agreed initially that they would walk round carefully and 'just take a look' but that discipline hadn't lasted very long. That was her fault, Olive knew, but the discovery of the last precious few yards of the most beautiful warm bronze dress-weight wool that was perfect for Tilly's colouring had been too good a bargain to risk losing, especially when the stall holder had confirmed that since Tilly was so slim there was just enough for a daytime dress and a matching jacket, which Olive had been able to bargain down to a truly unmissable price because it was the end of the roll.

Then, of course, Olive had wanted to get something for Agnes, and they'd soon found a lovely soft blue-grey wool on the same stall. Olive however, mentally scolded herself that there had not really been any excuse for her to let the girls persuade her to give in to a deep dark red for herself, even if the prices were good.

Despite the cold wind that was blowing, the

press of the crowd and the excitement of their bargain hunting had brought a warm glow to their faces, and Olive acknowledged that she was enjoying herself far more than she had expected. It was such a pleasure to have enough money to be able to treat the girls, thanks to letting out the rooms.

And as if their bargain-hunting shopping hadn't already been successful enough, when Tilly had complained how much she now disliked her 'childish' too-short coat, the stall holder reached beneath his stall and brought out the most beautiful rolls of what he'd explained was a blend of wool and cashmere.

'It's wot the toffs all have their coats made out of,' he told them as they huddled together under the stall's faded green and white striped awning. Olive could believe that. The wool was unbelievably soft and warm, and in the most beautiful jewel colours. Despite her habitual need to be frugal, in the end she wasn't able to resist either the fabric or Tilly's pleading look, though it was more than she'd planned to spend even after she'd haggled him down. And, of course, she then felt obliged to say that Agnes must have a new coat as well, so that they bought the coat fabric in a lovely warm brown colour for Tilly, and also in a soft air-force blue for Agnes. Both girls were thrilled to bits, despite the weight of the brown-paper-wrapped parcels they insisted were no problem at all to carry.

'What we need now is to find some lining fabric, oh, and buttons. Tilly, have you got those swatches of fabric the stall holder gave us so that we can match the shades up?' Olive asked.

Tilly nodded, but before they reached the stalls with the lining fabrics on them, Olive noticed a stall selling a range of pretty warm-looking tartans, fine enough for winter dresses.

'That would make very pretty party dresses for you both,' she pointed out to the girls.

Tilly pulled a face, wrinkling her nose as she objected, 'We'll look like schoolgirls in that, Mum. Oh, but look at that velvet.'

It was beautiful, Olive acknowledged, real silk velvet that slithered through her fingers when she touched it and in the most glamorous of colours: rich amber, warm rose, dark green, navy, and plum.

'It's a very good price,' the stall holder told them. 'French too. You'll not see this quality anywhere else.'

'Please, Mum,' Tilly pleaded, her eyes shining.

'I don't know, Tilly. We've already bought more than I planned. It is lovely, but the pile on the velvet is bound to flatten.'

'It's silk velvet,' the stall holder emphasised, overhearing her. 'You just give it a bit of a steam and it comes up like new. This rose colour would be perfect for you, with them dark curls,' she told Tilly.

'We've got lining fabric to get yet for your coats and buttons and everything,' Olive warned her daughter.

'Coats, is it?' the stall holder chipped in. 'Well, I'll tell you what I'll do. If you was to have a length of this silk velvet each then I'll throw in enough ordinary velvet for you to have a set of collars and cuffs made for your coats.'

'Oh, Mum,' Tilly breathed excitedly, and Olive acknowledged ruefully that she'd no chance of bargaining the stall holder down now, with her daughter looking so excited.

It was lovely fabric, though. Mentally she calculated how much they'd already spent. It would mean going over the budget she had set herself if they had the velvet, but she could afford to, thanks to the rent from the lodgers.

'Very well,' she agreed, 'but we'll need only two lengths,' she told the stall holder. 'Which colour do you like, Agnes?'

Agnes's reaction was to gaze at her with disbelief. 'Me? When you said two lengths I thought it was for you and Tilly.'

Poor Agnes – she had had so little, growing up, that she automatically expected to be excluded from treats, Olive thought.

'Of course you must have a new dress too, Agnes,' she told her firmly. 'Now which colour? This dark green will suit you, I think.' Holding the velvet up to Agnes, Olive saw that her whole face was illuminated with joy as, speechless with gratitude, Agnes could only beam at her. That look on Agnes's face made her decision all the more worthwhile, Olive admitted to herself, even if that did make her a sentimental softie.

'What about you?' the saleswoman pressed. 'I'll give you thruppence a yard off if you have three lengths.' She pointed to a roll of amber velvet. 'Perfect for you, that would be.'

'Oh, yes, Mum, do have it,' Tilly cajoled her. Olive reached out and touched the fabric. It was beautiful and she knew the colour would suit her. She paused and then shook her head, saying firmly, 'What do I need a party dress for?' before telling the stallholder, 'Just the two lengths, please.'

The velvet bought, they all agreed that a cup of tea and something like a nice fresh hot meat pie were needed to give them the energy to finish their shopping.

There were plenty of stalls selling food, but Olive insisted that they find a café. She didn't really approve of eating in the street, and besides, her feet needed a rest.

They found a welcoming café down a narrow side street, the smell of the hot pies they were selling making Tilly declare that her mouth was watering already.

The pies turned out to be as good as they smelled, hot and tasty, warming chilled fingers and filling hungry stomachs.

The women didn't waste much time in the café, though. The crowd milling around the market had grown throughout the morning, and Olive wanted to get their shopping done before it got even busier.

Once they had eaten their pies and emptied the generously sized pot of tea they'd had with them, the three of them headed for a stall Olive had noticed earlier that sold lining fabrics. The local dressmaker would charge her a little bit less, Olive was sure, if she provided her own lining fabric, thread and buttons, and make allowances for the time it would save her in not having to go out and buy them.

It was whilst she was carefully matching the swatches of fabric she had retrieved from Tilly that Olive suddenly realised that her daughter and Agnes had disappeared. Uncertainly she looked round. The market was busy; she didn't want them getting themselves lost in the bustling crowd. Then to her relief she caught sight of them hurrying towards her.

'You mustn't go off like that,' she scolded them vigorously. 'What on earth were you doing?'

'Oh, I just wanted to show Agnes some lace I'd seen earlier that would make a pretty collar,' Tilly told her airily.

'Just because you've persuaded me to let you have a velvet dress instead of a plaid one, that does not make you grown up enough to go wandering off without a by-your-leave,' Olive warned. 'There'll be pickpockets and all sorts here.'

'Yes, Mum,' said Tilly obediently.

When Olive turned back to finish choosing the lining fabrics Tilly and Agnes exchanged secret smiles. When they'd gone to the ladies' after they'd finished having their dinner Tilly had told Agnes that she wanted to go back to the velvet stall to buy the amber velvet for her mother, and immediately Agnes had said that she wanted to go halves on the cost with her. Now the amber silk velvet was parcelled up with their own and the two of them were excitedly anticipating surprising Olive with it when they got home.

*   *   *

The house was finally quiet, Tilly, Agnes and Dulcie all in their beds and Sally working at the hospital. Olive, lying in her own bed, was thankful to be able to rest her still aching feet. In the glow of her bedside lamp Olive could see the brown-paper parcels, open now, their string removed and carefully rolled into balls for future use, stacked on her dressing-table stool, including the amber fabric that Tilly and Agnes had surprised her with earlier in the evening. A tender smile curved her mouth, her eyes misting with emotion and maternal pride.

Of course she had remonstrated with Tilly, saying that she and Agnes had no business wasting their money on silk velvet for her when she had no need of a party dress. A party dress. The last time she had had one of those she had been Tilly's age. It had been pale blue silk and she had been wearing it the night she had met her husband, at a dance she had gone to with some friends. Jim had loved her in that dress, begging her to have a photograph taken of herself wearing it for him. She had loved dancing. She had loved Jim too, but she didn't want Tilly's youth to be like hers, over almost before it had begun, her life filled with the responsibilities of being a wife and a mother. She already knew what war did to young hearts and how it urged their owners to seize the moment in case it was snatched away from them. For a moment Olive's heart was filled with remembered pain. She had been widowed for so long that she rarely thought of how it had felt to be a wife any more, or how it felt to be loved by a man and to love that man back in return, and then to lose him.

This war would not be like that, she tried to reassure herself. Everyone said so. She hoped that they were right.

The papers were saying that the war would be over before Christmas, Hitler put in his place and the British Expeditionary Force brought back from France and Belgium. Mothers who had parted with their children, allowing them to be evacuated, fearing the worst and that London was going to be bombed, were now bringing them back, and Nancy next door was complaining that the streets were full of children causing mischief who should have been at school, except that the schools had been closed down when the children were evacuated, adding that she was glad that Article Row was free of children, and that Barbara Simpson hadn't decided to move back to London with their four. Olive didn't agree with her. She thought it was rather a shame that they could no longer hear the voices of the four young Simpson children.

Another week and they'd be at the end of October; two months and it would be Christmas. She'd have to start getting a few things in ready, and find out what her lodgers planned to do. Dulcie, she assumed – and hoped – would want to spend Christmas with her own family, but Agnes would be with them, and Sally possibly. She could get some wool and knit both Tilly and Agnes gloves and scarves for Christmas to go with their new coats. Perhaps she'd knit a set for Sally, as well, a nice bright red that would match the lining of her nurse's cloak.

Christmas. She'd have plenty of shopping to do

with her house so full, and perhaps the sooner the better. Nancy had been talking gloomily about the probability of food shortages and even rationing if the war continued. She needed to get started with making her Christmas pudding, Olive decided. Olive still used the recipe that had been her own mother's, given to her by the cook of the family with whom Olive's mother had been in service.

Somehow the thought of following her familiar routine helped to push away the fear that knowing they were at war brought.

War was such a small word with such a big meaning and overwhelming consequences. Olive reached out and switched off the lamp. It was church in the morning, and she'd be able to tell the vicar's wife about Sergeant Dawson offering to give her and Mrs Morrison driving lessons.

TEN

'It's St John Ambulance this afternoon,' Tilly reminded Agnes as they stood together outside the church after morning service. 'I hope I don't have to be injured again. Johnny Walton bandaged my arm so tightly last time it went numb.'

'Learning first aid isn't as bad as when we have to move all those sandbags that are supposed to be collapsed buildings, to get the injured out,' Agnes reminded her. 'Ted is on fire-watching duties for the street he lives in when he's not working nights. He says when there's a full moon he can see the barrage balloons as clear as anything, and right over to the river. Do you think that Hitler will really bomb us, Tilly?'

'I don't know,' Tilly admitted. People talked a lot about the war, but so far nothing really bad had happened, and it was hard to imagine what war was like, even though she knew that Britain's soldiers had been sent to France.

People were already complaining about the inconvenience of the blackout, and having bossy Air Raid Precautions wardens coming round threatening to fine you if you showed even the smallest chink of light. Plain daft, Nancy next door had said to Tilly's mother when she had been grumbling about it, when there wasn't a German in sight.

Where there had initially been a sense of purpose and determination because of the war, there was now almost a sense of anticlimax.

'Mum said that she was going to have a word with the dressmaker and arrange for us to go to her so that she can take our measurements for our new things.' Tilly gave a small sigh. 'I do wish that Mum would let me go to the Hammersmith Palais. I'm not a child any more, after all.'

'We'll be going to the church's Christmas Dance,' Agnes reminded her. To Agnes, going to any kind of dance was thrillingly exciting. She couldn't wait to tell Ted how kind Tilly's mother had been to her, and about her new clothes.

'Oh, the church dance!' Tilly pulled a face. 'That will just be boys and girls who are still at school. Dulcie said this morning at breakfast that the Hammersmith Palais is the very best dancehall in London and that it was packed with men in uniform last night.'

It wasn't men in uniform who occupied Tilly's most private thoughts, though, so much as one particular man in uniform – Dulcie's brother. In bed at night, when she closed her eyes, Tilly thought about how exciting it would be to dance with Dulcie's brother, picturing herself in her new dress whilst Rick swept her round the floor and told her how beautiful she looked. Of course, she couldn't say anything to Agnes about those thrillingly secret thoughts. They were far too private for that. And she certainly couldn't tell her mother. Tilly knew that her mother didn't entirely approve of Dulcie, and Tilly suspected that would mean that she would not approve of Rick either. She certainly didn't approve of Tilly wanting to go dancing at the Hammersmith Palais, but Tilly was determined to persist in begging her to let her go until her mother gave way. She was, after all, seventeen now, working, and properly grown up.

Several yards away from the two girls, Mrs Windle, the vicar's wife, was telling Olive, 'Sergeant Dawson spoke to me earlier about his offer to teach you and Mrs Morrison to drive. I must say it's a most generous and welcome offer. I believe he's already had a word with Mr Morrison and he's happy to agree. It will make such a difference to our WVS unit to have two drivers and a vehicle. I must confess I was beginning to have a most unchristian reluctance to listen to the bishop's wife talking about their drivers. I can't tell you how pleased I am, and how grateful too, to Sergeant Dawson and to you and Mrs Morrison, for giving up your spare time like this. This will make such a difference to our unit, and to those we'll be able to help.' Mrs Windle's face was pink with excitement. The vicar's wife was small and on the plump side, her grey hair tightly permed, her smile for Olive genuinely warm. Olive liked her, with her calm, practical manner, and her genuine concern for her husband's parishioners. The Windles, who were in their early fifties, didn't have any children.

'I just hope that I don't let Sergeant Dawson down and prove not to be able to learn,' Olive responded worriedly.

Mrs Windle patted Olive's arm and surprised her by telling her warmly, 'My dear Olive, of all the women I know, you are the least likely to let anyone down. I noticed this morning how happy little Agnes looks.'

'She and Tilly get on very well together,' Olive agreed. 'Tilly's persuaded Agnes to join the St John Ambulance and go along with her.'

'And of course they'll be coming to the church Christmas Dance. We've invited some of the Polish refugee families billeted locally to come along. It must be dreadful to be forced to flee one's home and country.'

'Terrible,' Olive agreed, slipping away from Mrs Windle's side as another parishioner claimed her attention. She went to have a word with Peggy Thomas, the local dressmaker, who lived a couple of streets away with her elderly mother.

She'd just finished making arrangements for Tilly, Agnes and herself to go round to be measured on Monday evening when Sergeant Dawson came up to her.

'I've had a word with the vicar's wife about the driving lessons.'

'Yes, she told me. It really is very generous of you.'

'I'm on nights this week so I thought we might make a start. Perhaps Thursday, if you can make it? Much easier for you both to learn in the daylight.'

'Thursday?'

'You're too busy?'

'No . . . not at all. It's just, well, I'm a bit apprehensive about it, I suppose,' Olive admitted with a small laugh.

'There's no need. You'll be a natural, I reckon.' He looked at his watch. 'I'd better get back. Iris isn't feeling too well at the moment.' He paused and then added, 'It's the anniversary today, you see . . . of us losing our lad, and she still takes it hard. We'll be going down to the cemetery later. She'd spend all day there if I'd let her.'

Olive gave him a sympathetic look. 'I know how I felt when I lost Jim but losing a child must be so much worse.' She glanced across at Tilly. 'So very much worse.'

'Iris still thinks that something could have been done – to save him, like.' Archie Dawson shook his head. 'I don't. Poor lad, I reckon he was glad to go and be freed from his suffering. I used to lie in bed at night listening to him trying to breathe. Really struggled, he did, wheezing and coughing . . .'

Olive didn't know what to say. Her throat felt choked with emotion. Had he been a woman she would have reached out and touched his arm but of course he wasn't, so that was impossible. All she could bring herself to say was a quiet, 'You must miss him dreadfully.'

'I miss what he might have been if he'd not been born so poorly. There was many a time when I'd be sitting at his bedside lifting him up to get air in to his lungs as he struggled to breathe, when I wished it was me that was so poorly and not him. He was such a brave little lad. Never a word of complaint, except towards the end one night he said to me, "Do you think I will die soon, Dad, only it hurts so much to live, and I'm that tired."'

Now the rules of convention had to be ignored as Olive gave in to her natural instincts and reached out to place her hand briefly and compassionately on Sergeant Dawson's arm.

'He's better off where he is now,' he told her simply, 'but Iris can't see that.' He cleared his throat and then looked across to where Tilly and Agnes were talking with several other young members of the local St John Ambulance brigade.

'Tilly's growing up into a fine young woman. One minute they're still at school and the next they're all grown up.'

Grown up? The sergeant's words jarred a little on her. Olive didn't want to think of Tilly being grown up. Not with a war on and all the temptations and difficulties that could bring for a young woman. She'd seen what could happen for herself with the last war: girls caught up in the patriotism and urgency of the moment, getting involved with and then marrying young men who had gone away to war and then, if they were lucky, had come back, but not as the young men they had been. And that was just those young women who had been lucky. She wasn't the only woman of her generation to end up widowed with a child to bring up. War gave young women freedoms they would not otherwise have been granted – she had seen that too – but those freedoms could exact a heavy price and she desperately wanted to keep Tilly safe from the pain she herself had known.

'Young Agnes is lucky to have found a billet with you,' the sergeant continued.

'Well, I don't know about that, Sergeant,' Olive demurred. 'I want to do my best for her, of course . . .'

'Something's troubling you?'

'In a way,' Olive admitted. 'Agnes isn't my daughter, of course, but I can't help feeling some responsibility towards her. She's become very friendly with a young man – Ted – she's met through her work at Chancery Lane underground station. He's a train driver. They've been meeting up at a café there. From Agnes's side it's all very innocent. So far as she's concerned he's simply teaching her the names of all the stations. He sounds respectable and well-meaning enough, but without knowing him or having met him . . .' Olive paused, knowing from Sergeant Dawson's expression that she didn't need to explain her concern in more detail. 'She's very young for her age,' she added, 'having only ever known life inside the orphanage.'

'Leave it to me, Mrs Robbins. Chancery Lane comes under our jurisdiction. It won't be any problem for me to call round there and ask a few discreet questions about this young man. You don't happen to have his surname, do you?'

'I'm afraid I don't, Sergeant, and you really mustn't go to any trouble.'

'It's no trouble. I'll have a walk round there during the week and see what I can find out. Meanwhile I'll see you on Thursday afternoon for your first driving lesson. Ernie Lord says I can collect the van any time that suits me, so would half-past two on Thursday afternoon be all right for you?'

Olive nodded. Now that the driving lessons were actually going to take place she felt far more apprehensive about them than excited, dreading both making a fool of herself by not being able to learn, and wasting the sergeant's time.

There was something about working nights that was intensely wearying, Sally thought as she suppressed a yawn. Maybe it was because the operations that took place on nights were emergencies, which meant that one was always somehow on the alert. Being on nights gave a person too much time to think because even on the ward, nights lacked the bustling busy routine of daytime shifts.

She had already been up to the ward to check on 'her' patients, and to make sure that they were recovering comfortably from their operations, talking quietly to the new junior nurse on the ward as she went with her from bed to bed.

'What are you doing that for?' the junior had asked her when Sally had leaned close to the bandaged stump of an arm that had had to be removed after being crushed when a barrel had fallen onto it from a brewery lorry.

'I'm just checking to see how it smells,' Sally had told her once they had moved away from the bed. 'That's something we can't always do when the patient is awake in case it frightens them. Stumps that aren't healing and are becoming infected smell of that infection,' she had gone on to explain.

The junior nurse had shuddered and pulled a face. Sally suspected that she would be one of those who didn't stick out her training.

'Cocoa?' Ward Sister offered. 'I'm just about to make some.'

'Yes, please,' Sally replied.

On nights at home in Liverpool, Callum had often been there to meet her and Morag when they had come off duty, walking them home to make sure they were safe.

Callum. Even without closing her eyes she could picture his face with its high cheekbones and the blue eyes she had once thought possessed a gaze that was both understanding and kind. Kind! He certainly hadn't been kind to her when he had called her selfish and cruel for refusing to welcome his sister's marriage to her father. It was true that with Callum blood was thicker than water, his loyalty to his sister far, far stronger than the relationship she had thought that they were beginning to share. The blood tie between her and her father, though, had not been strong enough for him to understand the revulsion she

205

had felt, and still felt, at the knowledge that he wanted to replace her mother with her best friend.

Olive hummed to herself as she hung out her Monday morning wash, pegging the sheets firmly to make sure they stayed on the line in the warm breeze. She'd just finished and was about to position the wooden prop to lift the line when Nancy's head appeared over the fence.

'Morning, Nancy,' Olive called out, with a smile, ignoring her neighbour's downturned mouth and disapproving expression.

'Mrs Morrison was telling me after church yesterday that Sergeant Dawson is going to be giving you and her driving lessons,' Nancy announced without any preamble.

'Yes, that's right,' Olive agreed, checking that the prop was fixed firmly into the lawn, before bending down to pick up her empty laundry basket. A couple of stray curls had escaped from the headscarf she wrapped round her head to keep her hair out of the way whilst she worked, and she stood up to tuck them out of the way, still smiling as she informed Nancy, 'It was Mrs Windle's idea. She had the offer of a van for the WVS to use but she didn't have any drivers. It's so kind of Sergeant Dawson to make the time to teach us.'

'Kind, is it? Well I've got to tell you straight, Olive, that that's not what I think and it wouldn't be what your late ma-in-law would have thought either.'

'What do you mean?' Olive asked, bewildered.

'What do you think I mean? Sergeant Dawson is a married man. And I don't think it's right or proper that he should be giving you driving lessons. It's all right for Mrs Morrison, she's got a husband to keep an eye out for her, but you haven't, and you know how people talk.'

Olive didn't know whether to laugh or be angry.

'I'm only warning you for your own good, Olive,' Nancy continued. 'A woman in your position, widowed, and with a teenage daughter to look out for can't be too careful about her reputation.'

'Nancy,' Olive protested, 'it's Sergeant Dawson who will be teaching me, not some stranger. And Mrs Windle has already said how pleased she is. It's for the war effort that I'm doing it.'

Nancy gave a disparaging sniff. 'You can say what you like, Olive, but I don't think it's right, a single woman like you spending time on her own with a married man, and I'm only telling you what your own ma-in-law would say.'

As Olive listened to Nancy's warning a surge of uncharacteristic anger filled her. She knew what Nancy was trying to do. She was trying to bully her into backing out of having her driving lessons. And besides, what Nancy was suggesting – but not coming out directly and saying – about her being alone with Sergeant Dawson possibly leading to some kind of hanky-panky on his part towards her was ridiculous. Sergeant Dawson was a respectable and an honourable man. Anyone who was in his company for more than a few minutes couldn't help but know that. Olive had come across her fair share of the other sort during her widowhood to know the difference. Oh, there had been nothing directly said by those men – some of them friends of her late husband and her in-laws, and most of them married – but it had all been there in the looks they had given her in private, the hints they had dropped suggesting that she, a young woman without a husband, must be 'lonely'. She had made it plain to all of them that she wasn't interested. The very idea was an insult! And Nancy's hints about Sergeant Dawson were an insult to him. Olive felt angry with Nancy on his behalf when the whole neighbourhood knew what a decent sort he was. She certainly trusted him. But even so, Olive knew that once she would probably have given in and done what Nancy wanted simply to keep the peace. Things were different now: there was a war on, and that was what she had to think about, not Nancy's disapproval.

She took a deep breath and then told her neighbour firmly, 'You might not approve, Nancy, but I think that Jim would. He'd want me to play my part and do everything I can to help others.' And with that Olive picked up her laundry basket and headed for her back door without giving Nancy the opportunity to come back at her. She was not a young girl like Tilly, she was a mature woman and one who was perfectly capable of judging for herself whether or not a man could be trusted, and what was and was not appropriate behaviour for her, without Nancy trying to tell her what to do, Olive decided determinedly, as she opened her back door and stepped inside without giving Nancy a backward look.

ELEVEN

'That was a lovely smooth gear change. You're really getting the hang of it,' Sergeant Dawson praised Olive as she drove down Article Row, changing through the gears as she did so.

Pink with delight and pride, Olive remembered just in time not to look at her instructor but instead to keep her attention focused on the road in front of her.

It was just over a month now since she had had her first lesson. The ending of British Summer Time and the shortening days meant that there were fewer daylight hours in which Sergeant Dawson could give both her and Mrs Morrison their driving lessons. She had been right to follow her own judgement and not listen to Nancy, Olive congratulated herself, because Sergeant Dawson's manner towards her had been all that she had known it would be: kind and friendly, but never ever stepping over the line that divided their relationship as neighbours and friends, mixed with a dash of professionalism from him as her driving instructor, from one that involved the kind of looks, comments and hints that would have warned her that he was looking for something else. She felt completely safe in his company, and knew that even her critical late mother-in-law could not have found anything to object to in his manner towards her.

Had things been otherwise she could not have relaxed and focused on learning to drive, Olive knew, as she waited automatically for that second when the clutch bit and depressed slightly when she pressed down the accelerator pedal, heralding the right moment at which to change gear. She could still remember how anxious she had been during that first lesson when Sergeant Dawson had demonstrated this all-important skill to her and she had sat next to him, privately unable to believe that she would ever understand the mechanics of changing gear, never mind actually driving.

Now she was familiar with such terms as double declutching, knew what the 'bite' point for changing gear was, could turn corners neatly and even reverse, and during their weekly WVS meetings she and Anne Morrison sat together exchanging tips and horror stories about their lessons, both ruefully admitting to each other how nervous they had been about that first lesson and how thrilled they were now that they were actually driving.

Olive hadn't forgotten Nancy's warning to her, but even though her response to it had led to a certain coolness between them on Nancy's side, Olive didn't regret her decision or her defiance. Learning to drive made her feel that she really would be able to do something useful, should the need arise. Times were changing and her sex was changing with it: today's women, with their men going off to war, were having to take charge of their own lives, make their own decisions, and take on the jobs that now needed doing. Today's women weren't shrinking violets who never stepped outside their front door without needing to ask a man's permission, and she certainly wasn't going to allow Nancy to tell her what she could and could not do.

'You can put your mind at ease with regard to young Ted, by the way,' Sergeant Dawson broke the silence between them after they had reached the far end of Article Row and Olive had turned left into its neighbour, Merton Road, which led eventually onto Chancery Lane.

'I've been making a few enquiries about the lad like I said I would and it turns out that he's generally regarded as a decent sort. Just to be on the safe side I had a word with him myself.'

When Olive forgot his instructions not to turn to look at him, he shook his head.

'All very discreet, I promise you. I've been into that café where he meets Agnes a few times now – thinks a lot of him, the owner of it does – so I arranged to be there one morning when he was coming off his night shift and I knew Agnes wouldn't be around and I made it my business to fall into conversation with him, like.'

The sergeant gave a small sigh. 'Lost his father when he was younger so now he's pretty much the main breadwinner for the family. I reckon he's a son any chap could be proud of.'

Guessing that he was thinking of his own lost

son Olive felt a stab of sympathy for him but she was too tactful to say that she had guessed what had caused his deep sigh.

Instead she said. 'I'm really grateful to you for going to so much trouble, Sergeant Dawson. You've put my mind at ease. Like I said when we first talked about it, it isn't up to me to tell Agnes what she can and can't do, but since she doesn't have a mother or any relatives of her own I can't help but feel responsible for her.'

'It's to your credit that you do. But you needn't fear for her with young Ted,' Sergeant Dawson assured her, noting approvingly how his pupil manoeuvred the van into position for the right turn that would take them onto Chancery Lane and from there onto Holborn itself, past Holborn Circus and then down to St Paul's Cathedral, where they would turn round and make their way back.

A November chill was griping the air now, mist and even fog rolling in from the river early in the morning and then again when the afternoon faded into an early dusk. Winter was round the corner and with it the rationing of butter and bacon from mid-December. Olive shivered a little as she concentrated on her driving. The first bombs of the war with Germany had already been dropped on the Shetland Islands; the *Royal Oak* had been sunk at her base in Scapa Flow by a German torpedo with the loss of over eight hundred men. The papers were warning about the danger to British shipping from German submarines and their deadly torpedoes. The red double-decker London bus in front of them pulled into the kerb at a bus stop, causing Olive to change down and wait for it to set off again because the road was too narrow and too busy for her to risk overtaking it. She didn't like overtaking, but Sergeant Dawson said that she was going to have to get used to doing so. The bus set off eventually, the rank smell of the diesel coming from its exhaust making Olive wrinkle her nose and think longingly of the comforting warmth of the vegetable soup she'd made earlier in the day for their tea tonight.

'I do wish that Mum would let us go dancing at the Hammersmith Palais, and stop treating me like a child, especially now that we've got our new frocks,' Tilly said wistfully, repeating a now familiar complaint as she and Agnes sat listening to the wireless whilst Dulcie read *Picture Post*. Olive had gone out straight after tea to a WVS meeting, and the three girls were on their own in the house as Sally was working nights.

'If you don't want your mother treating you like a kid, Tilly, then you should show her that you aren't and stop behaving like one,' Dulcie told her.

'What do you mean?' Tilly asked.

Dulcie gave a dismissive shrug. 'Well, for a start I'd never let my ma tell me that I couldn't go out dancing if I wanted to. I'd just tell her I was going.'

'I can't do that,' Tilly protested.

'Then go without telling her,' Dulcie told her.

Tilly gazed at her. 'You mean go to the Hammersmith Palais without Mum knowing?'

'Why not?'

'Oh, Tilly, you can't do that,' Agnes protested, shocked.

'Course she can, if she wants to,' Dulcie argued. 'That's if she's got the guts to do it and she isn't really too scared. All she's got to do is tell her mother that she's going somewhere else, like the pictures, and then go to the Palais instead.' Dulcie gave another shrug. 'Simple.'

'You mean lie to my mother?' Tilly asked uncertainly.

It would serve Olive right if Tilly did go to the Palais behind her back, Dulcie decided. She was well aware of the fact that her landlady disapproved of her and was determined to protect her precious daughter from what she saw as Dulcie's influence. It would be amusing to persuade Tilly to go behind her back.

'What do you want to do, Tilly? Only be allowed to go to boring church dances for the rest of your life whilst other girls are having fun at proper dances? If you ask me I'd say that it's your mother's fault if you have to lie to her to do what any other girl your age can take for granted. Of course, if you want to stay tied to your mother's apron strings all your life and never be allowed to make your own mind up about what you want to do, then that's up to you.'

Dulcie's challenging words were fanning the flames of Tilly's resentment of her mother's refusal to let her go to the Hammersmith Palais. Dulcie was right: her mother was wrong to keep on treating her like a child. She thought yearningly of how much she wanted to be allowed to be properly grown up. As Dulcie had said, other girls her age went to proper dances and their mothers didn't treat them as though they were still schoolgirls. A reckless determination took hold of her.

'Dulcie is right, Agnes,' she announced. 'We'll go this Saturday. We can tell Mum that we're going to the pictures, and then when we get back and she can see that we're perfectly safe then we can tell her where we've been. Everything will be all right then because Mum will understand that I'm old enough to go to proper dances,' Tilly insisted when Agnes continued to look uneasy.

Agnes was looking at her uncertainly but Tilly knew the other girl wouldn't go against her. Agnes was too gentle for that.

'It's the only way to make her see that we're properly grown up,' she insisted, adding, 'You don't want our new dresses to be wasted on church socials, do you, Agnes?'

'But how can we wear them to the pictures?'

Agnes had a point, Tilly recognised. But thankfully Dulcie had a solution for the problem.

'You'll just have to take them with you in a carrier bag and then change into them in the ladies'.'

Carried away by the excitement of fulfilling her ambition, Tilly nodded enthusiastically. It was wrong to deceive her mother, she knew, but something had to be done to prove to her that she wasn't a schoolgirl any more. Dulcie was right about that. The end justified the means, Tilly assured herself, soothing her conscience.

Later that night, when she and Tilly were in

bed, Agnes whispered across to her, 'Do you really think it's all right for us to go to the Hammersmith Palais without telling your mother, Tilly?'

'Of course it is,' Tilly assured her. 'Like Dulcie said, if we let her, Mum will keep on treating us like schoolgirls for ever.'

Agnes admired Tilly too much to doubt her, but the thought of lying to Tilly's mother, who had been so kind to her, was an uncomfortable weight on her conscience. At the orphanage lying was considered a very serious sin indeed.

She was still feeling worried and uncomfortable about Tilly's plans for Saturday night the next day, when she found Ted waiting for her at the entrance to the station, after work.

'Thought we'd have a cuppa together, if you've got time,' Ted told her gruffly.

'Of course I've got time,' Agnes told him as he fell into step beside her.

The familiar warmth of the café was a welcome relief from the cold wind outside, and Agnes nodded her head when Ted asked her, 'Cuppa and a teacake?' before making her way to 'their' table next to the window, from where they could look out and watch the world go by. Not that they could look through it now with the blackout in place. And even if they had been able to, there wouldn't have been much to see, Agnes acknowledged, as she waited for Ted to rejoin her. Not with it going dark by teatime, and no lighting of any kind allowed on the streets.

It wasn't long after Ted had given their order

over the counter before they were served, and Ted had poured them each a cup of tea.

'Summat's up,' he announced after noting the way Agnes's head drooped as she stirred her tea. 'Old Smithy's not been getting you upset, has he?'

Agnes shook her head. 'No, he's really nice to me now. Well, most of the time. Sometimes he shouts when his feet are bothering him.'

'So if it isn't old Smithy that's making you look so glum, what is it?' Ted pressed.

Reluctantly Agnes unburdened herself to him.

After he had heard her out Ted gave a soft whistle. 'That Dulcie's a one, isn't she?' he announced. 'Persuading Tilly to lie to her ma.'

'Tilly's been wanting to go to the Hammersmith Palais for ages,' Agnes told him, not wanting to portray her friend in a bad light. 'She says that once we've been and we get home safely then her mother will stop worrying and let us go without us having to pretend that we aren't doing.'

'I don't know about that,' Ted told her. 'Mas don't take kindly to being lied to.'

'Tilly says it isn't exactly lying. It's just pretending that we're going to the pictures,' Agnes defended her.

Ted could see that Agnes was getting upset so he didn't pursue the subject any further but inwardly he had already made up his mind that on Saturday night, come hell or high water, he intended to be at the Hammersmith Palais to make sure that Agnes didn't come to any harm. Poor kid. He could see that she didn't like the idea of deceiving her landlady but that she was too good a friend to Tilly to betray her.

He did have some sympathy with Tilly, though. There was, after all, nothing like being told you couldn't do something to make a person want to do it. But lying to her ma in order to do it – that wasn't a good idea at all – and Ted had a strong suspicion that it would all end in tears. In his home, had his dad still been alive, it would have ended up with his dad's belt being applied to the back of the offending child's legs.

All day Friday, Tilly's excitement grew. She dare not think about Saturday night when she was at work in case she went off into her favourite daydream – the one in which Dulcie's handsome brother suddenly materialised at her side and asked her to dance – and someone noticed and she got told off.

Of course she felt bad about deceiving her mother, but she tried not to think about that. Instead she thought about how exciting it was all going to be and how wonderful she and Agnes were going to look in their new frocks. A small pang of guilt did strike her when she thought about their new dresses. Mum had been so good about letting them have that velvet instead of the plaid, and the new clothes they'd had made from the fabric they'd bought at Portobello Market made both her and Agnes look ever so grown up. Even her mother had said so when they'd shown them off to her. Instead of feeling guilty she had to think instead about being grown up, like Dulcie had said, and proving to her mother that they were old enough to be treated like adults.

Whilst Olive put Tilly's growing air of tension and excitement down to the fact that her daughter would be wearing her new dress at the coming church dance, Dulcie, who knew better, observed it with slightly malicious glee.

Oh, it was going to be one in the eye for Tilly's mother, who treated her, Dulcie, as though she didn't really want her there, when she found out that Tilly had defied her. Olive's protective manner towards Tilly still irked Dulcie, reminding her as it did of her own mother's favouring of Edith. Well, let Olive go around with her nose in the air, thinking that her Tilly told her everything and thought she was wonderful; she'd soon find out that she was wrong. Dulcie knew instinctively that Olive would be hurt by Tilly's deception but she didn't care. Olive needed bringing down a peg or two. The fact that Dulcie's machinations might cause a rift between mother and daughter wasn't something that weighed on her conscience. Why should it? It was plain daft of Olive to try and keep Tilly a kid for ever. In a way she was doing them both a favour.

On Friday evening, when Tilly announced casually that she and Agnes were going to the pictures on Saturday night, Olive didn't think anything of it. Her head was full of all the things she needed to do for Christmas, only a month away now. She'd got a goose on order, and luckily she'd been able to get in a bit of a supply of butter from the grocer she always used, ahead of the rationing.

'I expect you'll be going home for Christmas, Dulcie?' she asked, her question causing Dulcie to frown. She hadn't really given much thought to Christmas, but now that Olive had mentioned it and made it plain that she expected her to go home because no doubt she didn't want her here, Dulcie felt like digging her heels in and being awkward.

'Well, I'd like to, of course,' she agreed, giving an exaggerated sigh as she added, 'especially with my brother expecting to be coming home from France on leave, but I don't think there's going to be room for me. Of course, if you don't want me here . . .'

'Of course we do, don't we, Mum?' Tilly immediately jumped in. 'It will be more fun if you're here, Dulcie. We always have a bit of a party on Boxing Day, don't we, Mum?'

'I'd hardly call it a party, Tilly, at least not the sort of party Dulcie would enjoy,' Olive responded pointedly, giving Dulcie a sharp look as though she guessed what she was up to. 'It's just a few of our neighbours, that's all.'

The news that Dulcie's brother would be home on leave over Christmas had brought a pink glow to Tilly's cheeks. She could hardly wait for tomorrow night and being able to ask Dulcie more about her brother without her own mother listening in and giving her that disapproving look.

'Well, I wouldn't want to put you out,' said Dulcie with pretend concern.

'You won't be putting me out, Dulcie,' Olive

221

felt obliged to deny. 'I just thought you would want to be with your own family.'

'But, Mum, Sally's going to be staying, and Agnes, of course, and it wouldn't be the same if Dulcie wasn't here,' Tilly protested.

It certainly wouldn't, Olive thought grimly, but with Tilly such a staunch supporter of Dulcie there was nothing she could say or do other than allow the subject to be dropped, and rework her shopping plans to make sure that she bought in enough to feed all of them.

As she said to Sally later, if it wasn't for all the inconvenience of the blackout rules, the ugliness of sandbag buildings, and the sight of so many ARP posts and air-raid shelters everywhere you wouldn't think there was a war on at all.

'It's no wonder people are calling it a phoney war.'

'It may be phoney for us here in London,' Sally agreed, 'but we had a young merchant seaman in today whose arm had to be amputated thanks to the wound he'd suffered when his ship was torpedoed by the Germans. He was telling us that the Germans are inflicting serious losses on our merchant fleet, and that the Government aren't letting on how bad the situation is. He reckons that it will be much more than butter and bacon that goes on ration soon, with so much having to be brought in to the country by sea.'

'Poor boy,' Olive sympathised.

'Yes,' Sally agreed. The young seaman had been visibly shocked when he'd been told that he would have to lose his arm or risk losing his life because of the gangrene that had set in to the crushed limb. He'd told her worriedly that merchant seamen, unlike men in the Royal Navy, did not get paid when they weren't actually working at sea, and she had really felt for him, his situation making her aware of how lucky she was, which reminded her . . .

'I'll be going out straight from work tomorrow afternoon,' she told Olive. 'One of the other nurses has got tickets for several of us for the matinée of the ENSA Drury Lane show. Apparently the theatres are really good about letting nurses have seats at a cheaper rate and when she asked me if I'd like one of them it seemed silly not to say yes.'

'I should say so,' Olive agreed. 'It will do you good to go out and have a bit of fun.'

'Yes, I think it will,' Sally agreed happily.

TWELVE

'Tilly, I don't think I want to go dancing after all.'

They were in their bedroom after what had felt like the longest day Tilly had ever known. So tense with nerves and excitement was she that she'd barely been able to eat her tea.

Agnes's words, along with the distinct tremor in her voice, had Tilly putting down the hairbrush to give Agnes an anxious but determined look as she told her firmly, 'Of course you want to go.'

'But what about your mother? She's been so kind to me.'

'Mum will be fine about it once we've been. We just aren't telling her because she doesn't understand yet that we're grown up. Once we've been then everything will be all right. You wait and see.'

Tilly had convinced herself of the truth of what she was saying and her belief in it propped up Agnes's wavering courage, although she did protest, 'Are you sure?'

'Of course I'm sure. If I wasn't then we wouldn't be going, would we?'

Her hair brushed, Tilly dipped her forefinger in her precious pot of Vaseline and then, with her tongue tip protruding slightly as she concentrated, she smoothed her dark eyebrows down and then very carefully Vaselined the ends of her long dark eyelashes as well.

Watching her, Agnes was impressed. Her own eyelashes and eyebrows were a plain mouse brown and she shook her head when Tilly offered her the jar of Vaseline.

'Knowing me, I'd probably end up sticking my finger in my eye.'

Her eyebrows and lashes done to her satisfaction Tilly reached for the Tangee lipstick that her mother had only allowed her to wear once she had started work. The lipstick looked orange but once on Tilly's lips it gave them a satisfyingly rosy-pink lustre that Tilly was convinced made her look much more grown up.

'Here, you have some,' she invited Agnes.

Hesitantly, Agnes took the lipstick. Living at the orphanage, she had been denied the opportunity to experiment with growing up in the way that other girls did and the movement of her hand as she applied the lipstick to her own mouth was shaky and uncertain.

'We'd better get a move on,' Tilly warned, turning to their shared wardrobe and opening its doors. 'Here's your bag and your dress.' She thrust both at her so that Agnes had no alternative other than to take them from her whilst Tilly removed her own dress from its hanger and quickly folded it up to put it into her own bag.

'Your mother is bound to ask what we've got in these,' Agnes warned Tilly as she eyed the over-filled bags.

'Not if we take them down into the hall and leave them there whilst we say goodbye. She'll be listening to the radio so she won't get up to see us off. She said how tired she was at teatime after Sergeant Dawson had her driving through the afternoon traffic. Come on,' Tilly urged. 'We've got to get changed yet into our skirts and jumpers as though we were going to the cinema.'

Upstairs in her own room on the top floor, Dulcie was also getting ready for the evening ahead, surveying her appearance in the full-length mirror. The dress she was wearing – pale blue silk, its V neck trimmed with a slightly darker shade of velvet ribbon, the same ribbon trimming its puffed sleeves – was cut on the bias, skimming her curves but not clinging to them. Dulcie knew where to draw the line and which side of that line she intended to stay. Other girls might make the mistake of dying their hair a too brassy blonde and wearing clothes that were too tight, but Dulcie never would. They could make themselves look cheap but she was certainly not going to. That sort of girl more often than not ended up having to get married quickly with a baby on the way and a life of hard-ship ahead of her.

Piling her curls up on top of her head and securing them there with some Kirbigrips that she'd been holding between her teeth, Dulcie paused to admire her own reflection. Classy, that's how she looked, she decided triumphantly. Her smile widened as she reflected on her other triumph of the evening – Tilly and Agnes's illicit attendance at the Palais. Olive might think that her precious daughter wouldn't listen to anyone but her, but Dulcie was going to prove her wrong.

'That's Dulcie going downstairs now,' Tilly told Agnes as she heard the tap of Dulcie's heels crossing the landing outside their room. 'Come on.'

'I can't go yet. I need the lav,' Agnes protested.

Downstairs in the kitchen, Olive too heard the tap of Dulcie's heels on the stairs and then the sound of the front door opening and closing, and frowned to herself. Tilly and Agnes were cutting it fine if they weren't going to miss the beginning of their film. She'd better go upstairs and hurry them along, Olive decided. Tilly could be such a daydreamer at times.

In her room, Sally hummed one of the tunes from the review to herself. She'd really enjoyed her outing with her fellow nurses, right from the moment at the hospital in the room where they'd all changed with Sister's permission, when Rachel had complimented her with a teasing, 'Well, don't you scrub up well?' as she admired Sally's appearance in her pretty hyacinth-blue dress, with its neatly fitted bodice closed by tiny pearl buttons and its softly gored full skirt.

'If I do I'm not the only one,' Sally had laughed in response.

It had been true. Eight of them had gone to see

the show, and seeing her fellow nurses out of their uniforms, with their hair down, anticipation of a happy afternoon out adding a soft glow to their skin and eyes, and wearing pretty clothes, made Sally think how attractive everyone looked.

'It should be a good show,' Rachel told Sally, linking up with her after they had all pulled on their coats and were heading for the door. 'Of course, some of the jokes will probably be a bit warm . . .' She paused and Sally laughed.

'Yes, I expect they will,' she agreed.

'Thank heavens you aren't the stuffy sort,' Rachel told her with evident relief, adding, 'Since the tickets haven't cost us anything I reckon we can splurge a bit and go by taxi. You go and hail a couple, Brenda,' she commanded one of the other girls. 'That blonde hair of yours is bound to have them stopping. A London cabbie never misses a blonde.' Rachel had been proved right a couple of minutes later when two cabs pulled up a few yards from them.

'What's this then?' one of the cabbies asked cheerfully. 'Nurses' day out? Matron know you're escaping, does she?' he joked as they split into two groups of four and piled into the cabs.

The show had turned out to be excellent, the comedian so funny that Sally had laughed until her insides ached. Best of all, though, had been the music and the dance routines, and Sally had itched to be twirling on a dance floor herself when the music had got her feet tapping.

After the show had ended all of them had agreed that the afternoon had been a success and that they should go out again together. Now, Sally hummed a few more bars of one of the songs . . .

The first thing Olive saw when she walked into Tilly and Agnes's bedroom was the bags on the beds. An attempt had obviously been made to fold the girls' new party dresses up small enough to fit inside them but it had not been successful, the dresses easily visible and recognisable.

The second thing she saw was the expressions on the girls' faces. In Agnes's case that expression was one of anxiety and guilt, but on Tilly's . . .

Disbelief followed by a pain as sharp as if someone had stabbed a knife into her heart gripped Olive as she looked in her daughter's face and saw defiance and, yes, the angry resentment.

Olive could hear her heart racing and pounding. She badly wanted to sit down, so great was her shock and distress, but she knew she mustn't, just as she knew she must not let Tilly see not just how shocked she was but how devastated and wounded. That her daughter to whom she had always been so close, whom she loved so much, should look at her now as though they were enemies shocked Olive to the core of her being. A part of her wanted to beg Tilly to tell her that it was all a mistake, to see her daughter smile at her and to feel her arms close round her, but another part of her reminded her that she was Tilly's mother and that she had a duty to her and to their relationship that must not be shirked.

So instead of pleading with Tilly not to look at her as she was doing, she asked coldly instead,

'Would you like to explain the meaning of these to me?' gesturing to the dresses but without removing her gaze from Tilly's face.

Whilst Agnes gulped with distress, Tilly showed no sign of guilt or remorse as she answered her boldly, and with some hostility.

'We were going to take them with us to the Hammersmith Palais and change into them there.'

Olive wanted to recoil as though she'd been struck, but she forced herself to say instead, 'So, you were lying to me when you said that you were going to the cinema tonight?'

'Yes,' Tilly told her, continuing fiercely, 'we had to. It's your fault for not seeing that we're grown up enough to go. Dulcie said.'

Now the pain inside Olive had turned to white-hot lava burning through her as she stopped Tilly with a sharp, '*Dulcie* said? I see. And what Dulcie says is more important than what I say, is it?'

She had known all along that Dulcie would be trouble and now she had been proved right.

On the other side of the room Agnes had started to cry quietly.

When Tilly didn't answer her but instead gave her a sulky challenging look, Olive told her, 'I'm ashamed of you, Tilly. Ashamed of you because you lied to me and ashamed because you no doubt forced poor Agnes to enter into your deceit with you.'

'It's your fault,' Tilly flashed back at her defiantly. 'I'm seventeen, I'm not a child any more. After all, I'm old enough to go out to work and do my bit so I can't see why you won't let me go to the Palais and why you want to stop me from having fun.'

Sidestepping her daughter, Olive went over to the beds and picked up the bags, her hands shaking a little as she did so.

'I am very disappointed in you, Tilly,' was all she could trust herself to say. How could Tilly, her Tilly, her beloved daughter, have done something like this? Tears tightened Olive's throat. She had never felt more alone, or more at a loss to know what to do. Automatically, as she turned towards the door, she announced emotionlessly, 'You will both stay here in your room, and you, Tilly, I hope will reflect on your behaviour.'

Standing beside her bed, Sally chewed on her bottom lip. The row going on below had been perfectly audible to her, and had filled her with disquiet. She liked and admired Olive, and of course what Tilly had planned to do was wrong, but the person who was really to blame, in Sally's view at least, was Dulcie, who Sally suspected had deliberately played on Tilly's vulnerability as she went through the natural youthful process of wanting to be 'grown up' and in charge of her own life.

In the hallway the clock still ticked and in the kitchen, the wireless was still on, Vera Lynn's voice spilling out into the empty room, familiar sounds in a familiar setting. But their familiarity could not offer Olive any comfort in the alien world she felt she now occupied. Tilly had lied to her, and not just lied to her but justified that deceit by blaming her for being the cause of it. Tears filled Olive's eyes. Agitatedly she brushed them away and went to the sink, reaching for the kettle and then putting it back. What comfort could a cup of tea give her? None. She sat down at the kitchen table and then stood up again, pacing the floor, wanting to go upstairs to beg Tilly to tell her that she was sorry, that she regretted what she had done and said, she wanted . . . she wanted Tilly to be a little girl again, running to her for the security of her embrace. But Tilly wasn't a little girl any more. Fresh pain filled her. Was Tilly right? Was she to blame for her daughter's deceit?

Upstairs in her bedroom Tilly sat down heavily on her bed, the exhilaration that had led to her outburst against her mother draining from her so quickly that she felt as though her legs wouldn't support her.

Had those really been tears she had seen in her mother's eyes just before she had left the room? Tilly had to swallow hard against the fear that suddenly loomed up inside her, the shock of it like running into an unexpected towering brick wall. She must have imagined it. Her mother never cried. Not ever.

On the other bed Agnes was gulping back sobs between demanding anxiously, 'Do you think your mum will send me away now because of us lying to her?'

'It wasn't you who lied to her, Agnes, it was me,' Tilly tried to comfort her. How awful to be afraid that you might be sent away. Tilly couldn't imagine how that must feel. Not really. Slowly, beginning like a drip of water that turned into a trickle and from that into a stream, Tilly felt the recognition of what she had done seep through her, and with it her guilt and remorse.

The house had settled down into an uncomfortable silence. Sally knew that she wouldn't be able to sleep. She felt too upset, both on Olive's behalf and Tilly's. What had happened wasn't any of her business, and she didn't want to interfere, but . . . Sally could remember how it felt to be Tilly's age and so desperately eager to be grown up. There had been an incident, over a tennis club dance she'd wanted to attend, and then another over her desire to be allowed to go out cycling with a quite unsuitable young man, during which she remembered hot words being exchanged.

'Darling, it's *because* we love you that we want to protect you,' she could remember her mother telling her gently. 'I know you can't see or understand that now, but I promise you that one day you will, and when you do you will thank us. You may think you are grown up but to us you are just as in need of our care as you were when you were a child, only in a different way. Imagine if, as a baby first learning to walk, we had let you walk without watching your every step, what kind of parents would we have been? It's the same now.'

Sighing to herself, Sally got up off the bed and opened her bedroom door. The house was still silent. The door to Dulcie's bedroom was closed.

233

Dulcie had not acted well in encouraging Tilly to lie to her mother, Sally thought, and their landlady was bound to hold that against her.

When Sally opened the kitchen door Olive was sitting at the table, her eyes betrayingly red-rimmed, the handkerchief she had been holding in her hand pushed quickly into the sleeve of her jumper when she saw Sally.

'I suppose you heard me having words with Tilly?' Olive felt obliged to say.

'Yes,' Sally confirmed.

'I can't believe that Tilly would do something like this – lie to me.' Olive had to bite her lip to stop it from trembling.

'I'll put the kettle on,' Sally offered, going over to the stove without waiting for Olive's agreement, and then saying calmly, once she had checked that it was full of water and had lit the gas beneath it, 'I remember having words with my parents about wanting to do things they didn't think I was old enough to do.'

Olive gave her lodger a weak but grateful smile when she poured the boiling water on the tea leaves and then brought the pot over to the table, before returning to the cupboard to remove two mugs, cream ones with blue spots on them, and blue handles, which reminded Sally of some her own mother had bought one year at Preston's annual Pot Fair.

Automatically Olive got up and went to the larder to get the milk jug, but it was Sally who poured their tea and who passed her mug to her.

'Tilly said it was my fault and that she'd had

234

to lie because of me.' The words, so painful to say, felt like sharp pieces of flint tearing at Olive's throat and her heart.

'I dare say she was so shocked at being discovered that she didn't really know what she was saying,' Sally offered comfortingly.

'Perhaps I have been too protective. But it was only for her own sake. She's so young. She doesn't know how hard life can be. I want her to have her youth whilst she can. I don't want to stop her from having fun, I just want her to be safe and to take her time growing up.'

'Would it help if I went to the Hammersmith Palais with them? Not immediately, of course, but if you wanted to let Tilly know that you do trust her to be properly grown up?' Sally offered.

Despite the angry words that had been exchanged upstairs, the kitchen still had the lovely comforting and comfortable atmosphere that Olive had created throughout her home, but especially here at its heart, its cosiness reaching out to warm the heart.

'I'd certainly far rather she and Agnes went with you than with Dulcie,' Olive admitted, absently tracing one of the lines that made up the checks on the kitchen tablecloth with the tip of her forefinger. Was Sally trying to say tactfully that she had treated Tilly like a child instead of recognising that she needed to know that she, her mother, trusted her? 'You get all sorts going to the Palais, from what I've heard, and Hammersmith itself has a bad reputation,' she defended her decision.

'I know nurses who've been to the Palais and

they say it's just about the best dancehall in London. I think they'd say if they thought it wasn't the kind of place one would want to go,' Sally offered tactfully, pausing to take a sip of her hot tea before wrapping her hands round her mug and then continuing carefully, 'Tilly is young, but she's not the sort of girl to have her head turned by the wrong kind of young man, or the sort of girl who would behave in the wrong way.'

Silently Olive digested what Sally had said, moving slightly in her chair and pushing it back a little from the table, its legs making a small scraping sound on the linoleum as she got up and began pacing the floor. Sally had offered her a face-saving way out of what was a miserable situation and she'd be silly not to take it, Olive acknowledged, stopping her pacing to turn to Sally.

'You're right. She isn't. And that's just as well with this war, and young people being what they are. Perhaps I have been too hard on her, but the last thing I want for Tilly's own sake is for her to meet some lad in uniform and then fancy herself in love with him and want to get married when he will have to go off to war and might not come back.' Olive sighed. 'I shouldn't be talking to you like this, Sally. You're only a girl yourself, and a very kind girl as well.' She sighed again. 'If you're sure you don't mind going with Tilly and Agnes, that would ease my mind an awful lot.'

'Of course I don't mind. I wouldn't have offered if I did,' Sally returned promptly. 'In fact, it will probably do me good. It's ages since I last went dancing and, by all accounts, the Hammersmith Palais is *the* place to go.'

'So Tilly keeps telling me,' Olive acknowledged ruefully.

From her favourite seat at her favourite table next to the dance floor, Dulcie was able to keep a close eye on everyone coming into the ballroom, and when an hour after her own arrival there was still no sign of Tilly and Agnes she gave a dismissive mental shrug and told herself that if Tilly was too soft to take her advice then that was her lookout, and more fool her.

Three girls she knew from school had taken the other seats at the table, the four of them exchanging nods of recognition, Dulcie well aware that the other three were covertly examining her appearance. Well, let them. It wasn't her fault if she looked better than they did.

'That good-looking brother of yours still in France with the army, is he?' one of the girls – Ida Walton – asked Dulcie.

'As far as I know he is,' Dulcie replied. 'Last time he wrote home he said how he'd been on leave in Paris.'

'Huh, Paris.' Rita Stevens, who was sitting next to Ida, joined the conversation. 'My brother Harry was there before he got sent home on compassionate leave when his wife died having a baby, and he reckoned that the women in Paris are all tarts and that any British soldier who goes with one of them is a fool.'

'Well, Rick certainly isn't that,' Dulcie said

smartly, ''cos if he was he'd have ended up married to Beatie Sinclair from Brewer Street, she's been chasing after him that hard.'

The other girls all laughed and the one sitting furthest away from Dulcie – Bettie Fields – asked her, 'Still working at Selfridges, are you?'

'Yes,' Dulcie confirmed.

'We're all thinking of going working in munitions,' Bettie told her. 'They reckon the pay's the best there is. Oooh, here's that lad coming over that danced with you three times last week, Rita.' She nudged her friend. 'And he's got a couple of pals with him.'

When she saw the three young men swaggering over to join them, Dulcie deliberately moved her chair away from those of the other girls. The young men were of a type and class familiar to her from her own family life, and Dulcie immediately mentally and somewhat scathingly dismissed them as being men she wouldn't want to dance with. For a start their suits were shiny and ill-fitting, they were wearing boots, not shoes, and their stridently cockney accents made her grateful for the fact that she had learned to speak in a much more refined way since going to work at Selfridges. Neither Olive nor Tilly, nor indeed anyone she had spoken to in Article Row, spoke with a cockney accent, and when Rita flashed her a look and apologised insincerely, 'Oh, sorry, Dulcie that there isn't anyone for you to dance with,' Dulcie was relieved rather than displeased.

Not that she wouldn't have minded someone buying her a drink, mind. It came to something when a girl as good-looking as she was had to sit all alone at a Saturday night dance without so much as having a drink bought for her.

The band was on form, playing all the popular numbers with a lively beat, the dance floor already a crush of couples – young women wearing their best frocks, the men – many of whom were in uniform, eager to take their partners onto the floor. A group of Italian-looking young men stood together at the edge of the dance floor, the dark-haired good looks catching Dulcie's attention. Not that there was any point in encouraging their attentions. Italian men wanted only one thing from non-Italian girls and it wasn't a discussion about ice cream, Dulcie thought witheringly. There'd been a couple of young Italians attending the same boxing club as her brother, and Rick had soon set her straight about them.

'They're only allowed to marry girls of their own sort,' he'd told her when the son of an Italian couple who ran a little shop round the corner from their parents' house had started waiting for her after school and offering to walk home with her. 'So you make sure you don't let them muck around with you, Dulcie.'

There'd been no need for her to ask him what he meant by 'muck around', nor any resentment on her part at his warning. After all, it had been Rick who had seen what was going on when their uncle Joey had started lying in wait for her at family get-togethers so that he could try to feel her up, pushing her into the darkest corner of the passage and then putting his hand on her budding breasts, before squeezing one of them so hard that it had hurt. Nothing had ever been said between them after Rick had come into the passage and seen what was going on, but later that week she'd seen her uncle in the street and he'd had a whopper of a black eye.

Ted looked round the packed dance floor of the Hammersmith Palais, the heat generated by the dancers bringing him out in a sweat that beaded his forehead. He shouldn't be here really. His ma had played holy heck when he'd told her that he was going out, because she'd wanted him to sit in with the kids whilst she went to the pictures with her sister, Ted's aunt Dottie. He'd stuck to his guns, though. He'd had to after what Agnes had told him. The poor kid had been in a real state over coming here tonight. Left to herself, Ted reckoned that she'd funk it, but from what she'd said about her, that Tilly was another matter and hellbent on defying her ma. In Ted's experienced view there could be only one outcome to the whole sorry mess and that was an all-out row and a lot of tears. One thing he was decided on, though, was that his Agnes wasn't going to get the blame, and if that landlady of hers tried to blame her – or worse still, turf her out – then Ted was going to have to set her straight.

His Agnes. Quite how it had happened that keeping an eye out for Agnes because she was so obviously wet behind the ears and incapable of looking after herself had turned into him starting to look forward to their teatime chats together, and then outright missing her when he couldn't see her, Ted didn't quite know. But it had happened, and although nothing had been said between them, Ted had decided that when the time was right, when she'd found her feet properly, and if she was willing then, Agnes was going to be his girl.

A little awkwardly he looked over his shoulder. Ted felt a bit iffy about Hammersmith. Not the Palais itself – that had a good enough reputation, and the management were certainly keen on checking who they let in. They'd given him the once-over with a bit of a sharp eye. No, it was the reputation that Hammersmith itself had that had made him feel wary. The East End of the west end of the city, some called it. Ted didn't know about that but he did know that to those who knew the city, who *really* knew it and had grown up knowing it at street level, Hammersmith was a hotbed of radical talkers, always wanting to stir up trouble. They'd had the IRA trying to bomb the bridge earlier in the year, and the only reason they hadn't got away with it was because someone had seen the bomb and chucked it into the river. Then there was the river itself, or rather the pathway along it. Got a real reputation, that had, for all sorts of goings-on and was a favourite haunt for the cheapest types of prostitutes. The Palais itself, though, was removed from all of that. People came from all over the city to dance there. It had one of the best in-house orchestras in the country – the famous Joe Loss Orchestra.

Ted had gone to a lot of trouble to make sure that he didn't stick out like a sore thumb when he got here. He'd been down to the public baths after work and had a really good soak, and then he'd gone home and dressed in his Sunday shirt and the tie that matched his one and only suit – his suit, like his tie, brown with a bit of a stripe in it. He'd Brylcreemed down his mousy hair and polished his shoes until he could see his face in them.

It took him an hour to crisscross the whole of the interior of the Palais, and then, and only then, when he had decided to his own satisfaction that Agnes wasn't there, did he make his way to the exit.

If she wasn't here then that meant that either Tilly had lost her nerve and changed her mind or something had gone wrong, by which Ted meant that Tilly's ma had rumbled Tilly's plot to deceive her.

Standing on the pavement outside the Palais, Ted reflected on what to do. There was no point in him going home. His ma had missed her weekly trip to the pictures now, and besides, if Tilly and Agnes were in trouble then he wanted to know about it, for Agnes's sake. Removing his flat cap from the pocket of the overcoat he had retrieved from the cloakroom, turning up his collar and pulling on his cap, Ted then shoved his hands into his pockets, hunching his shoulders against the dank fog-laden November air, as he set out for the underground.

THIRTEEN

Olive was alone in the kitchen when she heard the knock on the front door, Sally having gone out to meet her friends, and Tilly and Agnes still upstairs and very quiet.

Blowing her nose on the handkerchief she retrieved from her sleeve, Olive guessed that her visitor would be Nancy, who sometimes came round on Saturday evening for a chat whilst her husband went down to the pub on the next street. The last thing she wanted was to have Nancy, who was such a gossip, guessing that something was wrong and asking her a lot of questions.

Only it wasn't Nancy she could see standing outside her front door, when she switched off the hall light to keep the blackout, and then opened the door. It was a man.

Unable to make out his face in the darkness, Olive was wary about opening the door any wider, but whilst she hesitated a slightly nervous and young male voice told her, 'I've come to see if Agnes is all right. She was supposed to be going to the Hammersmith Palais. Agnes and me work together,' he ploughed on desperately into the silence.

Immediately Olive guessed, 'You must be Ted then?'

'Yes, that's right.' Ted was relieved to get a response.

'And Agnes told you, did she, that you would find her at the Palais tonight?' Olive's voice hardened.

'Oh, no, nothing like that,' Ted denied. 'Agnes isn't the sort to go saying anything like that.'

Softened by this response, Olive opened the door properly. 'You'd better come in.'

Taking off his cap, Ted stepped into the hall, glad of its warmth. Olive closed the front door and then switched on the light.

'Agnes is all right, isn't she? Only, she was a bit upset when she was telling me about what . . .'

'About what my daughter was planning to do,' Olive finished for him as she led the way to the kitchen.

'Well, I didn't want to say nothing about that,' Ted told her, ''cos it's none of my business, but I wouldn't want to think of Agnes getting into trouble, and there not being anyone to stick up for her.'

'Agnes is upstairs with my daughter,' Olive told him, going automatically to fill the kettle and then light the gas beneath it, waving Ted into a chair as she did so.

He looked a decent enough sort, and Sergeant Dawson had spoken well of him. Olive liked the fact that he was concerned about Agnes.

'I found out what Tilly was planning and I refused to let them go. I'm sorry if you are disappointed at not being able to see Agnes there,' Olive told Ted as she made the tea.

'No. I mean, I only went there 'cos I was a bit worried about her. I told her it was a daft idea and that they were bound to get found out,' Ted announced with male scorn for an ill-thought-out female plan. 'Told her too she should say summat to you about it and get it knocked on the head, but she said she couldn't on account of her and your Tilly being friends. Ta,' he added gratefully when Olive poured him a mug of tea and handed it to him.

Wrapping his cold hands round the mug, he told Olive, 'Once I'd seen that they weren't at the Palais I remembered how Agnes had said that she was feared that you might send her packing, her being only a lodger here, so I thought I'd come round just to make sure that you knew what was what.'

'You don't have to tell me that Agnes isn't the sort of girl to break the rules, Ted,' Olive assured him, touched by his obviously genuine concern for her lodger. 'I've made my feelings about what she's done very plain to Tilly and there's no doubt in my mind about where the blame lies.'

'Well, I dare say it's natural that she wants to go, it being the best place in London for dancing and everyone going there. I was a bit iffy about it meself until I got inside, Hammersmith being what it is, but the management there know what's what and there wasn't any trouble going on inside, that I could see.'

'That's very reassuring to know, Ted,' Olive thanked him gravely, hiding a small smile. Sergeant Dawson had said that Ted helped to look after his younger siblings and she could see that sense of responsibility in him when he talked about the Palais.

Ted drained the last of his tea and stood up.

'I'll be on my way then now that I know that Agnes is all right. Thanks for the tea.'

Dulcie tapped her foot irritably on the floor as she watched the three other girls dance off yet again with their partners. Not that she'd have wanted to dance with any of them, not for one minute. She could have been up there on the floor dancing. She'd been asked but she certainly wasn't going to waste her blue silk frock or herself on any of the no-hopers who'd come up asking her for a dance.

It wasn't in Dulcie's nature to question her own actions, never mind find fault with them. It was other people's fault that she wasn't dancing, not her own – because there was no one there good enough for her to dance with.

She felt a tap on her shoulder and braced herself, turning round impatiently, the words of sarcastic rejection dying on her lips, her eyes rounding as she looked up into a familiar face, her heart thudding so hard it took her several seconds to vocalise her recognition in an uncharacteristically stunned voice. She stared at the handsome man wearing an RAF uniform, and said in disbelief, 'You!'

It was David James-Thompson. For a minute

she was as shocked as a naïve girl who knew nothing might have been. But, of course, she wasn't a naïve girl and she had always known that Lydia's beau was the sort to break the rules, just as she had always known that eventually he would seek her out, she assured herself.

Suddenly the evening was full of promise and excitement, the glitter from the mirror ball twirling over the dance floor and the spotlights reflected in the sparkle of her eyes.

All she allowed herself to say was, 'You're in uniform.'

'You noticed then,' he teased her. 'I signed up for the RAF a week ago. Decided I couldn't bear to stand on the sidelines any longer. Pilot training begins next week.'

The RAF. Far more exciting than if he had joined the army, Dulcie thought approvingly.

'Thought I'd come on the off chance that you'd be here so we could celebrate together.'

Dulcie was over her shock now, and that fast beating heart had been firmly restored to its normal beat. There was no way she was going to allow him to know how thrilled she'd been to see him.

'Shouldn't that be something you're doing with your fiancée?' she taunted him instead.

'Possibly,' he agreed, unabashed, as he came to sit down beside her, taking the seat that had been Rita's and turning it round so that he was sitting facing her, his knees brushing against her thigh. 'Although at the moment she isn't very pleased with me for joining up. She and my parents think I should have arranged things so that I claimed exemption from military duty. Awfully boring doing that, though, especially when so many other chaps seem to be having so much fun. We like having fun, don't we, Dulcie?' he asked her with a knowing smile, reaching for her hand as he did so and then sliding his fingers through hers so that their hands were laced together with an expertise that told her that this wasn't the first time he had done something so intimate. The very fact that he knew what he was doing made David all the more of a prize and all the more exciting.

'We're two of a kind, you and I,' he told her, his eyes brimming with amusement and appreciation as though he knew what she was thinking.

David watched the battle going on inside Dulcie's thoughts and reflected in her gaze as caution fought with triumph. He hadn't intended to come here, after the row with Lydia about him joining up. He'd planned to have dinner with a couple of other chaps who'd enlisted at the same time, and then go on to a nightclub with them, but then suddenly he'd thought of Dulcie and before he'd really known what he was doing he was on his way over here.

She was a looker all right, and classy too, nothing cheap or common about the way she looked. David toyed with the idea of persuading her to leave the dancehall with him. He could take her to one of the quieter and more discreetly managed clubs he knew, somewhere where they could sit in the darkness together, but before he could say anything Dulcie was standing up and tugging impatiently on his hand as she demanded,

'Well, now that you're here we'd better dance, hadn't we?'

At the other end of the dance floor, on the elevated stage with its red curtains, the Joe Loss Orchestra swung into a waltz, and the lights were dipped.

The floor was packed with dancers, giving them no option but to hold each other close. He was a good dancer, leading her confidently, but then he would be, him being posh, Dulcie thought. Really, the two of them looked so good together that they could have had their photographs in one of those gossip columns in the newspapers, which showed you photographs of lords and ladies and the like. She looked far better with him than Lydia would, with her sallow skin and her bad-tempered face with its thin mouth. She wasn't surprised that David wanted to escape from his fiancée to be with her.

His fiancée. Dancing with another girl's fiancé was one thing, especially when she disliked that girl as much as she disliked Lydia, but once David was married to Lydia then things would be different. Girls who went out with married men were putting themselves on the wrong side of the respectability line and Dulcie had no intention of ever doing that.

Tilly couldn't sleep. She knew her mother had come up to bed. She'd heard her familiar footsteps on the stairs and then the opening and closing of her door, followed by the further equally familiar sounds of her mother going to the bathroom and then returning to her room. She'd also heard Sally coming in, humming some tune under her breath, her firm nurse's tread on the stairs. Only Dulcie was still out, but it wasn't because of that that Tilly couldn't sleep. Unlike Agnes, who was now making the small whuffling sounds she always made in her sleep.

Had those really been tears she had seen in her mother's eyes earlier? Tears caused by her? The weight of Tilly's guilt oppressed her. Being grown up wasn't just about doing what you wanted to do, she was beginning to recognise; it wasn't all about good things, it was about the consequences of those things as well. She had made her mother cry, and now that mattered far more to her than the fact that they had been found out and prevented from going dancing. There was a tight miserable pain inside Tilly's chest, and with it a fear. Previously she had believed that whatever happened in her life to upset her – like when the Benson sisters at school had started lying in wait for her and making fun of her – her mother could and would make everything all right again. But that had been before she had seen her mother's tears, before she had known that her mother was vulnerable.

The pain and guilt was too much for her. Throwing back the bedclothes, and trying not to shiver in the room's chill, Tilly felt in the darkness with her feet for her slippers, burrowing her toes into their warmth in relief. She didn't want to turn on the lamp in case she woke Agnes, but she was still able to retrieve her dressing gown from the post at the foot of the bed, quickly pulling it on and wrapping its cord round her. Her mother had been talking about making her and Agnes proper siren suits with hoods on them, to protect them from the cold should the air-raid siren go off and they had to spend the night in the Anderson shelter. Tilly had seen one of the suits in the window of Swan and Edgar. Bright red, its hood trimmed with swansdown, it had looked very warm and Christmassy, the pretty cosy image it portrayed very different from the reality of war rationing looming, and the increasing shortages of everything. All the best shops had their Christmas displays in their windows now: hampers with their lids thrown back to show what was inside in Fortnum and Mason; toys, of course, in Hamley's; women's clothes in the expensive dress shops in muted shades to tone with men's uniforms. Christmas had always been such a special time at number 13. Her mother had made sure of that. Quietly and quickly Tilly made her way from her own bedroom to her mother's.

Olive heard her bedroom door open. She had come to bed in the hope that sleep would stop her from brooding on the events of the evening, but sleep had proved to be impossible. Tonight, for the first time since she had been able to wrap her baby arms round her, Tilly had not kissed her good night. Olive had wept silently over that.

Tilly's mother's bedroom was filled with the familiar scents, which, blended together, became the scent that to Tilly was her mother: Pear's soap, freshly ironed laundry, the smell of clean rooms and a warm kitchen, lavender polish, and baking – her mother's scents. Tears of guilt and shame blurred Tilly's eyes but she didn't need to be able to see to find her way across the room.

'Mum, are you awake?' she asked hesitantly.

Olive turned to her daughter. 'Yes, Tilly.' She felt her bed depress under Tilly's weight.

'I'm sorry about what I said earlier, and about what I was going to do. It was wrong of me. I shouldn't have done.'

The wretchedness in Tilly's voice tore at Olive's heart. Sitting up in bed, she reached for her daughter and put her arms round her, her cheek resting on Tilly's downbent head.

'I'm sorry too, Tilly. Sorry that I haven't treated you, *trusted* you, as I should.'

Her mother's apology made Tilly feel even worse. Turning, she flung her arms round Olive and told her fiercely, 'You don't have anything to feel sorry for. It was me who . . . who lied.'

Stroking her hair back from Tilly's forehead, Olive told her sadly, 'I've been selfish, Tilly, trying to keep you as a little girl, when you aren't. I never wanted to stop you having fun, I just wanted to protect you. War makes people anxious to take what happiness they can, Tilly, when they can, especially the young. When we think someone we care for might be snatched from us, and with them our future happiness, it makes us all do things and take risks we wouldn't normally take. For young people that often means falling in love, being hurt.'

'I just wanted to go out dancing, but you're afraid that I might meet someone and fall in love and that they might be killed and then . . . I'd be like you were when Dad died. Oh, Mum . . .'

They held each other tightly.

'Sally has offered to go with you and Agnes to the Palais, just to help you find your feet there the first time you go.'

'You mean . . .' Tilly swallowed hard. This generosity on the part of her mother was too much for her to bear. Fresh tears fell.

'You'll have to take care of Agnes, Tilly. She isn't as used to thinking for herself as you are.'

'Can I stay here with you tonight?' Tilly asked.

Olive smiled in the darkness and drew back the bedcovers.

They were almost the last to leave the Palais and now, in the foggy darkness outside the dancehall, they stood facing one another on the pavement.

'Next time,' David told Dulcie, 'I'll take you somewhere a bit more exciting than this.'

So there was going to be a next time. A thrill of pleasure surged through Dulcie; not that she was going to let him see how she felt. Instead she demanded, 'Who says there's going to be a next time?'

'Not who but what,' David answered, 'and this is what says there will be.'

When he cupped her face in both his hands and gently drew his thumbs along her cheekbones, gazing down into her eyes as he did so, Dulcie could only gaze back at him. She'd been kissed before but never like this, like she'd seen people kissing in films, and no cheeky fumbling with her clothes either. David was a true gentleman. And awfully good at kissing. The only thing that could make right now any better would be being able to boast to Lizzie about it, but of course she could never do that.

'There'll be no seeing me again after you get married to Lydia,' Dulcie felt bound to warn him, but David merely laughed.

'Giving Lydia a wedding ring isn't going to stop me enjoying life, Dulcie.'

Deep down inside, Dulcie felt unexpectedly shocked. She knew that David didn't love Lydia, but to hear him speak so casually and uncaring made her wonder how serious he could ever be about any girl.

'It might not stop you enjoying life, but it will stop me from going out with you,' Dulcie insisted.

David was frowning now. 'If you're trying to persuade me not to marry Lydia, then I should tell you—'

'I'm not trying to persuade you to do anything,' Dulcie defended herself heatedly, not letting him finish. 'What I'm doing is telling you that I won't cheapen myself by providing a bit of fun for a married man. I think more of myself than to do that, even if you don't.'

David looked crestfallen. 'I'm sorry, Dulcie,' he said immediately. 'I didn't mean . . . That is, you know how it is with me and Lydia. She doesn't want me, she just wants who I am. You and I, we're two of a kind, I know it.'

'We aren't two of anything, and we aren't going to be.'

She meant it, David could see, and part of him admired her for her determination, even whilst most of him wished that she was more malleable. He might not have spent much time with her, but there was a quality about Dulcie that touched something in him that Lydia would never be able to reach. Perhaps it was a trait he had inherited from his Gaiety Girl grandmother that made him feel so at home with Dulcie, and if things had been different . . . But his parents, and especially his mother, would never accept Dulcie. And it was through his mother that ultimately he would inherit his wealth, just as it was his mother who was insisting on him marrying Lydia. David gave a brief inner shrug. Dulcie was a pretty girl but London was full of pretty girls. It wasn't in his nature to fight for what he wanted; it was easier instead to want something else, and more within reach, so he gave Dulcie another smile, and nodded in acceptance of Dulcie's decree before telling her, 'I'll get us a taxi,' and then stepping out into the road.

Almost by magic a taxi materialised through the fog, and within seconds David was helping her into it, whilst Dulcie battled against the dangerous temptation to wish that she hadn't closed the door quite so firmly on she and David getting together again.

She wasn't in any danger of falling for him, Dulcie assured herself as she let herself into number 13 – she'd made David tell the taxi to stop at the entrance to the Row because she didn't want Olive to hear the taxi and look out of her window to see what was going on – she wasn't that daft, or that soft. And she'd meant what she said about not seeing him again.

When she reached the top landing she saw that the door to Sally's room was open, a narrow oblong of light thrown by the bedside lamp. Then Sally appeared in the open doorway, wearing her dressing gown.

'I just thought I'd warn you that Olive caught Tilly and Agnes trying to sneak out earlier this evening,' she told her quietly

'So what if she did?' Dulcie hissed back. 'It's got nothing to do with me what Tilly does.'

'Except that you encouraged her. Olive was very upset, Dulcie. It wasn't a very nice thing to do. Olive is a decent sort and this is a good billet.'

'Look, it's not my fault if Tilly wants to go dancing. Serves Olive right, if you ask me, the way she carries on, fussing over that Agnes and treating me as though I'm something the cat brought in.'

Sally gave a small sigh. She'd only stayed up to warn Dulcie, thinking that the other girl might want to prepare an apology for Olive, but far from being remorseful Dulcie seemed to relish the trouble she had caused.

FOURTEEN

Tilly thought she was the happiest she had ever been – at least, she would have been were it not for the war. The new grown-up status now conferred on her by her mother meant that Tilly now felt she had to take her adulthood very seriously. That meant that whilst, of course, she was excited at the thought of going dancing at the Hammersmith Palais, she must also think about the war and all those who were involved in it.

Mr Salt, who was in charge of their St John Ambulance brigade had actually praised her at their last meeting for the attention she'd paid to his lecture about the correct way to use a stirrup pump, in case they were called upon to deal with any incendiary bombs.

It was Sally now whom Tilly admired and looked up to rather than Dulcie, although she had begged her mother not to say anything to Dulcie.

Reluctantly Olive had refrained from taking Dulcie to task, although she now felt even cooler towards her lodger than she had already done, and would have been very much happier if Dulcie had decided to leave.

Agnes, who had heard from Olive about Ted's visit and his concern for her now thought that Ted was even more heroic and had started blushing for no reason at all when he looked at her when they were having tea together in the café. Ted had told her to let him know when they were going to the Palais so that he could, in his own words, 'Go along as well and keep an eye on things.'

They were only a week away from Christmas and it had been decided that the girls would attend the Hammersmith Palais's Saturday night dance the day before Christmas Eve, since on Christmas Eve itself they would be going to the dance at the church hall.

All the shops had made a brave show of putting up their decorations in their windows, but of course there could be no Christmas lights because of the blackout, and it seemed to Olive as she did her Christmas shopping, queuing up with other housewives, that there was an atmosphere of weariness and irritation rather than of anticipation. And no wonder. So many of the shops seemed to have sold out of things, which meant shopping around to find increasingly elusive necessities.

Olive was glad that she had stocked up early. Her mother, having been in service, had instilled in Olive the importance of keeping a well-stocked kitchen cupboard, a habit also favoured by her late mother-in-law. Olive took it for granted that her own cupboards were always filled with fruit bottled in season, jams and pickles made from ingredients she'd bought from the barrow boys at bargain prices, and a good supply of tinned things, just as she knew to a nicety how to make a joint last from Sunday until Wednesday and how to make a tasty meal out of leftovers.

She'd heard several women complaining that they'd been unable to buy jars of mincemeat for their mince tarts, but she had plenty in her store cupboard. She just hoped that the goose she'd ordered would be big enough to go round. She'd got some sausagemeat on order for the sausage rolls she intended to make for her Boxing Day party, and she planned to cook a ham as well.

Her local greengrocer had promised her a nice bushy Christmas tree. Sergeant Dawson had offered to get her one from Covent Garden when he got one for the police station. Mrs Dawson wouldn't have a tree in the house since they'd lost their lad, he told her. She'd thanked him but explained that she'd already ordered her tree, and then on impulse she'd told him about her Boxing Day get-together and said that he and Mrs Dawson would be welcome if they fancied coming along.

They'd been busy in the Lady Almoner's office with patients who were well enough to get home in time for Christmas, which meant that there'd been lots of coming and goings. Most of their patients were in hospital insurance schemes, which paid their bills when they were in hospital. This meant extra administration for Tilly and her colleagues at this busy time of year.

When the tall dark-haired man in naval officer's

uniform came in at lunch time, Tilly was manning the office on her own, having volunteered to do so. First sitting in the canteen was always more popular than second because the food was hotter and you got bigger portions.

The officer was carrying his cap and smiled warmly when Tilly asked if she could help him.

'I hope so,' he answered. 'Only I'm trying to trace someone, a nurse, a friend from Liverpool, by the name of Sally Johnson, who I think might be working at St Barts. I've already tried St Thomas's and Guy's without any success.'

Tilly nearly fell off her chair. She was deeply conscious of the debt she owed Sally for offering to go with them to the Palais, and she was delighted at the thought of being able to do something for her in return, especially when it meant putting her back in touch with such a handsome and friendly-looking man. Of course, they weren't really supposed to give out people's addresses, but in this instance that surely didn't matter. Tilly couldn't imagine Sally not wanting her friend to be able to find her, especially when he had gone to such a lot of trouble to do so.

She gave him a beaming smile, unable to stop herself from bursting out, 'I know Sally. In fact she lodges with us. Oh, fancy you coming in and asking for her and me being here.'

'A happy coincidence indeed,' he agreed with another smile.

'Sally's on duty at the moment, but I'll give you the address. Although you'd be better not to call until this evening. Around seven o'clock would probably be best. It's number thirteen Article Row,' she informed him happily, only realising once he had thanked her and left that she'd been so excited that she hadn't thought to ask him his name.

Tilly hummed happily to herself as she got on with her work. She couldn't wait to tell Sally about her impending visitor.

Tilly didn't get the chance to tell Sally about the naval officer until they were both back at number 13, Tilly positively bursting with delight when she came in to find Sally in the kitchen with her mother.

'You'll never guess what, Sally. A man came into the office today asking for you, and he's coming round to see you tonight. At least, I think he is.'

Sally, who had been standing up, sank down into one of the kitchen chairs, the colour draining from her face, leaving her skin the colour of milk.

'A man, you say? Did he give you his name?'

Tilly shook her head. She could see that something was wrong and that Sally looked upset. Conscience-stricken, she told her lamely, 'He was ever so nice. Good-looking too. He said he was from Liverpool. I thought . . . I thought you'd be pleased to see an old friend.'

Somehow Sally managed to produce a wan smile although it was an effort. It wasn't Tilly's fault. Tilly was desperate to show her how grateful she was over her intervention with her mother with regard to the Hammersmith Palais visit. At Tilly's age she would probably have done the same thing.

'Oh, Tilly,' Olive shook her head reproachfully, 'you shouldn't have given him Sally's address without checking with Sally herself first.'

Callum. It had to be him. It couldn't be anyone else. Sally felt acutely sick. There was no point in upbraiding poor Tilly, though. She was now looking distressed enough as it was.

'I'm sorry if I've done the wrong thing,' Tilly said, looking flustered and guilty.

'No . . . it's all right,' Sally told her unsteadily, feeling obliged to explain, 'Callum's sister married my father after my own mother's death.'

Olive's breath escaped in an understanding sound of compassion whilst Tilly looked confused.

'I left Liverpool because I . . . didn't approve of the marriage. I dare say Callum hopes that time and distance have softened my feelings.'

'You don't have to see him,' Olive told her. 'I am quite willing to tell him that you don't wish to, Sally.'

Sally was tempted to accept Olive's offer. Seeing Callum was bound to be emotionally painful. But what if something had happened to her father? Anxiety speared through her.

'No. It will be better if I see him. That way I can make it plain to him that I haven't changed my mind.'

'I'm so sorry.' Tilly looked even more guilty and miserable.

'You weren't to know, Tilly. Callum is a very decent and respectable man. There would be no reason for you to suspect him of anything unpleasant. He's a schoolteacher.'

'He was in uniform,' Tilly blurted out. 'Navy. An officer's uniform, I thought.'

Sally disliked the reasons that her heart was bumping along the bottom of her ribcage even less than she liked the uncomfortable breathless feeling it was giving her. Callum meant nothing to her now. She didn't care what danger he might put himself into.

'When he comes, Sally, you can see him in the front room. You can be private in there, and I'm here if you should need me.'

Sally smiled her thanks to Olive, shaking her head when her landlady continued, 'We'll have tea now, I think. That way Sally's visitor isn't likely to arrive when we're halfway through it.'

'There's no need to change things for me,' Sally told Olive. 'I'm really not hungry at all, I'm afraid.'

Upstairs in her bedroom she looked towards the window, covered with its blackout cloth, as the law decreed. When she had first moved to London she had been afraid that someone from home – her father, Callum or even Morag herself – might try to get in touch with her, but as the weeks had gone by she had begun to feel safer. Nothing could protect her from the pain of what had happened, but at least she had felt protected from fresh misery. Until now.

It was just gone seven thirty when Callum knocked on the door to number 13.

Unable to stay on her own in her room as she had intended, Sally had gone back downstairs to the kitchen where Olive had been putting the final coat of icing on her Christmas cake. Watching her, Sally had immediately been transported back to her childhood and her own mother's kitchen. Tilly didn't realise how lucky she was to have her mother, but at least Sally knew what it was to have a mother's love, unlike poor Agnes, who was perched on a kitchen stool happily helping to cut out red berries and green Christmas trees from the marzipan to which green and red colouring had been added by Tilly as the two girls did their bit towards decorating the cake.

'I'll go,' Olive announced when they all heard the door, putting down in a bowl of hot water the palette knife with which she had been smoothing the royal icing, then removing her apron before heading for the door.

Sally let her go. It was going to take all the emotional and mental strength she had to face Callum.

When Olive opened the door to Sally's visitor, she felt very much as Tilly had done when she'd first seen him, liking his strong manly features and feeling reassured by his friendly smile. The uniform did its bit to establish him as someone to be trusted, of course. But then Sally had never said that he was someone who could not be trusted, and Olive could well understand why her lodger did not want to see him. She admired Sally's love and devotion for her late mother and sympathised with her feelings.

Callum's, 'I'd like to see Sally if she'll see me,' received a small inclination of Olive's head and a calm, 'Yes. She is expecting you. If you'd like to come this way . . . ?'

He wasn't wearing an overcoat, and since she wasn't sure what the etiquette was with regard to the naval officer's cap that he was carrying, she didn't like to offer to relieve him of it.

She showed him into the front room, its gas fire hissing warmly and its green, fern-print curtains drawn over the blackout fabric to give the room an air of cosy warmth.

Olive was very proud of her front parlour. She had redecorated it herself, painting the walls cream, with the picture rail painted the same green as the curtain pelmet. A stylish stepped mirror hung over the fireplace. The linoleum was patterned to look like parquet flooring and over it was a cream, dark red and green patterned carpet. The dark green damask-covered three-piece suite had been a bargain because there'd been a small tear in one of the seat cushions, and on the glass and pale wood coffee table, which was Olive's pride and joy, was a pretty crystal bowl that had caught her eye in an antique shop just off the Strand.

A radiogram in the same pale wood as the coffee table stood against the back wall behind the sofa, and Olive couldn't help but give a very satisfied glance around her front room before telling Callum that Sally would be right with him and then whisking through the door.

When Olive opened the hall door into the back room, Sally was already getting up from her chair, her face set and tense.

'I haven't offered him a cup of tea or anything,' Olive began anxiously.

265

'No, please don't,' Sally begged her. 'I don't want to encourage him to stay.'

In the hall outside the front-room door Sally took a deep breath and smoothed her damp palms against the pleats in her neat flecked tweed skirt. She'd bought the skirt on a shopping trip with Morag early on in the autumn before her mother had died. Morag had said how much the heather colours had suited her, bringing out the colour of her eyes, and had persuaded Sally to buy a pretty violet twinset to go with the skirt. She wasn't wearing that twinset now. Instead she had chosen a plain dark blue blouse.

She took a deep breath and pushed open the door.

Callum was standing on the hearthrug with his back to the fire, his hands folded behind his back. Seeing him in uniform was disconcerting. In her memories of him he was always wearing his patched tweed jacket softened by wear, a Tattersall checked shirt worn with a sleeveless pullover, and a pair of cavalry twill trousers. In his naval uniform he looked taller, stood straighter, the slight scholarly stoop she remembered gone. She looked away from him, aware of the pulse beating in her throat and the unwanted pang of longing seeing him brought her. His cap was on the coffee table.

'You're in the navy.'

It was stupid thing to say, but somehow the words had formed and were spoken, sounding, to her own dismay, almost like a reproach, as though she had the right to reproach him for doing something without her knowledge.

'Yes. Sublieutenant. I've just finished my training at the Royal Naval College at Dartmouth, and I should receive orders as to which ship I'm to join pretty soon.'

He paused and then came towards her, saying, 'Sally . . .' Immediately she stepped back from him, holding up her hands as though to ward him off, relieved when he moved away.

'Your father misses you,' he told her abruptly, 'and so too does Morag.'

'He's all right?' Sally couldn't hold back her anxiety.

Immediately Callum's smile deepened, as he said reassuringly, 'Yes, apart from the fact that he misses you.'

Sally stiffened and turned her head away as she told him fiercely, 'I miss my mother and I always will.'

'Sally, you aren't a child,' he told her in a sharp voice. 'I can understand your loyalty towards your mother but do you really feel she would want this? For you to cut yourself off from your father?'

'He cut himself off from her and from me when he married Morag.'

'You're being unfair.'

'*I'm* being unfair?' She made a small bitter sound. 'Morag married my father three months after my mother's death.'

'Your mother would never have wanted your father to be alone; she would have understood.'

'Understood what? That your sister, and my best friend, whom she had treated as another daughter, was offering him the . . . the comfort of an intimate relationship whilst she lay dying? And as for my father being alone, he would have had me. I'd like you to leave. Now. I don't want to talk about it. I don't know why you came here. After all, I've made my feelings plain enough. Your sister betrayed our friendship and the kindness my mother showed her.'

'Your mother encouraged them to be together.'

'Not in that way! You say that because it's what you want to believe, because Morag is your sister, but it isn't the truth.'

'Because you don't want it to be the truth? Your mother wanted your father to be happy, to be cared for and loved as she had cared for him and loved him. She told Morag so.'

'Do you really expect me to believe that? Well, I don't.'

'I thought better of you than this, Sally, I really did.'

Now his voice had become colder, sharper, critical, stabbing into the soft vulnerability of her emotions.

'Just as I thought better of your sister,' Sally defended herself. 'Now we've both been disappointed. How would you have liked it, Callum, if our positions had been reversed? It's all very well for you to come here and tell me how I should feel; you're bound to take Morag's side.'

'Sally, it isn't a matter of taking sides. Your father loves you and misses you. I know you were upset and shocked by their marriage, but surely out of your love for your father – and I know that you do love him – and the friendship that you and Morag shared, you can find it in your heart to accept that they genuinely want to be together?'

'What, and betray my mother, like Morag betrayed our friendship?' She shook her head. 'No. Never.'

'Sally, it's almost Christmas. A time for families to be together, to stand together, especially when we are a country at war. And besides . . .' He paused and looked at her and there was something in that look – a mixture of sadness and pity – that ripped at her defences and made her want to cry out to him, 'What about your loyalty to me and what we could have had? What about taking my side? What about understanding me?' But of course she didn't; couldn't when he had put himself so clearly on Morag's side.

She saw his chest rise and fall as he took a deep breath. Then he told her, 'I was hoping that you would agree to see your father and Morag before I had to tell you this, but obviously you won't. There's to be a child, Sally, due in May. Your father and Morag desperately want you to share in their joy.'

The room spun wildly round her, nausea clawing at her stomach, the sound of her vehement denial echoing inside her own head.

Callum caught hold of her, his hands gripping her upper arms as she fought against the faintness threatening to overwhelm her.

Above her she could see the once beloved face of the man she had hoped to spend the rest of her life with, a man she had thought so morally superior, so kind, so everything she could ever imagined wanting in a man and more; but who was now her enemy, and the pain inside her was so strong she thought it would break her apart.

'Sally?'

Was that yearning she could hear in his voice? If it was then it was a brother's yearning for her to uphold a sister, not a man's yearning for her love.

Bitterly, she shrugged off his hold.

'I don't want to hear any more,' she told him. 'I don't ever want to see you again, Callum, or them.'

'Have you no message for your father, Sally? He loves you and misses you.'

'Does he? Well, he will soon have another child to love in my place, won't he?'

She turned to the door and held it open, telling him, 'I want you to leave, Callum.'

Silently, his mouth grim, he collected his cap and walked past her to the front door where he paused to say, 'I thought better of you, Sally, I really did.'

'Maybe I thought better of you as well, Callum,' was the only response she allowed herself to make as he opened the door and disappeared into the darkness beyond it.

A child. Her father and Morag were to have a child. Revulsion filled her. Revulsion and anger, and pain. If things had been as they should, then it could have been her and Callum announcing the conception of their child this Christmas. Not only had her father and her once friend stolen her past and belief in the devotion of her parents to one another, like swans partnering for life; they had also stolen her future. She would never ever forgive them.

FIFTEEN

'So you're not coming home for Christmas then?'

Even as her mother asked the question, it was Edith she was watching, Dulcie thought resentfully as she observed her sister talking animatedly several yards away to a group of admirers, who had halted her progress across the crowded floor of their local working men's club where she had been singing.

Dulcie hadn't wanted to come to listen to her sister and she certainly hadn't wanted to listen to her mother praising her so dotingly for doing so, but she'd got caught out on Sunday after church when her mind had been on the previous evening and not what her mother had been saying to her, and too late she realised she'd agreed to join her family to listen to Edith's debut as a professional singer.

The club was a rectangular room with a bar occupying the full length of the wall at one end, apart from a door that led into a narrow passageway containing the ladies'. The gents' was outside in the yard where the brewery loaded the beer barrels into the cellar. Behind the bar was a kitchen where volunteers, who sometimes included Dulcie's mother, made up sandwiches sold at the bar under a glass cover. The distempered walls were stained with the cigarette smoke, which wreathed round the room, gradually rising toward the ceiling.

Behind the bar, with its mirrored back and glass shelves, the club's manager, overweight and sweating, was pulling pints whilst his wife and the barmaid washed glasses at the small sink.

Dulcie hated the place as much as the rest of her family seemed to love it. It was where the whole neighbourhood came to celebrate weddings, births and deaths, after going through the formal church proceedings attendant upon such occasions.

Since tonight was a 'social' night, which meant that the all-male membership was allowed to bring along their other halves and families, the place was packed, whole families, including grandparents, aunts and uncles, in some cases, crowded round the cheap shabby tables on equally cheap, shabby and mismatched chairs. A harsh light beamed down on the small stage, where Edith had performed, at the opposite end of the room to the bar. The whole place stank of stale beer, male sweat, and cheap cigarettes, Dulcie thought, fastidiously wrinkling her nose. A door in the middle of one of the long walls opened into the pool room – a holy of holies that women were not allowed to enter – and it was plain from a few all-women tables that some of the men had already taken advantage of that embargo to escape into it.

'No,' Dulcie answered her mother's question.

'Are you sure this landlady of yours wants you staying there over Christmas? It seems a rum do to me. You'd think she'd want her house to herself and not filled with lodgers. I know I would. Christmas is for being with your own folk.'

Her mother's words hit a nerve but Dulcie wasn't going to let her see that. Olive had been very cool with her since the night Tilly had rebelled, and Dulcie knew that her landlady blamed her, even if she hadn't said so. The truth was that hers was probably as welcome a presence at number 13 over Christmas as it would have been at her own home, Dulcie thought bitterly. Just as her mother would be fussing over Edith, so her landlady would be fussing over Agnes, making a big thing of her not having a family of her own. Not that Dulcie was going to tell her mother that.

Dulcie tossed her head, her blonde curls caught back in a pretty diamanté bow-shaped hair clip that she'd managed to get reduced, after she'd discovered that it had been slightly damaged. Dropping it on the floor earlier in the week and deliberately twisting the clip so that it didn't fasten properly had been easily done whilst Miss Timmins, whose eyesight wasn't very good, and who was really supposed to be retired but who worked one day a week had been in charge of the hair ornaments counter. Poor old Timid Timmy, as they all called her, had looked confused and blinked desperately, her thin, veined hands trembling slightly as she tried to examine the faulty catch. She had been easy for Dulcie to manipulate, and the departmental floor manager when summoned had agreed that the clip could be reduced. He might have given Dulcie a sharp look as she had paid for her purchase but she had felt triumphant rather than guilty. Just like she had felt triumphant that Saturday night at Hammersmith Palais, knowing that David would rather be with her than with his stuck-up fiancée-to-be.

Feeling triumphant was very important to Dulcie. It made her feel she was in her rightful place in the order of things.

'Actually,' she told her mother untruthfully, 'my landlady asked me especially as a favour to her if I would stay there over Christmas.'

'Oh, well, if she wants you there . . .' her mother responded, using a tone of voice that suggested to Dulcie that her mother couldn't understand why that should be the case. Immediately Dulcie's combative spirit was aroused.

'She does. She told me that she thinks of me as another daughter and that she doesn't know how she'd manage without me there to give her Tilly a few words to the wise when it's needed, me being older than Tilly and everything. Of course, I told her that I'm pleased to do my bit. Treats me ever so well, she does, just like I *was* her daughter really, always getting me little bits of treats.' Warming to her deception, Dulcie started to embroider the fabrication she had created.

'She took us all shopping to the Portobello Market the other week and she bought me ever such an expensive blouse, pure silk and French design, and—'

'Oh, here comes Edith now.'

The warmth for her younger daughter in her mother's voice as she interrupted her infuriated Dulcie, causing her to say unkindly, 'I don't know where Edith got that dress from but she's certainly not dressing anything like as well now that she hasn't got my wardrobe to raid any more. It doesn't suit her at all.'

'She looks lovely in it,' Dulcie's mother protested indignantly. 'Pink always was Edith's colour. I remember when she was born I had this lovely pink layette that I'd saved ever so hard for. The first new baby clothes I'd had. I had to make do with hand-me-downs for you and for Rick.'

'Oh, Mum, I thought I was never going to get over to you, so many people wanted to stop and tell me how well I'd done,' Edith enthused, laughing happily as she hugged her mother.

'More like they couldn't believe what you were wearing and wanted to get a closer look,' Dulcie told her nastily, causing the smile to disappear from Edith's flushed face as she turned back to their mother, looking tragic and upset.

'Take no notice of Dulcie, love,' their mother comforted Edith. 'If you ask me, Dulcie, it's just as well you aren't coming home for Christmas, the way you're always upsetting poor Edith.'

'It's just because she's jealous, Mum, because I

can sing and she can't,' Edith trumped Dulcie's earlier insult.

'Call that singing?' Dulcie returned, not to be outdone. 'It sounded more like someone was trying to kill a cat. And you missed that top note in your last song.'

'No I didn't.'

'Yes you did.'

'Dulcie, why do you always have to upset poor Edith?' their mother demanded.

'Why do you always have to take her side?' Dulcie shot back, taunting her sister, 'Mama's little girl who can't do any wrong.'

'Here comes Frank, Mum. I'll have to go. We've got to talk with the manager and the band leader about some future bookings,' Edith announced, ignoring Dulcie as she jumped up hurriedly.

Watching her sister walk away with the man who had swaggered up to them, a cigar stuck in his mouth, his thinning hair greased back from his beefy florid face, Dulcie asked, 'Who's that?'

'His name's Frank Lepardo, and he's Edith's agent,' her mother told her with obvious pride. 'He saw her singing the other week and went backstage to sign her up there and then, he was that pleased with her. He's a real impresario and he reckons that Edith is going to be big – bigger than that Vera Lynn everyone raves about. He's had one of the top ones from ENSA pleading with him to let Edith go on the wireless. Your sister is going to end up famous.'

Dulcie gave the two departing figures a cynical look. She knew men and she certainly knew what kind of man Frank Lepardo was. He had spiv and chancer written on him in letters as wide as the white stripes in his navy-blue suit.

'If you ask me, the only place Edith is likely to end up with him, is underneath him,' Dulcie told her mother bluntly, earning herself a furious look.

'I'll not have you talking about your sister like that. Frank Lepardo is a gentleman. Came especially to see me and your dad to get our permission to represent Edith, and he gave your dad ten pounds as an act of good faith.'

'And I'll bet Dad's lost it already down the dog track,' Dulcie said cynically.

It was more than likely that the real reason Frank Lepardo had gone to see her parents was to find out how naïve they were, she thought grimly, but she knew there was no point in continuing to warn her mother about Frank Lepardo. Anyway, why should she? It would serve Edith right to get what she deserved, the way she continually showed off and made out she was so special. Why was it that everybody was always against her, Dulcie? It wasn't right and it certainly wasn't fair.

The Christmas tree was up, decorated by Tilly and Agnes with the decorations that had been collected over the years and which Olive kept so carefully.

Agnes had gazed in delight at the pretty painted tin bird with its feather tail, amazed when Tilly demonstrated to her how it was also a whistle. Olive watching them had remembered the

Christmas she had bought the novelty decoration from a street market. Tilly had been only little then, entranced by the whistle herself.

This year there were no new decorations to add but they had no need of any. There were plenty to fill the Christmas tree, which they'd put up in the front room. Pretty electric lights of various colours shaped like flowers illuminated the tree, the fairy in her sparkly costume placed at the top. They'd even clipped on the old-fashioned metal candle holders, with their candles, a reminder of long-ago Christmases before electric lights had come in and, Olive had always thought, potentially very dangerous, especially around children. These, though, would not be lit; they were just there for decoration now.

Multicoloured paper garlands had been strung from the central light fitting in both rooms to the corners, adding to the festive décor.

Tonight, whilst the girls were out dancing at the Hammersmith Palais, she'd finish wrapping their presents and put them under the tree, once she'd made the pastry for her mince pies. The news that Dulcie was planning to stay had caused Olive to panic slightly over the fact that she had knitted sets of gloves with matching scarves and hats for the other three but not for Dulcie. Luckily, she'd been able to get some more wool and, by knitting frantically every spare minute, she'd managed to produce a set for Dulcie as well.

On her way back to the shops this morning, where she'd gone to collect her goose, her sausage-meat and the ham, she'd paused outside Holborn's famous bookshop, said to be one of the oldest in London, remembering the set of Beatrix Potter books she'd bought there for Tilly. She'd saved so hard for those books, and Tilly had been thrilled with them, even if Olive's mother-in-law had scorned what she considered to be a waste of money. Olive had been determined right from the start that her Tilly would have a proper education, so that she could hold her head up in the world.

There were sweets to put in the stockings she made for the girls from some cheap felt she'd bought, a sugar mouse for each of them, and some sugared almonds.

Upstairs the girls were getting ready for their night out. Tilly had almost been bursting with excitement over tea, and so had Agnes, who had told Olive shyly earlier in the week that Ted had mentioned that he might as well go along to the Palais, seeing as Agnes was going.

Guessing that Agnes was seeking her approval, Olive had nodded and told her, 'I think that's a good idea, Agnes, and very kind of Ted. There's nothing worse than going to a big dance, for the first time and then feeling left out because the other girls seem to know lots of boys and have partners.'

One member of the quartet from number 13 probably wouldn't lack partners or confidence, Olive thought wryly. She suspected that Dulcie would never be behind the door when it came to putting herself forward. She had convinced herself now, though, that it was better for Tilly to discover what Dulcie was for herself, instead of her criticising her and then having Tilly jump to her defence.

She could hear the girls clattering down the stairs. Tilly was first into the room, the air around her positively crackling with excitement and energy.

'Will I do, do you think, Mum?' she demanded, doing a swift twirl, the panelled skirt of her new velvet dress swirling round her.

Olive's breath caught in her throat. She'd seen the dress on before, but now tonight, looking at Tilly wearing it, she was filled with maternal emotion – pride combining with anxiety. The dress, with its sweetheart neckline, long sleeves and nipped-in waistline showed off Tilly's slender figure, the sweep of its panelled skirt making her look taller, revealing a hint of the woman that Tilly would become. Olive's heart ached with love, but of course she wasn't going to tell Tilly how beautiful she looked. Instead she told her calmly, 'I should think that dress would more than do for any dancehall, Tilly, even the Hammersmith Palais. The dressmaker really has done an excellent job with that velvet.'

The pretty gold locket that Tilly's father had given her mother as a wedding present gleamed softly against Tilly's skin. Her eyes had filled with tears when Olive had suggested she should wear it.

'Your dad would have been so proud of you, and it's right that you take a bit of him with you tonight to look out for you,' Olive had said.

281

Agnes's dress was just as pretty but a slightly different style to Tilly's, with a gathered skirt that added a bit of a curve to Agnes's thinness.

Olive shifted her attention from the two younger girls to Sally and Dulcie. Sally was wearing a quietly elegant silk dress in dark green that suited her colouring, whilst, predictably in Olive's opinion, Dulcie's dress, which was also silk, was very glamorous with a wrap round V-necked bodice and a straight skirt that flared out at the knee. The silk, a pretty pale green, was sprigged with soft pink roses with darker green stems and leaves, and a fabric covered belt cinched in Dulcie's narrow waist. A double row of fake pearls and matching pearl earrings in Dulcie's neatly shaped ears finished off her ensemble and she did look good in it, Olive was forced to admit – very elegant and stylish although the look was rather older than Olive felt suitable for a girl so young.

Olive didn't miss the challenging tilt of Dulcie's chin as they exchanged looks. There was nothing she could say, though, not without risking spoiling Tilly's night, and of course she didn't want to do that.

Instead she hugged her daughter and then Agnes, telling them truthfully, 'You all look lovely.'

Within minutes the girls all had their coats on and were going out of the front door, leaving the house feeling very empty and quiet without them.

An hour later Tilly was gazing round the interior of the Palais, still half unable to believe that she was actually here. The packed ballroom had been decorated for Christmas and everyone was in high spirits.

There was a large Christmas tree illuminated with multicoloured fairy lights in the entrance foyer, but well back from the doors so as not to break the blackout laws. Red and green paper garlands decorated the ceiling, coming from the walls to the huge glittering mirror ball suspended over the dance floor, whilst the male bar staff were wearing red waistcoats, and a cheery-looking Father Christmas, escorted by a bevy of pretty girls wearing short red dresses trimmed with white swansdown, went from table to table selling raffle tickets. The whole atmosphere was so exciting and filled with Christmas goodwill and fun that at first Tilly and Agnes could only stand and stare as they tried to take it all in.

'I never thought it would be like this,' Tilly gasped in delight. 'I mean, I knew it would be wonderful . . .'

When she stopped, lost for words, Dulcie informed her knowledgably, 'Well, it is the best dancehall in London,' before leading them all speedily to 'her' table, a move that Sally recognised was a good one, half an hour later as she looked to where some people were standing watching the dancing and reflected that she herself wouldn't have fancied standing up all evening. But then, aching feet were something she was familiar with, being a nurse.

Sally was used to the atmosphere of Liverpool's Grafton Ballroom, but she still had to admit that the Palais was impressive. No one could be here on a night like this and not be infected by the atmosphere of fizzing excitement and energy.

For Tilly, the atmosphere in the ballroom was almost magical, and she gazed round at her surroundings in thrilled delight, half unable to believe that she was actually here. The church hall could never compare with something like this. Her eyes widened as she watched prettily dressed young women and their partners take to the floor. She felt so . . . so grown up and special just being here.

'Oh, isn't this wonderful?' she mouthed to Agnes above the sound of the Joe Loss Orchestra.

'I hadn't realised it would be so big or that there'd be so many people here,' Agnes mouthed back, her own feelings tending more towards apprehension than excitement. She didn't much like crowds.

A waiter stopped at their table, asking if they wanted drinks.

'Lemonade for us,' Sally said firmly, indicating Tilly, Agnes and herself.

'Yes, and for me as well,' Dulcie surprised her by agreeing.

The reality was that whilst Dulcie would have a shandy if one was pressed on her, she had seen enough of what too much alcohol could do in her own neighbourhood to want to end up the worse for drink herself. There was Ma Bowker, who lived round the corner from her own parents, the whole family crammed into three rooms they rented in a tenanted house. Ma Bowker liked nothing more than rolling up her sleeves and laying into both her kids and her husband, giving them a real battering when she was in drink. Then there were the husbands who regularly knocked their wives about, and then 'up' after too much to drink; men who drank so much of their wages that there wasn't enough left to feed their families. Dulcie wanted no part of that. Her own father thankfully wasn't a big drinker. He liked his pint on a Friday and a Saturday, just as he liked his bet at the dogs, but that was all.

There were plenty of women dancing together, Tilly noticed, but when she suggested to Dulcie that they did the same, Dulcie shook her head firmly.

'It looks like you can't get a proper partner if you do that, and besides, we won't be sitting here long. The best-looking girls always get asked to dance.'

As though to prove her point, just as she finished saying this four young men approached their table. However, before they could so much as open their mouths, Dulcie was saying firmly, 'No, thanks, we aren't dancing right now. We're just waiting for our drinks.'

Dulcie's manner was rather different from what she had expected, Sally had to admit, ruefully.

'We can do better than that,' Dulcie explained. 'Much better. You've got to make sure that lads know how lucky they are when you agree to have a dance with them,' she informed Tilly and Agnes firmly.

Their drinks arrived, delivered by a smiling red-waistcoated waiter, and Sally paid for them using the money Olive had given her for that purpose when she'd asked Sally to keep an eye on what Tilly and Agnes had to drink.

Dulcie had told herself not to expect to see David. She'd achieved her goal and that was that. David might have said that they were two of a kind but Dulcie disagreed. He was posh – a toff – and he'd marry Lydia. To him she was just a bit of fun, a way of breaking the rules before he knuckled down to the right kind of marriage. Dulcie knew that, but she also knew where her own boundaries lay and she wasn't going to let David cross them. Besides, it made her feel good to realise that he'd rather be with her than Lydia. Lydia might look down her nose at her, but Dulcie could feel she had one up on her because Lydia's fiancé secretly fancied her. There was no way, though, that she was going to end up as David's bit on the side. That wasn't how Dulcie envisaged her future at all. Ultimately she would marry, and the kind of respectable man she wanted as her husband – a man with a good job, perhaps even in an office, who could afford to buy them a house like those in Article Row, or perhaps even in one of those new suburbs she'd seen advertised – would not want a wife who'd been carrying on with other men. Dulcie viewed her planned future without sentiment. All women had to marry – how else could they manage financially? But she was determined that her marriage would give her a better life than her mother and their neighbours had.

Dulcie had no illusions about herself. Men would always be attracted to her because of her looks, more the wrong kind of men than the right kind. It was up to her to make sure that when she let the wrong kind, like David, treat her to the good things in life, they did so on the understanding that she was merely trading with them the right to enjoy having a pretty girl on their arm, but not the right to expect sexual favours.

Living in Article Row, like working in Selfridges, was for Dulcie a step in the direction she wanted her life to go. Both conferred on her a certain status that, for all her mother's boasting about Edith's singing, allowed Dulcie to feel that she had moved 'up' socially from her background. She might milk these benefits for all that she could but there was no way she was going to risk losing them by going too far.

She looked at Tilly, flushed and excited. She had almost pushed Olive too far with that business of Tilly lying to her, Dulcie knew, which was why tonight she intended any report that Sally made back to Olive to be one that showed her in a good light and not a bad one.

To Tilly, filled with the excitement of the evening, simply being at the Palais was initially enough to fill her with happiness, but then eventually, tapping her foot in time to the music became a longing to be up on the floor and dancing.

Then Ted arrived, coming over to their table, to be welcomed by a shyly delighted Agnes, who introduced them.

Dulcie cast one look over Ted's plain honest face and shiny clean appearance, and immediately dismissed him as unimportant, whilst Sally duly registered Ted's discreetly protective manner towards Agnes and politeness to everyone else, and mentally agreed with Olive's judgement that Ted seemed a decent sort.

Ted, for his part, was glad to draw up a seat next to Agnes, and take charge of ordering the girls second drinks, rather than having to suggest that he and Agnes had a dance. He wasn't much of a dancer. He preferred to sit and watch, and it seemed to him that Agnes was of much the same mind.

The sensation of someone tapping on her shoulder, just as the band struck up for a new dance, had Dulcie stiffening, fighting against the betraying race of her heart, and trying to deny the name that immediately sprang to her lips.

Only the voice in her ear saying, 'I thought I'd find you here,' belonged not to David but to her brother, Rick.

'Rick, you're home!' Genuinely pleased, Dulcie turned round to find, not only her brother, but a whole group of other young men in army uniform clustered behind her.

'Got back this afternoon,' Rick told her, adding cheerfully, 'Is it OK if we join you?' and then calling for his comrades to collect some chairs, without waiting for Dulcie's reply.

There were five of them all together; Rick; a tow-headed young man with a northern accent, called Ned, who came from Manchester and who Rick said was their corporal; two boys from London, named Ian and Fred; and, a little to Dulcie's surprise, John Dunham, whose father was the builder for whom her own father sometimes worked.

'I thought you were going to join the navy,' she commented when John sat down next to her.

'I was, until Rick persuaded me to enlist in the army then as luck would have it we ended up in the same regiment – the Middlesex, 7th Battalion,' he said proudly, 'and the same company.'

From the minute she had seen Rick, Tilly's heart had been thumping with excitement and teenage self-consciousness. If anything he looked even more handsome than he had done before, bigger somehow, broader, and very manly and grown up in his uniform, with his dark hair cut close to his scalp. The other men looked shorn and rather forlorn with their short back and sides army-regulation haircuts, but in Rick's case the short cut only served to emphasise his well-shaped head.

'Mum won't be very pleased when she hears you've come down here. Not with Edith singing with ENSA,' Dulcie said somewhat sarcastically as she mimicked their mother's voice for the last few words.

Typically, though, Rick merely grinned. 'Yes, I heard all about that the minute I got through the door. Ta, yes, John, I'll have a beer, thanks,' he broke off as John was asking what everyone wanted to drink. 'Ma says that Edith's got an agent now.'

John was asking what Dulcie wanted to drink now but before she could show off her sophistication by announcing that she'd have a gin and it, Rick was telling his friend cheerfully, 'She'll have a shandy, John.'

'I was going to have a gin and it,' Dulcie told him crossly. 'And as for Edith's agent, he's a real spiv, and I told Mum that she was a fool for letting Edith take up with him, but of course she wouldn't have it. You know what she's like. She's always thought that the sun shines out of Edith's backside and now she thinks the same about this agent.'

'Ma said that you're having your Christmas dinner at your lodgings instead of coming home.'

'Yes. My landlady asked me in particular to have my dinner with them,' Dulcie fibbed, turning away so that none of the other girls could hear her.

Sally thanked the young corporal who was handing her her drink. She'd been a bit worried at first when Dulcie's brother had proposed that he and his friends join them, but the respectful manner in which the young soldiers were behaving towards them had calmed her fears. Dulcie's brother was a very good-looking young man, and it was no wonder that Tilly was looking at him with such admiration, Sally acknowledged ruefully. Once she had probably looked at Callum like that. The pain that thought brought her was swift and savage.

'What are we doing sitting here when we could be dancing?' Rick demanded jovially, giving Tilly an appreciative smile. She really was a looker, even if she was a bit on the young side. 'John, you dance with Dulcie,' he instructed, 'but mind she doesn't step on your toes; she's got two left feet,' he teased his sister, before holding out his hand to Tilly.

'Do you want to take pity on a poor soldier who hasn't seen a pretty girl in months and dance with him?' he asked with a warm smile.

Did she? Tilly was speechless with delight.

The corporal asked Sally up, causing Ted to reach for Agnes's hand and give it a little squeeze when she confided in him, 'I'm glad it's you that's asked me to dance, Ted, because I'm not very good at it at all. Because I was one of the oldest at the orphanage, I always had to be the boy when we did any dancing.'

Two minutes later they were all on the floor, Dulcie proving that she was as light on her feet as a proverbial feather, her steps confidently in perfect time with the music.

When Agnes whispered to him happily, 'Oh, Ted, you are ever such a good dancer,' Ted's chest swelled. Agnes felt so fragile and delicate, like something precious that he wanted to protect from harm. She looked a treat too in her new dress. He just hoped that one of those army lads didn't step in and catch her eye.

Tilly was in heaven, dancing on clouds of delirious excitement and delight. Never had there been such a wonderful Christmas gift, she thought giddily as Rick swung her expertly through the dance. But all too soon it came to an end, the light dimming to signal the interval between the orchestra's sessions. Then, just as the dancers were starting to disengage from their partners and drift off the floor, a young man wearing an RAF uniform jumped onto the stage and said something to the band leader, who nodded and then made an announcement.

'As a special request we're going to play the last waltz before the interval so that the flight lieutenant can share it with his new fiancée before he has to catch his train and get back on duty.'

Above the laughter and cheers of the crowd, the first strains of a waltz began. Rick had started to move back to their table, but since Tilly was still standing looking at the orchestra, he too stopped moving. The lights were still dimmed, couples swaying together, locked in their own personal worlds. Silently Tilly went into Rick's arms, trembling slightly when they closed round her. This was beyond heaven, this was . . . there were no words to name it, no previous experiences in her life with which to compare it. This was special, wonderful, a time out of time that would remain with her for the rest of her life, Tilly promised herself fervently as she instinctively moved closer to Rick.

The girls in Paris, at least the ones Rick had met, had been available – for a price – but dancing with them had not proved as tempting as dancing with Tilly, Rick acknowledged. He had felt her small betraying tremble when he had taken her in his arms, and now he was beginning to wonder if she would tremble as sweetly if he kissed her. And he did want to kiss her. The first time he had met her he had dismissed her as a pretty young girl, little more than a schoolgirl, really, but tonight when he had looked at her sitting with Dulcie he had seen a very desirable young woman. The music was offering him an opportunity to get closer to her that it would be a crime to ignore. A girl's head was surely designed to rest on a chap's shoulder, her soft curls brushing his chin. The low lights and romantic music were certainly designed to allow a man to whisper softly in his partner's ear that she looked lovely and that he was glad that she had chosen to dance with him.

Rick's breath against her ear sent desperately exciting shivers racing through Tilly's body, his compliment swelling a heart already tender with youthful adoration. Tilly lifted her head and looked up into Rick's face.

As Rick looked back at her the dim light seemed to enhance the delicacy of her profile and the shine in her eyes. He guided her arm around his side and then released his hand to lift it to her face to cup it as their movements slowed to a barely there sway. Enclosed by the crowd, lost in her own disbelieving delight, Tilly swallowed against the tension seizing hold of her.

Rick was going to kiss her.

Her heart gave a gigantic thump and then a series of flurried excited beats as he lowered his head toward her.

He *was* going to kiss her!

'The orchestra has stopped playing, in case you two hadn't noticed.'

Dulcie's sharp voice sliced into their privacy and its promise, shattering their intimacy. Instead of kissing Tilly, Rick drew his fingertip the length of her nose and then released her, guiding her back towards the table.

Sally, who hadn't seen what was going on between Tilly and Rick on the dance floor, was still concerned enough just by Tilly's now besotted expression to take hold of the younger girl's hand and pull her gently down into the empty seat the young corporal had just vacated to go to the bar, so that Tilly was sitting safely between her and Agnes and not therefore able to cosy up with Dulcie's handsome brother. Sally didn't need to ask herself what Olive would think of her vulnerable young daughter falling for Rick. Olive would not like it one little bit.

Dulcie, whilst equally aware of Olive's probable reaction to any burgeoning romance between Tilly and Rick, was less tactful with her brother than Sally had been with Tilly and a good deal more forceful, grabbing hold of Rick's arm to prevent him from following Tilly off the floor and then out of earshot of the others, hissing at him, 'And you can stop flirting with Tilly, and getting her all baby-eyed over you.'

'I was just dancing with her, that's all.'

'You were not just dancing,' Dulcie told him forthrightly. 'You want to watch out, Rick, because she's daft enough to fall head over heels for you.'

'So what if she does?'

Knowing what Olive's reaction would be if she could hear Rick, and guessing she'd blame Dulcie herself for sure, and probably throw her out, Dulcie asked her brother, 'That's what you want, is it, some daft kid getting soppy over you and then perhaps you ending up married with a baby on the way?'

Rick's horrified expression told its own story.

'I danced with her, Dulcie, that's all,' he defended himself.

'Yes, well, you'd better make sure you don't do any more dancing with her, 'cos I promised her mother that I'd keep an eye on her and that's exactly what I intend to do.'

That was a lie, of course, but it fitted too neatly into the story Dulcie had told her mother for her to be able to resist it.

'In fact, if you know what's good for you you'd better make sure she knows that you aren't available, because if she thinks you're messing with her Tilly, then her mother will be after you to put an engagement ring on her finger,' Dulcie insisted.

'I danced with her, that's all,' Rick repeated.

'Her mother won't see it that way. Not if Tilly goes home and starts telling her mum that she's falling for you,' Dulcie warned him.

Rick wasn't the sort to push himself onto a girl. He didn't need to. He normally had to fight them off, and he'd soon find someone else to flirt and dance with, Dulcie told herself as they both made their way back to the table.

Rick had taken his sister's words to heart. He liked Tilly, and her girlish and obvious hero worship had swelled his chest and increased his appreciation of her. However, Dulcie's warnings about the dangers of having Tilly fall in love with him had hit home. There was a lad in their platoon who'd got a girl into trouble just before he'd enlisted, and now he was a married man at nineteen and bitterly resented being tied down. Rick certainly didn't want that to happen to him. He'd have to cool things down between him and Tilly and keep his distance from her for the rest of the evening.

All Tilly's joy in the evening had gone. Rick was ignoring her. He hadn't even looked at her since they'd sat down after their dance, despite the imploring looks she'd given him. Now he'd actually turned his back on her to laugh with his friends as he sat two chairs away from her next to the quiet soldier who was sitting next to Dulcie. Tilly's misery was as intense as her earlier happiness had been, and threatened to overwhelm her.

Normally the sight of Tilly's unhappy face would have been enough to have Rick's resolve slipping. He liked Tilly, after all, and hated to see her looking so miserable, but Dulcie's warning about the likely reaction of Tilly's mother, coupled with his knowledge of the fate of his army mate hardened Rick's resolve. Flirting with a pretty girl, dating her, and even getting a bit sweet on her was one thing, but marriage – that was something different altogether. The last thing Rick wanted to do right now was tie himself down and become a family man. It wasn't easy, though, for him to ignore Tilly's distress when he asked other girls to dance. The poor kid couldn't hide what she was feeling. That was his fault for having encouraged her like he had, of course. Part of him wanted to act the big brother with her and warn her that it wasn't in her own interests to let any lad see her feelings so plainly, and that she should take a leaf out of Dulcie's book and act cool and dismissive around lads, but of course he couldn't do that. All he could do was make it plain to her that he wasn't the going steady or settling down type.

Agnes felt ever so happy. She was comfortable with Ted. He didn't make her feel awkward and shy. He understood without her having to say anything that she was content simply to sit at his side, and drink her lemonade whilst they exchanged snatches of conversation.

'Got anything fixed up for New Year's Eve?'
    The feigned indifference in John's voice didn't fool Dulcie. John had always been a bit keen on her, but she wasn't particularly interested in him. Her dad might go on about how lucky John's father was having his own business to hand on to his son – if you could call repairing chimneys and fitting new windows and doors and doing general repairs a business, which Dulcie did not – but Dulcie wasn't impressed. In her view John didn't have enough backbone about him. He was too

willing to go along with others – his dad, her brother, Rick, and of course her, if she had wanted him to do so.

In response to his question she gave a dismissive shrug. 'I've had a couple of offers, but I haven't made up my mind which one I'm going to accept yet.'

John nodded. Dulcie could see that he was disappointed but she didn't really care. The last thing she wanted was to be tied to someone as dull as John for New Year's Eve. If Rick was still on leave, then he could come here with her, she decided. That way she'd have a partner and the freedom to exchange him for someone else, if someone better came along.

The MC was announcing the final dance of the evening, an end that couldn't come fast enough, as far as Tilly was now concerned. Every bit as much as she'd longed to be here, she now longed to be at home. Especially now, with the last dance having been announced, and with it her last hope of Rick dancing with her again gone as he remained on the floor with the girl with whom he'd had the last two dances.

Tilly's heart ached with envy. Rick's partner was petite and blonde and full of confidence. Tilly had seen that from the way she'd showed off her dance steps when she'd first danced with Rick, twirling round so that the full skirt of her bright blue spotted dress rose up to show off her slim legs. She was pretty too, and fun. Tilly had seen the way Rick had laughed at something she'd said to him. It was obvious to Tilly that Rick preferred the blonde girl's company to her own and all she wanted to do was get home and give way to her tears.

SIXTEEN

Olive glanced anxiously at Tilly. Her daughter had been very subdued all day. At first Olive had put this down to the excitement of going to the Palais combined with her late night, but as the day had worn on and Tilly had showed no signs of reverting to her normal cheerful self, Olive's anxiety had grown.

Tilly had always loved Christmas so much, wanting to be involved in all the preparations for it, but today, when Olive had been busy baking and cooking, it had been Agnes who had done the most to help her, her excitement in sharp contrast to Tilly's withdrawal.

Now Olive, Tilly and Agnes were sitting in the church hall, watching the dancers enjoying themselves to music provided by the vicar's loaned radiogram. Several times Olive had urged Agnes and Tilly to get up and dance, but Agnes had protested that she wasn't a good dancer, and Tilly had simply shaken her head and said that she didn't feel like dancing.

Tilly saw her mother looking at her and bit her

300

lip. If she wasn't careful her mother was going to guess that something was wrong and then she would start asking questions and then . . . The last thing Tilly wanted was for her mother to know how silly she had been. Seeing her mother's face creased with anxiety made Tilly feel very guilty. There was no point in her continuing to make herself miserable over Rick, she told herself. He certainly wouldn't be sitting somewhere thinking about her and feeling miserable because she wasn't there, would he?

Just as she was thinking that, Mrs Windle came over, leading a young man wearing a St John Ambulance uniform.

'Tilly, Christopher is new to our congregation. He and his parents have just moved into number forty-nine Article Row, next to Mr Whittaker,' she announced. 'He doesn't know many people yet, so it would help him to make friends if you'd be kind enough to dance with him.'

He wouldn't get to know many people living next to Mr Whittaker, a veteran of the last war who was something of a recluse. Tilly's grandmother had always said that it was the disappearance of his wife and the gossip that had caused that had led to Mr Whittaker retreating into himself. The talk had been that she had run off with another man she had got involved with whilst Len Whittaker had been in France fighting for his country.

Now, with the vicar's wife smiling at her, Tilly got to her feet. She didn't want to dance but she was far too polite to refuse. The newcomer – Christopher – was pleasant enough looking, with his thick heavy fairish hair, and hazel eyes, but he was very quiet, and Tilly thought that he must be shy.

Trying to put him at his ease, she smiled and said, 'Are your parents here this evening?'

'No, my father isn't very well. He has a bad chest. The last war. He did have a job but he's retired now.'

Tilly was immediately sympathetic. 'Oh, I'm so sorry.' She paused, then told him, 'My own father died because of that war. I can't remember him because he died when I was very young.'

They'd reached the dance floor and Tilly turned to him but he stood back from her, his face going bright red as he told her fiercely, 'Before you dance with me there's something I have to tell you, and then if you don't want to dance with me you don't have to.'

'If you're going to tell me that you've got two left feet,' Tilly began to joke, brought out of her own misery by his obvious awkwardness and her own desire to help others.

'No.' He looked at her and then blurted out, 'I'm a conscientious objector – to the war you know. I won't fight. I don't believe in it.'

Tilly stared at him, and then said uncertainly, 'But you're in uniform.'

'Only to help those who need help. People call me a coward, and I suppose you'll think the same. But I don't care. I've seen what war can do.'

Tilly didn't know what to think. The music started up – a barn dance; she couldn't just walk away and leave him.

'I don't think you're a coward,' she told him truthfully. 'In fact I think you must have to be fearfully brave to refuse to fight.' She reached for his hand, pulling him into the dance, a protective feeling similar to the one she felt for Agnes filling her.

'Sergeant Dawson.' Olive gave the sergeant a warm smile when she saw him approaching her, his helmet under his arm.

'I've just come off duty and since I had to pass by on my way home I thought I'd call in and make sure that there wasn't any trouble. Sometimes young lads get a bit too full of themselves at this time of year.'

A bit too full of drink, the sergeant meant, Olive knew, but he was too discreet to say that.

'I'm surprised to see you sitting out instead of dancing,' he added.

'Oh, my dancing days are over. I've only come tonight because of Tilly and Agnes.'

Although she was smiling, Olive suddenly and unexpectedly felt a small pang of sadness. She used to love dancing; Jim had always said that she was as light as a feather on her feet.

'Me and Mrs Dawson used to really enjoy going dancing,' Sergeant Dawson told her, 'but that was before we had our boy, of course.'

Christmas must be a very sad and lonely time for the Dawsons, Olive thought, her sympathy for them driving away her own momentary sense of loss.

Sergeant Dawson was standing up, announcing, 'I'd better get on.'

'Oh, yes. You won't want Mrs Dawson worrying.'

'She'll have gone to bed. She doesn't sleep well and she says my snoring keeps her awake if she doesn't get off first. She prefers it when I'm working nights.' He was holding out his hand to her so Olive extended hers so that he could shake it, her hand almost engulfed by his, the feel of his skin against her own warm and roughly male. How long had it been since she had felt the touch of a male hand against her flesh in a caress of intimacy and love?

Quickly Olive snatched her hand free, guilt and confusion staining her face with hot colour. What on earth had got her thinking like that? She'd been a widow for sixteen years and never once during that time had she so much as thought of another man. She hadn't had the time or the inclination. And she didn't now, Olive assured herself, as she made herself focus on the dancers.

It was getting dressed up in her new frock that had done it, Olive decided. She knew she shouldn't have given in to Tilly's pleas to have something 'nice' made from the velvet she and Agnes had bought her.

On the dance floor Tilly tried to draw Christopher out of his shyness. Concentrating on him was far less painful than thinking about last night and the way Rick hadn't so much as looked at her after their dance, never mind asked her to stand up with him again. It must be as Dulcie had told her on their way home: Rick preferred older girls who

304

knew what was what and that he'd only danced with her because Dulcie had asked him to do so.

In the papers conscientious objectors were often vilified and labelled as cowards. But Tilly felt more sorry for Christopher than contemptuous of him for not joining up.

'What made you become a conscientious objector?' she asked him curiously as they stood together in the queue for the buffet table.

'I don't agree with wars and fighting, and killing people. Not after what the last war did to my father.' His gaze burned with intensity as he spoke.

'But the country has to be defended from Hitler,' Tilly told him.

He didn't make any response, turning away from her.

'Mrs Windle said that your family had only recently moved here, but most people are moving out of London, not into it,' Tilly persisted, trying to engage him in conversation.

'We used to live with my grandmother, but she died six months ago, and with me being in the civil service Mum said it made sense for us to move over here.'

Tilly nodded. There were a lot of Government offices in the Holborn area, including Somerset House.

'Mr Ryder from number eighteen, who's retired, used to work at Somerset House,' she informed Christopher, 'and Mr King, who owns six of the houses lower down the Row, used to have several tenants who worked in the civil service. Most of them have moved out now because of the war.'

When Christopher made no response Tilly suppressed a small sigh. She was a sociable girl who enjoyed the company of others and meeting new people, but trying to get him to talk was like drawing teeth, she decided ruefully. But good manners meant that she had to keep trying.

They'd almost reached the buffet table so she changed the subject and told him proudly, 'You must have one of the mince pies, and a sausage roll. My mother made them.'

He nodded and then blurted out, 'I'd prefer it if you call me Kit, not Christopher, and thanks . . . for dancing with me. I don't think the vicar really approves of me being a conscientious objector, only, being a man of God, he can't really say so.'

'You're still doing your bit,' Tilly told him stoutly, indicating his St John Ambulance uniform.

The dance finished early, in time for the midnight carol service. As Tilly told her mother, linking arms with both her and Agnes as they set off for number 13 afterwards, there was something special about singing carols on Christmas Eve.

At St Barts, Sally shared Tilly's feelings, her eyes stinging slightly with emotion when she left the chapel where one of the chaplains had just finished conducting the Christmas Eve midnight service.

'We never did get to manage that meal out together,' George Laidlaw told her, catching up with her as she walked down the corridor.

She'd seen the young doctor only briefly since

his return from his posting with their evacuated colleagues, their only exchange brief nods of recognition, and sometimes a few words as they went about their duties.

'The theatre lists have been busy,' she told him. 'With most of the staff evacuated and a reduced number of operating theatres, there's been more pressure on those that there are, especially with all the blackout accidents that have been coming in.'

'If you haven't already got a partner for the hospital's New Year's Ball, and you aren't on duty, perhaps you'd consider letting me take you to that?'

Automatically Sally opened her mouth to refuse and then closed it again. What was the point in looking backwards to what might have been?

'I'm not on duty, and yes, I'd like that,' she answered.

'You will?' George looked delighted.

Ten minutes later as she stepped out into the cold night air, her cloak wrapped warmly round her, Sally discovered that she was still smiling at George's obvious pleasure in her acceptance.

PART TWO

June 1940

SEVENTEEN

'Is there any more news about Dunkirk?' Tilly asked Olive anxiously, having raced home from work to change into her St John Ambulance uniform, ignoring the discomfort of its heaviness in the heat of the early June afternoon. Like the rest of the country, she had far more on her mind than herself.

'No real news, but according to Mrs Windle the troop trains are still full when they reach London, which must mean something.'

Dunkirk. How quickly the name had become familiar, so that over the space of a handful of days it was on everyone's lips, the echo of its horror and bravery the beat of everyone's heart.

Dunkirk – the beach beyond which the British Expedition Force had retreated until they could retreat no further, after the Germans had smashed through the supposedly unsmashable Maginot Line.

Dunkirk – from where not just the might of the British Establishment but the love and bravery of Britain's ordinary citizens, in their small vessels, had plucked the waiting men to safety, bearing them home across the Channel in voyage after voyage.

Olive and Tilly had seen what Dunkirk had done to once-proud fighting men. Olive manned one of the many WVS tea urns, and Tilly helped the walking wounded when they arrived at St Pancras station, one of the London stations into which troop trains came pouring to disgorge weary retreat-scarred men from the British Expeditionary Force; men who had left behind in France not only their guns and equipment but also their pride.

In three short days Tilly felt she had left her own youth behind her, just as those men had left behind them their dead comrades and their self-belief. The sight of grown men with blank expressions and eyes that constantly looked beyond her, as her St John Ambulance unit worked amongst the wounded, no longer shocked her as it had done that first day.

Men in dirty mud-spattered uniforms, rank with the dried sweat of fear, who couldn't look her in the eye; men with dirty bandages wrapped around wounds; men who broke down and wept with shame and relief when they were greeted with a hot cup of tea and a warm smile – Tilly had seen them all.

Because it was her turn to drive the WVS van, Olive said that she would take Tilly to St Pancras along with the members of her WVS unit she was due to pick up from the vicarage. Crouched in the back of the van, Tilly was filled with admiration for the way her mother drove, manoeuvring it with the new confidence the last few days had given her. Olive had even been co-opted into ferrying some of the walking wounded to various London hospitals for out-patient treatment.

The most seriously injured men and the stretcher cases had been sent to hospitals closer to the coast, Sally had told them. The London hospitals were only dealing with the more minor cases; cleaning up wounds, before the men travelled onward to take advantage of the two weeks of home leave they had all been granted.

One of Tilly's jobs had been to check with those arriving at St Pancras that they had sent off one of the postcards they had been issued with on arrival on British shores, to tell their relatives they were safe.

It was as she handed out postcards to those who, for one reason or another, had not already sent them that she had a glimpse of what was concealed behind the men's blank expressions, as though the thought of those waiting for them at home was the key that turned the lock on their emotions.

This evening the number of men filling the platforms seemed larger than ever.

Craning her neck, Tilly tried to see where the milling mass ended, as she and Agnes stood together with their bag of postcards and their instructions to send those men who looked most in need of medical attention to the St John Ambulance post behind them on the station's main waiting area, where they would be checked over and dealt with or sent on to hospital for further medical treatment.

Men were caked in a mixture of mud from the

retreat across France, sand from the beaches, salt from the Channel and, in some cases, oil as well. After three days Tilly had learned enough to know that oil meant the men had been rescued from torpedoed ships.

Down at the other end of the concourse, closer to the exit, her mother, along with various other WVS groups, would be serving the men tea and biscuits, the first drink, some men told her, they had had since leaving France.

A soldier, grey-skinned and dead-eyed, standing in the line a couple of yards away from them caught Tilly's eye. He was being supported by the man next to him, who looked equally done in.

'Grab these two,' Tilly told Agnes, the two girls stepping up to the men, and only just in time, Tilly recognised as the soldier being supported stumbled, and almost fell into her arms.

'Sorry, miss,' his companion, hollow-cheeked with exhaustion, his face grimy with oil and dirt, apologised. 'No offence.'

'None taken,' Tilly assured him, gesturing to her uniform. 'That's what we're here for. Has he got any injuries, do you know?'

She could almost see the soldier, who had been looking defensive and wary, relax a little at her words, as Tilly gently set the semi-conscious man back to his feet so that his companion could once again support him.

Tilly had learned that every soldier seemed to have a pal, a mate, someone from his unit who stood by him and for him, and who took charge of him when he was injured.

314

'Shrapnel in his leg. They wanted to hospitalise him when we came ashore but he refused. He's from up north – Newcastle – and he wants to get home. His brother's bought it, see, and he wants to tell his mam and dad himself. Doesn't want them to hear from anyone else.'

Tilly nodded and swallowed back her pity, telling the soldier, 'That's all very well but his parents won't thank him if he makes his own wounds worse. That leg needs attending to.' They both looked down at where fresh blood was seeping through the grimy bandage wrapped round the other soldier's thigh.

Tilly could see both relief and gratitude in the companion's eyes. 'Just as well he's out of it,' he told Tilly with an attempt at a grin. 'That's the trouble with these ruddy North-Easterners, they don't know when they're down.'

'Got to get home,' the injured man suddenly muttered, pulling away from his friend. 'Got to tell me mam and dad about our Tommy.'

He lurched forward and then stopped his eyes widening with shock before he looked down at his own thigh. Bright red blood was now soaking through the bandage. He put his hand on it and then removed it, staring at his own bloodstained hand.

He was haemorrhaging, Tilly guessed.

'Quick, Agnes, go and get Mr Ogden. Tell him we've got a haemorrhage. We need to lie him down and lift his leg up.'

Almost before she had finished speaking soldiers were moving into action, clearing a space, lying

315

their comrade down. Tilly had her first-aid kit with her, but it contained only the basics, she was reluctant to apply a makeshift tourniquet when there might be shrapnel in the wound that her actions could push in further.

The soldier had opened his eyes, and Tilly could see the panic in them.

'It's all right,' she told him softly. 'You're home now, and you're safe.'

'Gotta see me mam. Don't let me die before I've seen her,' he pleaded, tears filling his eyes and running down his cheeks, making clean runnels in the dirt.

'We won't let you die,' Tilly assured him. He had reached for her hand and she held it tightly, and kept holding it just as she held his gaze as Agnes returned with the leader of their brigade and two of the more senior members.

'It might be a shrapnel wound,' Tilly told the brigade leader quietly. 'He wouldn't let them hospitalise him when he came ashore. He wants to get home to tell his parents about the loss of his brother.'

The other members of the brigade were working quickly and efficiently to stem the bleeding as Tilly spoke, sliding a stretcher beneath the young soldier.

It wasn't until the soldier was being stretchered away that Tilly looked up and realised that one of the men who had assisted with him was Dulcie's brother, Rick, although she had to look twice before she could be sure that it was him. There was no sign of the good-looking charm on his face now. Even his curt nod in her direction in confirmation of his recognition of her was a world away from the easy manner she remembered. Not that she had any fondness for Dulcie's brother now. He had led her on, no doubt to boost his own ego, without thinking how she might feel about his behaviour. She had been such a naive girl then, she thought ruefully with the benefit of nearly six months of extra maturity behind her. An idiot, really, to be taken in by someone as vain as Rick, and not worth wasting her tears on. Well, she knew better now. She was a popular girl, with young men eager to take her out, but Tilly had learned her lesson in one sharp and very painful evening. She would never allow herself to be so gullible or easily hurt again. Nor would she ever be naive enough again to fall for a handsome face. In fact, she was off men, full stop, and had decided that instead of risking getting her heart broken she was going to concentrate on putting her energy into helping as much as she could with the war effort.

Her glance at Rick was cool and professional, letting him know that she wasn't the silly young girl who had quivered with delight just to be in his arms. Then she saw in his expression and bearing what she had seen in so many returning soldiers. It wasn't just the loss of friends and comrades that marked them, it was the loss of pride and confidence as well. They had been saved from potential death and imprisonment not by their own endeavours but by the endeavour of others, rescued from France's beaches like helpless

317

children, as one soldier had already described it to her.

'You stand there in line waiting, not knowing if you're even going to make it to the boats. Three days we were standing there waiting. It does something to you inside your head,' he had told her. 'It takes something from you that you know you'll never get back.'

Nodding brusquely at Tilly – how could a girl like her possibly understand the hell that had been Dunkirk? – Rick still felt raw and shocked by what he had experienced. Raw and shocked and shamed by the way they'd had to turn tail and run. It didn't matter how often he'd heard older, more experienced soldiers saying, 'He who fights and runs away lives to fight another day,' his pride, not just in himself but in his country, had been put through a firestorm from which he had emerged harder, angrier and determined to defeat the Germans . . .

Rick turned away from Tilly to rejoin the remnants of his unit. The lad who'd been stretchered away was seventeen. He'd lied about his age so that he could enlist with his older brother, the brother they'd had to leave behind in the mud with his head shot off and his brains splattered all over the road, after an aerial attack by the Luftwaffe. Rick had yelled out a warning but Tommy had been helping a young mother with her children, carrying a young boy too exhausted to walk, as they fled along with others, because the Germans were invading their country.

The mother and her children had died with

Tommy, and the dozens of others the Luftwaffe had sprayed with gunfire.

Tommy's brother had insisted on burying what was left of Tommy, after he had finished throwing up. Rick suspected that the boy had half hoped to be killed himself, watching the risks he had taken afterwards.

It wasn't glorious and heroic: it was dying on the roadside with your head blown open; it was blackened arms and legs separated from rotting bodies strewn along the road to the coast like lifesize dolls' limbs; it was fear and sickness, and screams of agony, both physical and mental; it was the fury and frustration of standing in line on the beaches whilst the Luftwaffe blew you apart and the sky above you remained empty of the RAF. It was seeing grown men cry for their mothers, seeing men die slowly over the long hours they waited for rescue; it was feeling that you would die of thirst but knowing you couldn't risk losing your place in the line.

And after that, being back here in London, seeing people who were clean and not injured and safe, and knowing that they were as alien to you now as though they belonged to a separate race.

It was knowing that nothing ever could or would be the same.

Rick couldn't risk speaking to Tilly because if he did he was afraid that he would tell her these things that could not be told to anyone, least of all a young girl like her.

It was gone eight o'clock in the evening before the flood of men was reduced to a trickle, and Tilly

319

and Agnes were free to leave their posts and make their way over to where Olive was handing over responsibility for the tea urns to a new group of WVS.

'We saw Dulcie's brother,' Agnes announced as they headed for the parked van, 'didn't we, Tilly?'

'Yes. I had to look at him twice before I was sure it was him,' Tilly told her mother. 'All the soldiers look so defeated. It really tears at your heart. It isn't their fault, after all,' she defended her countrymen fiercely. 'Everyone said that the Maginot Line would hold Hitler back. So many of them are angry with the RAF and blame them for not doing more to hold the Luftwaffe at bay whilst they were retreating.'

'I know,' Olive agreed. 'I suppose it's because the Government feel they need to hold back the RAF to defend the country.'

Tilly saw the looks her mother exchanged with the other WVS members she was taking back to the church hall.

'You mean in case Hitler tries to invade?' Tilly pressed her.

There was a brief silence and then Olive admitted tiredly, 'Yes.'

It had to be faced after all, Olive acknowledged as she drove back to the church hall. Hitler had smashed through the defences of every country he had invaded, and now France too had fallen, something that no one had expected to happen. What was to stop them being next?

'The Germans will target London first,' Hilda Blackett, one of the WVS, warned them all, her

320

voice sounding prophetically through the cramped stuffiness of the back of the van, where Tilly and Agnes were sitting hunched up to occupy as little space as possible.

'Well, if he does let's hope we're better protected than the BEF,' another woman said grimly.

No one challenged her because they had all seen and heard too much to do so, Olive recognised.

It seemed ironic now that she had worried so much that going dancing at the Hammersmith Palais might encourage Tilly to grow up too soon, when over the last four days she had had to grow up so brutally fast with what she was having to witness. Tilly couldn't be protected from the cruel realities of war, though, not when men not much older than she was herself were returning from Dunkirk with the horror of what they had seen and experienced stamped so clearly on them.

On previous occasions Tilly had enjoyed the drive back to the church hall, happy in the knowledge of a job well done, secretly marvelling at her mother's skill and very proud of the fact that she was the driver, but tonight the events of the last few days and what they meant weighed too heavily on her for that. The expressions on the faces of Rick and the young injured soldier refused to be ejected from her memory. Such grimness and pain couldn't be forgotten or dismissed. Tonight she would say a special prayer to add to all her other prayers for the young man she had tended, in the hope that he would live to see his mother.

*　　*　　*

News of the British Expeditionary Force's retreat and the desperate efforts to bring home as many of them as was possible might have the rest of the household at number 13 scurrying around and doing their bit, but Dulcie wasn't going to allow it to change any of her plans.

Tonight was Saturday night and she was dancing at the Palais just as she would have been on any other Saturday night – especially since Arlene at work had read out to them all the news of David's marriage with Lydia.

Not that she had ever expected anything else. He had as good as said himself that he had no choice, and it wasn't as though she had ever tried, or wanted to try, to change his mind. She had done what she wanted to do, proved what she had wanted to prove, and that was an end to the matter. If Arlene thought that it meant anything to Dulcie to have his engagement announcement read out to her then she was wrong. Nevertheless, the fact that Arlene had made a point of showing it to her had rubbed against Dulcie's pride, as had the sly, almost knowing look that Arlene had given her when she had made a comment about like always marrying like. Dulcie had longed to tell her that David might have married Lydia but he certainly didn't love her, but she had held her tongue. After all, she hadn't wanted David herself. Not really. Because if she had done then Dulcie knew she would have made sure that she got him, Lydia and marriage or no Lydia and marriage.

Even so, her pride demanded that the girls

she worked with now needed to be shown that she could get a beau who was even more handsome than David. She wasn't going to have them gossiping about her behind her back and laughing at her, just because David had paid her a bit of attention. That meant having a new and, of course, adoring beau she could flaunt in front of her work colleagues.

A couple of young Australian soldiers caught her eye, but Dulcie speedily dismissed them. They might be tall but they were also gangly. No, her new beau had to be handsome and stand out as special, someone better-looking than David and more eye-catching. She studied the groups of men clustered close to the bar, but they appeared too ordinary for her purpose.

She looked away and then tensed as a familiar group of Italian men came in. They always hovered on the edge of the dance floor, eyeing up the girls, but those in the know were wary of dancing with them, knowing perfectly well what they were after and that they were all destined at some stage to obey their mothers and marry a girl of their own sort. Tonight, though, there was a man with them whom Dulcie didn't recognise, and she knew she would have done if she had seen him before. For a start he was taller than the others – at least six foot, she reckoned – and broader shouldered too. He even held himself differently, standing tall with his head up, not surveying the dancers surreptitiously but instead focusing on listening to the other man who was talking to him Best of all, though, he was good-looking. Very good-looking, matinée idol good-looking, Dulcie thought with growing satisfaction, and smartly dressed as well. He stood out against the group he was with like a silver coin in a handful of copper, and Dulcie made up her mind there and then that he was ideal for her purpose.

Confidently she got up from her seat at the table, saying over her shoulder to the girl sitting next to her, 'Save my seat, will you, only I'm just going to the lav.'

Opening her handbag as though in search of a handkerchief, her head down, it was easy for Dulcie to stage manage accidentally bumping into her target and then dropping her handbag in supposed shock.

Of course he would pick it up for her, that was what men did and what Dulcie expected, but what she hadn't expected was that he would also give her a level look from amused brown eyes, as though he knew perfectly well that what had happened was no accident.

Dulcie, though, didn't respond to the knowing gleam in his eyes. Instead she thanked him prettily for helping to collect the powder compact and brush that had fallen from her handbag and then, as they both stood up, Dulcie making sure that she was close enough for him to be aware of the scent she was wearing – a tester she had 'borrowed' from Selfridges and which she would have to return – before saying in a deliberately husky voice, 'How kind of you to help me. I don't know what I can do in return, except offer to dance with you. I'm Dulcie, by the way. What's your name?'

No red-blooded man could possibly resist her. Dulcie waited confidently for his delighted response.

But instead he bent his head and told her calmly, 'Raphael – Raphael Androtti, and I must say, Dulcie, that I'm surprised that an attractive girl like you needs to pull a trick like that in order to get a dancing partner. What was it? A bet with your girlfriends?'

Dulcie was stunned into momentary silence. No man had ever spoken to her like that before. By rights he ought to be falling over his own feet with gratitude, and what did he mean, describing her merely as attractive? She wasn't attractive, she was beautiful.

'No,' she denied his allegation, telling him crisply – after all, she had nothing to lose now so there was no point in being sugary sweet with him – 'I don't need to make bets about getting someone to dance with me, especially not one of your sort.'

'One of my sort? What's that supposed to mean?'

His manner was now as hostile as hers was dismissive.

'You're Italian,' she told him, not mincing her words. 'Everyone knows that the only reason Italian men come down here is because they're hoping to get from one of us what they know they'd never get from an Italian girl. That's why no one wants to dance with them.'

'Except you.'

'I was just trying to be kind.'

'How charitable of you, if that were true. But it isn't, is it? I saw the way you looked at me when

325

you were sitting down. You targeted me deliberately. Why?'

'No, I did not,' Dulcie denied furiously.

The Italian gave an exaggerated sigh that lifted and then lowered his impressively broad chest and then told her very slowly, 'In Liverpool, where I come from, the only reason a girl drops her handbag in front of a man is because she wants him to notice her, and if you're going to try to convince me that it isn't the same here, then I'm afraid I'm going to have to tell you that I don't believe you.'

'I don't care what you believe,' Dulcie snapped.

'But you did want me to dance with you.'

'No.'

'So then why the dropped handbag trick?'

He wasn't going to stop questioning her until he'd got the answer he wanted, Dulcie recognised, and the only way she was going to get rid of him was by telling him the truth. That way she could satisfy her own pride by making it clear to him that it wasn't him she was interested in.

'Someone I work with has recently got married. Her husband – before they were married – was showing a bit too much interest in me, and I thought she'd feel better if she thought I was involved with someone else,' Dulcie lied smoothly.

'By seeing you dancing with me?'

'No,' Dulcie corrected him. 'By coming to Selfridges, which is where I work, on the makeup floor. If you'd danced with me and asked to see me again then I could have suggested that you come into the store.'

'Funny how wrong you can be about a person,' he told her. 'Somehow you don't strike me as the kind of girl who puts another girl's feelings before her own.'

'Well, that just shows what a poor judge of character you are,' Dulcie informed him, before stepping past him and marching back to her chair, her back stiff with disdain.

No one had ever spoken to her as the Italian had done, and now Dulcie was angry with herself for telling him as much as she had done. Still, she'd rather have him knowing the truth, or at least a fictionalised version of it, than have him thinking that she had actually been interested in him as a man. The girls in Liverpool could do what they liked, but at least she'd made clear that in London things were different and that she wasn't in the least bit interested in getting his attention.

At Barts Sally prepared to finish her shift. She had already worked two hours longer than she should have to help with the influx of wounded soldiers. Of the supposedly walking wounded, many had turned out to have far more serious injuries than they had wanted to admit to.

There'd been an awful lot of cleaning of hastily bandaged wounds to do, a lot of removing shrapnel from men who had borne the probing of tweezers with stoic silence, their tears only coming when they spoke in the darkness of the night about fallen comrades and those who had not made it.

Sally was supposed to have been going to the pictures with George Laidlaw after his own shift finished but when they finally met up in the main entrance to the hospital it was so late and they were both so exhausted that they agreed that a cup of tea at Joe Lyons was all they felt up to.

Their friendship had grown over the months. Sally enjoyed George's company and, of course, they had a shared interest in talking 'shop' and a shared understanding of what it meant to be dealing with young men whose battle scars weren't always only from their physical wounds.

Sally loved her job and the extra responsibility she had been given, but she wouldn't have been human if she hadn't grieved for those boys who came into the theatre and then left it with their lives saved but far too often without a limb. It would have been hard to talk as openly with anyone else as she could with George about her professional pride in being part of a team that saved lives, but her distress at this being at the cost of an arm or a leg.

'It's their acceptance of what they've been through that does it for me,' George told Sally as she poured them each a cup of tea. 'Some of the tales they have to tell . . .' He paused and shook his head. But Sally knew what he meant.

'I had to remove half a dozen pieces of shrapnel from a sergeant tonight who swore that all he'd got was a bit of a cut. He never made a sound, but afterwards he cried like a baby when he was telling me about having to leave a dog he'd befriended behind on the beach.'

'I had a young lad in, leg badly damaged, and I reckon we've been able to save it. He reckons he'd have bled to death but for the medic on the naval vessel that picked him up after the boat he'd been in had been shot to pieces.'

Sally nodded, and then picked up her cup so that she could avoid looking directly at him whilst her heart was still thudding so fast. She was a fool to react like that simply because he'd mentioned a naval vessel. Callum could be anywhere, and anyway, what did it matter to her where he was?

'Some date this is,' George was saying ruefully as he reached for her hand.

Sally let him take it, but her thoughts weren't really with him. His mention of the navy had been as effective at holing her defences as Germany's torpedoes were at holing British ships. Now the unwanted thoughts she had thought successfully blocked were pouring in. And not just thoughts about Callum. She was acutely aware that the baby Callum had told her about would have been born by now. Her father's child. Her half-brother or -sister. The child of betrayal and adultery.

No one in Olive's household was more aware of the number of lives that had been lost than Sally. The newspaper lists of shipping losses were something she made herself avoid. After all, why should she worry about Callum when he didn't mean anything to her any more? She had been out on several dates with George now, and she enjoyed his company. They shared similar tastes in music, both great admirers of Dame Myra Hess and her lunchtime piano recitals at the National Gallery, preferring to attend a concert rather than go out dancing, just as they preferred the theatre to the cinema. George had a good sense of humour, and a manner that made Sally believe that he had the makings of a first-class consultant, although she knew that ultimately his plans were to return to New Zealand and follow in his father's footsteps as a GP. George hadn't said anything to her about them putting their friendship on a 'going steady' basis, but Sally suspected that he would. And if he did, what would she say to him, Sally asked herself as she entered the hospital, ready to start night duty.

Sally exhaled painfully. The truth was that she liked George, but she didn't think that right now, with a war on, was the time to get involved in a serious relationship. She had seen the strain and anxiety on the faces of those girls who had serious boyfriends, fiancés and husbands. She'd miss his friendship if she turned him down and he left her life, she knew, but was she really ready to start going steady?

EIGHTEEN

'Come on, Agnes, we'd better hurry otherwise we'll be late,' Tilly exhorted.

It was one of their St John Ambulance evenings and, having spent an hour in the garden removing weeds from Sally's vegetable plot, they were now later than they had planned setting out for the brigade's meeting in the church hall.

With the return of the BEF from France, the WVS, the St John Ambulance and various other voluntary organisations were all working at full stretch, with volunteers being asked to put in as many hours as they could. This meant that Tilly and Agnes were returning home from work to quickly eat the meal Olive had cooked for them, before all three changed into their uniforms and dashed out of the house to join their respective voluntary groups. Olive was in particular demand because of her driving abilities and had even been called upon to drive a temporary ambulance to and from St Pancras to St Thomas's Hospital one evening when the normal driver hadn't turned up. Tilly and Agnes had gone from practising first aid to actually doing it, and as Tilly said to Agnes as they hurried to meet up with other members of their group, after the first few real wounds they'd had to check and dress, they'd been so busy that she'd forgotten to be nervous.

Christopher had reached the church hall before them and was checking through their main first-aid box.

Tilly nudged Agnes, telling her, 'Let's go and give Christopher a hand rolling those bandages.' He was standing with his back to them, dressed in stone-coloured cavalry twill trousers and a checked shirt with a Fair Isle-patterned sleeveless pullover on top. Tilly had noticed how some of the other members of their group avoided Christopher, turning their backs and refusing to speak to him, and their attitude made her feel sorry for him and protective towards him. He might be a conscientious objector and not prepared to fight but at least he was doing something towards the war effort.

'I didn't have time to change into my St John Ambulance uniform because Mum needed me to give her a hand setting up a bed downstairs for Dad. He's been bad with his chest these last few days and the doctor said that he didn't want him going up and down the stairs.'

Tilly knew from her mother that Christopher's father's health was declining, and Nancy next door had said that she reckoned he wouldn't see Christmas. Tilly hoped that Nancy was wrong. She knew how close Christopher was to his father, and she knew too how she would be feeling if it was her mother that was so seriously ill.

Half an hour later, when everyone had arrived and the tea urn had been filled, Lucy Higgins, whose father was an ARP warden came round with a tray of tea for them all, but when Christopher reached for a cup she deliberately jerked the tray away from him, so that he couldn't get a drink.

'Here, Christopher, this is for you,' Tilly announced, firmly handing him her own cup, before heading for the small kitchen to get a clean cup for her own drink.

Lucy Higgins appeared in the doorway, blocking her exit as she told her with contempt, 'You want to watch it, you do, making friends with that coward. Otherwise people will begin to think that you're just as bad as he is.'

'Christopher is not a coward.' Tilly immediately countered.

'Course he is. He's a conchie, and he's refusing to fight.'

'He objects to the war on moral grounds, not fears for his own safety.'

'Oh ho, moral grounds, is it?' Lucy mocked. 'He's a coward and a traitor, and he ought to be strung up. That's what my dad says.'

Lucy's unkindness and bullying manner towards Christopher left a bad taste in Tilly's mouth.

She was still feeling sorry for him when the three of them walked home together later in the evening, both her and Agnes having to walk a bit faster than normal in order to keep up with him, his speed no doubt because he was anxious to get back to his father, Tilly guessed.

She, on the other hand, would have liked to linger. The long daylight hours and June sunshine were a relief after the winter nights of blackouts and absolute darkness.

It had been a severe winter, with the loss of many, many sailors and a great deal of shipping, due to the successful attacks of Hitler's submarines on the navy-escorted convoys crossing the Atlantic and bringing much-needed supplies to the country. The convoys and the goods they carried were a vital lifeline for the country.

Despite the warmth of the June evening Tilly gave a small shiver. Everyone had been so confident when the war had first started, that they would have Hitler beaten within months, his army retreating back to Germany with its tail between its legs. The reality, though, was that it was the BEF that had been driven into retreat and now the whole counry was aware of how vulnerable Britain was. The fear of invasion was gripping everyone. Tilly knew that her mother was worrying about it, even though she wasn't saying so, and Tilly knew too that her worry was for her.

She felt afraid herself sometimes listening to people talking about the horror stories the refugees who had made it safely to London had to tell, especially those from Poland. Another shiver gripped Tilly. There were two Polish refugee families sharing a house in Article Row, two women with children, and an older woman.

According to Nancy, who made it her business

to know everything that went on in Article Row, the two women were sisters, and the elderly woman was their mother. Their husbands had been killed fighting against Hitler, whilst the eldest son of one of the women, a boy of fourteen, had been shot through the head by a German soldier for trying to protect the cousin the soldier had then gone on to rape, and who had shot herself with the soldier's gun rather than bear the shame of what had happened to her.

Tilly had guessed from the look exchanged between her mother and Sally when Nancy had told them all this story that it was both true and not an isolated occurrence.

She didn't dare let herself think about what might happen here in London if the Germans did invade and ended up marching on the city like they were now marching on Paris.

Sally wasn't the only one concerned about the important matter of 'going steady'. It was an issue that had been on Ted's mind since Christmas, and now, his feelings heated by the June sunshine and the sight of couples walking and sweet-talking together in London's streets and parks, he ached to tell Agnes how he felt about her and to ask her to be his girl.

There were problems, though. Ted was the sole breadwinner in his family, his earnings desperately needed to supplement the small income his mother received as a cleaner. The need for her services, and thus her income, had decreased since the start of the war with many well-to-do families leaving

London for the safety of the country for the sake of their children.

There was no way Ted could move out of the family home, a tiny rented flat provided by the Guinness Trust, and no way either that he could move Agnes into it as his wife, as he suspected it would be against the rules, and besides, his bedroom was no bigger than a cupboard and had room for only a single bed, whilst his mother shared the single bedroom with his two young sisters.

Agnes was a lovely girl and a very special person, who had blossomed from the shy shabby girl he had first met to a confident happy young woman. Even old Smithy was now putty in her hands, mellowed by her smile and her genuine kindness. Ted was happy that Agnes had found her feet – of course he was – but at the same time he was also worried that some other chap with better prospects and more to offer her might win her heart and steal her from him. For that reason he longed to be able to declare himself but how could he when all he could offer her was the prospect of a long engagement?

Rick downed his pint of beer. It had been a mistake coming here to the working men's club where his father's friends wanted to talk about the war and ask him questions. He still felt too raw for that. Dunkirk had left him feeling as though a layer of skin had been ripped from his body, leaving him sensitive to the lightest touch.

He had seen and experienced too much that

his mind and body wanted to forget and couldn't. Men – his comrades, his friends – left dead and dying during their retreat; good brave men, far braver and better than he. And then Dunkirk itself.

The dead and dying everywhere, like the tension that gripped them all as they stood in line waiting . . . waiting. He'd given up his chance of being the last onto one boat to allow an injured comrade to take his place. Rick reached into his pocket for his cigarettes. That act of generosity had saved his life, because the boat had been attacked by the Luftwaffe. He had seen it hit as he stood on the beach. He had heard the screams of the men dying in the hail of fire, or burned alive in the fuel it discharged as it caught fire. He should have been on that boat . . . His hands started to shake, making it impossible for him to light his cigarette.

He ordered another pint, drinking it quickly, trying to drown out his memories, but they refused to leave him in peace. The heat of the packed club brought him out in a sweat, the stale beer and cigarette smells filling his lungs and making him long for fresh air. Finishing his drink, he left the club, taking a deep breath of the mild late evening air as he headed homewards, his stomach heaving as he drew level with the chip shop and breathed in the smell of the cooked food.

Someone hailed him from inside the shop – Rita Sands, a local good-time girl. She had a reputation in the neighbourhood for being the girl that most of the local lads had had their first sexual experience with. Rick didn't stop.

Making his way home through the warren of backstreets of the East End, he was just about to cut down a narrow alleyway that was a bit of a shortcut, when he heard someone running after him, and Rita's voice calling, 'Hey, Ricky, hang on a minute, will you?'

Grimly Rick turned round, demanding, 'Leave me alone, will you, Rita? I'm not in the mood for company.'

Unabashed she told him, 'Bet I could get you in the mood.' She moved closer to him, putting her hand on his arm. Her hair smelled of grease and fish and chips. Rick wanted to recoil from her. Just as he had recoiled from the sight of his dead comrades? Bile filled his throat as he fought to stand where he was, just as he had done in France.

'Oooh, them's ever such strong muscles you've got there, Ricky,' Rita cooed. 'I'll bet it isn't only there that you've got them neither, is it? There's something about a man in uniform that makes a girl go weak at the knees, if you know what I mean.'

Rick knew what Rita meant all right. It was still light enough for him to see the way her breasts strained against her too-tight top.

He started to turn away from her, repelled by her sexual obviousness, but instead of letting him go Rita moved closer, flinging her arm round his neck and kissing him wetly on his mouth, her free hand moving to his groin.

'Come on,' she said, 'you know you want me really.'

Filled with revulsion, Rick shrugged her off, ignoring her outburst of insults and anger as he pushed past her, intent on putting as much distance between them as he could.

'Coward,' she called after him, jeeringly. 'Running away from me just like you ran away from the Germans.'

Rick stopped dead in his tracks. A red mist of rage descended on him, a desire to turn round and shake Rita until she took back her insulting words, not for his sake but for the sake of the men who would never come home, men who knew more about bravery and courage than someone like Rita could ever grasp.

His anger left him as abruptly as it had seized him. All the anger in the world wouldn't bring those men back, but he would damn well make sure that when he was eventually facing the Germans it would be those fallen men he would be fighting for.

NINETEEN

Dulcie eyed the neat row of lipsticks on the counter in front of her impatiently. It was Monday. They were always quiet on Mondays, her working day seeming to drag, not that there was anything interesting to look forward to for the evening at number 13, not with Olive trying to get them all to give Sally a hand with her vegetable plot. She'd rather go home and listen to her mother praising Edith than do that. And tomorrow night that was what she would be doing, she reminded herself, since tomorrow was her mother's birthday. She'd got her mother a lipstick for her birthday present, a pretty soft pink, and some powder as well. Her mother never took the trouble to make the best of herself, and having some decent cosmetics was bound to cheer her up. Her present was bound to be more expensive than whatever Edith bought her, Dulcie decided with some triumph. That should show her mother how wrong she was to favour Edith all the time. At least with Rick still at home on his post-Dunkirk leave, there'd be someone there to have a bit of a joke with.

Dulcie frowned as she looked down and noticed a small wrinkle in one of her stockings. Automatically she bent to smooth it away.

As she did so, from the other side of the counter she heard a male voice asking, 'So what exactly is it you'd want this boyfriend who isn't a real boyfriend to do?'

The voice and its amused tone were immediately recognisable. They had Dulcie standing up so quickly that she felt dizzy, which was no doubt why her face felt flushed, she decided as she stared up into Raphael Androtti's brown eyes.

Normally quick off the mark with a retaliatory comment, Dulcie for once was lost for words, finally managing only a defensive. 'Is this some kind of joke?'

'A joke? I thought we were supposed to be acting as lovebirds, not clowns. Of course, if you've changed your mind, and you've found someone else to play the role of doting boyfriend . . .'

He was turning to walk away. Caught off guard, Dulcie reached across the counter to stop him, protesting, 'No. I mean . . .'

'I've missed you.'

The smile and the not-so-softly spoken words were good enough to have come from the lips of any matinée idol worth his salt, as was the way in which he lifted his hand, about to touch her face, and then dropped it again as though realising where they were.

'Why are you doing this?' Dulcie demanded.

'You said you wanted me to.'

'Yes, I know that,' she hissed, 'but . . .'

'But what?' His voice became slightly louder as he demanded urgently, 'Have you changed your mind about me? About us? Please tell me that it isn't true and that you haven't.'

Somehow or other he had taken possession of her hand and was clasping it between his own.

He was enjoying this, Dulcie could see.

'You're overdoing it,' she told him. A quick look round the cosmetics floor showed her that the other girls were goggling at them from behind their counters, and that Arlene was looking astounded – astounded and envious!

Oddly, though, Dulcie felt less triumphant than she should have. That was because she liked being in control. She did not like someone else grasping the upper hand and directing the things she had planned to direct herself. It made her feel . . . Dulcie didn't want to think about how it made her feel or about being taken over by someone else, controlled by someone else. Didn't he realise that he was going too far? All she'd wanted was for him to come in and give the impression that he was keen on her, not act like they were already an item. Now she'd end up having to come up with a reason for them breaking up.

'The shop will be closing in couple of minutes,' she told him, wanting to get rid of him so that she could manage the impression he was giving when the other girls asked her the questions she knew they would ask.

His warm, 'I'll be waiting for you outside,'

wasn't the response she'd wanted, but she couldn't say anything, not with Lizzie standing within hearing distance.

Now he was giving her an openly languishing look, before turning on his heel and heading for the exit, just as the warning bell to customers to leave the store started to ring.

'Well!' Lizzie announced as soon as the bell had stopped. 'Who is he and why haven't you said anything about him?'

But before Dulcie could answer her, half a dozen of the girls were clustering round her, demanding, 'Where did you meet him, Dulcie?' 'Has he got any brothers?' 'Cousins?'

Then Arlene came and joined in, her nose in the air, malice in the look she gave her, before she said, with what Dulcie knew was mock concern, 'I don't want to spoil things for you, Dulcie, but your young man looks awfully foreign.'

'He's Italian,' Dulcie responded with a small shrug of her shoulders, as though she herself had never for a moment shared the thoughts she suspected were going through their heads. 'So what?'

'An Italian!' Arlene pretended to marvel, before adding mockingly, 'I suppose you met him when he sold you an ice cream.'

One of the other girls began to laugh.

'And the way he speaks . . .' Arlene rolled her eyes.

'He's from Liverpool,' Dulcie defended Raphael.

'An Italian from Liverpool.' Arlene dissolved into fits of laughter. 'Poor Dulcie, but then I

343

suppose you won't mind. Sometimes I do wish that my own standards weren't quite so high.'

'Don't pay any attention to Arlene, Dulcie,' Lizzie said stoutly after she and the others had gone. 'I thought your young man looked lovely.'

'He isn't my young man. He's just someone I know,' Dulcie told her crossly. Her plan seemed to have backfired on her, and that was his fault, not hers. If she did find him waiting for her outside then she'd give him a piece of her mind.

Only when she did find him waiting for her outside the staff entrance to the building, Dulcie discovered to her own surprise that her curiosity about why he had turned up in the first place was stronger than her desire to blame him for Arlene's mockery of her.

However, when he told her in response to her question, 'I was at a bit of a loose end, so I thought I might as well do you a favour,' Dulcie was more incensed than grateful.

'You overdid things,' she said, 'and now I've had to put up with the Miss Snotty Nose looking down on me even more because of you being Italian.'

They had been walking away from the building as she delivered this attack but now he had stopped walking so that Dulcie was forced to do the same, and the look in his eyes was far from warm as he demanded, 'Why should the fact that I'm Italian make her look down on you?'

'Because you aren't British,' Dulcie replied irritably. Surely it was obvious to him that him being Italian and foreign, an immigrant, meant that he could never be considered as good as someone who was really British. After all, everyone knew that was how things were.

'Actually I am British,' he informed her. 'I was born in this country, to parents who were also born here, and who, whilst being part of Liverpool's Italian community, have taken British nationality.'

'That doesn't mean anything,' Dulcie said dismissively. 'You look Italian, and you were with Italians when I saw you.'

'So I can't look Italian but be British is that what you are saying?'

Dulcie gave an exasperated sigh. 'This is boring and I don't want to talk about it.'

'It isn't boring to me,' he told her grimly. 'This is my country, a country I have enlisted to fight for and to die for, if necessary, but according to you because of my Italian ancestry I am not good enough for Britain – or for you? My grandfather would enjoy listening to you. It would validate and vindicate everything he believes.'

They had to stop walking for a minute to allow the crowd of people coming the other way to surge past them, giving Dulcie the chance to demand, 'Your grandfather?'

'Yes. It is to see him that I am here in London, to see if I can mend a family feud. You see, he abhors the thought of me being British just as much as you abhor the thought of me being Italian.'

'I don't abhor it,' Dulcie defended herself. She'd never heard the word 'abhor' before, but she could guess what it meant and she certainly wasn't going to let him know that it was new to her, she decided. She had to hurry to catch up with him as he strode off. 'But everyone knows that a girl who isn't Italian would be plain daft to get involved with an Italian chap when they always marry their own kind. Why doesn't your grandfather want you to be British?'

A shaft of sunlight beaming down as they crossed a road, highlighted the warm olive tint of Raphael's skin, catching Dulcie's attention. Here in the city, its buildings shutting out the sunlight, its dust filling her nose and its war-ready grimness all around her to be seen, that sudden glimpse of healthy vitally alive male flesh brought her an emotion she didn't understand. And because she didn't understand it, Dulcie refused to countenance it.

'Because he believes, as so many of his generation do, that our presence here in Britain is temporary,' Raphael told her. 'When he came here it was to work and send money home, to save up so that one day he too could return home. That was his belief and his dream. He and his contempararies do not consider Britain to be their home and their country because in their hearts Italy is that. They are fiercely proud of being Italian and they cling together in their communities because they are afraid if they do not, that they might forget and lose their traditions and their way of life. To Italians, family is all important, and family means not just husband and wife and children, but their whole community, to which they owe

346

their loyalty along with their loyalty to Italy itself.'

He paused as a bus that had stopped to pick up passengers set off noisily, disgorging fumes that made Dulcie fan the air with her hand, continuing once it had gone, 'When my father decided to become a British national my grandfather disowned him. He wanted my father to do as he had done and work to send money home to Italy but my father wanted to build a life here for my mother and for me. My father doesn't say so, but my grandfather's disowning of him hurts him. I would like to see them reconciled.'

'It won't please your grandfather to know that you've enlisted then, will it?' Dulcie pointed out practically.

'No,' Raphael agreed. There were deeper and more complex reasons why he wanted to speak to his grandfather, but he didn't intend to discuss those with Dulcie. He and his father had had several concerned discussions about the Italian Fascist movement in Britain, to which so many Italians belonged without really understanding the position in which it could put them in the eyes of the British Government, especially now with the country at war with Germany.

They had to stop to cross another road, the warmth of the sun making Dulcie begin to feel hot, hemmed in by the press of people on the busy street.

The movement provided Italian lessons for the children of Italians born in Britain, it provided meeting halls, schools, a place for Italian communities to be together, a small part of Italy and home in a foreign land. Only a small proportion of those who belonged to the movement were politically motivated and true fascists, and Raphael wanted to warn his grandfather against placing himself in that small group, especially as increasingly it looked as though Mussolini was about to ally himself to Hitler, and thus declare war on Britain.

He wasn't sure himself why he had elected to do what he had done with regard to Dulcie. It was true that he had had time on his hands, but he could have filled that time doing other things. It had surprised him to discover how much his pride had stung to hear Dulcie announce that he wasn't good enough for her, when her comment should have amused him. She was a shop girl, sharp enough when it came to her own wants, and ambitions, but oblivious to the political and social situations that were so important to him. If one of them should look down on the other then he should be the one looking down on her.

He stopped walking as they came to another crossroads.

'I'm sorry but I must leave you here.'

It was only after they had gone their separate ways and Dulcie was almost 'home' that she allowed herself to give vent to her feelings. Of all the cheek, him apologising to her for leaving her as though he thought that she had actually wanted his company, and would be disappointed at being deprived of it. Well, she wasn't. She didn't need anyone's company, much less that of a ruddy Eyetie. She was forced to admit to herself, however, for all that Arlene had affected to sneer at him, she'd seen the look in her eyes when they'd first clocked him. Eyetie or not, he was still a well set up and good-looking chap.

TWENTY

Sally pushed her hair back off her face, shading her eyes from the June afternoon sun as she looked up from the row of lettuces she had just been weeding around, leaning on her hoe as she did so.

'Looks easy hoeing, but it isn't.' The voice of Nancy's husband, Arthur, reached her from the other side of the garden fence. Arthur was a kindly gentle man, the complete opposite of the image of him that Nancy held up to others with her frequent references to Arthur's dislike of all those things that Nancy had decided were to be disliked. Now, as he filled and then lit his pipe, Sally laughed and agreed.

'Much harder. I've never been in full charge of a veggie plot before, although I helped my father with his.'

'Tea leaves is what you need. Soak them in vinegar overnight and then put them round your lettuces, and you won't get no slugs coming after them.'

Nancy's, 'Arthur, come and get a cup of tea,' over the hedge dividing the two gardens, had him giving Sally a farewell nod of his head before he dutifully headed for the back door where Sally could see Nancy standing with her apron on over her floral-patterned summer frock, her hands on her hips.

'Poor Arthur,' Olive commented, coming down the path with a tray of tea and two scones from the batch she had just baked, just in time to hear her neighbour calling out to her husband. 'He is rather henpecked. No butter for the scones, I'm afraid, but luckily I've got plenty of jam left from the batch I made last year. I'm really glad now that we've got rationing that I decided to sort out a stock cupboard last summer.'

'I've been thinking that perhaps we could get half a dozen hens,' Sally began five minutes later when the two of them were settled under the shade of the apple tree, enjoying their tea and scones. 'There's room for them, and I noticed a sign in the hardware shop as I came past the other day, advertising hen coops.'

'Well, I can certainly use the fresh eggs,' Olive agreed, 'but you can't be expected to look after the gardens and some hens, Sally. I feel a bit guilty as it is, watching you working so hard.'

'I enjoy it,' Sally told her truthfully, 'and you and Tilly and Agnes all give me a hand.'

'Well, if you really want to take it on, I'm all for it,' Olive approved. She looked up at the sky through the leaves on the apple tree.

'I can't imagine what it will be like to be invaded by the Germans, but that's what everyone says Hitler will try to do now that he's got France.'

'It won't be as easy to invade us as it was to invade France,' Sally said stoutly.

Olive gave her a wan smile. 'That's what everyone said about the Maginot Line – that he'd never cross it – but he did. I keep thinking of all those people who tried to escape.' She put her hand to her mouth and Sally knew that she was thinking of the women and children who had been killed by the Luftwaffe. She herself had heard the most graphic and awful stories from some of the injured soldiers they'd got at Barts, the words bursting from them as though they couldn't contain the horror of what they'd witnessed.

'If they do invade, they're bound to march on London.'

'We've got the RAF to hold them back, don't forget,' Sally tried to comfort her.

Olive gave her a troubled look. 'I worry for Tilly and Agnes, and you too, Sally. You are young with your whole lives in front of you, and I can't help thinking that if Hitler does invade you'd all be safer out of London.'

'If he succeeds in invading,' Sally told her gently. 'I personally don't think he will. If those of us who live and work here did desert London then what kind of message would that send out to him, and to our boys who are fighting for this country and for us? The BEF have taken a terrific blow to their pride. We need to show them, as well as Hitler, that we have faith in them.'

Olive looked at her lodger, taking in Sally's determined expression. 'You're right,' she agreed, adding, 'You have such a wise head on your young shoulders, Sally.'

'My mother's head, or rather her teaching.' Sally's smile softened and then disappeared, to be replaced by a look of sadness. 'I miss her so much. The trained nurse in me knew that she couldn't survive and that she would die, but as her daughter I couldn't bear to lose her.'

'Your father is still alive,' Olive began, but Sally shook her head.

'Not for me. I have no father any more. My father ceased to exist for me the day he married Morag. The man I knew and loved as my father could not have performed such a betrayal. I must finish this weeding before I have to go in and get changed for work. Arthur has recommended that I put tea leaves soaked in vinegar round the lettuces to keep the slugs off. I've never heard of that remedy before.'

Recognising that Sally had changed the subject because she did not want to talk about her father, Olive began to gather up their empty cups and plates. She couldn't really, after all, expect someone who had been as close to her mother as Sally had obviously been to understand the ache of emptiness and the fear of aloneless that came with the loss of a husband or wife, or to accept that sometimes the widowed partner felt driven by a need to fill that empty gap in their lives, especially when it was a man who had been widowed. Women were expected by their own sex to wear their widowhood as a form of respectability; men, on the other hand, were seen by that sex as poor creatures in need of the comfort that only a new wife could give. A widow's respectability was a fragile garment, easily tarnished and damaged, her behaviour constantly under the eagle-eyed inspection of other women. Olive could still remember the lectures she had been given by her mother-in-law in the months following her own widowhood, about the need to preserve her 'respectability' and that of her late husband's family. She had had no desire to marry again, though, Olive admitted. All she had wanted to do then was pour her love into her precious daughter. *Then?* What she meant was that all she had ever wanted to do was pour her love into Tilly, Olive told herself firmly.

'Well, I don't know why you've wasted your money on giving me this stuff, Dulcie, I really don't. Mind you, Edith can probably make use of it.'

Dulcie stared at her mother in outrage, opening her mouth to tell her that if she didn't want her present then Dulcie would take it back because there was no way that Edith was going to have it, her angry words converted to a yell of pain when Rick very deliberately nipped her arm.

'I'll have a bruise on my arm now,' she complained to him half an hour later as they left the house together, Dulcie to return to Article Row and Rick heading for the local lads' boxing club to meet up with his friends, 'What did you have to go and pinch me like that for anyway?'

'You know why,' Rick told her.

'Mum had no right saying she was going to give my present to her to Edith,' Dulcie objected. 'Why does ruddy Edith have to have everything? Mum said that she was going to give her that scent you gave her as well.'

'That's Mum's way, and making a song and dance about it won't change anything,' Rick advised as they set off down the street. 'Edith's always been her favourite.'

'Well, I don't know why,' Dulcie complained, still aggrieved.

'Ma's proud of Edith, Dulcie, because of her singing. Remember how when we were kids Ma used to tell us about how she'd won a prize for singing herself when she was at school?'

Dulcie nodded.

'Well, I reckon Ma favours Edith because of that. She wants Edith to have what she never did.'

'A greasy-hands-all-over-you agent, you mean?' Dulcie asked cynically.

Rick sighed and gave her a rueful look. 'You know the trouble with you, Dulcie, is that you can't just let things be. You've got to make your point, and have the last word, even if it means getting folks' backs up.'

They'd crossed the road and turned into another street whilst they'd been talking, any attempt Dulcie might have made to respond to Rick's accusation made impossible by the growing volume of noise.

'What's that?' Dulcie protested, raising her voice.

'Sounds like someone's having a bit of a set-to,' Rick told her unnecessarily as they both heard the sound of breaking glass joining the chants and jeers of angry raised voices.

Street fights weren't an uncommon occurrence in their neighbourhood, so Dulcie shrugged. Then they turned the corner and she could see the gang of youths up ahead.

'That's Mr Manelli's ice-cream shop they're throwing bricks at.' Dulcie stopped walking. 'They've got no right doing that. Ever so nice to us when we were kids, Mr Manelli always was, giving us an extra scoop of ice cream when we took Ma's baking bowl round on a Saturday to get it filled up for tea.'

As several more bricks were thrown into the broken window they heard a woman's screams from inside the shop.

'Come on, Rick. We've got to stop them.'

The sight of Dulcie, of all people, advancing on the jeering violent crowd of boys held Rick motionless for a second. But then he set off after her, calling out to the attacking mob, 'Come on, lads, what's going on?' The firm sound of his voice and the fact that he was in uniform were enough to bring a momentary halt to the attack. The youths turned to look at him, whilst Dulcie, to his bemusement, marched in between them and the shop front, her hands on her hips.

'You ought to be ashamed of yourselves, doing summat like this to Mr Manelli,' she told them. 'What's he ever done to you?'

'He's an Eyetie and a traitor, that's what,' the largest of the youths told Dulcie glowering at her. 'A ruddy Fascist, and him and his family want running out of the street and putting in prison like all the rest of his kind.'

'Give over, lads,' Rick counselled. 'We all know Mr Manelli – he's no traitor.'

'Well, if that's the case then how come the police have took him and the other Eyeties off to prison?' one of the other youths demanded, giving Rick a challenging look. 'My dad heard it from the police themselves. They've had orders to round up all the Eyeties and shove them in goal on account of them being Fascists and spies. 'Oo knows what's bin going on inside there?'

The mood of the mob was turning ugly, Rick recognised. If they chose to go on the attack again he certainly couldn't stop them by himself, and anyway, his first duty was to protect his sister, who was still standing in front of the smashed shop window.

Mentally Rick cursed Dulcie for getting them involved. He had no quarrel with the Manellis, but he couldn't hold the mob off by himself if they chose to turn their anger against him and Dulcie. Out of the corner of his eye he saw their local policeman crossing the top of the street. Quickly he hailed him, relieved to see him stop in mid-stride.

The sight of a burly policeman coming towards them at the run was enough to frighten off the mob, who quickly dispersed, leaving Rick to explain to Constable Green what had happened.

'That's the trouble when feelings start running high. Folks start taking the law into their own hands,' was his verdict on Rick's explanation of the mob's attack on the ice-cream shop.

Over an hour later, when Rick and Dulcie were finally on their own again, a still visibly terrified and sobbing Mrs Manelli having been handed over by Constable Green into the care of her neighbours and fellow Italians, Rick was finally free to ask his sister, 'What was that all about?'

'What do you mean?' Dulcie affected not to understand him.

Rick heaved a patient sigh and pointed out, 'We could have had those young idiots turning on us. Why take that risk?'

'Because I felt like it,' was the only answer Dulcie would give him.

Women and sisters – especially this particular sister, Rick thought in bewilderment – he would never understand them.

As she made her way back to Article Row, Dulcie was no more inclined to answer Rick's question to herself than she had been to him, other than to think that it had been high time she proved to a few people who thought they were so much better than her that they weren't. People like Edith, and Olive, and some of the girls at work, who thought they could look down on her and get away with it. And him too, that Raphael, who had tried to make out he was so much better than she was. Well, they weren't 'cos it was her that had had the guts to stand her ground and helped old Mrs Manelli, and not them!

Rick was just about to leave the boxing club and make his way home, when Raphael found him, having heard the story of Mrs Manelli's rescue whilst he'd been at the headquarters of the Italian Fascist Organisation.

He'd gone there in the hope of picking up some information about what had happened to the men who had been arrested in the early hours on 10 June, taken from their homes without warning under suspicion of being active Fascists. One of those men had been his grandfather, and naturally Raphael was concerned for him, an old man of eighty-one who was stubborn enough and foolish enough to cling to Fascism out of sheer cussedness.

The Italian communities, in Britain's main cities were all in shock over the night-time raids on their homes, their men being removed by the police, taken from their homes in the clothes they'd pulled on after being woken from their sleep, with no information being given about what was going to happen to them except that they were to be interned as enemy aliens.

Raphael had telephoned his father in Liverpool to discover that the situation there was even worse than it was in London. In London it was only those who were believed to be active Fascists who had been arrested. In Liverpool there had been a wholesale taking into custody of a huge swathe of the entire Italian adult male population. Only those, like his father, who had naturalised and become British citizens legally had escaped arrest.

Naturally the Italian community had flocked to their Fascist clubs, both for information and for comfort, especially those women whose husbands or fathers or sons had been taken.

In the heightened atmosphere within the club, the tale of Rick's heroic bravery spread like wildfire, causing Raphael to ask where he might find him. Since the Manellis were distant relatives and had no son of their own, it fell to him to thank Mrs Manelli's rescuer for his timely intervention.

Armed with the information, from a couple of young Italians who knew him, that he would more than likely find Rick Simmonds at his boxing club, and instructions about which bus he would need to catch to get there, Raphael headed for the bus stop, recognising only after he had left the club that Mrs Manelli's rescuer had the same surname as Dulcie. Raphael shrugged. Perhaps Simmonds was as common a surname to the East End as his own was to the Italian community. He had no intention of wasting time allowing someone like Dulcie to take up residence in his thoughts.

The warmth of the light June nights had brought people out into the city to stroll in its parks and see its shows, perhaps, Raphael suspected, aware of what was happening to France and thinking that they might as well enjoy their freedom whilst they could, although it was obvious that the people's mood was sombre. Everyone you talked to spoke in hushed or anxious voices about their belief that Hitler would try to invade Britain, often without admitting to their unspoken fear that he might succeed.

Like all those who had been rescued from the beaches of Dunkirk, Raphael had been granted two weeks' leave. That leave was already half over and in another few days he would be rejoining his unit of the Royal Engineers. He just hoped that before that happened they would know what had happened to his grandfather, not only for his grandfather's sake but, more importantly, for his father's. Raphael knew how desperately worried his father would be and how guilty he would feel, even though in Raphael's opinion his father had no reason to feel any guilt. He had, after all, over the years made endless attempts to be reconciled with his father, and it was the older man who had stubbornly refused all Raphael's father's attempts to make peace.

In the boxing club, Rick let the conversation going on all around him wash over him, as he stood at the bar. The club was busy tonight with young men in shorts and singlets working on the club's three punch bags, or lifting weights whilst the club's hopeful bantam weight contender for a local title was sparring in the ring under the stern eye of one of the ex-professional boxers who trained the young talent.

The building was run down, with chunks of plaster missing from the walls here and there, left like that, so the story went, by a pro from before the Great War, who'd had a habit of punching the wall if one of his sparring bouts hadn't gone well. Worn dark brown linoleum covered the stone floor, and in the winter the club got damp from the leak in the roof, which had been repaired with a sheet of corrugated iron.

It was here that deals were done that weren't always strictly on the right side of the law, from matches that were fixed to the selling of black market cigarettes. There was a small room off the bar that everyone knew not to go into when the door was closed because that meant that there was a 'meeting' going on that involved 'business'.

Rick still came to the club because he had boxed there for a while as a boy, and it was where his friends gathered, but his membership was merely a social one now. Tonight, though, Tom, his comrade in arms who had joined up with him and who had also gone through the hell of Dunkirk, wasn't in, and Rick wasn't in the mood to join in the speculation and talk of the possibility of Hitler invading England. Unlike him the other lads here hadn't tasted the reality of war as yet, some of them still raw recruits who had only just finished their basic training, others still waiting for their call-up papers and several in reserved occupations. How could they know how it felt to have been driven back by the Germans – to have to retreat as the BEF had done, abandoning its weapons and its artillery as it did so.

Rick knew he would never forget the silence that had greeted them when they had finally been put ashore in England, or the way that those dealing with the practicalities of their repatriation had avoided looking directly at them, as though ashamed of them. A shame they had all shared.

And if the shame of the retreat was hard to bear then the memories of what that retreat had involved were even harder to endure.

Rick was just about to leave when Raphael walked into the club, heading straight for the bar where he asked after Rick.

362

'Rick Simmonds?' the barman repeated. 'He's over there, heading for the door,' nodding his head in Rick's direction, and then adding warningly, 'If you've come here looking for trouble, mate, you've chosen the wrong place and the wrong man. Well thought of hereabouts, Rick is.'

'It's nothing like that – quite the opposite,' Raphael assured him, the sound of his Liverpool accent causing a couple of the regulars who were in the Merchant Navy to glance across at him in recognition of a voice from a well-known port.

Rick was outside before Raphael caught up with him, turning round when Raphael called out, 'Wait up, mate.'

Like the merchant seamen, Rick recognised Raphael's Liverpool accent. A quick glance at Raphael revealed a tall dark-haired broad-shouldered man with a soldier's bearing and stride, wearing army uniform and the badge of the Royal Engineers. Rick wasn't really in the mood for company but something about the other man's determined stride made him wait.

'Rick, Rick Simmonds?' Raphael asked. When Rick nodded, Raphael extended his hand to shake Rick's.

'Raphael Androtti. I just heard down at the local Italian club about what you did tonight for Caterina Manelli, and I wanted to thank you. She's family – a distant cousin.'

'It isn't me you should really be thanking,' Rick told him. 'It's my sister Dulcie. She was the one that got in between the mob and the shop.' Rick shook his head, betraying his continuing disbelief

363

that Dulcie of all people should have done such a thing and taken such a risk.

So Dulcie was related to Rick. Now there was a coincidence.

'I couldn't believe it when I saw what she'd done,' Rick admitted. 'She's not exactly the type to put herself at risk for someone else, isn't Dulcie.' He spoke openly, somehow finding the sight of Raphael's uniform making it easy for him to do so. Raphael might be Italian but he was a soldier, like Rick himself, and right now that formed a bond between them that meant Rick could speak frankly to the other man.

'Of course, once she'd got herself involved I'd no option other than to do the same. She is my sister, after all.' Rick shook his head. 'Women. I'll never understand them, doing something as risky and daft as that, just because old Mr Manelli used to put an extra dollop of ice cream in our bowl when we were kids.'

'I obviously owe your sister my thanks as well then,' Raphael told Rick. 'It's a bit late for me to call round at your home now, but—'

'You wouldn't find her there anyway,' Rick stopped him. 'Dulcie doesn't live at home. She's got digs in Holborn and a landlady who doesn't take too kindly to men she doesn't know turning up on her doorstep asking for her lodgers. Your best bet would be to go to Selfridges. Dulcie works there in the cosmetics department.'

Now was the time for him to come clean and tell her brother that he already knew Dulcie and where she worked, Raphael knew. That would be the right and honest thing to do. He battled with his conscience. He liked what he'd seen of Rick, and as a man honesty was important to him. However, he knew that Rick wouldn't like hearing about how he had come to know his sister – as her brother he was bound to be protective of her; that was only natural. In the circumstances it was best that he didn't say anything, Raphael decided, but that didn't stop him feeling guilty.

'I'll go and see her at Selfridges, as you suggest.'

'Will Mr Manelli be all right?' Rick asked him.

'I hope so.' Raphael reached into his tunic pocket to remove a packet of service-issue cigarettes, offering the pack first to Rick, who took one, and then lighting Rick's cigarette for him before lighting one for himself.

'Been in the army long?' he asked Rick.

'Joined up just in time to be sent out to France with the BEF. And you?'

'Same. We were working on an airfield down near Nantes when the order came to pull out. We were lucky. We got taken off the beach at St-Nazaire by a Finnish vessel and taken to Falmouth. Not that we thought we were going to be lucky at first, not when we'd seen all the RAF lot being given preference to get on board this warship they'd got at St-Nazaire, packed with women and children as well as the RAF. Poor sods. There wasn't any room for us.

Raphael narrowed his eyes and looked into the distance before telling Rick, 'The warship got bombed by the Luftwaffe – those on board didn't stand a chance.'

Both men drew heavily on their cigarettes in shared silence, each knowing why the other didn't speak.

Olive was in the kitchen when Dulcie came in. The girls had already gone up to bed taking their cocoa with them, but Olive had hung on downstairs. Not because she was concerned about the fact that Dulcie was still out, like she would have been had she been Tilly or Agnes. It was no business of hers what time Dulcie came in or where she'd been, only she had said that she was going over to her parents' because it was her mother's birthday, and the look on her face had said that it wasn't a visit she was particularly looking forward to.

Her walk back to Article Row took Dulcie around forty-five minutes and had given her time to think about what she had done, and once the euphoria of feeling that she'd triumphed over all those who thought they could look down on her by doing something brave had worn off, Dulcie had started to recognise the risk she had taken and to feel a bit shaky. The last thing she wanted as she walked into the kitchen, intent on making herself a spirit-strengthening cup of tea, was Olive, and the sight of her sitting in a chair as though waiting for her return brought Dulcie to an abrupt halt. No one had ever waited up for her. It was Edith her own mother worried about and sat up anxiously for, refusing to go to bed until she knew she was safely home. When Dulcie had pointed out that she had never waited up for her, her

366

mother had simply said that there wasn't any need for her to do that because she knew that Dulcie was perfectly capable of looking after herself. Not that Olive would be waiting up for her to get in, of course. It would be Tilly and Agnes she was sitting there for.

'Tilly and Agnes not in yet?' she asked Olive, as she headed for the kettle. Her mouth felt dry and her head ached painfully.

'Yes. They've gone up,' Olive told her, adding without intending to, 'You're later back than I expected.'

Dulcie had turned towards her, the kettle she had just filled in her hand, the light falling sharply onto her, causing Olive to gasp in shock when she saw the dried blood on Dulcie's cheek where a sharp-edged pebble – one of a handful thrown by one of the mob – had caught her and cut her skin. There were other marks on her clothes, dusty marks, and another cut on her leg.

'Dulcie, what on earth's happened to you?' Olive demanded, getting up to go and take the kettle from her.

Immediately Olive got close to her Dulcie recoiled, telling her abruptly and dismissively, 'There's no need to make a fuss. It's nothing. Just some lads who'd had too much to drink.'

When Olive's eyes widened in shock, Dulcie realised that her landlady was jumping to the wrong conclusion and she told her fiercely, 'It wasn't anything like that. I'm not daft enough to let any lads try doing something they shouldn't with me. It was all this fuss about the Italians

367

being Fascists and being taken away. A group of lads were throwing stones at the Manellis' shop window. Me and Rick told them to leave it out. Mr Manelli wasn't even there. The police had already taken him away.'

Olive had heard about the mobs going round attacking the premises of Italian businesses whilst she'd been at her WVS meeting and had been horrified by their behaviour, but somehow she hadn't expected to hear that Dulcie had stepped in to prevent one of those attacks.

Dulcie's mouth thinned when she saw Olive's expression and guessed what she was thinking.

'That's the trouble with people like you,' she told her sharply. 'You think that unless a person goes running around wearing something like a St John Ambulance uniform they're nothing, and you can look down on them.'

'Dulcie, that's not true,' Olive denied, but even as she spoke she recognised that there was a grain of truth in what Dulcie was saying.

'Yes it is,' Dulcie told her flatly.

'The doctor's been again this morning to number forty-nine,' Nancy announced over the hedge.

Olive paused on the steps to her back door, balancing the weight of the washing she had just been to collect from the local Chinese laundry more securely on her raised knee.

'It can't be long now, not with the doctor coming nearly every day. I said to my Arthur when they moved in that I didn't reckon the husband would last very long.'

368

Olive felt that sometimes Nancy took too keen an interest in such morbid subjects, almost relishing it when one of her dire warnings became true.

'Mr Long is very poorly at the moment,' she felt obliged to agree, whilst pointing out, 'But his son, Christopher, has told Tilly that they have every hope that he will rally and make some recovery. Apparently this has proved to be the case on more than one occasion in the past.'

Nancy merely shook her head, adding darkly, 'And that's another thing. If I was you I wouldn't let your Tilly get too involved with that boy of theirs, not with him being one of the conscientious objects. There's no saying where it might lead. Folk like them like putting the wrong ideas into other folk's heads, and you don't want your Tilly getting them kind of wrong ideas.'

'I don't think for one minute that anything like that is going to happen, Nancy. Tilly and Agnes have simply taken Christopher under their wing a bit because they are being good neighbours.'

'Well, you can say that, but—' Nancy began.

Her neighbour was like a dog relishing a particularly juicy bone it did not want to give up, Olive thought ruefully as she determinedly changed the subject.

'Has Linda settled in with her in-laws in Sussex now?'

Linda, Nancy's daughter, and her son-in-law, Henry, had evacuated themselves and their seven-year-old son to Sussex to live with her in-laws shortly after war had been announced.

'Oh, yes. Ever so glad to have her there, Henry's

369

mother is, and Henry's got a job working in partnership with an electrician that's already set up there. Mind you, Linda says that it's Henry that's bringing in most of the work, not this other chap, and she reckons that it's Henry who should be the senior partner. Henry's mother's lucky to have them living with her. There's nothing Linda doesn't know about running a house like it should be run. Of course, she's got me to thank for that. I have to say that Henry's mother doesn't have the same standards I've taught Linda. When we went and stayed with them the Christmas before last, there was that much dust on the picture rail in her hallway that she couldn't have dusted up there all year.'

Olive nodded. She knew from experience that there was nothing Nancy liked more than boasting about her daughter, but the weight of the laundry was beginning to make her arms ache so she excused herself and unlocked her back door.

Once inside she made her way straight upstairs so that she could put the clean linen in the airing cupboard, ready to change the beds on Monday.

When Nancy had first found out that Olive was sending her sheets and pillowcases to the Chinese laundry instead of washing them herself, she had affected to be shocked, but Olive didn't care. With five beds to change it would have been impossible for her to get all the bedding washed, dried and ironed every week, on top of everything else she had to do, including her WVS work.

Once she'd put the clean laundry away, Olive glanced at her watch and, seeing that it was almost half-past ten, she hurried back downstairs so that she could make herself a cup of tea and then sit down and enjoy it whilst she listened to *Music While You Work* on the wireless.

It was whilst she was listening to that that Olive found her thoughts wandering to the Longs. She wondered if she should call and ask Mrs Long if there was anything she could do to help, such as fetching her shopping for her. She didn't want her to think that she was being nosy, though, especially when Mr Long was so obviously poorly. Olive had no fears that Tilly might be getting too involved with Christopher in the way that Nancy had tried to imply. She knew her daughter and it was perfectly plain to her that Tilly thought of Christopher only as a friend. She certainly wasn't attracted to him in the way that she had been to Dulcie's handsome brother. Thinking of that reminded Olive of her exchange with Dulcie. She hadn't intended to get Dulcie's back up, and in fact she had actually, to her own surprise, felt concerned for her when she'd seen her cuts and bruises, but Dulcie wasn't someone who made it easy for others to be sympathetic towards her, Olive thought wryly. Quite the opposite.

She would go and see Mrs Long after she had had her dinner, she decided. It wouldn't be neighbourly not to do so. Olive could still remember how she had felt during the final weeks of her own husband's life. Of course, she had been younger than Mrs Long, and they had been living here with her in-laws, but you never forgot the awfulness of knowing someone you loved was going to die. She would certainly never forget the hours she had lain awake at night listening to his racking cough, and then the silences that had followed it, hardly daring to breathe herself as she listened desperately in the darkness for the sound of his breathing and only relaxing when she heard it.

Olive had decided to do a ham salad for everyone's evening meal, seeing as it was so warm, so she opened the tin of ham she intended to use, taking a thin sliver off the ham to make herself a sandwich for her lunch. The thin scraping of margarine she put on the bread didn't look very appealing, but Olive knew that with a bit of mustard and some lettuce her sandwich would be nice and tasty.

Once she'd eaten she checked the larder to make sure that there were enough boiled potatoes left over from the previous evening's meal for her to make some potato salad to go with the ham.

After removing her apron, Olive went upstairs to comb her hair and make sure that she looked tidy, setting her neat off-white straw hat on top of her newly brushed curls, and then opening her dressing table drawer to remove a clean pair of white gloves.

As she opened her front door, the Misses Barker from next door were walking up the Row, and naturally Olive stopped to speak to them. Spinster sisters and retired teachers, they always looked spick and span. Physically the sisters were very different. Miss Jane Barker, the elder of the two, was tall and thin, with a long bony face, whilst

Miss Mary Barker was smaller and plump. Olive's late husband, who had been taught by them at the local church school before they had retired, had often said that whilst Miss Jane favoured the stick, Miss Mary favoured the carrot, and that between them they had ensured that even the most unruly of boys along with the shyest of girls learned their ABC and their times tables.

Once 'good afternoons' had been exchanged, it was Miss Mary who told Olive excitedly, 'We've just seen the vicar and he's asked us if we'd like to think about helping out at the junior school. It seems that with so many families bringing their children back from evacuation, the Government is having to open some of the schools they closed at the beginning of the war.'

After they had parted company Olive reflected that the thought of going back to teaching had brought a definite spring to the sisters' steps.

When she reached number 49 she could see that the curtains were half drawn across the windows of the front room. Rather hesitantly she knocked on the front door, wondering if she had done the right thing when Mrs Long opened it and Olive saw how tired and distressed she looked.

'I'm sorry,' Olive apologised. 'Perhaps I've called at a bad time. I won't stay. I heard that Mr Long isn't very well and I just wanted you to know that if there's anything I can do to help – collect your shopping for you, that kind of thing.'

'Please do come in,' Mrs Long urged her, holding the door open wide, so that Olive felt obliged to step inside.

The immaculately clean hallway possessed a smell that Olive instantly recognised: the smell of carbolic and sickness and a certain fetid lack of air that came from trying to keep an invalid warm and a house clean.

Olive followed Mrs Long to the back parlour, in shape and size the same as her own but, because this house was tenanted, slightly shabby and down at heel. Dark curtains hung at the window, making the room dim and depressing. The small leather settee under the window had shiny patches on its arms where the fabric had worn thin, and the cupboards either side of the fireplace were painted dark brown, like the skirtings and doors. A table covered in a chenille cloth was pushed up against the wall adjoining the two rooms, three chairs tucked into it so that there was just enough room for the old-fashioned winged armchair with a leather footstool in front of it drawn up close to the fire: Mr Long's chair, Olive guessed.

'I'd offer you a cup of tea, but I'm expecting the doctor any minute,' Mrs Long told her. 'It's kind of you to offer to help but Christopher, our son, is very good and he calls and gets the shopping for me on his way home from work.' An expression of sadness shadowed her face as she spoke.

Poor woman, she was no doubt as anxious about her son as she was about her husband, albeit in a different way, Olive thought compassionately. Christopher's views on the war were bound to make life difficult for him, and what mother

374

wouldn't wish for a happy easy path through life for her child? Olive felt so sorry for Mrs Long. Thin and careworn, with an anxious expression and grey hair pulled back into a bun, she was looking into the hallway through the door she'd left open the whole time she was talking to Olive, her voice barely raised above a whisper. Olive, who had once been in her position herself, knew exactly what she was going through but was reluctant to say anything about her own experience. Mr Long was, after all, still alive, and Olive knew how desperately one clung to that and how desperately one hoped for a recovery. Telling her that she had lost her own husband might not be a tactful thing to do.

'Yes, this is the very latest colour,' Dulcie assured the customer who had spent the last half an hour hesitating over which lipstick to choose.

'And you can assure me that this lipstick was made here in England and not America? Only my husband wouldn't approve at all if I'd bought a lipstick that had taken up space in one of our convoys that could have been used for something much more essential to the war effort. He has a cousin in the navy, you see, and he's very conscious of the dangers to our brave sailors in crossing the Atlantic.'

'Our buyer would never countenance buying stock that risked sailors' lives,' Dulcie assured her customer without having a clue as to whether or not what she was saying was true, and privately thinking that her husband must be mean if he hadn't ever bought a bit of something to carry in his pocket and bring home for his wife.

Her reassurance seemed to convince her customer, who told her, 'Very well then, I'll take the lipstick.'

Last night's attack on the Manellis' shop had left Dulcie with several bruises and the angry cut on her face, which she'd done her best to disguise with some powder. Of course, the other girls had been curious about it, so she'd lied and said that she'd been scratched by a cat.

What had happened to the Italians was all over the papers, and at dinner time there'd been some snide comments from Arlene about the likelihood of 'Dulcie's Italian' being picked up by the police and imprisoned as an enemy alien.

For her own part, Dulcie had pretended not to notice, whilst talking to Lizzie in a very firm voice about how Raphael was in the Royal Engineers and how he was only at home because he'd been at Dunkirk. Not that she had done that for Raphael's sake, of course; she had done it for her own. She certainly wasn't going to have Arlene making out that she was romantically connected to an enemy alien.

The staff entrance to Selfridges was a dark shadowy place that seemed always to smell of oil and exhaust fumes, from the delivery vans and cigarette smoke from the workmen who hung around the entrance, snatching quick fags, and the late afternoon heat of the city emphasised those odours.

London's air as a whole smelled and tasted dry

and dusty to Raphael. For him it lacked the bracing salt tang of Liverpool's air, blown in over the Liverpool bar on winds from the Atlantic.

He'd arrived here well before six, determined not to miss Dulcie, knowing this was his last chance to see her and that he had a train to catch this evening to Liverpool, where his parents were waiting for news of his grandfather. Now he was leaning against a wall in the shadows opposite the store, waiting for her. He had managed to telephone his parents to discuss the dawn raids and they in turn had told him what had been happening in Liverpool. Not to them – Raphael's father was a British citizen, after all. He worked as warehouse manager down on the docks, a good job and one he had wanted Raphael to follow him into until he had realised how determined Raphael was to train as an engineer. That was how he had come to be in the Royal Engineers instead of the regular army.

Raphael saw Dulcie emerging from the building. He pushed himself off the wall, straightening up as he strode purposefully towards her.

Dulcie saw him and stopped walking, a surge of triumph and vindication reinforcing what she told herself she had already known: that although he had pretended not to find her attractive, he had been drawn to her all along. Irresistible, that was what she was, Dulcie decided smugly. Well, if he thought that all he had to do was turn up here to persuade her to grant him the favour of a date, he was quickly going to learn that it wasn't.

She waited for him to approach her, smiling a triumphant smile when he reached her, but instead of pleading with her to go out with him, he told her instead, 'I haven't got much time. I'm leaving for Liverpool this evening, but before I go I just wanted to thank you for what you did for Mrs Manelli. She's my father's second cousin, and since she doesn't have anyone of her own to thank you I'm doing it on her behalf.'

Raphael looked down at his feet in their polished army boots. Coming here like this was a duty he would rather not have had. Dulcie wasn't the type of girl he admired, and yet last night she had done something he admired very much indeed. He could see his own face in the gloss he worked into his boots.

He exhaled and raised his head, telling Dulcie, 'I'm not going to pretend that you weren't one of the last people I'd thought would do something like that, and I'm not going to apologise for thinking it either, but I am grateful to you.'

He hadn't come here to ask her out, and far from finding her irresistible he was practically insulting her. Dulcie glared at him.

'Grateful is it?' she challenged him. 'Well, you don't sound very grateful, and as for not apologising for thinking I was one of the last people you'd thought would do what I did, that just goes to show that you shouldn't go judging people and thinking things about them that aren't true. Just because I don't go round acting all holy and soft, that doesn't mean I don't know right from wrong. Those lads had no call to go acting like they did.

Always kind to us when we were kids, Mr Manelli was, even if he was an Eyetie.'

Raphael inclined his head in acknowledgement of her comment and then pushed back the cuff of his tunic to look at his watch.

Dulcie watched him. He was impatient to leave and she certainly didn't want to prevent him from leaving, so why, as he started to turn away from her, did she have to stop him by asking, 'Did you get to see your granddad?'

His, 'No,' was terse, and a signal that he didn't want to waste any more time talking to her, Dulcie suspected.

Well, that was all right by her; she didn't want to waste her time talking to him. She hadn't asked him to come here. He'd chosen to do that himself. She turned away in angry indignation.

'He refused to see me, and then yesterday morning he was rounded up with the others. They're keeping them at Brompton Oratory School for now.' Raphael paused and then said bitterly, 'He's eighty-one and for all his fiery Fascist talk, he's about as much danger to this country as a day-old child. They took them all before it was light; most of them were bundled off so fast they weren't even allowed to get dressed. I took some clothes down to the police station where they were holding my grandfather but they refused to let me see him.'

'What will happen to them?' She wasn't really interested, Dulcie assured herself. She wasn't so soft that she cared what happened to them, and yet deep down she knew that she did feel something that was more than mere curiosity.

He had no idea why he was talking to Dulcie in so much detail, Raphael acknowledged, unless it was simply because he needed to get what he was feeling off his chest to someone whose own emotions wouldn't be lacerated by what had happened.

'We don't know officially as yet. Although we have heard that the London detainees will be transferred to a camp at Lingfield racecourse in Surrey, prior to being interned. I must go otherwise I shall miss my train. Thank you again for what you did.'

'I don't want your thanks. I didn't do it for you.' The words were out before Dulcie could stop herself from saying them, causing her to hold her breath in case Raphael challenged her.

But to her relief he simply said, 'You may not want my thanks and my gratitude but you have them anyway.'

And then he was gone, striding away from her, tall and broad-shouldered in his military uniform, quickly caught up in the bustle and the crowds of Oxford Street.

She'd definitely go to the Palais this coming Saturday, Dulcie decided. She hadn't gone last Saturday – for one thing her mother's birthday present had left her a bit short of money, and for another she hadn't really felt like it. Not because Tilly and Agnes had shaken their heads when she'd asked them if they wanted to go with her – she'd been doing them the favour, not the other way around and if they chose not to accept it then that was their loss, not hers. Personally she'd thought them daft for going on duty with that St John Ambulance lot they'd got so involved with. In their shoes she'd have come up with an excuse rather than miss out on a good night's dancing.

TWENTY-ONE

'Tilly, Agnes seems very quiet. The two of you haven't had a fall-out, have you?' Olive asked her daughter, taking advantage of the fact that the two of them were alone as Agnes had been asked to stay on at work a bit longer because they were short-handed.

'No, of course not,' Tilly assured her mother. She had noticed herself that Agnes seemed a bit low but she had put that down to all the bad news in the papers. It made Tilly feel low herself.

The kitchen was warm with the smell of ironing, the kitchen door open to let in some fresh air. Tilly was helping her mother by folding the ironing, the two of them working companionably together. Sally was working nights and Dulcie had gone home to see her brother, who would be rejoining his regiment once his leave came to an end. Tilly gave a small sigh. She had really liked Dulcie's brother and when she had first seen him she had created all manner of romantic fantasies inside her head, most of which involved her doing something really brave, like saving his life, after which he clasped her to his chest and gazed deep into her eyes, telling her how wonderful she was.

Dunkirk, and what she had seen and heard from the soldiers rescued from France's beaches, though, had driven such silly school girlish daydreams right out of her head. Men weren't fairytale princes; they were human flesh and blood, marked by the things they had witnessed.

'I went to see Mrs Long today,' Olive told Tilly.

Tilly put down the petticoat she had been folding. 'Christopher's mother?'

Olive nodded, testing the heat of her iron on a damp handkerchief. Some women might spit on their irons to test their heat, but Olive's mother, having been in service, thoroughly disapproved of such common habits and had taught Olive to dampen a handkerchief and iron that instead. Having satisfied herself that it was hot enough to iron her smart cream linen summer skirt, she turned it inside out and slipped it on to the ironing board, carefully straightening its pleats.

'Is Christopher's father going to die?' Tilly asked anxiously. 'Christopher thinks he is. He doesn't say so but I can tell.'

'I think it's possible that he may, Tilly,' Olive answered her honestly, 'although naturally one hopes that he will not. It will be very hard for Mrs Long and Christopher if he does.'

'It must have been hard for you, Mum, when Dad died.'

They rarely talked about Jim's death. Although Olive had always made a point of talking to Tilly about her father, she had tried to talk about him in a light-hearted happy manner, wanting Tilly to know the best of her father rather than the dreadful final weeks of his life.

Standing at the sink, dampening the clean tea towel she was going to use to press her skirt with Olive then turned round and looked at her daughter. Tilly was growing up so quickly now. The war had done that.

'Yes,' she said simply, 'it was hard. I had your grandparents, of course. Your grandmother took your father's death very hard. I understand now much better than I did then how she must have felt. To have raised a child to adulthood and then to lose them is an unthinkable, an unbearable pain.'

'You must have missed Dad so much.'

'Yes I did. But I had you and that made it easier for me, Tilly. I had you to love and look after and I knew that your dad would want me to concentrate on you and not on his death. It will be harder for Christopher's mother than it was for me because they have been together so much longer, and hard for Christopher too.'

'Poor Christopher. His life is already difficult, with him being a pacifist. You have to be very brave to stick to your beliefs when other people don't always agree with them. I don't really agree with them myself, but that doesn't stop me being friends with Christopher.'

Her daughter definitely wasn't in any danger of falling in love with Christopher Long, no matter what Nancy might want to think, Olive acknowledged as she pressed the iron down hard on the pleats, filling the kitchen with sizzling steam and the smell of damp cloth.

Agnes felt so wretched. Even more wretched than she had felt when she had been told that she'd have to leave the orphanage, as she sat in the small back room off the booking office, hidden from public view, eating the fish-paste sandwiches Olive had made up for her lunch. She hadn't seen Ted for days, not since he had told her that he didn't think there was any need for them to have tea together any more now that she had settled in at the booking office. And she suspected that he was deliberately avoiding her.

Les, the new driver, on the other hand, she seemed to be bumping into all the time, but Les wasn't Ted. He didn't have Ted's kind smile nor his cheery whistle. She'd never thought that this would happen and that Ted wouldn't want to see her again. They had been such good friends – the best of friends – and Agnes missed him dreadfully. She couldn't sleep properly at night for thinking about him and worrying that he might have guessed that what she felt for him was more than just friendship.

Agnes didn't know when she had first realised that what she wanted most of all was to spend the rest of her life with Ted. She'd certainly known there was something at Christmas when he had hugged her and then kissed her quickly before releasing her. She'd wanted him to kiss her again but he hadn't and now he never would. A hard lump of emotion filled her chest, making it ache.

385

She felt so ashamed of herself, feeling like she did about Ted when he didn't want her to. That was a fine way to repay his kindness to her. She hadn't been able to bring herself to tell Tilly how she felt. Tilly was full of plans for what they could do together if the war continued, and once they were old enough. They could join the ATS or the WRNS, Tilly had said, and properly do their bit for their country. Agnes didn't want to go into uniform; she wanted to stay here where she could at least be close to Ted, but of course she hadn't told Tilly that, because she knew that Tilly would worry about her if she thought that she was unhappy over Ted. Tilly was like that.

She was so lucky to be living at number 13, Agnes acknowledged. She'd even got used to Dulcie's sharp tongue and had grown to realise that it didn't really mean anything and that it was just Dulcie's way. She couldn't imagine living anywhere where she could be happier, except of course if she was married to Ted and living with him. But that was never going to happen, Agnes acknowledged sadly.

TWENTY-TWO

Lying on the lawn under the shade of the apple tree in the back garden of number 13, taking a break from heeling in the new raspberry canes and blackcurrant bushes for Sally's fruit garden, Tilly looked up through the leaves towards the brilliant blue, early evening August sky. In the distance towards the south she could see white vapour trails and tiny barely discernible planes. Tilly's heart thudded with pride at the sight of them even though her stomach was churning with anxiety.

July had heralded the beginning of Hitler's attempt to destroy the RAF and thus leave the South Coast defenceless and ready for his invasion, and now, in mid-August, what was being called the Battle of Britain had begun in earnest, with aerial 'dogfights' taking place in the skies night and day, whilst the ground-based gun batteries did their bit to try to help the RAF.

The noise of heavy gunfire had now become almost as familiar to Londoners as the cries of its barrow boys and newspaper sellers.

There couldn't be many people who wouldn't

now recognise the heart-thrilling shape of an RAF Spitfire – or the fear-inducing sight of an enemy German plane, so familiar was the almost daily battle in the skies over the South of England between the RAF and the Luftwaffe.

London, especially Drury Lane and Piccadilly, were filled with men and women in uniform, especially RAF uniforms from Fighter Command's men based in the South of England, coming to the city to enjoy their leave by visiting the theatre and nightclubs.

British uniforms weren't the only ones to be seen either. In addition to the Free French of General de Gaulle, there were also Polish and Czech fighter pilots. And now that official military support from the colonies had arrived, there were servicemen from Australia, wearing their uniform hats pinned up at one side, from New Zealand, from Canada and, most recently, a contingent of airmen from Southern Rhodesia.

The Aussies were the most friendly and cheerful, and Tilly had been stopped more than once in the street by a smiling Australian wanting to know if she would 'show him where Buckingham Palace was', or making some other excuse to flirt with her. Such men though always took her refusal in good part, and Tilly had danced with some of them when the four of them – herself, Agnes, Dulcie and Sally – had gone to the Hammersmith Palais to celebrate Agnes's birthday in early July.

It was her own birthday on 7 September, a Saturday, and it had been agreed that since her mother would be on duty with the WVS that afternoon, her 'birthday tea' would be put off until the Sunday, and the four girls would have tea out together in London before going on to the Hammersmith Palais.

Tilly had felt quite envious of her mother earlier in the month when she had seen George Formby, who was filming *Spare a Copper* at the Ealing Studios, helping with the collection of scrap metal, something that Olive's WVS group took very seriously indeed. So seriously in fact that each member of the group had given one of their pans to the collection.

Tilly and Agnes had a St John Ambulance meeting this evening. Christopher wouldn't be going, though. He hadn't attended the last couple of weeks' meetings following the death of his father, feeling that his mother needed his presence at home. Poor Christopher. He had loved his father so much, and his death had increased his loathing of war.

As she left work for the day, Dulcie's thoughts were occupied with whether or not she was going to allow the good-looking Canadian, who had danced with her at the Palais the previous Saturday, to take her to the cinema, and admiring the nice tan the summer sunshine was giving her legs, meaning that she didn't have to wear stockings, so that she didn't see the man waiting for her until she had walked past him. He had called her name in a low urgent voice that had her spinning round in a mixture of disbelief anger and excitement, unable to stop herself from exclaiming, 'David!'

He was in uniform and it suited him, adding

to the devil-may-care manner that secretly she found so attractive. Not that she would ever admit that to him or anyone else, of course, especially now that he was married.

'Dulcie.' His delight at seeing her was obvious as he laughed and caught hold of her round the waist, swinging her off her feet and into his arms.

The unexpectedly familiar smell of him enveloped her – after all, his cologne was one they sold in Selfridges – further weakening her resistance. David, with his air of danger and excitement, appealed to a part of herself she had to struggle to control. But she did have to control it, she reminded herself.

'Put me down,' she demanded. 'Someone might see us, and tell your wife, and she certainly wouldn't approve of you being here, would she?'

'I don't care whether Lydia approves or not. She has her life, and I have mine.'

'The life of an RAF pilot who wants to do things that a married man isn't supposed to do,' Dulcie challenged him as he released her.

Her comment made him look deep into her eyes and tell her in a husky voice, 'There are so many things I'd like to do with you, Dulcie. I've thought about you a lot. We could have had a lot of fun together . . . we still can.'

Things like skulking around at the back of Selfridges, as though it were a back alley. Well, she wasn't the back alley type, and she wasn't going to be sweet-talked by David into becoming one, no matter how many jerky little bumps her heart gave just because he was here with her.

'Like I've already told you, I don't go out with married men,' Dulcie reminded him, before asking sharply, 'What are you doing here, anyway?'

'I'm on leave and in London – where else would I be but here hoping to see you whilst I still can. We've lost four pilots from our squadron this week, and two the week before. We have to live as much as we can whilst we can, Dulcie, because who knows which of us will be the next? I know what you said but I had to come and see you.'

He had moved out of the shadows now and it gave Dulcie a shock to see how the sunlight revealed harsh new lines either side of his mouth and a grimness to his expression. It shocked her even more to see how his hand trembled as he removed his cigarettes from his pocket and lit them each one.

Unfamiliar feelings of fear and panic turned her own body weak and cold. David was the last person she would have expected to talk about death.

'I've got only tonight here. Lydia's arranged some ruddy party she wants me to attend tomorrow – I should have gone straight home. I've got only a forty-eight-hour pass, but I told her I needed to come to London on RAF business. I have just this evening, Dulcie. Spend it with me. We could go out for dinner and then on to a club,' David urged her.

To her own shock, for a heartbeat of time she was almost tempted to agree, but David was a married man now even if he had claimed to her before his marriage that marrying Lydia would never be anything more than a duty he had been obliged to perform. David meant nothing to Lydia as a man, Dulcie suspected, it was his suitability and his connections she had married.

It wasn't because she felt she had a moral responsibility to recognise and protect their marriage that Dulcie was hesitating, though. It was because her instincts urged her to protect her own reputation. Once a girl crossed that line of respectability there could be no going back. Especially not when the man concerned was married. To Dulcie her reputation and her respectability were just as valuable assets as her beauty – important bargaining counters when the day came when she did want to get married and she had selected the husband she wanted. Just as Lydia and David's marriage was founded on her family's wealth and his family's country connections, she would be in a better position to get the kind of husband she wanted if she had something of value to trade with herself.

Dulcie knew all this by instinct, so that it only took a moment's hesitation before she was shaking her head and saying, 'I can't.'

'Yes you can. Oh, Dulcie, please,' David begged her reaching for her hand.

On the other side of the road, unobserved by either of them, Raphael, who had given in to an impulse to call and say 'hello' to Dulcie whilst he was in the area, saw David take Dulcie's hand.

He was in London on family business – Enrico Manelli, like his own grandfather and along with over seven hundred other Italians, had lost his life

392

when the *Arandora Star*, the ship transporting many of the Italian 'aliens' from Liverpool to Canada for internment, had been sunk by a German U-boat.

Some families had lost whole generations of male relatives, since, during their incarceration at Warth Mills near Bury in Lancashire, fearing that they would be separated, families had privately swapped papers so that family groups could stay together.

The trauma of so many deaths had affected everyone in the Italian community. Raphael's own father had been consumed with guilt about Raphael's grandfather and the fact that he had died without them being reconciled. Raphael had come to London during his leave to see Caterina Manelli to offer her his condolences. He didn't know where the sudden impulse to come here to Selfridges to see Dulcie had come from, and had excused his behaviour to himself by telling himself that Dulcie might want to know what had happened to the Manellis.

Watching her now, though, he could see that his presence was hardly likely to be welcomed. So he turned and walked away.

Tugging her hand free from David's, Dulcie repeated, 'I can't,' adding, 'I'm already seeing someone this evening.' It wasn't a complete lie, because she was anticipating seeing the Canadian. 'I must go.' She didn't want to stay in case David tried to persuade her to change her mind.

'*Dulcie, please.*'

There was real anguish in his voice but she

refused to listen to it, walking away from him so quickly that she was almost running, the flared skirt of her summer dress swirling round her legs in the speed of her retreat.

Agnes had been lingering so long outside the steps to Chancery Lane underground, that she was beginning to feel sick with anxiety and the fear of disappointment. She was waiting here after work in the hope of seeing Ted, whom she knew would be coming on duty. Agnes knew that what she was doing was 'wrong', and that it wasn't acceptable for a girl to lie in wait for a man, especially when that man had already made it plain that he didn't want anything more to do with her, but not knowing what it was she had done wrong and why Ted was ignoring her was making her feel so miserable that she had to see him.

It was a busy time of the evening, with people going home from work and others starting evening shifts, in addition to all the people in uniform, so many more of them now than there had been at the start of the war. Even Mr Smith had joined the Home Guard, as the Local Defence Volunteers were now called.

Agnes stiffened as she caught sight of Ted. He hadn't seen her – yet. Determined not to lose the opportunity to speak with him she screwed up all her courage and plunged into the mêlée of people, her heart pounding so heavily she thought it would burst through her skin. She reached the door to the café at the same time as Ted, the colour leaving his face when he saw her.

Already he was turning away from her. Desperately, Agnes grabbed hold of his arm, pleading with him, 'Ted, please, what's wrong? Why don't you want to be friends with me any more?'

The sight of Agnes's pale pleading face made Ted want to take her in his arms and hold her tightly, not something he would normally have even considered doing in public and in full daylight, but such was the effect of seeing her after all the weeks of avoiding her that his emotions threatened to get the better of him. But he couldn't and must not let them, he reminded himself. Things weren't good at home. His younger sister had been poorly all summer, coughing and wheezing so badly that they'd had to have the doctor, and that had cost money, even though they were in a hospital savings plan. The doctor had said that it was the dry dusty air in London that was affecting little Sonia's lungs and that she'd be better off living in the country, but there was no way Ted's mother would allow her two young daughters to be evacuated without her, and they were over the age at which she could have been evacuated with them, so all they'd been able to do was to buy the medicine the doctor had recommended and keep Sonia inside as much as possible. Ted's sister's illness meant that his mother needed his wages even more. Only the previous night, lying awake in bed listening to Sonia coughing, Ted had known that the door had finally closed on any chance he might have had of courting Agnes.

Now, manfully, Ted put his own feelings to one side.

'The thing is, Agnes,' he began carefully, 'when you and me used to get together you was still finding your feet at work, so to speak. It was like, well, a sort of business relationship. I couldn't stand back and see you get yourself in a mess and perhaps leave the underground. I reckoned it was my duty to help you out a bit.' He could see Agnes's face crumpling, and he had to harden his heart and deny his own feelings, telling himself that it was better this way and that he was doing it for her. There was no sense in him starting something between them that could never go anywhere. Better to be cruel now to be kind to her for the future.

A business relationship? Did Ted mean that they had never really been friends at all? He must do.

'It's different now. You've settled in, and there's no call for you and me to get together any more. I reckon you're a real credit to what I've taught you and to yourself,' he added, trying to soften the blow. He was hurting her, he knew, but it was surely better to hurt her now?

So now she knew. Ted hadn't fallen out of friends with her, because he had never thought of them as friends in the first place. Agnes felt mortified. She wanted to run away and hide, but of course she couldn't. She could only nod her head and accept what Ted was saying to her, and then let him go.

She cried all the way home. In fact she cried so much that she could hardly see where she was going, only managing to stop just before she reached Article Row, extracting her handkerchief

396

from her pocket and doing her best to rub away the signs of her misery.

Olive wasn't deceived, though. She was alone in the kitchen when Agnes came in, her head down and her shoulders bowed in defeat.

Down at the bottom of the garden the greenhouse door was open and she could see Tilly inside it, picking the tomatoes Olive had told her they needed for tea. Knowing that she would be several minutes, Olive seized her chance, going over to Agnes, taking hold of her hands and telling her gently, 'I know that something's upsetting you, Agnes. You haven't been yourself for weeks now. Why don't you tell me what it is?'

Olive's sympathy was too much for Agnes's fragile composure. Fresh tears started to fall as the story of her feelings for Ted and his lack of them for her came flooding out in fits and starts.

Once Olive had discreetly established that nothing that shouldn't have happened between them had happened, and that Ted had not taken advantage of Agnes in any kind of way, Olive led Agnes to a chair and pushed her gently into it.

Young love could hurt so much. She could still remember the pain she had felt when she had discovered that the boy she had secretly admired for weeks had sent another girl a Valentine card.

'I know what's happened hurts dreadfully, Agnes, but it will get better, I promise you. Why, I shouldn't be surprised if this time next year there'll be another boy in your life who makes you forget Ted completely.'

'No one could ever make me forget Ted,' Agnes

sobbed, crumpling her already damp handkerchief into a wet ball.

'Oh, Agnes . . .' Olive kneeled down in front of her and took her in her arms, rocking her as though she were a small child. There was nothing she could say or do to make things better, Olive knew. Compassionately, she stroked Agnes's head.

Poor child. She was so young and so vulnerable. Somehow Olive couldn't see her own Tilly being so overwhelmed and cast down with misery in the same situation, but then Tilly hadn't experienced the same loss and childhood that Agnes had. She'd have to have a word with Tilly, and Sally too, to warn them not to mention Ted to Agnes.

'Tilly will be coming in, in a minute,' she told Agnes, releasing her and getting up. 'Why don't you go up upstairs and bathe your eyes with some cold water, Agnes, and then when you come down again I'll have a nice hot cup of tea waiting for you?'

The day did bring some good news, though. Well, sort of good news, Olive thought as they all listened to Winston Churchill's wireless broadcast to the nation that evening, silence between them as they concentrated whilst he spoke, Olive's eyes filling with tears as he thundered the words.

'The gratitude of every home in our Island, in our Empire, and indeed throughout the world, except in the abodes of the guilty, goes out to the British airmen who, undaunted by odds, unwearied in their constant challenge and mortal danger, are turning the tide of the World War by their prowess

398

and by their devotion. Never in the field of human conflict was so much owed by so many to so few. All our hearts go out to the fighter pilots, whose brilliant actions we see with our own eyes day after day . . .'

When the speech finally came to an end, all of them exchanged looks, the emotional silence between them, as they digested what Mr Churchill had said, broken by Olive saying firmly, 'I think we should have a cup of tea.'

Sally was still thinking about Winston Churchill's speech the following day at work. His words stiffened one's spine and lifted one's spirits.

All the serving men on men's surgical were talking about it and Sister had had to issue a ban on them discussing it for an hour to calm things down in the ward before the consultants' morning rounds.

Privately all the nurses knew from the evacuated staff that one harsh reality of the RAF's fierce defence of the country was the number of young men in military and other hospitals with the most dreadful kinds of wounds, not just missing limbs but terrible burns and disfiguring facial injuries. She herself this morning, when Matron had called for volunteers willing to go down to help out when needed on the now busy wards of the evacuated main hospital, had added her name to the list.

She told George about this later in the day as they left the British Museum together, George having asked Sally if she'd like to attend one of Myra Hess's lunchtime concerts there.

'I'll be on duty down there as well,' George told her.

Sally wouldn't be leaving London permanently, of course; relief staff would only be called upon for short periods of a couple of days or so when necessary, and Sally hoped it wasn't too selfish of her to feel glad about that. She had settled in so well at number 13 that it felt like home to her now and she would have been reluctant to leave.

The music had been uplifting and, combined with her existing feelings, had Sally surreptitiously wiping the betraying signs of emotion from her eyes as she and George stepped out into the afternoon sunshine.

She saw that George had noticed, though, and as they became part of the crowd walking away from the British Museum he reached into his pocket and produced an immaculately clean handkerchief, which he handed to her with such an understanding smile that Sally warmed even more to him, that feeling growing when he confessed, 'I've never been able to listen to Beethoven without being in danger of disgracing myself and being overcome with my feelings, and Myra Hess does play so very well.'

'Doesn't she just,' Sally agreed, carefully patting her eyes, before handing George's handkerchief back to him with her thanks. After that somehow it seemed perfectly natural and right that he should take hold of her hand, and that when he suggested that we hop on a bus and take advantage of our time off and the good weather to walk in Hyde Park,' Sally had no hesitation in agreeing.

'This is what I miss about home,' George told her later when, still hand in hand, they were walking through the park. 'Greenery, fields and the countryside.'

'Hyde Park is hardly the countryside,' Sally laughed.

'No it isn't, but at least it's green,' George smiled.

The park was busy with others doing exactly what they were doing – strolling in the sunshine – in the main groups of young men and women in various uniforms.

'I do so admire the young men who've come from the Dominions and the Commonwealth to fight for Britain,' Sally told George, as a group of Aussies with their distinctive hats strolled past, obviously off duty.

'We come because we want to, because we do love our Mother Country,' George told her solemnly, stopping walking, his own voice low as he stared into the distance, perhaps seeing, Sally thought, a different landscape of green fields halfway across the world.

Unable to stop herself, she squeezed his hand, her eyes full of the emotion she was feeling as he turned back to her. They were standing in the shadow of one of the trees, and when, after a brief look round, George bent his head and kissed her, Sally didn't push him away. It was a tender kiss, a sweet kiss full of hope and promise, she recognised, as she nestled closer to him and he took advantage of her movement to take her properly in his arms, a new beginning for her, for them both, with the birth of a new relationship.

George's kiss was firm but respectful, and it touched Sally's heart that she could feel his heart thudding so fast and the faint tremble of his arms. He was such a genuine, likeable, nice man, so easy to be with. And easy to love?

'I've been wanting to do that since I first saw you,' George confessed after he stopped kissing her, which made it easy for Sally smile and easy too for her to put serious thoughts of love to one side.

Their kiss had changed things, though. Now, as they continued their walk, they moved much closer together, George's arm now round her waist, holding her to him, and when they stopped to watch some young naval ratings rowing on the Serpentine, it felt natural and right to Sally to put her head on George's shoulder.

'I've enjoyed today,' George told her as they made their way back to the hospital.

'So have I,' Sally told him.

They looked at one another and smiled, and Sally felt her heart lift.

The future suddenly looked much brighter, despite the threat of war, and the sadness she had felt for those poor wounded boys.

TWENTY-THREE

Things had changed an awful lot since the first time Tilly and Agnes had gone dancing at the Hammersmith Palais, Olive reflected ruefully, as she watched all four young women giving their appearances final checks in the hall mirror. In the small space the rustle of their party frocks mingled with the sound of high heels on the linoleum either side of the hall runner.

'How do we look, Mum?' Tilly demanded, twirling into the back room, her face alight with happiness and excitement.

'You all look lovely,' Olive assured her truthfully. She had been so anxious that first night she had watched them leave; now her concern was more for the young men who would have to deal with three stunning-looking confident young women, all intent on dazzling them, and one shy one whose quiet sadness was almost bound to draw their compassion.

Tonight would be Tilly's first really 'grown-up' birthday, and the first she would not be celebrating at home, although of course they were having a traditional birthday tea tomorrow, at Tilly's request. Today, though, the four girls would be having their tea at a Joe Lyons restaurant before going on to the Palais, and Tilly was as excited about that as though they were dining at somewhere like the Ritz. If Olive suspected that Sally might have preferred to spend her Saturday off with her doctor friend, who she mentioned increasingly in her chats, Olive wasn't going to spoil either Tilly's evening or Sally's generosity by saying as much. Even Dulcie seemed to have made an effort on Tilly's behalf, as Tilly had told her that Dulcie had instructed the young Canadian airman she had met at the Palais to make sure he brought plenty of his pals along with him, informing Olive earnestly, 'so that we have lots of dashing partners. Dulcie says the Canadians are best, Mum, because they look smart in their uniforms, and they're very respectful. Dulcie says they don't flirt like the Australians, or the Poles, so we won't have to worry about them making a nuisance of themselves.'

Tilly and Agnes were wearing the pretty floral sateen cotton dresses Olive had had made for them after another trip to the Portobello Market. This time there had been several characters there who Olive had thought distinctly shady, a sign, so Sergeant Dawson had told her when she had mentioned this to him, of the increase in black market trading.

Sally's dress was pale blue with darker blue polka dots, the colour suiting her auburn hair and pale skin, whilst Dulcie was wearing a pink cotton skirt, the cotton embroidered with small black bows, and a black fine-knit top with pink bows at the neckline and on the puffed sleeves.

It was a warm enough night for the girls to insist that they didn't need heavy coats and that their simple stoles would do.

Tilly looked so grown up in her new dress, wearing the pearl clip-on earrings she had persuaded Olive to let her borrow. The war was changing their lives, making the girls grow up so fast.

'You know what to do if the air-raid siren goes off?' Olive couldn't help saying, forced into a rueful smile when four voices chorused together, 'Yes, run for the nearest shelter.'

It had been a shock at first when German bombers had been seen over London on the night of 24 August, but the RAF had seen them off and bombed Berlin in retaliation. Although there had been plenty of scares since then, with the air-raid sirens going off at night with increasing frequency, disturbing everyone's sleep when they all had to troop out of their beds to the nearest shelter – which in the case of Olive's household was the Anderson shelter in the garden – after the first shock Londoners had begun to take the air raids in their stride. After all, they had the ground batteries with their heavy-duty 'ackack' guns, and the RAF, to protect them.

The girls had decided to have their tea at the Joe Lyons in Leicester Square but two buses had gone past them without stopping, obviously full already.

'Here's another, and it's slowing down,' Tilly cheered.

'It's going to Covent Garden, though, not Leicester Square,' Agnes pointed out.

'Never mind, let's just get on it,' said Dulcie, giving Tilly a push in the direction of the now stationary bus. 'We can walk the rest of the way.'

Tilly hesitated but the conductor was getting impatient and called out, 'Are you girls getting on or not?'

'We're getting on,' said Sally, stepping forward, the others following on behind her, clambering onto the platform and holding on tight.

'It's standing room only down here,' the conductor told them, reaching for his ticket machine. 'Upstairs, if you want a seat.'

Taking care to keep her skirt away from the stairs, Tilly went up first, followed by the others, half gasping and half groaning in protest as the bus lurched to an unwieldy halt at the next stop to allow more passengers to get on.

Agnes gave the café where she and Ted used to meet a forlorn look from the seat where the four of them had squashed up together at the back of the bus, and Tilly, who knew from her mother what was causing Agnes's low spirits, affected not to notice, trying to distract her by pointing out a group of French military on the other side of the road, insisting that one of them had definitely looked like General de Gaulle.

'Pooh, the French, they're nothing. The Canadians are much better,' Dulcie announced as their bus came to a halt at a stop just short of Covent Garden.

Covent Garden was relatively quiet as it was too early for the evening's ballet-goers. The girls decided to cut across to Leicester Square via the backstreets to avoid the crowds Dulcie had warned them would be filling the square.

'You should have seen it yesterday. You could hardly move for uniforms, most of them RAF. I suppose they deserve a bit of time off after all this fighting they've been doing.'

They had already walked down one street, when Sally broke into Dulcie's conversation to demand, 'What's that?' She looked upwards towards the sound they could all now hear – a sound that was growing louder and more ominous by the second, its dull droning now becoming a rumbling roar.

Up above them the sky was darkening, the light shut out by the mass of aircraft swarming towards the city.

'Oh Gawd, it's them. It's the Germans,' Dulcie gasped, reverting to the cockney accent she was normally so careful to keep hidden.

Tilly gulped in shocked silence, feeling Agnes's arm trembling against her own.

Sally continued to stare upwards in horror. There must be hundreds of them: black bombers surrounded, escorted, protected by fighter planes, too many of them to count, the noise they were making as they flew over making conversation impossible. It was like a nightmare, so unbeliev-able and unthinkable that surely it couldn't be happening. Not here in London. The Germans could not be here overhead in such a huge force that they almost blocked the light out of the sky.

Where was the RAF? Why were the ack-ack guns silent?

In disbelieving terror the girls stood rooted to the spot as though shocked into a trance.

'They're heading for the docks,' Dulcie, who knew her East End, broke the silence, mouthing the words to them, the four of them wincing as, hard on her words, they heard the sound of an explosion quickly followed by another and then another, huge plumes of smoke billowing up toward the skyline.

Never had the wail of air-raid sirens sounded so unnerving and doom laden.

'Come on,' Sally yelled. 'The nearest shelter will be the one in Leicester Square.' They started to run, their speed hampered by their heels and the summer-heat-greasy cobbles of the pavementless alley.

'Oh, ruddy hell,' Dulcie swore as her heel caught between two cobbles. The air around them was thick with the acrid smell of smoke drifting in from the bombed docks, the sound of sirens filling the air. Dulcie tried to free her heel with an impatient movement of her foot and then gasped in shock when the heel refused to come free, her own violent movement pitching her forward onto the cobbles. She put out her hands to save herself but it was too late.

It was Tilly looking back who saw her, calling out to the other two, 'Stop. Dulcie's fallen over.'

Sally tried to catch hold of her, all too aware of their danger, but Tilly had already turned back, Agnes going with her, leaving Sally with no option but to do the same. They were so vulnerable out here in plain view, and she was thankful that it was the docks and the East End the bombers were attacking, and not the city itself.

'Dulcie, are you all right?' Tilly dropped down on her knees at the same time as Dulcie struggled to get up.

There was blood on her forehead and what looked like a large bruise already swelling above her eye.

'Of course I—' she began, her sudden gasp of pain slicing off her words, as she sank down again.

'I think Dulcie's hurt,' Tilly said to Sally, who had just reached them. 'There's blood on her forehead and—'

'Dulcie?' Sally queried, immediately the professional trained nurse.

'It's my ankle. I must have turned it when I fell. I'll be all right once I'm standing up.'

'We'll help you,' Tilly began, but Sally shook her head, her heart sinking as she looked at the unnatural angle of Dulcie's foot, and saw the bruise on her forehead.

'Well, come on then,' Dulcie demanded impatiently. 'Help me up.'

'Dulcie, I need to look at your ankle. I think you may have broken it, and you've hurt your head. Do you feel sick, at all, or dizzy,' Sally asked her crisply. There was no point in her mincing her words, but she didn't want to frighten Dulcie more than was necessary by telling her that the bump to her head could result in delayed concussion.

'No, I don't feel sick,' Dulcie told her crossly. 'I just want to get out of here.'

The sound of another bomb exploding was so loud that she had to stop speaking.

'You can't,' Sally had to tell her. 'You won't be able to walk on that ankle. We'll need to get you some proper medical help.'

As a nurse Sally could recognise from the look on Dulcie's face how shocked and frightened she was, even though she was trying not to show it, but there was nothing she could do to help her.

It was too late now to regret coming down this empty back alley with no sign of either a shelter or an ARP post. Normally Sally would have stayed with Dulcie and sent Tilly and Agnes to get help, but she was very much aware that Olive, even though she had not said so, expected her to keep the two younger girls safe. As she worried about who needed her the most, a fighter plane screamed overhead, causing them all to duck and Dulcie to wince with fresh pain.

Tears were rolling down Agnes's face, and for once even Tilly was subdued and quiet.

But then it was Sally's turn to be shocked when Dulcie told her in a thin but determined voice, with a jerk of her head towards Tilly and Agnes, 'You'd better get those two to safety, 'cos if anything were to happen to them Olive would have my guts for garters. I'll be all right here until you can send some help. Jerry isn't going to come dropping any bombs down this back alley when he's got the whole of the docks and the East End to bomb.'

They would leave her anyway, Dulcie reasoned to herself as she spoke, so she might as well be the one to send them away as lie here and wait for them to say they were going to leave her. In their shoes she wouldn't waste a minute – not even a second – in running for safety, so why should they? And she certainly wasn't going to have them thinking she was scared, even though she was. So scared that she secretly felt like begging them not to leave her, but of course she couldn't do that. Her pride wouldn't let her. If her own mother was here right now she probably wouldn't stay with her because she'd be worrying about her precious Edith. She was nothing to these girls, just like they were nothing to her. She'd be daft to think that they'd care about her feeling frightened and alone.

What Dulcie said made sense, Sally knew, but before she could say anything, Agnes, who up until now had been crying silently, suddenly stopped and said fiercely, 'We can't leave Dulcie here. It wouldn't be right. I'm staying with her.'

Dulcie stared at Agnes. Agnes wanted to stay with her. Agnes, who she had tormented and, yes, bullied and who was so unsure of herself that she never said a word, was standing there telling Sally that she was staying. Dulcie couldn't believe it. Agnes's face became a tearful unfocused image she had to blink her eyes to get back into focus. She wasn't crying, or if she was it was only because of the pain in her ankle and because her head hurt, and not because of the aching pang of emotion she could feel inside her heart.

'No, it wouldn't,' Tilly agreed. 'If Dulcie has to stay then we're staying with her. We're all in this together, friends together, and friends don't go and leave each other, they stick together.'

Friends! Dulcie had never wanted friends. She'd never believed in them. Friends was just a word that meant palling up with someone because they were useful to you, and then dropping them when they weren't. It didn't mean risking your own life to be with them when you were free to walk away from danger and they weren't.

'It's best if you go and get help, Sally,' Tilly added. ''Cos you'll know what to say, and me and Agnes will stay here with Dulcie.'

Tilly plonked herself down on the cobbles next to Dulcie as she spoke, the skirt of her dress billowing out around her.

She wasn't going to be able to budge Tilly and Agnes, Sally recognised. Dropping down on her haunches she demanded, 'Let me have another look at your ankle, Dulcie.' Perhaps it was only sprained and not broken. But another closer inspection showed Sally that Dulcie's ankle was quite definitely broken.

'Should we try and get Dulcie's shoe off?' Tilly asked, eyeing the now swollen flesh puffing over the strap on Dulcie's shoe.

Sally shook her head. 'No, her shoe will help to give the broken bone some support.'

In the immediate anxiety of worrying about what to do, the ongoing bombing was something that Sally had pushed to the back of her mind, but now it couldn't be ignored. Over towards the docks and the East End, they could still hear bombs exploding. It felt as though they'd been here in the alleyway for hours but a glance at her watch told Sally that they had actually been there only just over fifteen minutes.

'We can't stay here, it's too dangerous.' The words were spoken before Sally could halt them. 'I'll stay with Dulcie. You two run for the shelter.'

'No,' Tilly refused firmly. 'If we can't all go, then we should all stay. We're in this together, and we should stick together.'

There was a moment's silence, during which they all looked at one another, and then winced as another bomb exploded.

'If me and Tilly made a chair with our hands, perhaps we could carry Dulcie and you could run on ahead, Sally, to get help. We used to make chairs that way at the orphanage,' Agnes suggested

Sally's training told her not to risk moving a patient until they had been assessed by a doctor but with the lives of three other young women to worry about, she knew Agnes's suggestion made sense.

'We could try,' she agreed. The three of them could try to get Dulcie to her feet and if they succeeded then she could support Dulcie whilst the other two formed their chair.

Sally took a deep breath, warning Dulcie, 'It's going to hurt when we get you upright. Whatever you do don't try to move your foot or put any weight on it.'

Dulcie nodded, resolving inwardly that no

matter how much it hurt she would manage to deal with the pain. And not just for her own sake, she recognised with a stab of shock; she wanted to do it for the sake of the girls who had offered to stay with her.

Five minutes later, sweating and feeling sick from the pain, like a knife slicing into her, that had been beyond anything she had ever had to bear, Dulcie was standing up, her head and her ankle pounding. Sally supported her on the side of her broken ankle, whilst Tilly and Agnes stood behind her carefully forming a seat for her with their hands.

Dulcie had more guts than she had expected, Sally admitted as she lowered her patient onto the makeshift 'seat' as gently as she could. She knew how much pain Dulcie was in from her broken ankle, and she was concerned too about that bump on her head, but Dulcie had not uttered one word of complaint or one protest when they had lifted her up. Sally's estimation of her had risen a great deal as she witnessed this stoicism.

They could make only slow progress, Dulcie's arms round Tilly and Agnes as they carried her, all three of them urging Sally to go on ahead, Tilly calling out to her that they would be fine, before telling Dulcie, 'It's a pity we haven't got some of those Canadian airmen here to help us.'

'What, and let them see me looking like this?' Dulcie joked back. 'No, thank you.'

It couldn't be far to the nearest ARP post, surely, Sally reasoned as she ran to the end of the alleyway following the dogleg of a slightly wider empty street round until, to her relief, she could see where it opened out into Leicester Square.

The bombing seemed to have stopped, and wasn't that an ARP post at the bottom of the road?

'Hey, you, miss. What are you doing out here? Can't you see there's a bombing raid going on? Didn't you hear the sirens going off?'

The man confronting her was wearing a tin helmet, an ARP band on his arm, his face and voice both evidencing his irritation.

'There's been an accident. My friends need help. One of them has broken her ankle. I'm a trained nurse but we need help,' Sally told him breathlessly.

'What the devil . . . ?' The ARP man turned back to the post, with its covering of sandbags, and shouted into it, 'Hey, Fred and Bert, get out here, will you?'

Two men emerged, one of them cramming his tin hat onto his head as he did so, the other finishing a cup of tea.

'We've got some girls needing help. What . . . ?' he ducked automatically as up above them the sky darkened as the German bombers turned for home. The sound filling the air now was of their engines and thankfully not the explosion of more bombs.

The other girls had just reached the first part of the dogleg and had paused for a minute because Tilly had a bit of a stitch in her side, when they too saw the German aircraft overhead.

They'd just started off again, Tilly and Agnes

both ignoring the pull on their now aching muscles from the effort of carrying Dulcie, when suddenly one of the fighters escorting the bombers peeled off, screaming from the sky to head directly toward them.

For a second they all froze, and then Dulcie told the other two to run. 'Go, leave me . . . just run.'

'Quick,' Tilly urged Agnes, 'that doorway over there.'

It wasn't easy to run and carry Dulcie but somehow they managed it, sheltering in the narrow doorway as best they could whilst machine-gun fire from the fighter plane rat-a-tat-tatted over the cobbles in flares of bright burning flames. The plane had come down so low that they could see the pilot in his helmet as the fighter's guns fired another burst of bullets, the girls wincing as some struck the side of the building, narrowly missing the doorway.

'What are we going to do if he comes back?' Agnes asked.

'You two are going to run, now, before he does,' Dulcie answered ruthlessly.

'We aren't leaving you,' Tilly told her. She was more frightened than she had ever been in the whole of her life, but there was no way she was going to leave Dulcie here on her own to be gunned down by that German pilot.

'He'll get us if he turns back,' Dulcie told her grimly. 'He knows we're here.'

'Then he'll just have to get us, won't he, Agnes?' Tilly declared. 'Because we aren't leaving you.'

Agnes nodded. She was surprised how calm she felt. But then what did it matter if she was killed? Not having Ted in her life any more was worse than being killed. At least that only hurt you once. Not seeing Ted hurt her every day.

'Tilly, Agnes, where are you?'

'That's Sally,' Tilly said unnecessarily, poking her head round the corner of their protective doorway to call back, 'We're here.'

At the other end of the street, the German plane banked and turned, with menacing intent, but then unexpectedly, and to their relief, instead of coming back it rose up and turned again before heading south at speed, leaving the sky clear for the girls to see the Spitfire following it, chasing it across the sky.

Thankfully, the three girls exhaled, no words necessary as they clung together. The smoke-tainted London air had never tasted sweeter.

Sally and the three men ran down the street, Sally offering up thanks for the girls' safety. When she had seen the deathly bulk of that plane filling the other end of the street, she had been so sure that they would be killed. Now the relief was making her feel shaky and weak, but she was a nurse and she still had a job to do. She pushed her own feelings to one side, as they reached the girls and the men took charge, making a fresh, stronger chair for Dulcie.

'We'll need to get her to hospital,' Sally told the men. 'Barts will be best. I work there.'

'We'll try and get an ambulance sorted out for you once we get back to the post, although you'll probably have a long wait. The docks and the East End have taken a real hammering. There's hundreds been left dead, we've heard.'

Now that it was over the girls were silent, simply looking at one another with marvelling gazes, too filled with relief at their escape to be able to speak, other than to thank their rescuers. Besides, there was no need for words now. The bond that had been formed between them all in those terror-filled moments when they thought they would die, meant that they each knew exactly what the others were thinking and feeling.

In the air-raid shelter with the other WVS workers, Olive prayed that the girls would be all right. The Germans were bombing the docks and the East End, not Hammersmith, she tried to reassure herself. Mrs Weaver, the oldest member of their group, got out the knitting she always seemed to have with her. Olive envied her, wishing that she too had something to occupy her hands, even if the only thing occupying her thoughts was the safety of her daughter.

The girls had just reached Barts, Sally having decided that she would feel happier if Tilly and Agnes were with her rather than leaving them to make their way from the ARP post to the air-raid shelter and from there to home on their own, when the second wave of bombs were dropped on the docks and the East End.

The hospital was busy with the constant arrival of casualties from the bombing, and although strictly speaking Sally did not work in the Emergency Department, and was not on duty anyway, she insisted on being allowed to go there with Dulcie, pushing her wheelchair herself, to save the overbusy porters having to do so.

'What's going to happen to me?' Dulcie demanded.

'A doctor will examine you and then you'll have to have that ankle set and put in plaster. They'll take a look at that bump on your head and keep you in for a day or so to make sure that you aren't suffering from concussion,' Sally told her, handing her over to the ward sister. 'Don't worry, Dulcie. Everything will be all right. I'm going to offer to go on duty now, so I'll be here and I'll see if Sister will let me come down and see you later once they've made you comfortable.'

Dulcie, her defences weakened by pain, turned to Tilly and Agnes and told them emotionally, 'What you two have done for me tonight, I'll never forget. Never.'

Each of them holding one of her hands, they looked at one another whilst Sally looked on. They all knew that what had happened, what they'd shared, had forged a very special bond between them.

'I've never been bothered about having friends,' Dulcie continued. 'I've never seen the point 'cos you always know that when it comes down to it someone who says she's a friend will put herself first. I'd do the same myself. But tonight, well, you've taught me different; you've shown me what friendship really is. You've given me something that no one else has ever given me and I won't ever forget that. From now on the three of you come first with me, and that's a promise.'

Facing danger together bound people in a very special way, Sally acknowledged, listening to Dulcie. Tonight they had all individually and together shown a strength and a desire to put one another first that was the very best of human nature. Tonight a relationship had been forged between them that would last for the rest of their lives.

'Friends?' Dulcie asked gruffly.

'Friends,' Agnes, Tilly and Sally answered her, all four of them reaching out to place their hands one on top of the other.

It was daylight before Tilly and Agnes arrived back at number 13 to find Olive waiting anxiously for them. They had spent the night in a large public shelter close to Barts Hospital and had had to wait for the all clear to go off before they could leave.

Over hot strong cups of tea, Tilly told her mother what had happened, her daughter's matter of fact, 'Dulcie wanted us to run for safety and leave her but, like Agnes said, we couldn't do that,' leaving Olive torn between surprise that Dulcie of all people should have shown such selflessness, pride in Tilly's bravery and shaky relief that they had all made it to safety.

'Dulcie will have to stay in hospital until they say she can leave,' Tilly continued, 'and Sally said that when she is allowed out her leg will still be in plaster.'

'Has anyone told Dulcie's family what's

happened?' Olive asked. 'Only if they haven't, I'd better go round and let them know.'

'No one's sent a message, as far as I know,' Tilly answered her, hesitating before adding, 'Dulcie's family live on the edge of Stepney, and by all accounts that got badly bombed.'

Olive nodded. 'I know. We heard about it last night after the all clear.'

What Olive didn't want to say was that the ARP official had also said the devastation in the East End was beyond description and had spoken of stumbling across bodies, so many people had been killed.

The plain unvarnished truth was, according to the ARP official, that those in charge of areas like Stepney had simply not done enough to make plans in the event of a serious bombing raid.

'You and Agnes have had a tiring night – why don't you try and get a couple of hours' sleep instead of going to church this morning, and I'll try and call round on Dulcie's family? I've got their address from when she first came here.'

'Me and Agnes thought that we'd go up to the hospital this afternoon, Mum, and see how Dulcie is. We felt really bad about leaving her there last night, didn't we, Agnes?'

Agnes agreed.

'Of course, Sally will be there to look out for her,' Tilly acknowledged before adding, 'Dulcie was ever so brave, Mum, telling us to go and leave her.'

'Yes, she was,' Olive was forced to admit.

*   *   *

Later that morning, though, setting out to tell Dulcie's family what had happened, Olive felt more concerned about the danger her own daughter had been in than she was about Dulcie. Not that she wished any harm on the girl, she assured herself as she headed for Stepney, but there was no getting away from the fact that helping Dulcie had put her own daughter's life at risk and that was something Olive didn't like at all.

Even though, mercifully, Holborn and the City of London beyond it had escaped the ravages of the bombing, the Germans having concentrated on the docks and the East End, there was still a pall of smoke hanging in the air, as Olive set out on what she knew would be a long walk, the pavements busy with ARP wardens, firemen and the police, as well as some of the more adventurous Londoners themselves, come to see the damage inflicted on their city.

Olive didn't want to risk catching a bus, though, even if she could find one that was running, in case it couldn't take her very far.

Not knowing what to expect, she found the sight of familiar buildings still standing, their sandbags still in place, reassuring. Her route took her past St Paul's, thankfully untouched, but when she paused to look at the cathedral an elderly shabbily dressed woman standing close to her said, 'St Paul's might be standing now but them Germans will be back, you mark my words. Practically done for Stepney, they have. I was lucky I'd gone to the Tilbury shelter, off the Commercial Road, 'cos our whole street's bin flattened.'

Olive made a small sound of sympathy.

'My daughter reckons we'd be better off sheltering in the underground, but we was barred from doing that last night at Liverpool Street station. I'm off out of here this afternoon. Putting us on coaches, they are, to take us somewhere where they can rehouse us, so I thought I'd come have a look at St Paul's just in case it ain't standing when they bring us back.'

Already apprehensive about what she might find in Stepney Olive was now increasingly anxious at the old lady's words, especially when she got closer to the area and saw how many people were trudging around in family groups, carrying bundles of possessions, the blank look on some of their faces giving a hint of what they might have been through.

Olive had almost reached Stepney when she had to stop because of the ARP men turning people back, and explaining that it was too dangerous for them to go into the area because of the number of bombed and collapsed buildings.

When Olive told them where she was heading, though, after consulting a street map she was told she could go ahead, and given instructions of how to get there.

It seemed that because Dulcie's family's home was in a street on the city side of the area, the houses were still standing, although by the time she got there Olive felt that she was almost choking on dust and smoke.

It was Dulcie's mother who opened the door to Olive's knock, her facial resemblance to Dulcie plain, despite her careworn appearance. However, the relief on her face when she opened the door changed to apprehension when she saw Olive standing there.

Thinking that her anxiety was on Dulcie's account, Olive made haste to tell her, 'It's all right; Dulcie's all right. I'm her landlady . . .'

But to her surprise, instead of greeting her news with relief, Mrs Simmonds simply said sharply, 'Oh, yes, of course Dulcie would be all right, knowing her.' She was looking past Olive now and out into the street. 'It's our Edith I'm worried about. She's a singer, you know, and she's going to be famous. She's got a top agent looking out for her,' she told Olive proudly, fresh apprehension colouring her voice as she added, 'She was singing last night at a club up the West End. I just hope she's all right.'

'I'm sure she will be,' Olive tried to comfort her. 'The West End wasn't bombed at all, according to what I've heard. But about Dulcie . . .'

'What about her? She's been causing trouble, I suppose. That's Dulcie all over. She's always been difficult and hard work.'

Although privately Olive might have agreed with the other woman's comments, somehow hearing them spoken by Dulcie's own mother made her feel unexpectedly protective of her lodger so that she said firmly, 'I think I'd better come in.'

'Well, if you must, but this place won't be what you're used to. Always singing your praises, Dulcie is, and telling us what a lovely house you have and how much at home you've made her; how you think so much of her and treat her like a daughter, asking her to look out for your Tilly.' Mrs Simmonds gave a sniff of disdain. 'Always going on about Tilly and Agnes and Sally, she is, saying what good friends to her they are and how much they think of her. Of course, she only does it to upset Edith, and why I don't know. I couldn't have asked for a better daughter than Edith, good from the minute she was born, Edith has been, and sing – she's got the voice of an angel.' Fresh anxiety showed on Mrs Simmonds' face. 'Worried to death about her, I am, and I shan't have a second's peace until I know she's safe.'

Olive's thoughts were whirling after Dulcie's mother's revelations about what Dulcie had said to her. Normally Olive would have wondered what on earth had made Dulcie create such a fabrication, but after listening to Dulcie's mother praising her younger daughter whilst criticising her elder, Olive suspected that she knew the reason for Dulcie's behaviour. Against her will she felt sympathetic toward Dulcie, her compassion aroused at the thought of a child – any child – being rejected by its mother in favour of a sibling. It was no wonder that Dulcie was the way she was.

Mrs Simmonds showed Olive into a small, cramped and dark back room, lifting some clothes off a chair and putting them down on the table so that Olive could sit down.

'Them's our Edith's stage clothes. Course, they cost a fair bit, they did, but then like she says, she's got to look the part if she's to get the good

425

jobs. Her agent reckons she's going to be bigger than Vera Lynn. I just wish I knew she was safe.'

'Of course you must be worrying,' Olive agreed. 'That's the price we mothers have to pay for loving our children, isn't it? I don't like to add to your worries, but I thought you'd want to know that Dulcie had a bit of an accident last night. She ended up with a broken ankle, and they're worried that she might have concussion.' Olive paused, waiting for Dulcie's mother to express alarm and concern and then, when she made no comment, continued quietly. 'She's in hospital – Barts – I expect she's told you that Sally is a nurse and works there. You'll want to go and see her, of course.'

'Well, ordinarily I would, I suppose, but I can't go anywhere now, not when I'm so worried about Edith. It's a pity our Rick isn't here. He could have gone to Barts and seen her.'

Olive stood up. She had felt sorry for Dulcie's mother before she had met her, and in some ways she still did now that she had seen how careworn she was, but it went against all Olive's own feelings about motherhood to hear the other woman speaking so unkindly and uncaringly about her elder daughter. It was surely a mother's duty to love all her children, because if she did not then who would?

Despite her feelings, Olive still managed to say politely as she left, 'I hope you have some news of Edith soon.'

'They say there's dozens dead in Stepney, and even more in Silvertown, and they've hit the

Woolwich Arsenal and the Docks. Dulcie's dad was summoned first thing this morning to go and help clear some of the buildings that got blown up. He's a jobbing builder.'

Olive nodded her head and then turned away. There was nothing she could say that would lighten the burden of anxiety the other woman was carrying. Only the safe return of her daughter Edith could do that. Olive knew how it felt to love one's daughter but Dulcie's mother had two daughters, not one.

It was with some troubled thoughts in her head that Olive made her way home, glad to have them interrupted when Sergeant Dawson called out to her when she walked past the church hall. He was wearing his Home Guard uniform rather than his police uniform and he told her that he and some of the rest of their local Home Guard had gone over to the East End as soon as it had come light, to do what they could to help.

'Some of the houses in Silvertown have come down like a pack of cards,' he told Olive as they walked towards Article Row together,

'There's whole families just walking around with nothing but the clothes on their backs and nowhere to go to. And they're the lucky ones.'

'We just weren't prepared,' Olive said unhappily, 'and these poor people have paid the price for that.'

Her ankle still ached but the pain was nowhere near as bad as it had been, even if the plaster cast on her leg was driving her mad already, just like Sister, who had told her that she was to stay in bed and not move, and who had said, when Dulcie had told her that she wanted her handbag because she wanted to put her lipstick on, that she was in a hospital, not a dance hall, where she'd be staying until they were satisfied that she wasn't going to suffer from delayed concussion.

Last night, racked with pain, her emotions overwhelmed by the relief of being alive and the kindness the other girls had shown her, and despite the flood of injured bomb victims being rushed into the hospital and filling the ward, Dulcie hadn't really been aware of what all those injured people had meant.

This morning it was different. This morning her mind was as sharp as a knife, picking up on the conversations going on all around her as the occupants of the other beds talked about what they had experienced. And the more she heard the more anxious about her own family Dulcie became.

It wasn't until Sally, on her tea break, came into the ward to see her that she was able to ask the question uppermost in her mind.

'How can I find out which streets have been hit?' she asked Sally urgently. 'Only I've heard people saying that Stepney got it pretty badly.'

'I can't help you, Dulcie; I wish I could,' Sally was forced to admit. She'd been in the operating theatre virtually all night as patient after patient was wheeled in, all of them victims of the bombing and most of them badly injured. There had been one little baby boy they'd had to operate on. He'd been eighteen months old and his right leg had been so badly crushed that they'd had to amputate it. Sally had seen the surgeon wiping away tears as he looked at him. She had cried herself afterwards. It was impossible not to be affected by such things.

Worst of all, George had told her, were the people who came in asking if their loved ones had been brought in, hoping desperately to find them alive when George knew that they were in the morgue.

Such had been the shock of the night's bombing that Winston Churchill himself had been in the East End this morning to reassure people and praise them for their courage, so Sally had heard from another nurse.

'I expect we won't know properly which streets have been hit until we get tomorrow morning's papers. How are you feeling? How's your ankle? Is it giving you much pain?'

'Just a bit of a twinge, and I'd be feeling a lot better if Sister would tell me where my handbag is and let me put my lipstick on.'

Sally laughed. 'I've got your bag. I took it with me when I went on duty to keep it safe. I've got to get back on duty now, but I'll get it for you when I have my next break.'

'There's no point in us all going,' Olive had told Tilly and Agnes. 'They'll only let Dulcie have one visitor, and you'll be able to see her tomorrow, Tilly, when you're back at work. Besides,' she'd reminded them, 'you've both got St John Ambulance this afternoon, haven't you?'

429

Olive had her own reasons for wanting to see Dulcie on her own.

From her bed in the middle of the ward Dulcie was able to watch when visiting time came and the ward doors were opened to admit the surge of anxious relatives waiting to see their loved ones.

Although she pretended she wasn't doing so, Dulcie's gaze searched quickly amongst the visitors, looking for Tilly and Agnes's familiar faces. Not that she expected to see them, just because last night she'd gone and made a fool of herself, saying what she had.

The stream of visitors turned to a trickle, and Dulcie told herself that she wasn't in the least bit concerned that hers was the only bed without a relieved relative standing next to it.

And then Dulcie saw Olive coming towards her, carrying a copy of *Picture Post*, which she dropped on the bed, to lean over, take both of Dulcie's hands in her own and say emotionally, 'Dulcie, that was so generous and selfless of you last night to tell Tilly and Agnes to save themselves and leave you. I do thank you for that, my dear.' As she spoke Olive squeezed Dulcie's hands gently in her own. For a moment neither of them spoke and then, to Olive's own shock as much as Dulcie's, Olive leaned down and gave Dulcie a hug, telling her fiercely, 'I'm glad they didn't leave you, Dulcie, and I'm glad that you're safe. Number thirteen wouldn't be the same without you.'

'You mean it would be a lot better,' Dulcie couldn't resist quipping as Olive released her to smile ruefully.

'I might have thought that once, I admit, but I don't think it any longer. I'm sorry about your ankle. Oh, and your mother sends her love.'

'You've seen Ma? Are they all right? Everyone's been saying that Stepney got hit badly with the bombs.'

Olive's heart ached anew for Dulcie when she saw her genuine concern.

'Your parents are fine and the street hasn't been touched. Your mother is a bit anxious about your sister, though, because she was out singing somewhere last night and still hadn't come home.'

'Oh, yes, Ma would be worrying about her.'

There was a raw ugly animosity to Dulcie's voice now. Instinctively Olive reached for her hand again and held it, telling her, 'We're all looking forward to you coming home. We can put a bed up in the front room for you until you can manage the stairs. Nancy next door has a spare single we can borrow and I'll ask Sergeant Dawson if he'll give her Arthur a hand moving it round.'

Home? That was what number 13 was to her now, Dulcie recognised, with a stab of shock.

'I know that things haven't been all that good between you and me,' Dulcie told Olive, determined to clear the air between them, 'but they're going to be different now that me and the others are going to be friends.'

'I'm very glad to hear that, Dulcie, because after what you did last night, I can't think of anyone I'd want Tilly to have as a friend more than you.'

'Dulcie says she's like a second daughter to you,' Dulcie's mother had told her, so as she stood up when the bell rang to signal the end of visiting time, Olive leaned forward and kissed Dulcie on the cheek and then gave her another hug.

'We'll all be thinking about you, and Tilly will be in to see you tomorrow.'

TWENTY-FOUR

The first thing Agnes heard about on Monday morning when she got to work was that people had tried to shelter in the underground, despite the fact that the Government had said that the underground was not to be used as a shelter.

'Had some poor souls here from the East End,' Smithy told her. 'Bin walking around all day, they had, on account of their own houses being blown up and them having nowhere to go. It will be even worse tonight after last night's bombing. I'd heard there was four hundred at least killed last night.'

Agnes shuddered and went pale. 'We saw them on Saturday night, the bombers. We were going out for our tea and we saw them come over, then Dulcie got her heel stuck in the cobbles and broke her ankle and this German plane saw us helping her.'

'Sounds like you had a lucky escape.'

'We did,' Agnes agreed in a heartfelt voice, thinking no more about what she had said as the queue built up at her ticket window and she got to work.

By the time Ted finished his shift at five o'clock that afternoon, though, the story about Agnes's lucky escape had been passed on amongst the staff, its details embroidered with each telling so that when Ted heard it from one of the other drivers, the story was that Agnes had been badly hurt when a bomb had blown up in front of her.

The shock and despair that gripped him as he listened to the other driver was like no pain Ted had ever experienced. Agnes, his Agnes, was badly injured, and could be lying in hospital at death's door. In that moment Ted knew that he would give up his own life willingly if only Agnes could be saved. Knuckling the tears from his eyes he made his way up the steps and out of the underground station into the smoke-tainted late afternoon air. He'd go round to where she lived, ask them, beg them, to tell him which hospital she was in and then he'd go and see her and he'd . . . Ted lifted his downbent head to blink back his tears and then came to an abrupt halt, because there, less than three yards in front of him and walking away from him was Agnes. He blinked, thinking he must have conjured her up from his own imagination, but then she dodged a group of commuters coming the other way, and he knew she was real. His heart surged and bounded with joy and relief. He ran after her, catching hold of her arm so that she turned toward him.

'Ted!'

'You're safe! I thought . . . I heard that you'd been badly injured.'

'No, Dulcie broke her ankle when we got caught up in the bombing, but I'm all right.'

All around them the tide of moving humanity ebbed and swelled but they were both oblivious to it, oblivious to everything and anything except one another.

Agnes told him disjointedly, 'I thought, that is . . . I didn't think you wanted to be friends with me any more.'

'No! Agnes.' Ted was reaching for her hand and holding it, clasping it tight in his own, his face working as emotion gripped him. 'You mean the world to me, Agnes,' he told her hoarsely. 'There's nothing I wouldn't do for you. You're the best girl a chap could ever meet.'

They stood on the pavement looking into one another's eyes, still holding hands.

'Then why haven't you wanted to see me?' Agnes asked him.

'It was for your sake, because . . .' Ted paused and shook his head, fighting to control his emotions, '. . . it was for you, Agnes, because I wanted you to be free to find someone who could give you all the things that I can't.'

When she looked bewildered, he explained bleakly, 'You know how we live. Mum couldn't manage without my wages. The girls are only nine and eleven. It will be years before they are earning. I haven't got anything to offer you, Agnes.'

'You've got your love. I don't mind waiting, Ted. Not for you.'

When he didn't say anything she told him

practically, 'It won't be that long before the girls are grown up, not really, and then when they're bringing in a bit of money, you and me can marry and we can find somewhere a bit bigger, so that we can all live together.'

'You deserve better than that, Agnes.'

'There couldn't be anyone better for me than you, Ted. I've been that upset and miserable, thinking that you didn't want me. Last night, when that fighter plane came straight at us and Dulcie told us to run and leave her, all I could think was that I didn't care about living if living meant being without you.'

'Agnes.'

She raised herself up on her tiptoes and very daringly kissed him full on the mouth.

'*Agnes!*'

The rough note of emotion in his voice made her tremble with happiness and then he was kissing her back, and telling her how much he loved her, and Agnes knew that this was the happiest day of her life.

'Does this mean that we're going steady now?' she asked Ted breathlessly once he'd stopped kissing her.

'It could be years before we can get married,' Ted warned her.

'I don't care,' Agnes told him. 'Just as long as you love me.'

'Of course I love you. How could I not do when you're the best girl in the world?' Ted told her emotionally.

* * *

Of course, Olive had to be told, Agnes's face so alight with love and happiness as she explained what had happened.

Agnes was very young but Olive suspected that she was the kind of girl who, once her heart was given, would stay true to that first love all her life.

'Ted wants us to get engaged. He said it will tell other lads that I'm spoken for, but he'll have to save up for a ring first, so we thought we'd get engaged at Christmas. He's going to tell his mum that she's not to worry and that he'll still be handing his wages over to her for her and the girls.'

'I'm glad that Agnes isn't going to marry Ted yet,' Tilly told Olive later when they were on their own. 'I wasn't so sure how it was going to be when you first said about taking in lodgers, Mum, but now I'd hate it to be any different. Agnes and Dulcie and Sally – well, they're like family now.'

Family.

Tilly was right, Olive thought. The girls she had taken in originally as lodgers as a means of earning some money had now all found and made their own special places in her heart: Agnes, who had been so vulnerable and in need of love; Sally, so practical and hard-working and yet with such a terrible sadness to bear; Dulcie, whose influence on Tilly she had feared and resented and who she had judged on Dulcie's challenging manner, and who now, she had discovered, beneath that outer defensive attitude hungered for a mother's love.

They were her girls now. Her London Belles,

Olive thought with a surge of maternal love. The girls, her girls, reminded her of the joyous sounds of the many different bells of London's churches, and how that sound lifted the spirits of those who heard them, just as the sound of the girls' laughter and happy chatter lifted her spirits. Life had brought them together, and Olive prayed that life would keep them together and safe through the darkness that lay ahead, and that their hearts would always ring true.